Praise for the novels of

WILBUR
SMITH

"Read on, adventure fans."
THE NEW YORK TIMES

"A rich, compelling look back in time [to]
when history and myth intermingled."
SAN FRANCISCO CHRONICLE

"Only a handful of 20th century writers tantalize
our senses as well as Smith. A rare author who
wields a razor-sharp sword of craftsmanship."
TULSA WORLD

"He paces his tale as swiftly as he can with
swordplay aplenty and killing strokes that come
like lightning out of a sunny blue sky."
KIRKUS REVIEWS

"Best Historical Novelist—I say Wilbur Smith,
with his swashbuckling novels of Africa. The
bodices rip and the blood flows. You can get lost
in Wilbur Smith and misplace all of August."
STEPHEN KING

"Action is the name of Wilbur Smith's game
and he is the master."
THE WASHINGTON POST

Wilbur Smith is a global phenomenon: a distinguished author with a large and established readership built up over fifty-five years of writing, with sales of over 130 million novels worldwide.

Born in Central Africa in 1933, Wilbur became a full-time writer in 1964 following the success of *When the Lion Feeds*, and has since published over forty global bestsellers, including the Courtney Series, the Ballantyne Series, the Egyptian Series, the Hector Cross Series and many successful standalone novels, all meticulously researched on his numerous expeditions worldwide. His books have now been translated into twenty-six languages.

The establishment of the Wilbur & Niso Smith Foundation in 2015 cemented Wilbur's passion for empowering writers, promoting literacy and advancing adventure writing as a genre. The foundation's flagship program is the Wilbur Smith Adventure Writing Prize.

For all the latest information on Wilbur, visit: www.wilbursmithbooks.com or facebook.com/WilburSmith.

David Churchill is the author of *The Leopards of Normandy*, the critically acclaimed trilogy of novels about the life and times of William the Conqueror. He was also the co-author on previous Wilbur Smith titles, *War Cry* and *Courtney's War*.

Also by Wilbur Smith

Non-Fiction

On Leopard Rock:
A Life of Adventures

The Courtney Series

When the Lion Feeds
The Sound of Thunder
A Sparrow Falls
The Burning Shore
Power of the Sword
Rage
A Time to Die
Golden Fox
Birds of Prey
Monsoon
Blue Horizon
The Triumph of the Sun
Assegai
Golden Lion
War Cry
The Tiger's Prey
Courtney's War
King of Kings
Ghost Fire

The Ballantyne Series

A Falcon Flies
Men of Men
The Angels Weep
The Leopard Hunts in Darkness
The Triumph of the Sun
King of Kings
Call of the Raven

The Egyptian Series

River God
The Seventh Scroll
Warlock
The Quest
Desert God
Pharaoh

Hector Cross

Those in Peril
Vicious Circle
Predator

Standalones

The Dark of the Sun
Shout at the Devil
Gold Mine
The Diamond Hunters
The Sunbird
Eagle in the Sky
The Eye of the Tiger
Cry Wolf
Hungry as the Sea
Wild Justice
Elephant Song

WILBUR SMITH

WITH
DAVID CHURCHILL

LEGACY OF WAR

ZAFFRE

All rights reserved, including the right of reproduction in whole or
in part in any form.
First published in the United States of America in 2021 by Zaffre,
an imprint of Bonnier Books UK
80–81 Wimpole St, London W1G 9RE
Owned by Bonnier Books
Sveavägen 56, Stockholm, Sweden

Typeset by IDSUK (Data Connection) Ltd
Printed in the USA

10 9 8 7 6 5 4 3 2 1

Hardcover ISBN: 978-1-49986-235-5
Canadian paperback ISBN: 978-1-49986-236-2
Digital ISBN: 978-1-49986-234-8

For information, contact
251 Park Avenue South, Floor 12, New York, New York 10010
www .bonnierbooks.co.uk

I dedicate this book to my wife, Niso.
From the day we first met she has been a constant and powerful inspiration to me, urging me on when I falter and cheering me when I succeed. I truly do not know what I would do if she were not by my side. I hope and pray that day never comes. I love and adore you, my best girl, words cannot express how much.

KENYA, JUNE 1951

In the flickering, smoky light cast by torches of burning brushwood, Kungu Kabaya looked past the slaughtered goat lying in the middle of the abandoned missionary chapel towards the men, women and children watching in fearful expectancy.

There were around sixty of them, members of the Kikuyu tribe and 'squatters', as the white farmers called their black labourers. For no matter how hard a squatter worked; no matter how long he, or his father, or even grandfather had lived on the farm; no matter how skilfully he had built the hut in which he and his family lived: he only stayed on the farm with the farmer's blessing and could be expelled at any moment, with no right of appeal.

Kabaya cast his eye towards a separate group of around twenty squatters, men and women alike, who had been selected to take part in tonight's ceremony, and he nodded to the one at the head of the line. He was thin and gangly, no more than eighteen years old. With a young man's reckless bravado he had volunteered to be the first to take the oath. But as the gravity of his decision weighed upon him, his courage was giving way to anxiety and trepidation.

Kabaya approached him and put a fatherly arm upon his shoulder.

'There's nothing to fear,' he said, speaking quietly so that only the youngster could hear him. 'You can do this. Show them all that you are a man.'

The five men Kabaya had brought with him to the ceremony glanced at one another and gave nods or smiles of recognition as they watched the young man straighten his back and hold his head up high, his confidence restored. They had all served with Kabaya in the King's African Rifles, a British colonial regiment, during World War Two, campaigning in Ethiopia against Mussolini's Italian armies and then in Burma against the Japanese. They had watched as he had been promoted from private to company sergeant major within five years. And for each of them there had been times when Kabaya had found the words to keep them going in times of hardship, or given them courage when the fighting was most fierce.

When they came home to East Africa to discover that their military service had earned them neither human rights, nor decent jobs, Kabaya and his men had turned to crime. Their gang was one of many that emerged in the teeming shanty towns that had sprung up around the Kenyan capital, Nairobi, but it swiftly became the most powerful. The gangsters had become rebels and still they followed Kabaya. Whether a soldier, a criminal or a terrorist, their boss had a genius for leadership.

Kabaya stepped back to leave the young man alone in the middle of the floor. As he did, his second in command, Wilson Gitiri, sat beside the goat, placing the wickedly sharp, long-bladed panga knife with which he – like all of Kabaya's men – was armed, on the floor by his right hand.

Kabaya was a tall, handsome, charismatic man. He was highly intelligent, confident in his ability to win people over by reason and charm as well as fear. Wilson Gitiri was malevolence personified. He was shorter in stature than his commander, but he was as barrel-chested as a bull. His face was criss-crossed with thick welts of scar tissue. His eyes were permanently narrowed, forever searching for possible threat. His hair was plaited into tight braids that were gathered in a ridge that ran from the back to the front of his scalp like a soldier's forage cap. His presence in the chapel was an act of intimidation.

An earthenware jug, a battered tin cup and a length of rope had been placed by the head of the goat. Gitiri poured a small measure of thick, dark, viscous liquid from the jug into the cup, before replacing both vessels in their original position.

Minutes earlier, Gitiri had removed one of the goat's legs with a single blow from his panga. He had skinned the severed limb, cut the muscles away from the bone and diced the uncooked flesh into twenty cubes, which he piled in a wooden serving bowl. This, too, sat on the floor beside the animal's body.

Kabaya glanced at Gitiri to ensure he was prepared.

Gitiri nodded.

Kabaya said, 'Repeat these words after me . . . I speak the truth and vow before God, and before this movement of unity . . .'

'I speak the truth and vow before God, and before this movement of unity,' came the response, like a parishioner following his pastor's lead.

The oath-taking began as Kabaya spoke and the young man repeated the next lines:

That I shall go forward to fight for the land,
The lands of Kirinyaga that we cultivated.
The lands which were taken by the Europeans
And if I fail to do this
May this oath kill me . . .

Gitiri stood, holding the tin cup in one hand and the wooden serving bowl in the other. He held out the bowl. Kabaya took a piece of raw, bloody meat and offered it to the young man, saying, 'May this meat kill me . . .'

The young man, whose eyes kept darting towards Gitiri as if he dared not leave him out of his sight, hesitated. Kabaya glared at him, his eyes fiercer, more demanding this time. The young man took the meat, repeated, 'May this meat kill me,' and put it in his mouth. He chewed twice, grimaced, then downed it in one swallow.

Gitiri held out the cup. Kabaya took it from him and said, 'May this blood kill me . . .'

The young man repeated the words and drank a sip of blood from the tin cup.

The other Kikuyu tribespeople in the hall looked on in awed, horrified fascination as two separate strands in their culture were woven into a single binding cord.

Solemn blood-oaths had long been central to Kikuyu life, though in the past they had been restricted to elders rising to the highest councils of the tribe. Within the past seventy years they had been converted to Christianity and were familiar with the rite of Holy Communion: the blood of Christ and the flesh of Christ, expressed in wine and wafer. This was a darker, deeper, more African communion. It spoke to the very core of their being and everyone, from the youngest child to the most snowy-haired grandparent, knew that any oath taken under such circumstances was a sacred, unbreakable vow.

Kabaya intoned the last lines of the oath, and the young man repeated after him . . .

I swear I will not let the white men rule our land forever . . .
I swear that I will fight to the death to free our lands . . .
I swear that I will die rather than betray this movement to the
  Europeans . . .
So help me God.

Kabaya dismissed the young man, who walked back towards the main mass of his people. A knot of other youngsters grinned at him and applauded their friend. But he did not share their joy. He had looked into Kabaya's eyes and understood that the words he had sworn were deadly serious. He would only live as long as he obeyed them.

One after another, the chosen squatters took the oath, some with enthusiasm but most because they were too terrified to refuse. There were only five men and women left to be sworn in when Kabaya pointed to a man in late middle age and said, 'You next. What is your name?'

'Joseph Rumruti,' the man said.

He was not a tall man, nor strongly built. He had thin, bony limbs and a small pot belly. His scalp was almost bald and his beard was mostly grey. When he said his name he did so diffidently, as if he were apologising for his very existence.

'I am his wife, Mary Rumruti,' the woman next to him said. Like her husband, she seemed meek and submissive.

Kabaya chuckled. 'Mary and Joseph, eh? Is your boy Jesus here tonight?'

The men on either side laughed at their leader's wit.

'No, sir, we have no son,' said Joseph. 'The Lord did not see fit to bless us with children.'

'Huh,' Kabaya grunted. 'So, Joseph . . . Mary . . . it is time for you to swear the solemn oath. Repeat after me—'

'No.' Joseph spoke as quietly as before.

A tense, fearful silence descended upon the hall.

'Did I hear you say "No"?' Kabaya asked.

'That is correct,' Joseph replied. 'I cannot take your oath for I have already made a pledge, in church, in the sight of God, that I will have nothing to do with you and your renegades, or any other men like you.'

'Woman,' Kabaya said, looking towards Mary. 'Tell your man to swear the oath. Tell him to do this, or I will make him swear.'

Mary shook her head. 'I cannot do that. I have taken the same pledge.'

Kabaya stepped up close to Joseph, towering over him, his veneer of civility falling away to reveal the iron-hearted warrior within. His broad shoulders seemed to swell beneath his khaki shirt, his fists clenched like the heads of two blacksmith's hammers. Kabaya's eyes glowered beneath his beetling brow.

'Swear the oath,' he said, speaking as quietly as Joseph had done, but with a chilling undercurrent of menace.

Joseph could not look Kabaya in the eye. His head was bowed, his body trembling with fear.

'No,' he repeated. 'I cannot break my word to God.'

'You are not the first person to defy me,' Kabaya said. 'They all swore the oath in the end, and you will too.'

'I will not.'

The tension in the hall tightened still further. One man shouted, 'Take the oath, Joseph! For God's sake, take it!'

'Listen to your friend,' Kabaya said. 'Heed his words.'

Only those closest to Joseph could hear him say, 'I will not.'

Kabaya heard.

'I have had enough of this foolishness,' he said. 'I will make you swear.'

To Gitiri he said, 'The rope.'

Gitiri walked to where the dead goat lay. He put down the cup and bowl. He picked up the rope. Each movement was slow, deliberate, almost as if they too were solemn components of the oathing ceremony.

He faced Kabaya and tied the rope into a noose with about two feet of its length protruding from the knot.

Kabaya nodded.

Gitiri put the noose over Joseph's head. He tightened it until it was snug against Joseph's throat, then he stepped behind Joseph, holding the end of the rope.

'One last chance,' Kabaya said. 'Will you swear?'

Joseph shook his head.

Kabaya said to Mary. 'Take the oath and I will spare you.'

Mary stood taller, squared her shoulders, looked up at Kabaya and, to his face, declared, 'No.'

Kabaya gave a shake of his head and shrugged, as if he did not want to take the next step but had been left with no choice. He nodded at Gitiri.

Gitiri closed the noose more tightly against Joseph's neck. Gitiri's expression betrayed no emotion.

Joseph was struggling to breathe.

'Look at me,' said Mary, and he obediently turned his eyes towards her.

'This can stop now,' Kabaya said. 'You can go free. Just swear.'

Joseph did not respond.

Again Gitiri pulled the noose, slowly constricting Joseph's throat, completing the task in tiny fractions.

Kabaya looked over to the rest of his men, picked out three of them with his finger and nodded in Mary's direction. They took up station around her, brandishing their machetes.

The two remaining men, the ones armed with rifles, raised their guns at the crowd, which recoiled, pressing closely to the mission walls.

'If you will not save yourself, save her,' Kabaya said to Joseph.

'Don't!' Mary cried. She started intoning the words of the 23rd Psalm. '"Yea, though I walk through the valley of the shadow of death, I will fear no evil . . ."'

There was a murmur from the crowd, a rumble that formed the word, 'Amen.'

'You prepare a table before me in the presence of my enemies. You anoint my head—'

Kabaya lost his patience. 'Do it,' he ordered.

The soldiers obeyed their commanding officer. Gitiri gave a brutal tug on the rope, tightening the noose so violently that it smashed through Joseph's larynx and crushed his windpipe.

As his body collapsed, Mary screamed. The other three men hacked at her with their machetes, slicing into the arms she raised in a futile attempt to protect herself, and butchering her body. Within seconds she was lying dead beside her husband and her blood was bathing them both.

Kabaya looked at the corpses with indifference. He glanced at the final three oath-takers. They were huddled together, their arms wrapped around one another's bodies.

'Take the oath,' Kabaya said.

In desperate voices that cried out to be believed, they did what they were told.

LONDON

'Before we go any further, I'd like to propose a toast,' said Saffron Courtney Meerbach, raising her glass of champagne. 'To Gubbins . . . who brought us all together, and without whom none of us would be here today.'

'To Gubbins!' chorused the other five men and women seated around the table in the small French bistro.

They had met there at her invitation as a nod to days gone by. The restaurant was an old haunt for them all. It was off Baker Street in central London, a stone's throw from the headquarters of the Special Operations Executive, the wartime intelligence agency in which all but one of them had served. Brigadier Colin Gubbins was their commanding officer.

'By God, he was scary though, wasn't he?' Leo Marks, a small man with a puckish smile added. 'I still have nightmares about the first time he fixed those eyes of his on me. Classicists among us will recall the basilisk, the mythical Greek snake that could kill with a single glance. Well, dear old Gubbins made the basilisk seem like the Sugar Plum Fairy.'

Of all the people at the table, only one had joined in the toast out of politeness, rather than enthusiasm. He was tall, with the chiselled features, tousled dark-blond hair and perfect tan of a Hollywood star. But there was a slight hollowness to his cheeks and, occasionally, a haunted look to his cool, grey eyes that spoke of a man who had seen and experienced horrors beyond any normal human imagination. He was not the only one around the table of whom that was true.

'Tell me, my darling,' Gerhard Meerbach said in a light German accent, as he reached across the table and took his wife's hand. 'I understand how Gubbins links you all together. But how do I owe my presence here to him?' Gerhard gave a wry shrug of the shoulders. 'I was on the other side.'

'Because, dearest,' Saffron replied, 'it was Gubbins who packed me off to the North German plain in late April '45, to try and find our missing agents, including Peter . . .'

Peter Churchill gave a modest nod of his bespectacled head as Saffron continued, 'Had I not been there, I should never have followed the trail of the high-value prisoners that the SS were hoping to trade for favours with the Allies all the way to . . .'

She was about to say 'Dachau', but stopped herself. She didn't want that hellish nightmare intruding on their gathering.

Instead she said, 'All the way across Germany and into the Italian Tyrol, where . . . where I found you, my darling . . . and thought I'd arrived too late . . .'

The sudden, vivid memory of Gerhard's skeletal, feverish wreck of a body lying on what seemed to be his deathbed took Saffron unawares. She could not speak for the lump in her throat and had to blink back the tears before she could mutter, 'Sorry,' to the rest of the table. She pulled herself together, took a deep breath and with a forced briskness added, 'But I hadn't . . . and everything was all right, after all.'

Silence fell across the table. They all had their own bitter memories and understood how shallow the emotions of war were buried, how the pain could creep up on one at any moment.

Peter Churchill knew what a decent English gentleman should do at such a moment: lighten the mood.

'I say, Saffron,' he piped up. 'It seems to me that you're hogging the limelight in the matter of the Gubbins–Meerbach connection. After all, if I hadn't been stuck in the same concentration camp as Gerhard, we wouldn't have been on the same grim charabanc ride across the mountains. Thus I wouldn't have been able to keep him more or less alive . . .' He glanced towards Gerhard. 'You were in the most terrible state, old boy, we thought you were a goner for sure . . . And I only happened to be on the bus thanks to Baker Street's determination to keep sending me into Occupied France until I finally got caught. Ergo, the Law of Gubbins applies to me too.'

'Then I agree, I must also thank Brigadier Gibbins,' Gerhard said. 'And I thank you, Peter, from the bottom of my heart. I would have died without you.'

'Think nothing of it, old boy. Anyone in my shoes would have tried to help. Inhuman not to.'

Gerhard nodded thoughtfully. He frowned as he collected his thoughts and the others gave him time, knowing that there was something on his mind. Then he said, 'Here we are, talking about the war. I can't help but think of the terrible things I saw . . . You know I was imprisoned, but before that I spent three years on the Russian Front. I was at Stalingrad, almost to the very end. I saw what was done to the Jews – the firing squads, the gas vans. All my closest friends were killed.

'Sometimes I feel cursed by fate to have had to endure so much horror, so much suffering and death. But then I tell myself, no, I am blessed, truly blessed, for I have experienced a miracle. I stumbled to the edge of the grave, but I did not fall in. I lived.'

Gerhard looked at the others, knowing that they had suffered as much, or more than him, and that they shared his feelings in a way most ordinary people could never do. He went on, 'And when I awoke from the sleep of death, the first thing I saw was an angel . . . Saffron, my true love.

'I would like to propose a toast. And I have been wondering what we should be drinking to . . . Good fortune, maybe – or love, or friendship, or peace – but what I would like to toast is what we all share . . .' He raised his glass. 'To life, the greatest blessing of all.'

They drank again and then their food was served. Up to this point, Peter Churchill's wife Odette, a slender, dark-eyed brunette had been happy to listen while the others talked. Now she spoke in a French accent.

'I am sure you will understand, Gerhard, that it was not easy for me, the thought of having lunch with a German . . .'

'Of course,' Gerhard replied.

'But then Saffron wrote to me and I learned how you two had met before the war and fallen in love, and Peter told me that you had both been at Sachsenhausen at the same time. I realised that you had been a victim of the SS, just like me. Now we have met and, well, I can understand why Saffron fell in love with you.'

'*Merci beaucoup, madame,*' said Gerhard, with a nod of the head.

Odette gave a quick, sparkling smile before composing her features and replying with equal formality, '*Je vous en prie, monsieur* . . . But there is one thing of which I am curious. Did you ask Saffron's father for permission to marry his daughter? I would very much like to know how he reacted when he heard his daughter was marrying a German.'

Gerhard grinned. 'Good question! And I am not just any German. My family and Saffron's have a certain . . . ah . . . history . . .'

'My father killed his,' said Saffron, in such a casual way that no one was sure how to respond.

That process was made all the more tricky when Gerhard remarked, in an equally offhand tone, 'It is only fair to say that my father had been trying to kill her mother, who was at that time, his mistress.' He paused for a beat and then added, 'Though she was actually in love with Mr Courtney.'

'Well, that's Africa for you,' said Saffron casually, while the others were trying to work out who had been killing, or loving, whom.

'My dear, this is too fascinating, and one day you must tell me the whole family history,' said Odette. 'But for now I would like your husband to answer my question.'

'And I shall,' Gerhard assured her. 'As you know, I was very ill when Saffron found me. It took me several months in a Swiss sanatorium to recover, although even then, I was still weak. All that time, Saffy was at my side. Anyway, when I was finally well enough to travel to Kenya, which the doctors agreed was the perfect place for me to complete my cure and regain my full strength . . .' He paused and glanced around the table. 'It's paradise, you know, a Garden of Eden. And Saffron's home, the Lusima Estate . . . *ach*, I don't have the words to describe how beautiful it is. So, I still haven't answered your question, *madame* . . .'

'Indeed not,' said her husband, 'but I'm greatly enjoying your failure to do so. *Garçon*! Another two bottles of wine, if you don't mind.'

'We took the train to Genoa,' Gerhard went on. 'From there we sailed to Alexandria, where we boarded another vessel that took us through the Suez Canal and down the coast of East Africa to Mombasa. Saffy's father Leon and her stepmother Harriet—'

'Who is the loveliest stepmother any woman could hope to have,' Saffron interjected.

'. . . were waiting on the quayside to meet us. Leon took us to lunch and of course he hadn't seen his daughter in years—'

'Four, to be precise.'

'. . . so I sat there for most of the meal while they caught up with each other's news.'

'I dare say you were quite relieved not to be the topic of conversation yourself,' Churchill observed.

'Absolutely . . . Then, after the puddings had been eaten, Harriet stood and said, "I think it is time for us girls to go and powder our noses." I had no idea what she meant by that. But they walked away and I realised they were going to the ladies' room . . . and I was alone with Saffron's father . . .'

L eon Courtney assessed the tall, thin, war-ravaged thirty-five-year-old man sitting opposite him as thoroughly as he might any other investment his family was going to make.

Not bad, so far, he thought to himself. *Impeccable manners, respectful to me, charming to Harriet, plainly dotes on Saffy. Top marks, too, for letting us get on with it and not trying to make himself the centre of the conversation. Not a show-off. Nothing like his bloody father. Now let's see what he's made of . . .*

'Would you like a glass of brandy with your coffee?' Leon asked.

Gerhard gave a half-smile. 'I'm not sure my doctor would approve.'

'Nonsense. Nothing like brandy to buck a man up.'

Gerhard looked at Leon, eye to eye, letting him know that there was a strong, confident character behind that ailing façade. He gave a wry dry chuckle.

'On second thoughts, yes, thank you, I will have a brandy. I suspect that I may need it.'

'Good man.'

Two coffees were served, accompanied by the brandies, both doubles. Leon knew, but Gerhard did not, that there was a pleasant garden at the back of the hotel at which they were dining, where one could sit in the shade and be waited on hand and foot. Harriet was under strict instructions to take Saffron outside and remain there until further notice.

'I'll send a boy to fetch you when we're done,' Leon had said.

'Go easy on the poor man,' Harriet had warned him. 'He's not well and Saffron adores him. If you make an enemy of him, you'll be making an enemy of her too.'

Leon had grunted at that, but he loved his daughter very deeply and had learned to trust and respect her. She would not have chosen this man, let alone waited all war for him, unless he deserved it. Still, Leon wanted to see for himself what his prospective son-in-law was made of.

He let Gerhard savour his first sip of brandy and said, 'So, you want to marry my daughter, eh?'

'Yes, sir,' Gerhard said, no pleading or ingratiation in his voice, a straightforward statement of fact.

'You know that I will kill you if you ever harm a hair on her head.'

Gerhard surprised Leon. He gave another one of his gently amused smiles and replied, 'If I ever harmed Saffron, you would not need to kill me. She would already have done it herself.'

Leon could not help himself. He laughed. 'Well said! Of course she would. But could you defend yourself against her, eh?'

Gerhard shrugged. 'At the moment, no, I could not defend myself against a small child. But when I am well again and have my full strength, I am not a bully, Mr Courtney – not like my father – but I am not a weakling either, and . . .' He paused, grimaced, thought for a second and said, 'I flew my first combat mission over Poland at dawn on 1 September 1939, the first morning of the war. I was on active duty continuously from then until my arrest in September 1944. Looking back, let me tell you what I can truly be proud of. I always did my best to care for the men under my command. I was awarded some of the highest medals for gallantry that my country has to offer. And finally, the most important thing . . . All those medals were stripped from me, along with my rank, when I stood in a Berlin courtroom and refused to save myself from prison by swearing my loyalty to that murderous lunatic Adolf Hitler.

'I tell you this, Mr Courtney, so you appreciate I am not a weak man, either physically or morally. We both know that Saffron will never, ever let a man dominate her. But also she could never love a man who let her dominate him. And she does love me. So we are equal.'

Yes, you are, Leon thought. *My girl has truly met her match. That's why she didn't let go of him. She knew she'd never find another.*

'I dare say you've thought a bit about this moment,' he said. 'Asking for my daughter's hand in marriage – wondering how I'd take it, eh?'

Gerhard smiled. 'A bit, yes . . .'

Leon grinned. 'Me too. I had a long list of questions for you. Don't think there's any need for them now.'

'Thank you, sir.'

Leon's expression grew serious. 'A lot of people here in Kenya lost family, men they loved. Some may give you the benefit of the doubt, but most won't. It won't be easy. Not for you, not for anyone . . .'

'I imagine not.'

'But Saffron loves you with all her heart, I have no doubt of that.' Leon gave a knowing chuckle. 'That's the only way we Courtneys do anything – flat-out, way over the limit.'

'I knew that from the moment we met,' said Gerhard. 'When Saffy came flying off the Cresta Run and landed in the snow at my feet.'

'Ha! That's my girl! And now I also have no doubt that you love her too – and that you're nothing whatever like your father.'

'That's true, for sure. I have spent my entire life trying to be nothing like my father.'

'Then I would be delighted, and proud to welcome you into our family, Gerhard. I ask no more than, love my girl and make her happy. As long as you do that, you will have my friendship, my support and my help if ever you need it. And if you don't . . .'

Leon let the words hang in the air for a moment, then summoned a waiter.

'Be a good chap and send a message to Mrs Courtney. She's in the garden with my daughter. Tell them that it's safe to return to the table.'

'We stopped off in Nairobi to get our marriage licence and we had the service a few days later in the chapel at Lusima,' said Saffron.

'The choir were workers from the estate,' Gerhard said. 'I thought the choirs in Bavaria were good, but my God, those African voices . . . It sounded like angels singing.'

'Of course, that was when my darling husband discovered that he actually had two fathers-in-law, not one—'

'Oh, but that's too much, even for you, darling!' laughed the sixth member of the party, Brigadier Gubbins' former secretary Margaret Jackson.

'No, it's true,' Gerhard assured her. 'Lusima is huge, more than one hundred thousand acres.'

'Much more,' Saffron murmured.

'About one tenth of it is farmland, and all the workers come from the Kikuyu tribe. But the rest of the land is kept wild and the people who live there are Maasai, who roam across the country, herding cattle. Saffron and I have built our own home there, by a watering hole where the animals come to drink. We called it Cresta Lodge, after the Cresta Run in St Moritz, where we first met.'

As he spoke, Gerhard could see the others being seduced, as he had been, by the idea of the private African kingdom where Saffron had been born and raised, a world away from the grey, foggy, bomb-scarred streets of post-war London.

'While the lodge was being built, we lived with Leon and Harriet, but I was managing the project, so I often camped at the site,' he said. 'One morning I woke up before dawn, which is one of the very best times for seeing game, so I decided to go for a walk. It was quite chilly, because Cresta Lodge lies at an altitude of around seven thousand feet and the nights are cold at that height. The air was still and clear, and the loudest noise was the buzzing and chirping of insects around me.

'There are some low hills behind the house, and I was heading towards them when I saw a big, dark shape moving behind the top of the rise ahead of me. It still wasn't quite light, so I stopped to look more closely and I realised it was an elephant, a great bull, coming over the brow towards me. More shapes appeared, another bull and then the females and young, all in a line. A couple of the babies were holding their mothers' tails with their trunks as they trotted along behind them.

'I remember being struck by how gentle and loving the mothers were to their children, and how serenely the herd moved across the landscape. But at the same time, there was a kind of equal, but opposite impression that these were the mightiest and potentially deadliest creatures I had ever seen. They were like huge, grey, living tanks, trampling everything in their path. I stood absolutely still as they walked past me, no more than thirty yards away, partly because I didn't want anything to disturb this magical sight, but also because I thought, "I don't want to get that big bull angry!"'

The story was heard in silence and greeted with appreciative smiles and laughter. 'Encore!' Leo Marks called out.

Gerhard grinned. 'If you insist . . . Some nights, I would drive home after the building work stopped, because, well, as great as it was to camp out under the stars, it wasn't as great as being with Saffron. There are two or three main tracks that cross the estate. They aren't tarmac, or anything like that, but the earth is packed hard, so you can drive at a decent speed. One night I was coming up to a corner that goes around a grove of trees, so you can't see around the other side. You'd think that's not a problem. I mean, there are no other cars on the road. So I went around the corner at quite a speed because I was in a hurry to get home and, right in the middle of the track, was a female rhino with her young. She took one look at me and went away up the road with her kid at her heels. Let me tell you, the great big, leathery, fat backside of a female rhino running away from you is not a pretty sight. But it is a lot more attractive than the sight of the same rhino from the front, charging in your direction.'

Gerhard paused and added, 'Another time I drove into a pride of lions who were having an orgy that reminded me of a few Berlin clubs I knew, back in the wild days before the Nazis. But that is a long story and not suitable for a respectable restaurant in broad daylight.'

'Tell us about the native population,' said Peter Churchill. 'One sees rather disturbing stories about Kenya in the press these days. You know, those rebels—'

'The Mau Mau,' Saffron said.

'That's the bunch. Do you get any trouble from them where you are?'

'Not yet, thank heaven,' said Saffron. 'The Mau Mau belong to the Kikuyu tribe. The Kikuyu are farmers and we have quite a few living and working on the part of the estate that's given over to farmland and plantations. But out in the wild, where Gerhard and I live, the people are Maasai, cattle herders, and they aren't involved in Mau Mau at all.'

'The chief of the Maasai on the Lusima estate is an extraordinary man,' Gerhard said. 'He's called Manyoro. Many years ago, when Leon was a young army officer, Manyoro was his sergeant. Leon saved his life.'

'Manyoro was injured in a fight with a rebel tribe called the Nandi,' Saffron explained. 'My father carried him on his back for days to get him to the sacred mountain, Lonsonyo, where his mother lived, so she could treat Manyoro's wounds. She was a healer, she had amazing powers, I've experienced them myself. Ever since then, Manyoro and my father have considered themselves to be brothers.'

'But surely a white man can't be that close to a black man, not in a place like Kenya,' Marks said. 'From what I can gather, the place is stuffed with bloody idiots who think Negroes are one step removed from monkeys.'

'It is, and they do,' Saffron agreed. 'But as you say, they're bloody idiots.'

'Trust me, Leo, Manyoro is a second father to Saffron,' Gerhard said.

'Poor Gerdi.' Saffron leaned over and gave her man a consoling pat on the back. 'He thought he'd survived the third degree after he'd got past Daddy Courtney. Little did he know he was in for another talking-to from Manyoro.'

'He made it as plain as Leon Courtney had done – if I hurt Saffron in any way, he would be my mortal enemy.'

'He was only like that because he loves me so much. Once I'd assured him that I knew I'd found the right man, he gave Gerhard a huge hug, and started giving me a lecture instead.'

Gerhard grinned. 'You should have heard him. He was telling Saffy that she had to give me many, many children—'

'I've managed two so far, one of each, and that feels like quite enough.'

'What are they called?' Margaret asked.

'Alexander, who's four, and Nichola, who's two. But we always call them Zander and Kika because that's how they say their names.'

'Did you bring them with you to England?'

Saffron's face fell as she gave a shake of the head. 'No. We thought about it, of course. But it's much better for the children to be at home with their grandparents and their nanny, surrounded by people who love them. They'd have been miserable traipsing around Europe with us, too young to understand what was going on or where they were.' She smiled wistfully. 'I got a letter from Harriet this morning. She wrote about how happy Zander and Kika are and what fun they're having, being spoilt rotten by everyone. She was only trying to reassure me, but of course it made me weep buckets.'

'I think you're doing the right thing,' Margaret said, patting Saffron's hand. She looked at Gerhard. 'I'm so sorry I interrupted your story.'

'Don't worry,' Gerhard said. 'I was only going to pass on the final command that Manyoro gave Saffy. He said that when she grows older, it will be her solemn duty to find new young wives for me and make sure that they behave and produce even more offspring.'

'I say, that's the spirit!' Churchill exclaimed.

'Pah!' Odette snorted, in true Gallic style, rolling her eyes at the idea. She smiled and said, 'Look, everyone, here comes Pierre!'

The others looked towards the kitchen, from which the chef and proprietor Pierre Duforge was emerging, wiping the sweat from his forehead as he came towards them.

'Ah, *mes amis*,' Pierre said as he reached the table. 'It has been too long since I saw you all. And Odette . . .' He paused and swallowed hard. 'It is an honour, truly, to serve you again at my table. I saw your film, the one with Anna Neagle playing your part, and my dear wife, she had to stop me from standing up in the cinema and shouting, "I know the real Odette!"'

Odette smiled. 'Thank you, Pierre. It's a pleasure for me also to be back here once again.'

As a fellow SOE veteran, Saffron knew the story of Odette Sansom, as she had been called back then: her exploits as an undercover agent in Occupied France; her capture by the Gestapo; the torture she had suffered, and her appalling mistreatment in Ravensbruck concentration camp. But having spent the post-war years in Kenya, she had no concept of how famous Odette had become.

'I want to pay you my sincere respects,' Pierre continued. 'And to offer my most profound sympathy for what you had to endure. The things those filthy Boches did to you . . . they're no better than savages.'

He sensed a sudden air of silent embarrassment descend upon the table and stammered, 'D-d-did I say something wrong?'

Gerhard smiled reassuringly. 'No, Pierre . . . it is just that I am a filthy Boche. But you are right. Some Germans were bloody savages and they did things that shame me to the depths of my soul. But most of us are not like that. We are no better or worse than anyone else.'

'Look at it this way,' said Leo Marks. 'I'm a Jew and I'm breaking bread with him.'

'I do not wish to offend anyone. Please, I insist, let me give you this meal, as the Americans say, "on the house".'

'Thank you, Pierre, that's very kind,' said Odette. 'And don't worry. You meant well. All that matters is the war is over. Now we can live in peace.'

Saffron took Gerhard's hand and looked into his eyes. They had been reunited for six years, but it still felt like a miracle to have him by her side.

'Amen to that,' she said.

Pierre Duforge regarded himself as a man of discretion. But he was also a businessman, and in the current state of the austerity-ravaged British economy it was not easy to keep a restaurant afloat. The lack of decent food for his customers only made matters worse. Whenever Pierre went home to France, the market stalls were laden down with vegetables, fruits, meats, cheeses and all manner of breads and pastries. Why, he asked himself in profound bemusement, did the British still choose to starve themselves?

As he walked away from the table, his conscience fought with his need to make money. He knew customer confidentiality was an important part of his trade, but these were desperate times; cunning and opportunism were needed to survive. Finally he told himself, *This is just a little thing. It will cause no harm to anyone. And I did give them a meal for free.* Making sure no one was watching him, he ducked into his office and dialled the number of a regular customer, who happened to be a reporter on the *Evening Standard*, one of London's two main local newspapers.

'Come quickly!' he whispered. 'Odette herself is here with a table of her old comrades. And my waiter heard one of them saying she had just come from Buckingham Palace.'

The reporter had a word with his picture editor. They agreed that this was a story that might interest Londoners on their way home from work. And so, when Saffron, Gerhard, Odette and the others emerged from the bistro they were met with the dazzling burst of a camera flash, and a quick-fire series of questions from the reporter.

Odette took the intrusion in her stride, having become accustomed to being a public figure. Gerhard was baffled and a little uneasy at the questioning. It brought back memories of previous interrogations that he would rather have kept buried. But Saffron laughed it off.

'It reminds me of being a deb, back in the thirties. I was forever being photographed at parties with young men who were supposedly about to marry me.'

Gerhard looked at her with a raised eyebrow.

'Oh, don't worry. None of them were remotely interesting. They were either hopelessly shy or ragingly oversexed. You know, wandering hands and all that. Believe me, darling, you were a complete revelation.'

She lowered her voice so that no one else could overhear.

'You always knew exactly what to do with your hands.'

Kabaya had made sure that the bodies of Joseph and Mary were buried on the night they died. He was back in Nairobi by the time dawn broke the following morning. But for the next several days, he brooded.

The squatters had been warned that anyone who said a word of what had happened to the authorities, be it their farm boss or the police, would be punished in ways that would make the deaths they had witnessed seem merciful. Even so, there was a danger someone might find it impossible to keep their mouth shut. If they talked, the buried bodies might be discovered.

Something had to be done. Ten days after the killings, Kabaya and his men returned to the farm, late at night. He commanded the squatters who had sworn the oath to demonstrate their loyalty to the cause by rounding up every squatter on the property, including women, children and old folk who had not been at the oathing ceremony. They were ordered to bring digging implements.

The assembled squatters were marched to the spot where their two friends' remains were buried. Kabaya set them to work exhuming the bodies. In the light of flickering torches made from bundled twigs, every man, woman and child was made to remove at least some of the earth, so that none could later deny that they had taken part.

The weather had been hot, with periods of blazing sunshine interspersed with torrential downpours. The bodies had been decomposing fast. The sight and smell of the two corpses was enough to turn the strongest stomach. People were retching, holding their hands to their mouths and noses, or vomiting on the ground beneath their feet. A handful fainted and collapsed unconscious, looking like dead bodies themselves.

Kabaya wanted the bodies destroyed. He lined the squatters up. One after another, they had to step up to the place where the exhumed, putrefying bodies lay.

One of Kabaya's men handed each a machete. They were ordered to hack off a piece of the body in front of them: a toe, a fingertip, an ear, a slice of fat and skin, or a chunk of jellified meat. Next, they were told to pick up the stinking, festering morsel that they had carved and press it to their mouths, like some Devil's communion wafer.

'Break your vow of silence and your flesh will be corrupted like that,' Kabaya told the squatters.

The fragments of Joseph's and Mary's desecrated bodies were gathered up and taken to a nearby patch of woodland, where they were scattered as carrion for animals, birds and insects. Within a few days, there was no trace of Kabaya's victims to be found. Without bodies to prove death there could be no case against him. He could rest easy.

The squatters had no doubt that Kabaya would not hesitate to kill and torture again. No one told the full story of what had happened to anyone who might report it to the police. But human beings cannot help but talk among themselves. Stories spread, even if no more than vague, nightmarish rumours.

For many months there had been talk in the native and colonist populations about bizarre ceremonials at which terrible oaths were sworn. These were embroidered with further tales, often magnified and distorted in the telling, of ritual killings and cannibalism.

The men responsible for these terrible things called themselves *muhimu*, 'the important ones'.

But the white settlers had a different name for the rebels. They called them the Mau Mau.

Saffron and Gerhard mingled in the crowds of people thronging the courtyard in front of the Wilkins Building at University College London. The flights of stone steps that rose towards the classical portico, the ten mighty columns that stood guard over the entrance and the dome that rose behind them, were as encrusted with soot and grime as every other building in London. But nothing could diminish the imposing splendour of the institution. Nor could the strain of living in a country still suffering rationing and austerity, six years after a war it was supposed to have won, dim the joy on the faces of the families gathered there.

This was graduation day for the university's medical students, the moment when proud parents could boast that their child had qualified as a doctor. As the medics poured out of the building in their doctoral gowns and tasselled velvet caps, clutching their diplomas and scanning the courtyard for their families, Saffron kept her eyes peeled for one particular student.

'At least he'll be easy to spot,' Gerhard remarked.

The majority of the newly qualified medics were white. A small number were Asian. But those of African or Caribbean descent could be counted on the fingers of one hand.

'There he is!' Saffron cried, catching sight of a bespectacled young man, with the tall, slender physique and dark brown-black skin characteristic of the Nilotic tribes of East Africa. 'Benjamin!' she shouted, frantically waving her hand.

Gerhard looked on with an amused smile. It was rare to see Saffron acting with such girlish enthusiasm. But then, he reflected, Benjamin was Manyoro's son. Leon Courtney had paid for him to study in London. And though she was several years older than him, without a drop of blood in common, Saffron felt as strongly as any older sister would do on their younger brother's big day.

Benjamin saw them and his face lit up with a broad grin as he waved back. But something distracted him. He held up a hand to say, 'Hang on,' before dashing away down the steps.

'Hmm . . . there's someone more important than you,' Gerhard said.

Saffron smiled. 'I can't wait to meet her.'

Five minutes later they discovered what the fuss was about.

'Goodness, she's ravishing,' Saffron declared.

'She certainly is,' Gerhard agreed, as an ebony vision in a yellow silk sundress walked towards them with the feline grace of a prowling leopard, her head raised with the regal carriage of a princess. Gerhard felt that she might at any moment raise one of her white-gloved hands to flick a dismissive wave at the pale-faced Britons who gawped, open-mouthed, as she strolled by.

She seemed to Gerhard's eye like an African version of Botticelli's Venus. She had a high forehead, with tumbling black curls, rather than golden locks; perfectly arched eyebrows, but with deep brown eyes, rather than pale ones; the nose as fine, but the lips fuller and more sensuous.

Gerhard had lived with fifteen years of ceaseless Nazi propaganda about the superiority of the Aryan race. One look at this woman proved what ludicrous nonsense that was.

Saffron met Benjamin with an exuberant hug.

'Benji! I'm so proud of you!'

Gerhard could see the shocked looks on the faces around them. People were not used to respectable white women throwing their arms around black men.

'Saffron, may I introduce my fiancée, Wangari Ndiri,' Benjamin said, with manners as impeccable as his command of English.

'I'm so pleased to meet you, Saffron,' Wangari said as Saffron gave her a welcoming kiss on the cheek. 'Benjamin always speaks very highly of you and your family.'

'Well, we couldn't think more highly of him,' Saffron replied.

Gerhard contented himself with a firm handshake for Benjamin and a lighter one for Wangari.

'So,' he said, 'would you care to join us for a picnic? I certainly hope so.' He picked up a large wicker picnic hamper. 'I would hate to think I had been carrying this around for nothing.'

'That's very kind of you,' Benjamin replied. 'But I'm not sure—'

'Oh, do,' said Saffron. 'I've so been looking forward to catching up with you.'

'We'd be delighted,' said Wangari, taking charge of the couple's social arrangements.

Saffron beamed. 'Wonderful! I thought we could set up camp on Primrose Hill. We'll catch a cab and be there in no time.' She took Wangari's arm in hers as they walked out of the UCL gates and onto Gower Street and said, 'Now, you must tell me all about yourself. Manyoro didn't mention a word about you.'

'Perhaps he thought it best to be discreet. You see, my father is Chief Ndiri.'

'The Kikuyu leader?' Saffron asked, with surprise.

'Yes.'

'Oh, that explains it.'

'Why's that?' Gerhard asked.

'Different tribes, darling. For the son of a Maasai chief to marry the daughter of a Kikuyu is like, ah . . .'

'The son of a German industrial dynasty marrying the daughter of a wealthy British landowner?'

'Just like that,' Saffron agreed, 'only worse.'

'It's ridiculous,' Benjamin snapped. 'In this day and age we shouldn't be bound by outdated notions of tribalism. Wangari and I are Kenyans and we are Africans. National self-determination and continental unity – that's where our future lies.'

'I wish you the best of luck,' Gerhard said. 'We're still trying to get rid of tribal rivalries in Europe after two thousand years of supposed civilisation.' His face brightened. 'Aha! A taxi!'

Gerhard hailed the passing black cab. The two ladies sat on the passenger seat, with the men facing them on the jump seats. Saffron continued her gentle interrogation of Wangari and discovered that she too had recently graduated, receiving a First Class degree in Law from the London School of Economics. She and Benjamin had met at a public meeting at the LSE organised by left-wing students and academics under the banner, *End the Empire Now*. Speeches had been given by Indians and Africans involved in the fight against colonialism, and various Labour and Communist politicians who supported them.

'A friend of mine knew Benjamin and invited him to come along,' Wangari said.

'We started talking, and discovered we were both Kenyan, and that we shared a similar vision for our nation,' Benjamin added.

'At the end of the day, we went to a pub nearby and of course the conversation was all about the need for independence and social change,' Wangari smiled. 'So we fell in love over Marxism and warm beer.'

'How romantic!' Saffron remarked, with irony.

The taxi driver dropped them off at the foot of Primrose Hill, across the road from London Zoo. As they walked through the park that, come rain or shine, war or peace, provided some of the finest views of the city, Benjamin spoke in a voice that was all too often silenced in Kenya: that of the educated, articulate African, making the moral and political case for his freedom.

'Your father is a good man and my father loves him very much. But the fact remains that your father owns the land and mine does not. Yours has a vote and mine does not. Yours belongs to the one race that rules all the other races, and mine does not. So long as those things are true, then Kenya will be a land of injustice and oppression. And we cannot tolerate that.'

'Can't you see, Saffron, that Benjamin and I have a duty to our people?' Wangari's voice was gentle, but her resolve was clear. 'It is because we have been given so much, and are so privileged, that we have to give back to those who are not so lucky. We have to use our talents to make their lives better.'

Gerhard nodded appreciatively. 'Well said. I felt the same way when I was your age. I wanted to use my family's money and industrial power to make life better for the poor. That never happened – or not yet, anyway. But your ideals are noble, and I applaud them.'

'Thank you.' Benjamin sounded pleased, but also surprised. 'My ambition is to dedicate my life to the fight to end colonialism and create a new, free Africa.'

'And I will stand beside you, my love,' said Wangari.

Saffron looked at the two of them: so proud, so gifted and so much in love. Yet her mind was filled with trepidation.

'Will you make me one promise, Benjamin?' she asked. 'Tell me that you won't make this a war between our people. I couldn't bear to think of you as my enemy. It would break my heart.'

'And mine too,' he replied. 'But if your people are not willing to talk – if they refuse to be reasonable or fair – what else can we do but fight?'

'We can be friends,' said Gerhard. 'It is a beautiful day. The grass is green, the view is magnificent, the women are beautiful and charming. Let the future take care of itself. For now we have climbed far enough up the hill, and I have carried this hamper so long my arm is about to drop off.'

'You should have carried it the African way, on your head,' Wangari said. 'Much easier.'

'Now she tells me!'

They stopped and all talk of politics ceased as they looked down from the top of Primrose Hill and saw the view across the skyline of London. The dome of St Paul's was visible, and Big Ben too.

Saffron opened the hamper and produced a tartan picnic blanket on which she laid plates, knives and forks. Next came four crystal wineglasses, followed by a bottle of champagne, wrapped in a damp cloth to keep it cool. Gerhard popped the cork, poured them each a glass and they drank to Benjamin's success, and Wangari's too.

Saffron then made Benjamin's and Wangari's eyes widen in amazement, as she opened a series of greaseproof paper packages to reveal piled slices of smoked salmon and roast beef, fresh tomatoes, a crusty loaf of home-baked wholemeal bread, half a dozen large brown hard-boiled eggs and a punnet of strawberries.

'How did you get hold of food like this?' Wangari asked. 'The food in England is terrible and the rationing . . . ugh!'

'I have English and Scottish cousins who live on large farms. I rang them a couple of days ago and said I needed emergency supplies, and they sent them on the overnight trains.'

'How long are you over here?' Wangari asked.

'We're only in England for a couple more days,' Saffron said, 'and then we're moving to Germany.'

'I have family business that needs attending to,' Gerhard said. 'And I fear that, unlike this delightful occasion, it will be no picnic.'

Cricket was traditionally seen as a peculiarly English sport, played by gentlemen dressed in white, who interrupted the game with breaks for lunch and tea. The rules were baffling, but impeccably observed. The spectators watched in silence, with polite applause for good play, even by the team they opposed. But what was also English, though less obvious to the casual spectator, was that beneath its civilised veneer, cricket was a dangerous, even brutal sport. The bowler was perfectly entitled to aim a very hard ball at the batsman's head, or the more delicate parts of his anatomy, with the specific intention of hitting them as painfully as possible.

Such a battle was taking place in the Kenyan White Highlands at the Wanjohi Country Club, or 'the Wanjo' as it was known to its members, where the annual match between the club's First Eleven and a team of officials from Government House, the colonial administration in Nairobi, was taking place. The African sun blazed down upon the immaculately mown turf of the club's cricket pitch. The rolling brown hills stretched away towards the Aberdare Mountains on the horizon. Uniformed native servants offered the elegantly dressed spectators afternoon tea, or something stronger if they preferred.

Meanwhile, in the middle of the pitch, a large, angry man called Billy Atkinson was walking towards the end of his run-up, pushing a stray shank of sweaty black hair from his forehead. Billy Atkinson was the Wanjo's secret weapon. A Yorkshireman by birth, he was the quickest bowler in East Africa and the meanest, too.

The man facing him appeared to be as outmatched as an elderly spinster climbing into a boxing ring to face the world heavyweight champion. Ronald Stannard was short, skinny and narrow-shouldered. His eyes peered out from a round pair of National Health spectacles. His thinning, reddish-blond hair was covered by a moth-eaten old cricket cap.

Leon and Harriet Courtney were standing in the shade of the verandah that framed the cricket pavilion to one side of the ground.

'Look, darling. Stannard's about to get his fifty,' Harriet said. 'Mind you, Atkinson doesn't seem very impressed.'

A short while earlier, as Stannard had walked out to bat, Atkinson had come up to him, a towering mass of muscle and menace and growled, 'I'm going to knock tha' bloody block off.'

Stannard had not responded. He was used to dealing with bullies. From his first day at school the rough boys had used him as a human punchbag. At the age of eleven, forced to take part in cricket lessons against his will, he had discovered, to his amazement and everyone else's, that he had a natural gift for the game: a combination of hand–eye coordination, balance and timing that can't be taught. That talent put him in the school team and silenced his persecutors. Now he was putting it to good use in adult life.

No matter how fast Atkinson had bowled, Stannard smashed him to every corner of the ground. The least sporting spectators were roused from their refreshments and gossip to pay attention as this unlikely paragon rattled up forty-eight runs, two shy of the landmark score of fifty.

Leon had been glad of the distraction. He visited the Wanjo as seldom as possible. The place held too many memories. He could still feel the pride of watching Saffron, aged seven, compete here in a showjumping event in which she was the youngest competitor and came within a hair's breadth of victory. But likewise he had never rid himself of the terrible pain of watching his first wife, Eva, suffer a fatal miscarriage. He could see her as she lay in agony on a wooden dining table, her limbs thrashing in a fit brought on by eclampsia, her lifeblood draining away before his eyes. Every time he came back to the Wanjo that image was more vivid than the time before.

There were, however, some events at the club that could not be avoided if one wished to remain part of Kenyan society, and this was one of them. Every major landowner in the region had arrived to see the match, along with wives and children. Many of the most senior men from Government House had come to watch their team. The Chairman of the Wanjohi Country Club, Sir Percival Potter, was hosting a dinner-dance afterwards. Business would be conducted over whiskies, brandies and gin and tonics. The latest political gossip would be spread. The opportunity for Leon to gather intelligence and make his own opinions known was too good to miss.

The talk so far had been about the unrest in the Kikuyu community and the growing influence of the Mau Mau, especially among the young men of the tribe. Leon had spent much of the afternoon lost in thought, wondering whether his own Kikuyu workers would fall under their sway. Ronald Stannard had managed to make him think of something else.

Leon watched as Atkinson pawed the turf a couple of times, then started moving, gathering pace until he was sprinting as he approached the wicket.

'I'd rather face a charging bull elephant,' Leon muttered as Atkinson hurled the hard, red ball at Stannard, twenty-two yards away. The ball was travelling at almost ninety miles an hour as it hit the ground. It reared up off the sun-baked, heavily rolled pitch and sped like a missile towards the centre of Stannard's face.

Harriet gasped and she raised her hand to her face in horror at the sheer hostility of Atkinson's attack.

Stannard hit the ball when it was barely two feet from crashing into the bridge of his nose. A sharp crack echoed like a gunshot around the ground as he sent it hurtling across the emerald-green outfield until it collided with the boundary fence in front of the pavilion: four runs.

The spectators burst into wild applause. Those who were sitting jumped to their feet to register their admiration as the Kikuyu boy changing the metal numbers on the scoreboard moved Stannard's score from forty-eight to fifty-two.

The captain of the Governor's XI, Arthur Henderson, was the non-striking batsman. Amid the applause, he walked down the wicket to have a word with his team's hero.

'Damn well played, my boy,' Henderson said.

'Thank you, sir,' Stannard replied respectfully, for his skipper was also the most senior member of staff on the team.

'Now, we don't want to make the local chaps look foolish. Not good for their morale, or their authority with the natives. I'd be grateful if you didn't linger too long at the crease.'

Stannard understood what his captain was saying. He was being ordered to get out. He played three more venomous shots that were his own, unspoken way of telling Atkinson what he thought of him. Then he lobbed an easy catch back to the next bowler, the local vicar, who was so amazed that one of his slow, innocuous deliveries might have deceived the mighty batsman that he almost dropped it.

Henderson gave a nod of approval.

As Ronald Stannard left the field, raising his bat to acknowledge the applause, he thought of how proud his widowed mother would be when she read his letter describing the match. Here he was, a grammar-school boy, the son of a factory foreman and a sorter on the production line, being cheered from the pitch by the smartest men and women in Kenyan society. Even the native servants were cheering his performance, along with their masters and mistresses.

This, Stannard thought, was one of the happiest days of his life. The happiest would be when he was allowed to score a century. He had no doubt he would achieve it.

'Ah, Courtney,' said Sir Percival Potter, waving him over with a hand whose first and index fingers were wrapped around a cigarette, 'come and say hello to the hero of the hour.'

'My pleasure,' said Leon.

He glanced around, to make sure he was not deserting Harriet, spotted her engrossed in after-dinner conversation

with three other wives, and strolled over to join the chairman
of the Wanjo.

A waiter appeared holding out a tray of drinks. Leon took
a brandy and soda and nodded his thanks as Sir Percival said,
'Stannard, this is Leon Courtney, a man worth knowing.'

'I'm very pleased to meet you,' said Stannard, blinking
nervously.

His handshake was soft and damp. His dinner jacket was ill-
fitting and obviously second-hand. He was holding what looked
like a glass of orange squash. It hardly seemed possible that he
was the same young man as the fearless batsman who had been
the sensation of the day.

Little did Leon know, but Harriet and her friends were at
that moment speculating whether Stannard's performance in
bed would be as athletic and daring as his batting, or as meek
and mild as his off-the-field demeanour. This was, however, an
entirely theoretical debate. Ronald Stannard was a virgin who
had never so much as kissed a woman.

'Congratulations,' Leon said. 'Splendid innings.'

'Thank you very much, sir,' Stannard said.

'How long have you been on the staff at Government House?'

'About three months. I joined the Colonial Office a year ago.
This is my first overseas posting.'

'And what do you make of Kenya?'

Stannard looked from Leon to Sir Percival, trying to balance
his desire to give Leon a straight answer with the knowledge
that both he and Sir Percival were highly influential men whom
a young, junior official would be unwise to offend.

'I think the situation is more complicated than I realised
before I arrived.'

'Well played,' said Leon, with an appreciative nod of the
head, for he could see how carefully Stannard had dealt with
the question and how unsure the young man must be feeling at
an occasion such as this.

Having been born, bred, raised and educated in Africa, Leon
did not give a damn about the nuances of the British class

system. But he could hear that Ronald Stannard spoke with a regional accent, rather than the clipped, upper-class tones of the other colonial officers who had played in or attended the match. They would have had their jobs fall like ripe fruit into their laps. Stannard must have had to work his way up. To many members of white Kenyan society, not least those who were hiding their own humble origins, that would make Stannard an object of disdain. To Leon Courtney, it was an achievement to be applauded.

'I was just explaining to young Stannard that I am considered to be quite the liberal by some of my club members,' Sir Percival said. 'As you know, I regard the white man's purpose in Africa to be a moral one. We have a duty to prepare the natives for the day when they will be ready to run their own nations. I doubt it will be in our lifetimes, but even if we do not see the fruits of our labours, we must still plant and nourish the seeds, eh?'

'I completely agree, sir,' Stannard said. 'To me, the only justification for empire is the good it can do for people less fortunate than ourselves. What do you think, Mr Courtney?'

'We have that duty, certainly. But we need to move a lot faster towards granting Kenya its independence.'

Stannard looked surprised. 'How interesting. Why do you say that?'

'Partly as a matter of principle. I've always had more faith in the native peoples' abilities than most in these parts.'

'You should be aware, Stannard, that Leon's views make mine seem positively conservative. He is looked on as a dangerous radical by every other white man in this room,' Sir Percival said, chuckling. 'He's just so damnably rich that no one dares say so to his face.'

'A few of them have said so, loudly ... and rudely,' Leon said. 'But I'm not as bleeding hearted as they think. I reckon it's in our self-interest to give more control to the people and keep their goodwill. Better that than have Kenya torn from our hands and lose everything.'

Stannard frowned. 'Do you really think there's a chance of that?'

'Bloody Mau Mau animals ...' Sir Percival muttered. 'They're a bunch of savages. Apes in human form.'

'Well, I certainly don't condone what the Mau Mau are doing,' Leon said, 'though their victims so far seem to be restricted to their own people.'

'They'll be coming after us next, mark my words.'

'They may well, Percy, but if we want to outwit our enemy, we should pay attention to what he says and wants, and why he's here in the first place.'

'I can tell you exactly why he's here. Ingratitude, greed and the pernicious influence of Bolshie agitators.'

'Do you think there's more to it than that, sir?' Stannard asked Leon, and suddenly Leon saw a hint of the brave bats-man in the young man's watery eyes.

You think there's more to it, don't you, lad? he thought. *Right then, I'll tell you what these other stuffed shirts won't.*

'In my opinion the Kikuyu have genuine grievances, and the reason that some of them have resorted to violence – which, I say again, I deplore – is that when they tried to make their case peacefully, no one paid a damn bit of attention.'

'Oh really, Leon, that's a bit much!' Sir Percival protested.

'Well, how would you feel if all your land was taken by peo-ple from another country?'

'You've taken a large slice of it yourself!'

'Yes – which is why I do my damnedest to respect the tradi-tions and knowledge of the people who live on it.'

'How do you do that?' Stannard asked.

'The Kikuyu have farmed here for centuries. They're better at it than half the damn fools who came out to this country from England without the first idea about local conditions. Those same fools refused to learn from the Kikuyu. Instead they prohibited them from selling most of their crops on the open market, giving white farmers a virtual monopoly.

'I think that's wrong. Worse, it's plain stupid. We should use their knowledge to everyone's advantage. So I let my farmers work land of their own, within my estate, alongside the work they do for me. I buy their crops off them at a fair price. I take it all to market and, yes, I sell for more than I paid, but not much more, and my people know it. And another thing . . .'

Leon paused for a moment. *Oh hell, I've really mounted my hobby horse now*, he berated himself. *What the hell, might as well ride it.*

'Young Kikuyu men can only get a wife once they have land of their own, with which to support a family. But there isn't enough land on the territories set aside for the Kikuyu. That means the young men can't acquire any, and so they can't marry. It's hardly a surprise if they become frustrated and angry. I make sure that my young Kikuyu get land, so they can start their own families. The result is I have much happier, more productive workers.'

'Like the Cadbury family,' Stannard said. 'They gave their workers houses, playing fields, schools . . . everyone loved them. My father was a foreman at the Bournville factory. He thought the Cadburys were royalty.'

'Did you say your father worked . . . in a factory?' Sir Percival asked.

'Well, I don't claim to be royalty,' Leon said, ignoring the chairman's expression. 'But I like to think my people are content and don't see any reason to rebel.'

'And that's good for business,' Stannard said.

'Exactly . . . Tell me, Stannard, were you in the war?'

'No, sir, I was too young. I was called up in March '45, but by the time I'd completed my training the war in Europe was over. There was talk we were going to be shipped to the Far East, but the Americans dropped the bomb before that happened.'

'Well, a lot of young Kikuyu men served in the King's African Rifles. In the first couple of years of the war they saw action in East Africa against Mussolini's mob. Then they were shipped out to Burma. They saw some tough action against the Japs, conducted themselves damn well. You'd agree with that much, at least, Percy, surely?'

'Can't deny it, they made first-class soldiers.'

'Quite so. And when the war was over, they had the same reaction as their white comrades. They'd gone to fight for the Empire, now they wanted something in return. That's why so many British soldiers voted Labour in the '45 election and kicked poor old Winston out of Number Ten. I'd never in a month of Sundays do any such thing, I might add—'

'Thank God for that,' sighed Sir Percy.

'. . . but I could see their point. And I can see the Kikuyu veterans' point, too. They stuck their necks on the line and when they came back, nothing had changed. Bear in mind, these men spent time in India during the war. They know about Gandhi and they've seen India gain its independence. Hardly surprising they think, "I'd like a bit of that."'

'But Indians are civilised,' Sir Ronald objected. 'They had cities, writing, mathematics and all that long before we got there. They were far readier for independence than the African.'

'The African doesn't agree,' said Leon. 'He may be wrong, but he wants the chance to find out. That's why this is a matter of self-interest. I'm a businessman and I don't want to lose my business. So I say, let's make a deal – they get more say in governing the country, we keep most of our land. Trust me, if we don't make that deal we're liable to lose the lot.'

'No we aren't,' Sir Percy insisted. 'That's the point. They don't have the means or the might to beat us.'

'Gandhi beat us.'

Before Sir Percival could argue the point further, the club's maître d', a stately, bald Kikuyu in a sharply pressed charcoal grey suit, walked up to the three men, waited until Sir Percival had acknowledged his presence and then whispered a few words in his boss's ear.

Sir Percival frowned as he listened, then murmured, 'You're quite sure about this?'

The maître d' nodded.

'Then I think we should deal with the matter immediately. Get everything ready and we'll be with you in a few minutes.'

The maître d' nodded and walked away.

'What was that about?' Leon asked.

'One of the boys was caught trying to steal food from the kitchen. Cheeky little bugger had been going through the dirty plates and picking off bits of uneaten meat.'

Stannard looked aghast. 'But . . .'

Sir Percival patted him on the shoulder. 'Sorry, my boy, must dash. If you want to watch the action, Leon, we'll be in the yard behind the kitchens. I'm going to round up a few of the other chaps. Best be discreet, though. Don't want to worry the memsahibs.'

The Wanjo chairman disappeared into the crowd of guests. Stannard watched him sidling up to another group of male guests for a brief, conspiratorial conversation and then saw the looks of excitement on their faces as Sir Percival walked away.

'What's going on?' Stannard asked Leon.

'How long have you been out here?' Leon replied.

'Almost three months.'

'Huh . . . Time you saw the real Kenya. Follow me.'

Stannard was standing with Leon Courtney and another twenty or so party guests, formed up on one side of a courtyard where delivery vans unloaded foodstuffs and other goods for the Wanjohi Country Club's kitchen, dining room and bar. Lamps mounted on the walls and headlights from cars that had been drawn up across the open end of the yard illuminated the scene. The gentlemen members smoked cigars, cradled freshly poured drinks and chatted among themselves. Their faces bore the flushed, sweaty look of white men, wearing formal attire in hot climates, who have eaten and drunk a great deal. The conversation was good-humoured, even joshing, like spectators waiting for a rugby match to begin.

Across the far side of the wall, facing Stannard and the others, a similar number of Wanjo staff members were assembled. They were mostly black, with a scattering of Indians, all in their various uniforms: chefs and their minions, waiters and waitresses, barmen and scullery maids. The Indians were talking to one another, but the Africans looked on in silence, their faces sullen, devoid of animation. They were waiting and watching while their masters gave their little display.

A wooden dining chair, like the one on which Stannard had sat for dinner, had been placed in the centre of the yard, with its back facing towards the kitchen. The maître d' stood beside it, next to a young man, barely more than a boy, who wore the blue trousers and white top of a junior cook. This, Stannard realised, was the alleged food thief.

Stannard found he could not take his eyes off the boy. His face seemed as blank as all the others, but the longer Stannard looked, the more he detected the sign of the boy's fear: the widened eyes, the chewed lip, the way his Adam's apple bobbed as he swallowed.

Stannard found his stomach tightening anxiously.

'What's going to happen to him?' he asked Leon.

'Wait, watch . . . and keep your thoughts to yourself.'

'But . . .'

Leon Courtney was forty years older that Ronald Stannard, but he was taller, broader in the shoulder and imbued with the kind of authority a man acquires after a lifetime of leadership. He looked at Stannard with stern eyes.

'Not a word, do you hear? For your own good.'

'Yes, sir.'

A gentle ripple of applause broke out, reminding Stannard of the sound that had greeted him as he walked to the batting crease that afternoon. Sir Percival had emerged through the kitchen door and was striding across the yard, holding a horsewhip.

'Oh, dear God . . .' Stannard gasped and fell silent as he sensed Leon's disapproval.

Sir Percival looked at the maître d' and said, 'If you'd be so good . . .'

'Yes sir,' the maître d' replied.

He ordered the boy to take off his shirt and undo his belt. Stannard could see that the uniform trousers were too big for the boy's skinny waist, so he now had to hold them up with one hand.

The maître d' moved the boy so that he was standing with his back towards Sir Percival.

'Hands here,' the maître d' said, tapping the top of the dinner chair.

The boy gripped the chair. His trousers fell down. The white men cheered.

'So it's not true about their cocks!' one hooted. 'Thieving bastard's got a tiddler!'

Stannard knew what it felt like to be jeered at, to be helpless and humiliated. He was ashamed to be part of the same race as these crowing loudmouths, and he could not bear to see what was about to happen. Suddenly he felt an iron grip around his bicep.

'Don't make an exhibition of yourself,' Leon hissed at him. 'Stand up straight. Eyes front.'

Stannard forced himself to obey. He saw the boy's hands clenched round the wooden chair-back. He saw his head bowed in shame and knees quivering with fear. He heard Sir Percival announce, 'The penalty for theft, as laid down in club rules, is fifteen strokes of the whip.'

'Hear! Hear!' one of the men in the dinner jackets said.

Sir Percival raised his right arm and pulled it back, holding the horsewhip diagonally behind him. He took a sight on the accused boy's buttocks, then swung his arm and brought the thick whip down to strike a wicked blow that made its victim wince in pain as a welt began to form across the top of his thighs.

The maître d' pulled the food thief up straight and put him back in position for the second blow.

One after the other, the strokes rained down upon the boy's naked body, criss-crossing his thighs, buttocks and back in a pattern of raised skin, bruised flesh and the occasional glint of blood where more than one strike had hit the same spot.

The boy cried out on the third stroke as the pain became more than he could bear in silence. By the sixth he had started to cry. Sir Percival, meanwhile, was scarlet-faced, his chest heaving with exertion, for he was well into his late sixties, overweight and unfit.

As the chairman paused to mop his face, the black servants looked on impassively. Stannard felt their silent rage at the cruelty and injustice they were witnessing.

The boy had been accused of stealing food that had been discarded by the men and women for whom it had been cooked. It was obvious the lad was in need of a decent meal, and Stannard was willing to bet he had parents and siblings who were equally malnourished. What possible harm had he done?

The longer it continued, the stronger Stannard's feelings of physical nausea. The boy's humiliation disturbed him the most. The physical wounds would heal, but the mental ones would fester for years. Stannard understood why Courtney was convinced that an accommodation had to be made with Kenya's native people. The pent-up rage emanating from the onlooking staff was almost tangible, yet the whites who were egging Sir Percival on seemed oblivious to the troubles they were storing up for themselves.

By the tenth stroke, Sir Percival appeared to be struggling.

'I say,' someone declared, 'poor old Percy's in danger of a heart attack. Anyone else want a go?'

'I'll do it,' another replied.

'Attaboy, Quentin!' came the shout as a man emerged from the scrum and marched towards Sir Percival.

He was old enough to be Stannard's father and considerably fatter than the man he was taking over from – indeed, he was obese. He carried his weight like a weapon with which to bully anyone smaller or weaker than himself.

Something made Stannard glance at Leon Courtney. He had his eyes fixed on Quentin and his face bore an expression of loathing that seemed out of keeping with the self-confident, generous nature Courtney had demonstrated earlier.

'Let me help you with that, old boy,' Quentin said.

'Much obliged,' Sir Percival wheezed, handing over the whip.

Quentin smacked it gently against his palm a couple of times, then went to the boy and said something to him. The words were too quiet for anyone else to hear, but Stannard could see the boy's eyes widen. Whatever Quentin had said had made him frightened.

With good reason. The last five strokes were delivered with a brutal fury. Each one drew blood; the beaten boy howled and brought a deeper look of savage satisfaction to Quentin's face.

When it was over, the boy let go his grip on the chair and collapsed to the ground. Quentin stood over him for a moment, like a hunter over his dead prey, then walked to the other club staff and strolled past them, smacking the whip against his palm.

The message was clear. Quentin would do the same to any black Kenyan who broke the rules. Stannard was overcome with disgust at this vile sadist and the supposed gentlemen who were encouraging him on. He felt his stomach heave, his throat gag, and he bent over and was violently sick.

Billy Atkinson saw Stannard bent double, puking his guts out on the tarmac.

'Aye, like I said, soft,' he crowed.

His teammates, who had spent the afternoon running across the outfield fetching the balls that Stannard had hit to all corners, took delight in seeing their sporting tormentor humbled.

Stannard went out onto the lawn outside the clubhouse to get some fresh air. He was still there, trying to clean the mess off his clothes and shoes, when he felt a tap on his shoulder. He turned to see his captain, Arthur Henderson, who said, 'A word with you, young man.'

Stannard followed him to one side of the path.

'That was a damn poor show, making an exhibition of yourself. I take it you had too much to drink.'

'No sir, I would never do that,' Stannard replied. 'I'm teetotal.'

Henderson looked appalled. 'Good grief!' he gasped. 'What was it then, touch of the dicky tummy?'

'No, sir, it was . . .' Stannard had suppressed his feelings once, when Leon was there to restrain him. But this time he could not stop himself. 'I just couldn't bear it, sir.'

'Bear what?'

'Seeing a native worker being beaten, sir. It was . . . completely unforgivable.'

Henderson's eyes narrowed. 'What do you mean by that?'

'Well, sir, if Britain stands for anything, it's the rule of law. Surely that's what we're supposed to be spreading throughout the Empire. Seeing a native being beaten like that, without any chance to put his case . . . It was barbaric, sir, and . . . well . . . it made me sick to see British men behaving that way and no one lifting a finger.'

'I never heard anything so pathetic in all my days,' Henderson said. 'Let me tell you why we're here. Forget all that white man's burden nonsense about giving the lesser races the benefits of our civilisation. The only thing that matters is keeping Kenya in the Empire. We've lost India. We're losing Malaya. It's a matter of time before the West African colonies and the Caribbean islands go too. But Kenya is the one jewel left in the imperial crown and we are not letting it out of our hands, d'you hear?'

'Yes, sir.'

'As for tonight's show of discipline being barbaric, well, it probably was. But do you think any African would treat a thief any better? The Kikuyu beat their miscreants with a club called a *kiboko*. Believe me, young man, that boy thought he'd got off lightly just getting a few strokes of a whip.'

'Yes, but—'

'But nothing. I spent five years in Somaliland. They believe in Muslim law there. That boy wouldn't have been given a whipping, they'd have chopped his bloody hand off.' Henderson paused. 'Listen, Stannard, if I'd not seen you play cricket I'd have had you marked down as a lily-livered bleeding heart, and had you shipped back to England on the next boat out of Mombasa. But no one can face fast bowling the way you do without a bit of backbone, so I'll tell it to you straight.

'Those chaps you saw cheering their heads off because a young black man was being whipped are scared witless. They know that they, and their wives and children, are outnumbered a hundred to one by the natives. They live in dread of the day when the masses rise up against them. The only way we can keep a grip on the place is to make the blacks more scared of us than we are of them. The moment they scent weakness, or loss of conviction in the white population, the game's up.'

'Then surely it would be wise to come to some kind of peaceful settlement, sir.'

'And what do you suppose the Kenyan nationalists would think if they heard we wanted to parley? They'd know at once that it was a sign of weakness, proof that we'd lost faith in our ability to hold on. We have to keep grinding their noses into the dirt. We can't let up for a second. Believe me, Stannard, it's them or us.'

Quentin De Lancey had greatly impressed the gentlemen of the Wanjohi Country Club by stepping in and giving a misbehaving servant the thrashing he deserved. He was leaning against the bar, accepting free drinks while he gave his admirers the benefits of his wisdom.

'I've been out here thirty years, give or take, and my views remain what they have always been. The black man is nothing but vermin. Oh, I know there are some who like to dress up in fancy suits and play at being civilised, but mark my words, they're savages under the skin.'

'And they breed like rabbits, particularly the damn Kukes,' said another Wanjo man, using the term by which the colonists referred to the Kikuyu. 'We're going to be swamped soon, if we're not careful.'

'Well, you know what they say,' said De Lancey. 'The only good Kuke is a dead Kuke. They're no use as workers. Lazy buggers, never do what they're told, always complaining.'

'What do you make of this Mau Mau business? You've heard the stories, I'm sure. It's time someone at Government House put a stop to it, I say.'

'There's only one way to put a stop to it,' De Lancey replied. 'Say what you like about old Adolf, but he had the right idea about dealing with people who are a threat to one's race. We have to deal with the Kukes once and for all.'

'The only good Kuke, and so forth.'

'Correct. And we won't be able to sleep easy in our beds until all the Kukes are good Kukes. Do I need to say more . . .?'

'No, De Lancey, you don't. I think we all take the point very clearly.'

There were about a dozen men clustered in a knot around the bar. Every one of them had understood what he was suggesting. And not one had disagreed.

The Schloss Meerbach had been built by an industrial emperor to match the country home of a king.

In the early 1850s, Maximilian II of Bavaria invited the steam engine magnate Gustav von Meerbach to stay at the royal residence of Hohenschwangau Castle. Gustav was impressed by this hilltop fortress that looked medieval yet was newly built, with all the creature comforts that the mid-nineteenth century had to offer. He purchased a swathe of land along the hills that rose from the shores of the Bodensee, the long, narrow lake that separated Bavaria from Switzerland. Having found the spot with the most picturesque views, he commissioned a residence of his own.

A gentleman might have ensured that his castle was smaller and less ostentatious in its decoration than his host's pride and joy. But, like some of his descendants, Gustav was no gentleman. He built a monument to himself that matched his character. It was undeniably impressive, even magnificent. Yet it was monumental, almost bullying in its severity.

Gerhard and Saffron were staying at Schloss Meerbach while he saw to his family business. The first item on the agenda was a family meeting, held around a table in the library. Ceiling-high, black oak bookshelves filled with leather-bound volumes, unopened for decades, ran along the two long walls of the rectangular room. At the far end, mullioned windows provided views across wooded hillsides to the lake, while the fourth wall was dominated by a massive stone fireplace, surrounded by the stuffed hunting trophies, displays of weaponry and armour, and portraits of stern, glowering von Meerbach men that were the typical ornaments throughout the castle.

As she looked around the table, Saffron paid little attention to these mementoes of the past. She was more interested in the men and women around her. To Saffron's right sat Gerhard's mother Alatha. She had been bullied and abused by both her husband Otto and her older son Konrad, but retained her dignity. She was over eighty, and the suffering she had endured could be seen on the lines traced across her graceful, fine-boned features. Yet she somehow possessed an air of serenity as if, after so many years of stormy weather, she had finally found safe harbour and calm waters.

The same could not be said of the woman seated opposite Alatha. Trudi von Meerbach, the first wife of Gerhard's older brother Konrad, exuded bitterness and anger. It made her a difficult woman to be around, but Saffron could understand why Trudi was emotionally scarred. Barely a decade had passed since Konrad had told her that he was divorcing her on his terms and that if she resisted she would, in his words, 'Spend the few remaining days of your life in a slave-labour camp.'

Saffron's eyes came to rest on a tall, elegant, immaculately dressed man, seated opposite her, whose silver hair only added to his handsome dignity. He smiled at her and she was about to speak to him when Gerhard, seated at the head of the table, rose to his feet.

'Good evening,' he said. 'As you know, I was for some time unable to contribute to the management of the Meerbach Motor Works. That is why, three years ago, before the Federal Republic of Germany came into being, I asked Isidore Solomons to become our Chief Executive Officer. For me, it was an easy decision. I trusted Isidore completely and I knew he had an unmatched understanding of our family's portfolio. But for him, the situation was not so simple. Our family has, in the past, treated him appallingly, so he had every reason to refuse my invitation. But he did not and I am profoundly grateful to him for that. So now let me hand over to a man I am proud to call my friend – Isidore.'

'Thank you, Herr Meerbach,' Isidore said with the due formality of a man addressing his boss. He gave a nod of the head to Alatha. 'Countess . . .'

'Good morning, Isidore,' she replied with a fond smile, since she had known him since he was a boy.

Like his father before him, Isidore had been the von Meerbach family lawyer. Before taking on that role he had fought with distinction in the First World War and been awarded the

Blue Max, Germany's highest award for gallantry. Alatha had been disgusted by the way her oldest son had treated such a loyal servant to their family and country.

For Saffron, 'Max' was also the code name by which she had known Isidore when they first met in pre-war Switzerland, barely twenty-four hours after her encounter with Gerhard. It was Isidore's account of how Gerhard had helped the Solomons family escape Germany, in defiance of his brother's will, that had made Saffron certain that she had found the right man.

'So,' Isidore said, 'I have been asked to consider the current state of the Meerbach Motor Works, assess its future prospects and give my advice as to the best course for the future. But, however distressing this may be, I must begin with the man who is not here – Count Konrad von Meerbach. No one knows where he is now, or even whether he is still alive. The same is true of his second wife, Francesca, who is also known by the nickname Chessi.'

'Yes, when we were best friends at school . . . Chessi and Saffy,' Saffron said sadly, more to herself than the rest of the table.

Isidore glanced at her and then continued, 'Both have disappeared. The count remains a wanted man, a pariah, regarded as a war criminal by the Allied powers and the state of Israel.' Isidore paused for a moment and looked around the table. 'I apologise if my description seems too harsh.'

'On the contrary, it is no more than the truth,' Gerhard said. 'Please, carry on.'

'Very well. I have been able to establish that the company's reserves of foreign currency were removed from its bank accounts in the two weeks before the end of the war in Europe. At around the same time, a number of the most important works in the art collection here at Schloss Meerbach were cut from their frames and removed, and have not been seen since. It is possible that other members of the Motor Works board took the company's money. Allied troops may have stolen the artworks. But the most likely explanation is that the count and countess fled the country, taking the money and canvases with them.'

'So he's a thief as well as everything else,' Trudi hissed.

'Well, the paintings were the count's personal property, so he could not be accused of stealing them. But smuggling them out of Germany and into another country would be a serious crime. As for the company funds, the count was of course the largest single shareholder in Meerbach Motor Works, but that did not entitle him to embezzle company money. That was a criminal act, and the loss of crucial financial reserves has had a damaging impact on the company's ability to recover in the past few years.

'Equally significant has been the stain the count's wartime activities has left on the name and reputation of the Meerbach Motor Works . . .'

Isidore paused. Saffron was looking at him with a hand raised slightly off the table, wanting to ask a question.

'But, Max, surely that applies to almost every major German company,' she said. 'Forgive me, I don't wish to be insensitive, but they were all caught up in the Nazi war effort, or the Final Solution, in one way or another.'

'Yes, but our company bears the name of an SS general. And as the representative of an American corporation told me . . .' The meeting had been conducted in German, but now Isidore switched into English. '"I'm real sorry, Izzy, but that sure is bad for the brand."'

'The American was right,' Gerhard said. 'That's why I dropped the "von" from my name. I didn't want to be connected to Konrad.'

'I always thought the "von" was a ridiculous, *arriviste* affectation,' remarked Alatha, whose own family could trace their aristocratic lineage and title back to the twelfth century. 'The Meerbachs added it to sound smarter than they really were.'

Saffron could not help but smile, knowing how much Alatha must have relished the opportunity to skewer the pomposity of men who had caused her so much grief. But returning her attention to the matter at hand, she asked Isidore, 'Are you suggesting that the company should change its name?'

'My suggestions go further than that,' he replied. 'I am suggesting it should no longer belong to the Meerbach family at all.'

Isidore Solomons took a careful look at the faces of the other six people in the room. So far as he could tell, only Trudi von Meerbach seemed upset by what he had suggested. But she always looked infuriated, so he decided to ignore her and carry on.

'The situation in Germany is more favourable now than at any time in the past forty years. The economy is booming, creating demand for our products, and we are also developing export markets. There is little doubt that the Meerbach Motor Works can prosper in the future as it has in the past. But from the day it was founded, this company has been led by a member of the family. So now I must ask – does anyone here want to take on that responsibility?'

Isidore was met by silence. 'Gerhard,' he asked, 'may I speak to you and your family as a friend?'

'Of course.'

'Very well, then. I believe that the actions of the past two counts have left you all with a cursed inheritance. You will not be free to pursue happy, fulfilling lives as long as you are weighed down by this damn company – and this damn castle, for that matter.'

Gerhard thumped the table with the flat of his palm, to signal his hearty agreement.

'I've always hated it.'

'I couldn't agree more,' said Alatha. 'So soul destroying!' She glanced at her son. 'Do you remember, darling, when your father threw us out and we went to live in my pretty villa in Grünwald? Such an improvement!'

'Then you will not, perhaps, object to my advice,' Isidore resumed. 'I have been approached by a number of parties interested in purchasing various family properties, including the Motor Works, the land surrounding the factory, the castle and the estate. I am confident that we can achieve good prices. You might wish to receive some of the payment for the Motor Works in the form of shares in the purchasing company. In this way you could benefit from future growth. I would also counsel you to keep a small portion of the land in the castle estate – a few hundred metres of lake shore and a little woodland, perhaps – for your private use.'

'How much do you think the sales would bring in?' Gerhard asked.

'I cannot give you an exact figure, but if we can get buyers bidding against one another, I would hope to achieve a total in excess of ten million marks.'

'Otto used to boast that he was worth more than a hundred million,' Alatha said, dryly. 'And that was forty years ago.'

'Ha!' Gerhard exclaimed. 'I can remember you and I, Mother, sitting at a board meeting in, I suppose, '34 or '35 while a company accountant said we were as wealthy as the Rothschilds and the Rockefellers.'

'But one wouldn't wish for that now, though, darling. It would be too much . . . grotesque.'

'I agree,' Gerhard said. 'I am tempted to say we should give all the proceeds to charity. But I leave that decision to each individual.'

'There is one problem . . .' Isidore said. 'Until Konrad von Meerbach is formally declared dead, he retains his majority shareholding in the company, which means that the bulk of proceeds from any sale go to him.'

'That's outrageous!' Trudi exclaimed, and Saffron agreed.

'There must be some way you could get around that, Izzy,' Gerhard said.

'We cannot pay him, of course, since we do not know where he is and his known bank accounts have been frozen by order of the US Treasury. And you all have a claim against Konrad for embezzling assets in which you had an interest, so you could demand his money as compensation for your loss. But I think that the fairest solution is for Konrad's money to be put in trust for his children until such time as there is proof that he is dead, or still alive.'

'Then perhaps Mother, Trudi and I should take a vote, since we are the other shareholders present,' Gerhard said. 'The motion is simple – do we agree that Isidore should proceed with the sale of the Meerbach Motor Works, and the Schloss Meerbach? All in favour, raise your hands.'

The vote was unanimous.

'In that case, let us adjourn for lunch.'

'Before we do,' Isidore said, 'there's one last item of business to consider, isn't that right, Countess?'

'Oh yes, so there is, I'd almost forgotten,' said Alatha. 'Excuse me one moment . . .' She got up from the table and walked to the door, opened it and said, 'You may come in now, gentlemen.'

She returned leading four men, who all bore the tough, craggy look of men who'd done many years of hard, manual labour, and not stinted on tobacco or alcohol during that time. They were wearing suits whose fabric, never high quality to begin with, had been made shiny in places with wear. But the suits were cleaned and pressed and the shoes beneath them shone as brightly as a guardsman's boots.

As they reached the table and stood, shuffling nervously, Alatha said, 'Would you like to do the honours, Herr Schinkel?'

'Thank you, Countess,' said the biggest of the four, a tough, almost menacing figure, who was holding a polished wooden box in hands so ingrained with oil that no amount of cleaning could ever completely remove the stain. He approached Gerhard, who rose from his chair to greet him.

The two men shook hands and then Schinkel said, 'Me and the lads here all served in the Luftwaffe. Not pilots like you, of course. We were mechanics.'

'You should be proud of that,' Gerhard said. 'We could never have left the ground, let alone come home safely, without the work you men did.'

'Thank you, sir.' Schinkel's face was softened by the smile that crossed it. 'Much appreciated.'

'And sincerely meant, I assure you. Now, what can I do for you?'

'Well, me and the lads, we were all proud of you. Having a famous ace like you, part of the family we've worked for all our lives—'

'And our dads before us,' another of the men said.

'Well, it meant a lot to us.'

Gerhard's face fell. Hearing him be accused of treason, how-ever unjustly, must have been almost as shaming for these men as it had been for him.

'I'm sorry if you ever felt that I let you down. I promise you that—'

'Oh no, sir, we never felt that, not for a single second. See, we were all socialists, the proper kind, not like Adolf's lot, National Socialists, my arse . . .' Schinkel suddenly realised he'd let him-self get carried away. Blushing like a maiden, he gulped and said, 'Sorry, Countess, ladies.'

'That's quite all right, Herr Schinkel,' said Alatha. 'Any man who speaks well of my son can do no wrong in my eyes.'

The men all laughed. 'Stop cursing and tell him what we've done,' another of them said.

'Yes, well, when we heard you were coming back home, after all these years, we made something for you. As a token of our appreciation, like.'

Schinkel held out the box.

'Thank you,' said Gerhard, opening it.

The inside of the box was lined with rich, black velvet that set off a gleaming metal flask within. Gerhard lifted the flask out of the box. It was made of two parts: the main body was matt, and as Gerhard looked at it more closely he saw it was brushed steel, but worked to a finish as perfect as any precious metal in a jeweller's store. A second, gleaming piece of metal, which Gerhard thought must be chrome-plated, fitted like a lid across the top, with a screw-cap in the middle to let drink in and out.

Though it was small and slender enough to fit inside a jacket pocket, the flask was surprisingly heavy in his hand. He said as much to Schinkel, who nodded.

'That's because it's milled from solid steel, just like one of our engine blocks. We thought it would be fitting.' He paused and added, with a nod towards the flask, 'We wrote something for you too.'

He turned the flask over and there were three words: *Immer in Einsatz*.

Gerhard smiled and showed it to Saffron.

'"Always in action",' he said, in English. 'It's the motto of the Luftwaffe.'

'Well, you can forget about going into any more action, darling husband of mine,' she replied, speaking in German so the men would understand. 'I worked far too hard to keep you alive to let you get into trouble now.'

As Gerhard gave a rueful shrug, the men all laughed. Then he said thank you once again and then, as any good officer should, took the trouble to speak for a moment to each of the men, inquiring about their families, asking them if there was anything he could do in return and making a careful mental note of their replies. Saffron, too, joined in the conversation, making sure that they knew that even though she was British, she was touched by their loyalty to her man.

Athala escorted the men from the room, assuring them that the cook had prepared a hearty lunch and that they were not to stint on the beer.

'I have it on good authority that if you skip work this afternoon, the boss will not mind.'

Gerhard, meanwhile, had gone to speak to Isidore.

'I hope it wasn't too hard for you, hearing all that Luftwaffe talk.'

'My dear boy, if it had been hard for me, I would not have let them in the room. No, I was just musing on the irony that you and I, who are by far the most decorated warriors that this household has ever seen, also share the distinction that the Nazis wanted to kill us.'

'Very true,' said Gerhard, 'but listen. Those were good men, and there are thousands more like them. So whatever we do with this company, and whoever we sell it to, none of our people must end up unemployed. Do you hear me? Not one.'

*

An hour later, the family were taking coffee in a small sitting room when Saffron approached Gerhard and Isidore, who were chatting about the upcoming Olympics in Helsinki.

'I'm sorry for breaking in,' she said. 'But it seems to me that there's one important matter arising from this morning's meeting that we really need to discuss.'

'Go on . . .' Isidore said, with the air of a man who knew what was coming next.

'It's Konrad. He's like a ghost hanging over everything. We don't know if he's alive or dead. If he's alive, we don't know where he is, or what he's doing, or even what he's stolen from everyone else. We have to find out.'

'Maybe,' said Gerhard. 'But do you really want to go looking for him?' He gazed into Saffron's eyes. 'You have never met Konrad, but if you did, you would see at once that this is a man driven by hate, like other people are driven by desire for money, or fame, or sex. And I think that Francesca has become like him. I saw it in their eyes when they came to my trial. They wanted me to suffer. That was all that mattered to them. I don't want you to become their enemy, too.'

'I already am,' said Saffron. 'In Francesca's eyes, I stole the man she loved from her when I fell in love with you. And my father took Konrad's father Otto from him.'

'If you know that these people hate you, Saffron, is that not an argument for leaving them alone?' Isidore asked. 'Gerhard was telling me how much you long for a peaceful life. Konrad is a very dangerous man. If we begin a serious search for him, who knows how he might react?'

'Yes, there's a risk,' Saffron said. 'But it's one we have to take. We won't have peace until we deal with Konrad. We should talk about that. We need to make a plan.'

'Very well then, we will talk,' Isidore said. 'But not in Germany. Even now, you know, I don't feel entirely safe. There are people here for whom nothing has changed. But I will be back in Zurich this weekend. Perhaps then . . .?'

'Fine,' said Saffron. 'Zurich it is.'

The Mau Mau had yet to strike at their colonial rulers, yet the idea of their presence somewhere out there, watching, waiting, preparing to strike, had spread fear like a viral epidemic, infecting the entire white population. People were demanding that something must be done, though no one knew quite what. The authorities could not strike back at an enemy they could not see. But as the cries for action grew stronger it was decided that a Special Constabulary would be formed.

At two o'clock one morning, with the waning moon no more than a silver sliver, Kungu Kabaya and Wilson Gitiri crouched in a drainage ditch that ran beside a dirt road. Across the way stood a small mud-brick building with a corrugated iron roof: the local police station.

Three weeks earlier, workmen had erected a second building. It was a low, squat structure made from reinforced concrete and it stood about twenty yards away from the station. Wooden posts, ten feet high, had been driven into the ground at regular intervals, forming a perimeter around the new structure. Barbed wire was strung between the posts to form a protective fence, with a double gate facing the police station, also constructed of wooden poles and barbed wire. It was secured by a heavy chain.

A convoy of trucks had come and gone. Their cargo had been unloaded. The natives who transferred a stream of heavy wooden crates from the trucks to the new building were believed to be loyal to their white masters. The contents of those cases were supposed to be secret, as was the purpose for which they were intended. But the terrifying power of the blood oaths outweighed any loyalty to the Crown, and there were precious few secrets from the Mau Mau any more.

Kabaya checked his watch. 'Go,' he whispered.

Gitiri raised his head above the side of the ditch, looked around to make sure no one was watching and ran across the road, bent low, before coming to a halt beside the fence. He was carrying a pair of long-handled cutters. They made short work of the barbed wire and Gitiri fashioned an opening big enough for a man, or a case filled with rifles, to get through. He turned towards the ditch and gave a quick thumbs-up.

Seconds later, Kabaya was scurrying to his second in command, followed by three other men. All of them had empty army backpacks hanging from their shoulders.

One after another they crawled through the gap in the fence, then ran up to the bare concrete wall of the blockhouse. They were confronted by the only way in or out: a thick steel door as impervious to gunfire or hand grenades as the concrete around it.

It would take an artillery shell or a bomb to smash into the building. Kungu Kabaya had neither. Yet he believed that he could get in. He looked at his watch and muttered under his breath.

'Come on . . . Come on . . .'

Maina Mwangi was the police constable on duty. The night watch had never traditionally been a particularly arduous task. The country around the police station was white-owned. The colonists drank too much. They committed too many acts of adultery for the tastes of the pious men and women who cooked their food, cleaned their houses, washed their clothes and worked their farms. But they were seldom guilty of criminal offences. And if any African stole anything from them, their white masters almost always administered their own rough justice without recourse to the police.

For years, Mwangi and his fellow constables had been able to doze through their night duty without any fear of disturbance. In recent months, however, the white farmers and their families had seen the Mau Mau in every shadowy movement in the night and had heard their approach in every unexpected noise. Barely an hour earlier, he had answered the phone to hear a terrified white woman pleading with him to come to her aid.

'They're out there, the rebels – I know they are, the murderous swine. I can hear them and I'm all alone, my husband's away in Nairobi. Come here now, boy, now!'

Mwangi had driven out to her farm, a couple of miles from the police station, to find a loose tool shed door being tapped against its frame by the gentle breeze, and an empty oilcan rolling across a patch of stony ground.

Mwangi had taken the woman's hands in his, looked into her eyes and said, 'There are no bad men out there, memsahib. I promise you this. I have checked for myself and I know it to be true.'

Back at the station, Mwangi had another duty to perform. Every two hours, he was required to leave the station and patrol the blockhouse perimeter. He looked up at the clock on the wall opposite his desk. It was time for his patrol.

He put on his cap, picked up his torch and walked out of the police station and across the bare earth towards the gate. In the bright light from his torch he could see that it was closed and the chain was locked in place.

Mwangi continued for a further twenty paces or so. The torch beam played back and forth casually, the sign of a sentry who does not expect to see anything out of the ordinary. Then he stopped. Something was wrong.

He examined the fence again, more carefully. The beam illuminated a void: the empty space where wire no longer ran. Someone had cut their way in.

The police in Kenya, like those in Britain, were not routinely equipped with firearms. Mwangi had only a truncheon to defend himself as he ducked through the hole.

He stood up. Now his torch was shining on solid concrete walls.

Mwangi began a circuit of the blockhouse.

He was halfway round when he saw them: five men crouched beside the steel door.

Every one held a panga in his hand. They looked at him with cruel, merciless eyes.

Kabaya stood up, pointed to Mwangi and said, 'You're late.'

Maina Mwangi was another war veteran. His application to become a policeman in 1946 had been accompanied by an exemplary record of military service and a glowing testimonial from his former CO. But he, like Kabaya, bore a deep and abiding grudge against the British Empire that had been so willing to use his people in war, yet reluctant to respect them in times of peace.

Mwangi grinned as he handed over the key to the blockhouse.

'I was delayed. A white woman feared there were rebels around her house.'

'Not tonight,' muttered Kabaya. He opened the door and they entered the building.

The treasure they were seeking was piled around the three walls of the interior space: wooden crates, each filled with ten Lee–Enfield rifles, and metal boxes of ammunition. They were intended for the white authorities' latest response to the Mau Mau threat: an armed militia called the Special Constabulary, comprised of native Kenyans from tribes hostile to the Kikuyu, commanded by settlers who had military or police experience. Kabaya would have loved to have taken all the weaponry. But his time and manpower were limited; he had to be selective.

He picked out four crates, at the top of a pile and easy to get hold of. They were lifted to the ground and laid on the concrete floor. Using a short crowbar, Kabaya jemmied open the locks on a number of ammo boxes.

He and the four men shovelled five-round clips of .303 cartridges into their rucksacks. Mwangi stood by two unopened boxes while they worked. Each had a single metal handle running along its top face, like a suitcase. The gun crates bore simple rope handles at either end.

Less than a minute had passed before all five men's packs were full and loaded onto their backs. They formed a human chain, linked by the gun crates: five men, four crates between them, holding the handles in front and behind them. Mwangi brought up the rear.

As Kabaya stepped into the open air he cupped his hands over his mouth and emitted a strikingly accurate imitation of the call of a Verreaux's eagle owl: a low, growling, almost coughing sound that bore more resemblance to a grumbling panther than the hoot of a normal owl. It was answered by the noise of a diesel engine starting up.

Kabaya led his men in a steady jog to the fence. One after another they bent low through the hole in the wire, taking care to maintain their grip on the crate handles. Mwangi followed the others across the open ground to the road. A van bearing the name 'Kishanda Valley Dairy' painted across its sides was waiting there.

The men loaded their cargo. Kabaya moved towards the cab, while the others walked round to the rear, ready to jump in. Mwangi grabbed Kabaya's sleeve.

'I want to go back.'

'No time,' Kabaya replied, glaring at him.

Mwangi let go. 'There are Stens, I'm sure. Give me two men. I can find them.'

'Two men . . . and two minutes. One second more and we go without you.'

Mwangi nodded. The strongest man in the squad, able to carry the heaviest loads, was undoubtedly Gitiri. But Mwangi found his presence so unnerving that he dared not ask him for help. He chose two less powerful companions and led them at a sprint across the road, under the fence and into the blockhouse. Inside, he flashed his torch around the piled crates. The beam darted impatiently up and down and from side to side, Mwangi muttering exhortations to himself, until it came to rest on the black capital letters: STEN MK VI × 10, at the bottom of a pile.

He closed the heavy steel door behind him, said, 'Only God can hear us now,' and yanked the top crate in the pile, crashing it to the floor.

The other two men pulled away the heavy wooden boxes until they reached the crate that Mwangi had picked out.

'Take it back to the truck,' he ordered them. 'I will follow. Go!'

He began another frantic search for ammunition. In his head he was counting down the seconds from one hundred and twenty. He had reached fifteen and was about to give up and run for it when he found what he wanted: a box of the 9 mm ammunition that the Sten guns fired, and beside it another identical container.

Mwangi grabbed hold of the two boxes' handles and headed out of the blockhouse. As he ran towards the fence he could hear the sound of the van starting up its engine again. By the time he had scrambled through the hole, ignoring the barbed spikes tearing at his scalp and back, the driver had shoved the gear lever into first.

The van was already moving as Mwangi crossed the road. He ran up behind it, hurled the two cans through the open rear doors and dived forward, head first.

Two of the other men caught hold of Mwangi's torso. For a few seconds he was dragged behind the vehicle, the toes of his boots ploughing furrows in the damp earth. Then his comrades gave a heave and he tumbled into the cargo bay.

The men reached for the van's flapping, clattering rear doors. They pulled them to, then hammered on the steel partition of the driver's cab.

The driver put his foot down and the van sped away, bumping and jolting on the rough road surface. And as he thought of the cargo that the vehicle now carried, Kungu Kabaya's heart was filled with a malevolent ambition. There had been years of oppression and anger, months of planning and preparation. Now, at last, he was ready to go to war.

'Here it is,' said Gerhard, tapping the heavy oak of the boardroom table. 'The place where I was sitting when a sycophantic little rat called Paust boasted to Konrad about how he and his underlings had removed all the Jews from the company workforce. Then the chief accountant, Lange, said that stuff Mother mentioned about how disgustingly rich we all were.'

'Was that the same day you asked your brother for the five thousand marks?' Saffron asked.

'Pretending that I wanted to buy myself a fancy sports car? Yes, that was the day.'

'And you gave it to Izzy.'

Gerhard nodded.

'Little did you know you were making sure that a girl who had no idea you even existed would one day fall in love with you.'

'If I'd known that I'd have asked for ten thousand!' Gerhard laughed. 'Come on, let me show you the factory – while we still own it.'

It was the day after the family meeting and Gerhard had taken Saffron to the Meerbach Motor Works. She had imagined a single factory, a large one no doubt, but a single building. In fact, the works sprawled across a site that covered a number of square kilometres. At the company's height there been not one giant workshop but eight, churning out aero-engines to power the Luftwaffe. Of these, two had survived the Allied bombing raids in good enough condition to be brought back into service, producing power units for civilian aircraft manufacturers. A third was in the process of being rebuilt. The other five were little more than husks of rubble, bent metal and broken glass, overgrown by brambles and bindweed.

As they made their inspection, stopping to talk to the workers, Saffron was struck by the extraordinary contrast between England and the new West Germany. The country that had won the war seemed exhausted by the effort. Everyone was poorly fed and penny-pinching, ruled by a brave but sickly king whose decline seemed emblematic of a country whose empire was falling to pieces, with no sense of what might replace it.

But the German workers that she and Gerhard met were fired with determination to rebuild their nation from scratch. They looked healthier and less shabbily dressed than their British counterparts. They were certainly better fed. When she and Gerhard took lunch in the workers' canteen, she was amazed to be served with thick, juicy pork chops, swathed in fat. No one in Britain had eaten anything so indulgent since before the war began.

Gerhard noticed the contrast, but his impressions were more personal. His name ensured that everyone he spoke to was unfailingly polite and respectful, but there were undercurrents that spoke of unhealed wounds and unrepaired divisions among the men and women in the company's offices and workshops. Some made a point of saying how proud they were of him as a fighter ace who had stood by his principles. But others conveyed a different message in the lack of enthusiasm with which they greeted him.

'What a bolshie man that was,' Saffron said after one such encounter.

'Bolshie?' Gerhard looked at her quizzically, unfamiliar with the slang.

'Oh, you know, rude, uncooperative, generally disagreeable. Short for "Bolshevik", I suppose.'

'Ah, well, I imagine that man was the opposite of Bolshevik,' Gerhard replied. 'Konrad wasn't the only Nazi fanatic in the company. My guess is maybe one worker in three here voted for Hitler in '32 and one in ten was a Party member. Some of those did it to get ahead at work, but many would have been like Konrad. You know – true believers. I'm sure some still are. To them, I'm the man who betrayed his Führer and his country.'

'But most people don't think that, surely?'

'Great God, no . . . but how many does it take?'

*

'Lock the door,' ordered Heinrich Stark, as a sixth man joined the five already gathered in the janitor's storeroom.

Stark reached into his jacket pocket and took out the golden party badge that signified his status as one of the first 100,000 members of the National Socialist German Workers Party. Of all the thousands of workers who had once toiled at the Motor Works, only one other – Konrad von Meerbach himself – had been entitled to wear such a badge, a fact that both men regarded as a shared honour. Though one was the company president and the other a shop floor foreman, they saw one another as equals in their devotion to Adolf Hitler.

Stark knew that von Meerbach was still alive and he believed, as an article of faith, that Hitler was not really dead. He would one day return, like a resurrected Messiah, to reclaim his Reich. The others agreed with him. And they were as offended as Stark to see Gerhard, the turncoat, strutting around the factory.

'A man who's so ashamed of his family name that he tries to change it,' one of them had sneered.

'With a stinking English bitch of a wife!' exclaimed another.

'We must keep a constant watch on von Meerbach.' Stark emphasised the 'von' to show that he was not prepared to accept its removal. 'Who knows what trickery he is up to?'

'He's already put that filthy Yid in the boss's old office,' another said. 'I bet he's planning to sell us to his Zionist friends.'

'You're not wrong,' Stark confirmed. 'One of our brothers works at the castle. There was a family meeting yesterday. The Yid sat with the traitor at the head of the table. He was overheard by one of the maids making plans to sell the family's holdings.'

'This is how they behave when the count's back is turned.'

'Well, you know what kind of a worm the traitor is. He always resented the count for his power and strong principles. He would do anything to ruin everything his father and brother built here.'

As the other men nodded, with murmurs of agreement, Stark continued. 'That is why we have to keep track of what he is up to. Where he goes. Who he sees. If there is the slightest reason for suspicion, believe me, men, I will make sure the information reaches the right ears.'

There was a frantic knocking on the door.

'Who's there?' snapped Stark.

'It's me,' a muffled voice cried. 'Werner. For God's sake let me in.'

The door was opened. A tall, heavily built man came in. He was breathing heavily, pushing his fair hair from a red, perspiring forehead.

'They just got a message at the motor pool. Herr Meerbach wants a Jeep for himself and his wife. He wants to show her the site.'

Stark told Werner, 'I want you to follow him.' He threw him a Volkswagen key. 'Here, take my car, it's in my usual parking place. Follow them. Make sure they don't see you.'

Werner grinned. He'd done his share of dirty work. He knew the dark arts of tracking and surveillance.

'Don't worry. It'll be like old times.'

'Then go. There's no time to lose.'

Werner left as quickly as he'd arrived. The other men grinned at one another. Maybe that bastard would sell their business out from under his brother. But they, and the men who controlled them, would make him pay a heavy price for his betrayal.

Gerhard slowed the US Army surplus Jeep to a halt at the edge of an expanse of cracked concrete and crumbling asphalt, pock-marked by craters left by Allied bombs, still waiting to be filled in. Summer sunshine had given way to heavy cloud, blown in by a chilly north-east wind. Saffron had spent the past month in sleeveless dresses and sandals, but today she was glad of her cotton jumper, flannel trousers and flat brogues: 'sensible shoes', as her stepmother Harriet would have called them. The Jeep was open. The wind that buffeted them as they drove only made everything colder. Saffron had been grateful for the pair of fine leather gloves she'd tucked away in the tan-coloured Hermès shoulder bag she wore slung across her body.

'Welcome to the Motor Works' private airfield,' said Gerhard, climbing down from the Jeep.

Once he'd helped her alight from the vehicle, Saffron looked across a flat landscape, featureless except for the dominant, rusting iron skeleton of what must have been an enormous building, about half a mile away. It was hundreds of metres long and as tall as the nave of a cathedral.

'What's that?' she asked, pointing towards the black ruin, etched against the slate grey sky.

'That's the old Zeppelin shed,' Gerhard replied. 'Where they kept the airship that my father flew to Africa at the start of the first war.'

'With my mother aboard?'

'Absolutely . . . And thirty-seven years later, almost to the day, here we are. But that isn't the reason I brought you here.'

'So what is?' Saffron asked, wrapping her arms around Gerhard's waist and pulling their bodies together.

She loved being close enough to smell him. She had bought him a bottle of Floris No. 89 cologne a few Christmases ago, knowing how well its classically masculine wood-and-citrus perfume would suit him. Gerhard had taken the hint and worn it ever since, and the way it combined with his natural male musk was intoxicating. Above all though, it was the scent of her man that reassured Saffron that, having once been parted from him for so long, he was completely with her now.

'Well,' he murmured, looking deep into her eyes in a way that only added more spice to the warm feelings simmering inside her. 'I have a confession to make. I have had two great loves in my life—'

'Two?' Saffron pulled back. Her emotions chilled as quickly as they had heated. 'This had better not be about another woman.'

During the war Saffron had killed two men in hand-to-hand combat. She had told Gerhard as much, without going into details. Now there was a cold, hard look in her eye that told him how dangerous a predator she could be.

But Gerhard took a risk and pushed her a little closer to the edge. Giving a carefree shrug he said, 'I admit a female is involved.'

Saffron's eyes narrowed. His tone had been teasing, but she still had her guard up.

'Go on . . .' she said.

'Well, she was small and her name was Baby,' he said. 'She wasn't the prettiest thing you ever saw, a little dumpy from some angles, but when I got inside her . . . *ach* . . . she really made me fly . . .'

'You beast!' Saffron exclaimed, trying very hard not to find it funny as she beat her bunched fists against his chest. 'You're talking about a bloody aeroplane, aren't you?'

Gerhard burst out laughing, which only made her hit him harder. He knew that she was playing at being angry. But it was wise not to push her too far.

'You're right! I confess!' he cried. 'The Grunau Baby was the first craft I flew solo. She was a glider. Some mechanics set up a winch, mounted on the back of a truck over there.' He pointed across the airfield. 'Then the rope was attached from the winch to the nose of the glider. The winch started turning, the glider was pulled forward, faster and faster and then suddenly I was up in the sky and . . . *ach!* There is nothing in all the world as incredible as making love to you. But flying is the next best thing. An Anglo-American pilot called John Gillespie Magee wrote the most beautiful poem about flying called "High Flight". His words come back to me every time I fly: "Oh! I have slipped the surly bonds of Earth, And danced the skies on laughter-silvered wings."'

He looked at the sky. 'The moment I got up there, alone in the sunlight, the sound of the air rushing over the wings . . . I felt free. Konrad had done everything he could to make my life hell, but when I was flying he could not touch me. And it all started here.'

He looked at Saffron. 'So, do you forgive me?'

'I'm not sure,' she said. 'I'm thinking about it.'

'Maybe I can help make up your mind.'

He took her in his arms, pulled her close to him and gave her a long, deep, intensely passionate kiss that left her insides melting and her knees about to give way.

'That helped,' she said, gathering her breath as they pulled apart.

'Maybe I could help some more,' Gerhard growled, and Saffron was about to let him try when she caught sight of something over his shoulder.

'Wait,' she said, putting a hand to his chest. 'Why is there smoke over there?'

Gerhard gave the sigh of a man denied his pleasure, then followed the line of her hand. He saw that something was burning, not far from the old Zeppelin shed.

He gave a shrug and said, 'How should I know? Does it matter?'

'I think it does, we should find out.'

Gerhard could sense her concern.

'All right . . . let's go.'

The smoke was coming from a campfire burning in front of a small shack, cobbled together from rusty sheets of corrugated iron, bits of wood and a large oblong of camouflage material that Gerhard recognised was an old Wehrmacht groundsheet. A rusty bicycle was leaning against the side of the hut. A black pot was hanging from a tripod over the fire.

'Someone's having a brew-up,' said Saffron. 'Making a cup of tea,' she added, by way of explanation.

'Coffee,' Gerhard replied with a grin. 'They're German.'

As they drew closer a man emerged from the shack, wearing field-grey battledress trousers and a matching blouson, stripped of all its ranks and unit badges, open to reveal a dirty white vest. He was unshaven. There were deep lines across his weather-beaten face and heavy bags under his slightly bloodshot eyes. His hair was shaved close to his scalp on the sides of his head, with an unkempt brown and grey mop on top.

One of the sleeves of the man's army top was empty. His remaining hand was holding a cigarette to his mouth. *Hand-rolled*, Saffron noticed as they drew to a halt a few metres from where the man stood. He took one last drag as he watched them through narrow, suspicious eyes, threw the cigarette to the ground, and asked, 'Who the hell are you?'

Gerhard smiled affably and held out his hand.

'Gerhard von Meerbach,' he said, and Saffron had to suppress a smile at the way he had reverted to his full name. 'And this is my wife, Saffron.'

The man stood straight, eyes wide, quickly doing up the buttons of his top as he asked, 'Count Konrad's brother? The fighter ace?'

Gerhard nodded.

'I heard you were dead,' the man said. 'In the camps.'

'Almost – I was very ill. This is the first time I've been home. I wanted to show my wife the place where I learned to fly.'

The man's face broke into a broad grin. 'I remember! You went up in that glider – you wouldn't know, but I was working the winch.'

'But that's incredible!' Saffron exclaimed. 'Gerhard was telling me about it.'

'Herr von Meerbach had a gift for it, ma'am, I could tell. I'd seen the test pilots at work, putting our engines through their paces. I could recognise a real flyer when I saw one.'

'Well, this is a stroke of luck,' Gerhard said. 'What is your name?'

'Ferdinand Posch. But everyone calls me Ferdi.'

'And you were in the army, eh?'

'*Panzergrenadiers* – motorised infantry, Army Group Central.'

'Russia . . .' Gerhard murmured.

'That's right. Summer of '41, cutting through the Ivans like a scythe through grass till a truck I was in got hit by a shell, outside of Minsk. That's where I lost this.'

He pointed to the empty sleeve.

'I'm sorry,' Saffron said.

'Don't be. Best thing that ever happened to me. No more Russia.'

'Yes, you got a good deal,' Gerhard agreed.

'Were you there too?' Ferdi asked.

'Three years. What happened after you were wounded?'

'I got shipped home, came back to the Motor Works and they gave me a job as a security guard.'

'Well, at least you still had two legs,' Gerhard said. 'You could run after an intruder, even if you couldn't hold on to him.'

Ferdi laughed. 'But there weren't any intruders. No one would be that mad. They knew what the count would do to them.'

'Do you have any family?' Saffron asked.

'Got a sister, lives in Stuttgart. But I haven't seen her in years.' He eyed his two unexpected guests. 'Let me get you some coffee – the real stuff, not that ersatz shit we had to drink back then. Oh, sorry, ma'am, didn't mean to offend you.'

'That's all right, Ferdi,' Saffron assured him. 'I'm used to military language. Don't get out your best china, I can drink from an old mess tin. I've done it often enough before.'

Ferdi laughed. 'I like your wife, sir. She's not one of those fancy society types who looks down their noses at the common man – not like some I could mention.' He opened his mouth to say more, grimaced and said, '*Ach*, what am I doing chattering when my guests need their drinks?'

Two hundred metres away, crouching behind a small gap in the sixty-metre-high wall of the Zeppelin shed, Fritz Werner relished his good fortune. He had chosen the giant ruin as his hiding place because it provided cover and the widest outlook. No matter where the traitor and his English bitch went on the airfield, there would be some point within the building from which he could observe them.

And then, by chance, they'd driven towards him. For a moment he'd been concerned. What if they were coming to inspect the place for themselves? It was the most prominent landmark, only natural that they'd want to take a look.

He'd taken precautions. You didn't serve eight years in the *Geheime Staatspolizei*, the secret state police, otherwise known as the Gestapo, without having the rules drilled so deep into you they were automatic, even after a six-year gap. His car was well hidden. He had faith in his ability to escape detection.

For some reason they stopped by the hut used by the one-armed tramp who played at being a security guard.

That bastard von Meerbach's got good taste in women.

Werner took a good look at her through his field glasses. She was tall, slender but enough meat on her to give a man something to hold on to. Dark hair, blue eyes; then she smiled with such brightness that he wanted to punch her.

He thought back to the Russian women they used to arrest during his two years in Smolensk – 'suspected partisans'. Find a pretty girl, let the lads have a go. Take her out onto some waste ground and put a bullet through the back of her head. Those were the days.

The von Meerbachs were standing around the fire, getting into a proper old conversation.

He frowned.

Why in God's name do you want to talk to a tramp?

Ferdi dragged a couple of rusty oil drums towards the fire.

'Sit yourselves down.'

He went into the hut and emerged with a couple of battered tin cups.

The water in the pot was now boiling. Ferdi took the pot off the stove, then opened the paper packet. Saffron caught the smell of coffee before he emptied it into the pot.

'Got to let it settle,' he said.

'Would you like something stronger in yours?' Gerhard asked, taking his new flask from his jacket. 'Brandy, Martell Cordon Bleu, taken from the castle this very morning.'

'Thank you, sir,' Ferdi said.

Gerhard poured in a healthy slug and then looked at Saffron, who was cradling the hot cup in her bare hands.

'No thanks,' she said. 'This will do me. Thank you, Ferdi, I—'

Her sentence was cut short as something in the Zeppelin shed caught her eye: a glint of light amid the gloomy shadows of the ruin. She decided it must be sunlight striking an old window, and turned her attention back to Ferdi.

'You were about to say something, before you made the coffee.'

Ferdi shrugged. 'I don't want to sound rude or disrespectful—'

'Feel free to say what you please.'

'Very well, but let me fix my smoke first.'

He took a battered tobacco tin from his trouser pocket, followed by a packet of papers. Within seconds he had fashioned a perfect roll-up and struck a light from a match, all with one hand.

Saffron applauded gleefully.

Ferdi grinned as he sucked on the cigarette. 'The countess,' he said. 'Rolling a cig in her presence? She wouldn't have stood for that and she'd have made sure I suffered for it.'

'Really?' Gerhard said, casually. 'I used to know her when we were young. She wasn't like that back then.'

'Maybe it was the count who made her that way.' Ferdi spat a shred of tobacco off his tongue. 'Don't know why I'm telling you this. Could get me into trouble. But I was here when they left. Saw them both go.'

Gerhard and Saffron looked at one another.

'You mean, at the end of the war?' said Gerhard.

'*Ja*, right at the very end. But they didn't go together. She went first, in a standard plane. He went a few days later. You should have seen that thing – fuselage like a V2 rocket, four jet engines—'

'Four?' Gerhard gasped incredulously. 'There were no four-engined jets in 1945.'

'There was at least one, sir, because I saw it with my own eyes. Looked like something out of a comic book. God in heaven, you should have heard the sound it made when it took off. Went up like a bullet . . .' He pointed his hand to the sky. 'Boom! And the next thing I knew it was out of sight.'

Saffron's heart was pounding. She wanted to shake every last shred of information out of the man in front of her.

'That sounds like an incredible aircraft,' she said.

Ferdi nodded. 'Oh yes, if we'd had a few squadrons of planes like that—'

'Probably as well we didn't,' said Gerhard, 'or those maniacs would still be ruling us now.'

'What makes you think they aren't?' Ferdi asked. 'They didn't all leave. And they weren't all caught. Trust me, they're out there, waiting for a second chance.'

'Let's hope they don't get it,' said Saffron. 'Those two planes – do you know where they went?'

'No. They both took off from the main runway and went in that direction.'

'West,' said Gerhard, following the line Ferdi was pointing.

'That's right – but, see, the countess's plane turned south, over the lake.'

'Towards Switzerland?'

'I reckon. Makes sense, doesn't it?'

'How about my brother's plane?'

'That kept going – but like I said, gone in the blink of an eye. Could have gone in any direction after that and we'd never have known.'

'Did they take anything with them?'

'I don't know – it's a few years now . . .'

'Take your time,' Saffron said.

'Let me think . . . it's coming back to me . . . I know the count didn't take hardly anything – maybe a case, but nothing more than that. There wasn't room in that space machine.'

'And the countess?'

'*Ja*, that's it,' he murmured. 'She had more. Personal luggage for herself, but also there were wooden boxes, not very big but as heavy as lead, the lads who loaded them said. And long brown tubes . . .' Ferdi looked at Gerhard. 'You know those tubes the intelligence boys used to keep their maps in, all rolled up?'

'Yes, absolutely.'

'They were like that, but bigger.'

So that's where the pictures went, Saffron thought.

'Did the count tell anyone about his plans?' she asked, knowing that the answer was almost certainly 'no'.

'He didn't file a flight plan, if that's what you mean.' Ferdi grinned. 'The only person who'd have known was the pilot. But he vanished, just like the count.'

'You mean he never came back from the flight?'

'That's right – did a runner. Left his wife and little kiddies too. He was a decent lad, Berni, never thought he'd do a thing like that.'

'What was his surname?'

'Sperling,' said Gerhard, before Ferdi could answer. 'He was the company's chief pilot. I remember him from the old days. And you're right, Ferdi, I don't see him as a man who'd desert his family. You don't happen to know where he lived, do you?'

'I don't have an address, but he used to live in Friedrichshafen . . . Now, what was his wife called? Something like Klara . . . maybe Kora . . . No, Katya, that's it. Try the phone book. Can't be too many Katya Sperlings in Friedrichshafen.'

Saffron had been listening to Ferdi. But she saw the movement from the Zeppelin shed again.

'There's something going on over there.'

'*Ach.*' Ferdi shrugged. 'It's probably a deer. There's a few out there.'

'Do the deer round here carry binoculars? I saw a glint over there a few minutes ago. What's the best way into the shed from here?'

'You could drive in through the front. They took the main doors down years ago.'

'Did you see anyone drive in within the past hour or so?'

'No, but I was taking a nap before you got here. They could leave the car round the far side and sneak in without anyone seeing.'

'Is there a back door?'

'There was, but it's overgrown.'

'Damn!'

Ferdi smiled. 'There is another way though. You'd never see it, but I've got in that way. Go round the back. Look for a rusted iron pipe pointing at the wall. Follow the line of the pipe. When you see the bushes, get on your hands and knees and crawl. You'll see where to go.'

Saffron nodded. It was risky but she was determined to find out what was going on. Her husband wouldn't approve but her old instincts kicked in. Then she looked at the terrain between their current position and the shed.

Two hundred yards away at most, she thought to herself. *Maybe one-fifty*.

The land between them was open, but to the left was a line of ruined buildings: the old control tower, a smaller hangar and a couple of other structures. They would provide cover.

'Here's what's going to happen,' she said. 'You and I, darling husband, are about to have a furious argument. I'm going to storm off. Give me five minutes. Then both of you get in the Jeep, and drive towards the Zeppelin shed, fast as you can. If there really is a man watching us, you have to get there before he smells a rat and tries to get away. Okay?'

'Get out of here, I'm sick of you,' Gerhard said.

It took a fraction of a second for Saffron to realise he was acting the part. She leaped to her feet and started screaming at him. She'd been speaking German, but she switched to English.

Gerhard stood too and stepped across to her, his body tense, fists clenched, eyes blazing. He was shouting in German, making sure that anyone listening could hear and understand him.

Saffron slapped him, not hard enough to do any damage. She turned on her heel and stalked towards the empty building, with the insults of her husband echoing in her ears.

Fritz Werner was laughing. What a story to tell the boys tonight! The traitor and the bitch screaming at each other in two separate languages.

Then a thought came to him.

Why in God's name talk to a tramp?

And then his blood chilled as the answer struck him: an answer that had been staring them all in the face for years, yet somehow never occurred to anyone. Why would it? Posch was just a tramp, subhuman, not worthy of a moment's consideration.

But he's not just a tramp, is he? He's the airport security guard. He was here during the war. Which means he might have been here at the end, when anyone in the SS hierarchy was running like hell for the nearest exit from the Fatherland.

Werner did not know how Konrad von Meerbach had escaped, or where he had gone. No one other than the most senior men, whose own identities were unknown, were in possession of that information. But the count was still alive, and not in Germany, that was for sure. And how else would a man who had his own private airfield escape?

'*Scheisse . . .*' Werner whispered to himself.

He had to get back to his car.

He was about to get to his feet when he saw the men by the fire walk towards the Jeep. Then, he saw a fleeting shadow in the corner of his eye.

There's someone else in here!

Werner turned his head a fraction, saw the person darting between two blocks of fallen masonry.

It's that English bitch!

A smile creased the corners of Werner's mouth.

She wants to take me by surprise. Two can play at that game.

Saffron had made her way to the back of the Zeppelin shed. The clouds had thinned a little. The sun was making a brave attempt to emerge.

The pipe was as Ferdi had described it. It looked like a section of railing, hollow, a couple of inches in diameter. *Could come in handy*, she thought.

She picked it up and made her way towards the thick mass of tangled brambles. She saw an opening, but a few thorn-covered branches had fallen across it. The vegetation gave way to hard, rough rubble, then solid brick and suddenly she was into the Zeppelin shed itself.

She saw the remains of wooden partitions, broken windows and a door. It looked like an office, probably used by the man who ran the place and his admin staff. She stayed on her knees, keeping herself under cover as she crawled to the front of the office. When she reached the partition, she rose up enough to see through the shards of shattered glass that clung to the window frame. It was a magnificent sight. The massive walls rose up into the air on either side, stretching away into the distance. There were four or five places where the wall had collapsed, either in part or to the ground, like the holes left by missing teeth. High above her arched the bare steel beams that had once supported the roof.

Saffron spotted the car, an old pre-war VW parked behind a pile of fallen rubble. From the front entrance it would be invisible.

She crept out of the office towards the car, clambered up the rubble and looked across the vast open expanse.

You could line up an entire infantry division in here, with all its vehicles and equipment – how am I going to find one or two men?

She narrowed the search. Her quarry would be on the right-hand wall of the shed, facing Ferdi's hut.

There was a shadow, the outline of a man, crouched, like she was.

He was heavily built, short blond hair, wearing a smart but well-worn black suit. His eyes were directed outwards, towards Ferdi's campfire.

Saffron made her way silently across the floor of the shed. She'd been highly trained: all those hours in the wind and rain, on the west coast of Scotland, creeping up on instructors posing as German soldiers, learning how to play a deadly game of Grandmother's Footsteps. The final fifteen metres took her almost thirty seconds.

She stepped out from behind her cover.

She was directly behind the man's position.

Except, he wasn't there.

And then she felt hard metal jabbed into her back and heard a guttural German command.

'Drop the pipe.'

Saffron's mind flashed back to a book she had learned by heart, the SOE combat manual *All-In Fighting* and, within it, Lesson No. 30(b), 'Disarm From Behind'.

It was a basic tenet of SOE training that one could always escape being held at gunpoint. If the man with the gun wanted to shoot you, he would have done so already. Nor was he expecting resistance. The first priority was to do everything to make your opponent feel that he had won.

Saffron dropped the pipe. She slumped her shoulders. Her head dropped.

'If you want to live, do exactly as I say,' Werner snarled.

He had survived every torment that living hell could throw at him. The Red Army, the partisans, the bitter cold, the blistering heat, the lunatic delusions of idiot commanders in Berlin. He knew that if none of them could beat him, a rich man's wife stood no chance. In his mind he was no longer an employee, but back in the war zone. And his thinking now was the same as it had been then: do whatever you have to do to survive. Sort out the consequences later.

Saffron whispered, 'Please . . . Don't . . .'

She heard him chuckle. 'This is what happens when you send a woman to do a man's job.'

It was like a strange, brutal dance: four separate, virtually simultaneous movements executed with perfect coordination to create a single physical expression. And SOE agents spent almost as many hours practising it as ballerinas did at the barre.

One: Saffron twisted sharply to her left, rotating around her left leg as she spun round to face Werner.

Two: she brought her left arm, bent in a V-shape, over Werner's right arm. Then she pulled it tight, clutching his gun-hand close to her body, trapping it between the crook of her elbow and her armpit, with the end of the barrel sticking harmlessly out behind her.

Three: as the gun went off and the bullet flew away harmlessly into the cavernous hangar, Saffron moved her right knee upwards, as hard as she could. She harnessed all the momentum of her spinning body as she aimed for Werner's crotch.

Four: Saffron's right arm used the power of that same motion to jab hard at Werner's chin. She led with the heel of her palm, going for a knockout blow.

Most men went down if you hit them in the testicles and the face at precisely the same time. But Werner, too, had lost none of his wartime combat skills, nor his instant, reflexive response to an attack. He twisted his hip enough to take the force of Saffron's knee against his upper thigh, rather than between his legs. And he bobbed his head like a canny boxer so that her hand struck the side of his face, rather than the point of his chin.

The blows hurt, but they weren't enough to knock Werner out.

Now they were in a fight. The carefully scripted moves in the instruction manual were discarded in a chaotic flurry of lashing limbs and twisted bodies.

Werner aimed a vicious headbutt at Saffron's face.

She ducked, turned her upper body and felt a shock of pain as his forehead hit the point of her shoulder.

Werner yanked his trapped arm out of Saffron's grasp.

She swung her right hand down in a karate chop against his forearm, forcing him to drop the gun.

Werner kicked at Saffron's legs, hitting her shins and causing her to stumble backwards. But even as she was losing her balance, she had the presence of mind to kick the fallen gun out of reach.

Werner launched himself forwards, tackling her around the waist and driving her backwards to the ground. He lay on top of her, pressing her down with his greater weight, trapping her wrists in his hands. He sat back on his heels, still astride her, let go of her arms and fixed his hands around her throat.

He was going to kill her. Saffron knew that for sure. His face was contorted in blind rage, rational calculation long since replaced by raw, animal bloodlust.

She clawed at Werner's face, but he leaned back and her hooked fingers fell short of his skin. She tried to force her arms between his and prise them apart, but he was too strong for her.

She was unable to breathe. He was crushing her larynx and trachea. In another few seconds her throat would cave in. Her ears were filled with a formless, hissing, crackling noise. Her eyes could barely see.

Now her arms were flailing at her side.

Saffron was blacking out. The darkness was closing in.

Her right hand bumped against something hard, cold.

The pipe.

She gripped it. With her last, failing reserves of strength she whipped her arm up and hit the metal shaft as hard as she could against her assailant's body.

Somewhere in the distance a car started and revved hard.

Fritz Werner had forgotten how much he enjoyed killing people. It had been so long since he'd been able to relish the last moments of a dying human being. His attention was focused on Saffron's face as he squeezed the last drops of life out of her. The smack of the pipe against the side of his ribs took him by surprise.

It wasn't a hard or painful blow, but it was enough to make him loosen his grip for an instant.

Saffron hit Werner again, harder this time, as she felt the glorious rush of air into her lungs. That hit was enough to knock him half off her, easing the downward pressure on her body so that she could wriggle out from under him.

As she was gasping for air, Werner was scrabbling across the dirt floor towards his gun. It was less than a metre from his outstretched fingers.

Saffron's mind was still slow, her reactions dull.

Werner's hand grasped the gun.

She swung her arm.

He raised the gun. His finger tightened on the trigger.

Saffron smacked the pipe against his outstretched arm with all her strength, a fraction of a second before the gun went off, breaking his right arm just above the wrist. The bullet ricocheted off the floor.

Then she did what she had intended when the fight began: hit out and not stop until her enemy was incapable of retaliation.

Werner was on his knees, curled over, with his back towards Saffron, who was standing over him. He was trying to cope with the pain from his shattered arm when he felt the next blow from the pipe: an excruciating explosion on one side of his lower back, catching him in the kidneys. She hit his other side in exactly the same place.

Saffron kept hitting and moving, changing her position to enable a steady, relentless succession of strokes.

Through the pain, Werner was aware of the deliberate, calculated way in which he was being worked over. The woman wasn't just some rich man's pampered pet. She was a professional. She knew what she was doing. He couldn't have done it better himself.

Werner heard a car and audible over its engine another sound: a victim's desperate, plea for mercy.

'Please . . . don't hit me any more.'

He realised the voice was his.

'Don't move, or I'll kill you,' said Saffron.

Werner stayed where he was.

Saffron had acted impulsively; it was in her nature. She saw a threat and went to investigate, confident she possessed the resources and training to neutralise the danger. She had given her instructions to Gerhard so firmly, so definitively, that there was no room for discussion. It was only when she disappeared into the remains of the old control tower that he'd asked himself, *Why did you let her do that?*

'She knows what she's doing,' he said.

Ferdi considered that claim as he worked on another one-handed roll-up.

'You reckon there's anyone in there?'

'She has a gift for it.'

'How long before we follow her?'

Gerhard checked his watch. 'Just under four minutes.'

'I get it. Here . . . have a drink.'

He gave Gerhard a bottle, watched Gerhard's face as the raw spirit hit the back of his mouth.

Gerhard returned the bottle to Ferdi and said, 'I spent three years drinking the crap the Russians claimed was vodka. Compared to that, this tastes like the finest cognac.'

Ferdi laughed.

'Do you go into the main works much?' said Gerhard.

'Sure. I pick up my pay, use the showers, get a hot meal in the canteen.'

'And you keep your eyes open, ear close to the ground?'

Ferdi nodded. 'People think I'm that crazy deadbeat who lives on the airfield. They say things they wouldn't if they took me seriously . . . if they thought I was paying attention.'

'But you are . . .?'

Ferdi nodded.

'Would anyone want to send someone out to spy on me?' Gerhard said.

'There's a group of old Nazis, serious, hardcore types. Some of them have been workers here since the old days, but some have turned up in the past few years – old SS men, getting jobs from their friends.'

'Are they organised?'

'Can't say. You hear stories about different groups, not just here, across the country . . . Gangs that get war criminals out of the country, people who dream about taking back power – madmen, the lot of them . . .'

'*Ja,*' Gerhard agreed. 'But dangerous madmen.' He looked at his watch – a minute to go.

The sound of a gunshot rang across the deserted airfield and suddenly they were both up and running for the Jeep.

As Gerhard clambered into the driver's seat his voice was a hoarse, anxious whisper: 'Oh Jesus . . . Saffron!'

He rammed the gearstick into first, floored the accelerator and the Jeep sped across the short stretch of concrete apron towards the Zeppelin shed. Gerhard yanked the wheel hard left and the tyres sent up a cloud of dust and pebbles as they skidded into the building's gaping maw. He had a second to get his bearings.

Ferdi was shouting 'Over there!', pointing to the left.

He saw Saffron, and his immediate thought was, *Thank God, she's all right.* Then he saw that she was using some kind of implement to attack the curled up body of a man, lying like a discarded sack of potatoes at her feet.

The Jeep pulled up a few metres away from Saffron and the two men got out. Gerhard caught her eye and they exchanged a brief, unspoken understanding. His instinct was to run to his wife and hold her tight, but there was no time.

The man was a hefty brute: tall, beefy. Gerhard knew at once that he was ex-SS. Something about him brought back memories of Gestapo men in Russia and camp guards at Sachsenhausen. Somehow she had managed to reduce him to a beaten, quivering wreck.

'I know that man.' Ferdi looked at Gerhard and said, 'You were right about your wife, sir. She's got a gift for it all right.'

'Bang on the dot,' said Saffron. 'Thanks.'

'It looks like you didn't need us,' Gerhard said.

'Not until now.'

Gerhard frowned. 'There are red marks around your neck. Are you all right?'

Saffron shrugged. Her voice was hoarse. 'He tried to strangle me.'

She turned her attention to Werner, stepping around his body until she was standing by his head. She tapped his skull with the pipe, hard enough to hurt, but not inflicting further damage.

'Do what I say and you may still live,' she rasped. 'Nod if you understand.'

Werner nodded.

'Good boy. Now roll over onto your back, with your arms underneath you.'

Werner did as he was told.

Saffron pressed the tip of the pipe onto Werner's forehead. 'Stay there.'

'God-damned English whore!' Werner snarled.

'Actually, I'm Kenyan,' Saffron replied.

She pressed down on the pipe and the pressure on his forehead ended Werner's insults with a gasp of pain.

She coughed, clearing her throat. A little more clearly now, she said, 'Ferdi, could you please find something suitable for tying wrists and ankles?'

'Yes, ma'am.'

Ferdi scurried away and returned with lengths of electric cable, wrapped in dirty black rubber. Werner's ankles were bound and his hands tied behind his back. A longer length of cable was slipped through the bonds at Werner's wrists and ankles, then tied so that it was taut. His range of movement was now virtually non-existent.

Saffron gave the pipe to Gerhard.

'Feel free to use this.' She stood over Werner, opened his jacket and patted his flanks. 'No other weapons,' she murmured. 'Let's find out who you are.'

She rummaged through Werner's jacket and trouser pockets. Her haul included his wallet, identity card, Meerbach Motor Works employee card and keys, as well as a small amount of loose change.

'Would you like to interrogate him or shall I?' she asked Gerhard.

'It's your field of expertise,' Gerhard said. 'If we're ever flying an aeroplane, I'll take charge.'

'Good plan. But tell me, do you agree that this big lump has SS written all over him?'

'Without doubt.'

'No question,' added Ferdi.

'Tell me, Herr Werner,' Saffron asked, 'are you still working for your old employers?'

Werner spat at her. The saliva fell short.

'I'll take that as a yes. Who sent you to follow us?'

Werner glared at her silently.

'I assume you understand how interrogation works, Herr Werner. Sleep deprivation, disorientation, unpredictable gaps between interrogations, those sorts of things. But it takes a long time, and we don't have that. Nor can I be bothered to beat information out of you. There's nothing else for it. We'll have to get rid of you.'

Werner shouted, 'Help! Help! Someone . . . !'

Gerhard drew back the pipe, ready to silence Werner, but something stopped him. He had flown hundreds of combat missions against enemy pilots who were trying to kill him and never had the slightest hesitation in shooting them down first. But he didn't have the capacity to hit a defenceless man, no matter how loathsome.

Saffron can do that, he thought to himself. *She can do whatever is necessary.*

Now he understood why she had been selected for service in a network of undercover spies, saboteurs and assassins, and how she had survived.

Saffron saw him hesitate. 'It doesn't matter,' she said, resting a hand on Gerhard's arm. 'There's another way to shut him up.'

There was a ragged piece of long-discarded rag, caked in many years' worth of accumulated filth and dust, lying on the floor not far from where Werner lay. Saffron bent down and picked it up. The fabric was badly frayed and it was easy for her to rip it in two. She crammed one piece between Werner's teeth, shoving it in like stuffing into a chicken. Then she sealed it in place by rolling the other piece into an improvised bandana, wrapping it over Werner's mouth and knotting it tight at the back of his head.

'Stay calm,' she said. 'Breathe evenly through your nose. That way you won't suffocate.'

She turned to Gerhard and Ferdi.

'I know what we have to do.'

'Are you sure I can't give you any money?' Gerhard asked, as they dropped Ferdi off at Friedrichshafen Stadt station. 'You've taken a great risk to help us.'

The one-armed watchman grinned.

'Most fun I've had in years. Besides –' he tapped his small, battered suitcase – 'there's nothing in here but money. Years of back pay.' He shrugged. 'I've not had anything to spend it on but grub, a little booze and tobacco.'

'And you're certain your sister won't mind taking you in?'

'We're family. What choice does she have?'

'Goodbye, then,' Saffron said, giving him a peck on the cheek. 'And good luck.'

'Remember,' Gerhard said, 'if you ever want to come back, I'll make sure you still have a job waiting for you at the Motor Works.'

Ferdi lifted his hand in salute. 'Thank you sir . . . ma'am.'

He turned and went off to catch the Stuttgart train.

'You won't be able to give him a job if you sell the company,' Saffron said to Gerhard as they watched Ferdi make his way across the station concourse.

'I'll have a clause written into the sale contract,' he replied. 'I mean it.'

'I know you do.' She looked up at her husband. 'I love you very much.'

'And I love you too, my darling. Now, let's find Frau Sperling.'

There was a line of phone booths near the station entrance, each with a local directory, and there was only one *K. Sperling* in the book. Saffron made the call, reasoning that it would feel less threatening to Katya Sperling if she heard a woman's voice.

It worked. Katya agreed to meet them at a café near her apartment block.

'But I can't stay long. My eldest can look after her brother and sister. But she's only twelve, so I'll need to get back.'

Katya had once been an attractive woman: the kind a dashing pilot would pick as his wife. But six years as a single mother had put lines on her face, bags under her pale blue eyes and grey in her brown hair.

'Berni used to talk about you a lot, sir,' she said. 'I remember we went to the cinema one week and there was a newsreel about the fighter ace who had shot down so many Russian planes.' She gave a sad smile as she looked at Saffron. 'Your husband was so handsome in his flying gear, ma'am. All the girls were swooning, like he was a film star. Berni said to me, "I helped teach that man to fly."'

'That's true,' Gerhard agreed. 'He's a good man.'

'Was,' said Katya. 'I know he's dead. He must be. He wouldn't have gone six years without getting in touch with me and the kids. Not my Berni.'

'He might not be able to,' Saffron said. 'If he's in hiding somewhere.'

'He'd have found a way. He told me he would. Before he left, that last time, he said, "I have to fly the count out of here, but when this damn war is over, I'll send for you all, I swear." And he meant it. I know.'

'Did he tell you where he was going?'

'No . . .'

Saffron's spirits fell. But Katya went on.

'Not exactly. But he said that the count had managed to get hold of a wonder-machine that no British or American plane could ever catch. And he told me, "Look at an atlas and ask yourself, where can I find safety in a single flight? That is where we will be."'

'Did he mean Switzerland?' Saffron asked.

'No, I don't think so. He had already gone there, a short while earlier, but in the normal company plane. Why would he need a wonder-machine, just to cross the Bodensee?'

That confirms what Ferdi said about Chessi's escape, Saffron thought.

Katya said, 'There's something else, you know, that Berni used to tell me. The count used to talk about you, sir . . . and you, ma'am. They weren't nice, the things he said. He wanted to hurt you both.' She looked at Saffron and Gerhard in turn, then said, 'So you're planning to find him?'

Gerhard shrugged.

'When you do,' Katya Sperling said, 'make him pay for what he's done. He took my man away from me and left my children without a father. I want him to burn in hell.'

'I understand,' said Saffron. 'Really . . . I do.'

'There you are, sir,' said the Schloss Meerbach's chauffeur, opening the garage doors. 'I knew you'd come back one day, so I've made sure to keep her in perfect working order. Good as new, she is.'

'Ahh, well done, Heini,' said Gerhard in a tone of appreciation, as he ran his hand along the gleaming scarlet bodywork of his pre-war Mercedes 540K cabriolet. The bonnet stretched out in front of the windscreen, flanked by the unbroken swoops of gloriously curvaceous metal that flowed over the front wheel, down below the doors and up over the rear.

'Brings back memories, doesn't it, darling?' he said.

'Mmm . . .'

Saffron had wrapped a silk scarf around her neck to cover the strangulation marks that were now turning a vivid shade of purple and black. It hurt her to swallow and her breathing felt constricted. Her mind, though, was not on those relatively minor discomforts, but on that first night together in St Moritz. All these years later, her body still came alive at the thought of their first kiss, the first touch of his naked body against hers, the first time that they had made love.

Saffron permitted herself a brief moment of self-indulgence, then brought her mind back to the here and now. She and Gerhard had not yet discussed what had happened between her and Werner in the abandoned hangar. They shared a war veteran's distaste for revisiting past battles. She had survived. Werner was incapacitated. For now, at least, no more need be said.

Gerhard was focused on his car.

'Is there any petrol in the tank?' he asked.

'Oh yes, sir,' Heini answered. 'Filled her up myself this morning. Knew you wouldn't be able to stay away from her.'

'You know me too well!' Gerhard fished in his pocket for a key and gave it to Heini. 'This belongs to our hire car. Could you please take it back to Munich Airport in the morning?'

'Certainly, sir.'

'Excellent.' Gerhard extracted two fifty-Deutschmark notes from his wallet and handed them over. 'This should cover the balance of the bill and your train ticket home.'

'Thank you, sir.'

Heini beamed. By his reckoning there was more than enough here for the bill, a first-class ticket and a decent meal washed down by a couple of foaming steins at the Löwenbräukeller in Munich along the way. Tomorrow promised to be a fine day out.

Half an hour later, Gerhard's Mercedes was growling softly along the three-kilometre drive that led to the public highway, waiting for the chance to be let loose and roar. Saffron was relaxing in the passenger seat. She had passed the first two years of the war as a driver-mechanic and would have had no difficulty in controlling a machine as big and powerful as the 540. But now it was right that Gerhard was at the wheel. It restored the balance between them.

'When are you going to tell me where we're going?' she asked.

'I'm not. It's a surprise.'

'You realise that's a high-risk strategy with a girl like me? You know, the type that actually likes to know what she's doing.'

'Then it's a risk I'll have to take.'

'You seem oddly unbothered by the prospect of making me very cross.'

'Perhaps that's because I won't.'

'You're making me quite cross already.'

'I think you're doing that all by yourself.' Gerhard rested a hand on her thigh. 'Don't worry. This is a nice surprise. I promise.'

'Hmm . . .'

The sun was beginning to set as they crossed the border, and it was almost dark by the time they stopped for dinner at a roadside restaurant south of Bad Ragaz. By then they had been over all the information they had gathered during the day, concluding with Berni Sperling's last words to his wife: that he was going 'somewhere I can find safety in a single flight'.

'Do you agree with Katya that it can't have been Switzerland?' Saffron asked.

'*Ja*, I do,' Gerhard replied. 'There are plenty of ways to get from our side of the Bodensee to Switzerland without attracting attention, why take a jet plane? It would be simpler to row across.'

'So what's left? Virtually all of northern Europe was in Allied hands by the end of April '45. Sweden was neutral . . .'

'But so far as we know, Konrad was in Berlin up to the last weeks. He wouldn't go all the way south to the Motor Works, only to turn back again and fly over the American, Russian and British forces. I don't care how fast his plane was, that's a crazy risk.'

'And the Swedes would hardly have welcomed him with open arms. Yes, they gave the Nazis' iron ore, but they didn't want to be a haven for war criminals. Everyone knew about the camps by then. SS officers were humanity's enemy.'

'It would have to be somewhere that still had a government sympathetic to Germany.'

'Like Spain or Portugal,' Saffron said. 'They had fascist leaders. Still do, come to that.'

Gerhard gave a sigh as he shook his head at the madness of the world.

'Franco and Salazar . . . still clinging like limpets to power.'

'Could Konrad's plane have got that far?'

'I don't know for sure – I've been trying to work out what it was that Ferdi saw. I know the Luftwaffe had two companies developing multi-jet bombers during the war – Heinkel and Arado. I think only the Arado ever took to the air.'

'Can you remember its range?'

'Less than the big Allied bombers, that's for sure. Jets use up a lot of fuel and the Arado wasn't as big as one of your Lancasters, or a Flying Fortress. They could fly three or even four thousand kilometres. The Arado couldn't get nearly as far.' He shrugged. 'I don't know, maybe fifteen hundred kilometres, something like that.'

'How far would that get Konrad?'

'From the Motor Works? Hold on, I can't work this out and drive . . .'

Gerhard pulled the car to a halt by the side of the road and closed his eyes, imagining his way across the map from southern Germany to the Iberian Peninsula.

He nodded and said, 'If the plane was an Arado, with the range I'm estimating, Sperling could get to north-east Spain – the coast of Catalonia.'

'Which would have been safe,' Saffron said.

'Absolutely.' Gerhard started up the engine and pulled onto the road as he added, 'And the good news from his point of view is that the journey would have taken him over the northernmost area of Italy, which was still in German hands up to the very last days. He'd fly across the western Mediterranean, where there would have been light Allied naval and air force presence. All their effort was being focused on the push to Berlin.'

'If he got to Spain, he could have stayed there, or gone on to Portugal, or to South America. He could be absolutely anywhere. Damn! We aren't any closer to him than we were to begin with!'

'That's not like you,' Gerhard said.

'What isn't?'

'Letting your emotions cloud your reason. It seems to me we're much closer. You know the Chinese proverb – a journey of a thousand miles begins with a single step? We know, or can reasonably assume the first step . . . two, in fact, because we know where Francesca went. Once we have that, we can start looking for the next step, and the one after that.'

'You're right.' Saffron laughed to herself. 'Maybe I'm just hungry. I go mad if not fed at regular intervals.'

'Then when we next see a decent-looking restaurant we'll stop and have some dinner.'

Gerhard led Saffron into a bistro off the highway.

'Before we eat, can I freshen up?' she asked.

'Of course.'

'While I'm doing that, maybe you could put Herr Werner back in touch with his friends.'

'Good idea,' said Gerhard. 'We've put enough distance between us and them.'

The restaurant had a payphone for its customers' use. Gerhard called a number in Ravensburg, north of Friedrichshafen. A man answered.

'Listen carefully,' Gerhard said. 'This is the lost property department. We know you are looking for something you have lost. You will find it in Workshop Seven.'

'What are you talking about? Who are you?'

'You heard me. Workshop Seven. Goodnight.'

Gerhard waited for Saffron and they were led to their table.

'Did the message get through?' she asked once they had been seated.

'I sent it. Whether they act on it is up to them.'

They ate. Gerhard drank a glass of wine with his meal. Saffron, as the passenger, allowed herself two. Most of their conversation was the normal chit-chat of husbands and wives, as if they had made an unspoken pact to set harsh realities aside, for now at least, and act as though they were still on a pleasant European holiday. Only once did the events of the day intrude.

'Were we right, do you think, to let Werner live?' Saffron asked.

'Absolutely,' Gerhard replied. 'It would have been murder. We'd have been no better than them.'

'But it's a risk. What if they work out that we're looking for Konrad?'

'How would they do that? Werner saw us talking to Ferdi. He doesn't know what we were discussing and Ferdi's no longer there, so they can't ask him.'

'It's still a loose end.'

'All right, suppose they do find out. Suppose they discover that we know about Chessi's flight to Switzerland and Konrad's flight to Spain, or wherever he went. Suppose they tell Konrad. So what? Now he'll be afraid we're coming after him. He'll wonder whether he needs to run even further away. Good. I hope he loses a lot of sleep.'

'You're right,' Saffron said. 'Let him be the one to worry. Now, I know it's very wicked, but I think I might have some pudding.'

Happily replete with food and wine, Saffron dozed off as Gerhard drove them on the last leg of the journey. He smiled to himself as the road signs flashed by, delighted that Saffron was missing all the clues to their destination. When they were a couple of minutes away from their arrival, he gently shook her shoulder and said, 'Wake up.'

Saffron came to, blinking. Her throat felt sore.

'Where are we?' she yawned.

'Almost there. You've been asleep pretty much since we left the restaurant.'

'Oh . . .' She looked out of the window. 'This looks familiar, like I've been here, but it didn't look like this. Does that sound completely barmy?'

'Not at all. Last time you were here, everything was covered in snow.'

It took a second for the hint to work its way through Saffron's sleepy brain. Then her eyes widened, a huge smile crossed her lips and she cried out, 'St Moritz!'

'That's right. I took the liberty of making a call while you were packing, back at the Schloss. It's the height of the summer season but I know the manager pretty well and—'

'You didn't get us a room at the Suvretta House, did you?'

A smile wreathed Gerhard's face. The Suvretta House was where they had spent their first night together, Saffron's first night ever with a man.

'Actually I got us a suite. The same—'

He didn't have to finish the sentence. Saffron gave a shriek of delight.

'Oh, you clever man! You clever, clever, wonderful man!' She was rapidly thinking ahead as she added, 'I am so glad I got some sleep, because I'm going to keep you up all night.'

The four torches cut through the dust in the air of the abandoned workshop. It had started to rain soon after nightfall and the light sparkled on the drops falling through the gaping holes in the bomb-damaged roof. The torch beams played back and forth until one stopped and a voice cried out, 'Over here!'

Heinrich Stark ran over to where his comrade was standing. In the torchlight he saw his VW. But where was Werner?

Stark pulled a wartime police-issue Mauser HSc pistol from his raincoat and stepped towards the car.

'Careful,' he said to the men on either side of him. 'This could be a trap.'

He kept his light on the bulbous little VW. The other beams swept the air to either side.

'Can't see anyone,' one of the men said.

'Me neither,' another replied.

'There could be booby traps,' warned Stark.

He had reached the car. The passenger window was slightly open. He placed the end of his torch by the gap and examined the interior. The seats were empty, there was nothing in the footwell. There appeared to be no sign of any tampering with the wiring under the dashboard.

Stark thought he heard something: a faint tapping sound.

He jerked his hand up to signal silence. The men around him stood still. Stark waited a few more seconds. He heard the noise again.

It was coming from the front of the car.

Stark went round and opened the bonnet. He shone his torch.

He had found Fritz Werner.

The former Gestapo agent was stuffed into the VW's small luggage compartment like meat into a sausage. He was barely conscious, badly beaten and unable to tell Stark what had happened to him. Someone, presumably the count's traitor brother, had spotted him and somehow managed to overpower him.

In Stark's opinion it must have been an ambush. He had heard stories of Werner's time in Smolensk. The Russian partisans had spent years trying to kill him, but he'd been too tough, too cunning and too brutal for them. It beggared belief that von Meerbach could have beaten him in a fair fight.

But what had Werner revealed to his assailants? He'd evidently provided Stark's home telephone number. His wallet, keys and every scrap of identification were missing, so all that information was now in enemy hands. God alone knew what other secrets he had given up.

If he talked to the traitor he can damn well talk to me, Stark thought. But Werner wouldn't be able to say a word to anyone without medical attention.

He and his men dragged Werner from under the bonnet. Someone had known how to tie knots because it took them several minutes to untie the cables around their comrade's wrists and ankles, and the one that linked them.

They placed Werner onto the back seat, where he lay, immobile and unspeaking, showing no signs of life except the occasional grimace of discomfort.

'Oswald, you come with me,' Stark said, picking the biggest and strongest of his men. 'The rest of you go home. And not a word to anyone about what happened here, do you understand?'

Stark and Oswald drove to Friedrichshafen, stopping along the way to procure a bottle of cheap brandy from a bar manager who was sympathetic to their cause. They poured half the bottle over Werner. Oswald took a few hefty slugs. Stark abstained. They went to the hospital and carried Werner between them into the emergency room.

'My friend has had a bad fall,' Stark said. 'I'm afraid he had drunk a great deal.'

'He had bad news from home,' Oswald said, breathing pungent, boozy fumes over the receptionist. 'We were trying to comfort him.'

'I see,' the receptionist replied, examining the three of them with disapproving eyes. 'And what is the injured man's name?'

'Schmidt.' Stark was grateful that there was at least one thing to be gained from the theft of Werner's personal possessions. 'Frank Schmidt.'

'And might I ask who you are . . . for our records?'

'My name's Müller and my friend is Schneider.'

He had chosen the three most common surnames in Germany. Suspicion now replaced disapproval in the receptionist's expression.

'Well, take a seat, Herr Müller, and the doctor will be with you shortly.'

Werner was admitted for examination. Stark and Oswald were told that their presence was no longer required. Visiting hours, they were informed, were from two in the afternoon until eight in the evening.

'Thank you, Doctor,' said Stark. 'I will come back here as soon as my day's work is done. As you can imagine, I'm very worried about my friend.'

The doctor nodded, waited until the injured man's companions had departed and began his detailed examination of the patient. It was plain at once that the story that Herr Werner had fallen was patent nonsense.

When the patient's clothes were removed, the stench of brandy disappeared with them. His breath did not smell of alcohol and his eyes were not bloodshot. The doctor ordered a blood test, to be on the safe side, but if he were a betting man he'd have wagered a thousand Marks that this man had not had a drop to drink that night.

The bruising on his torso might possibly have been caused by a fall, but it seemed more likely to be the result of repeated blows by a hard object. Meanwhile, the marks around his ankles and wrists were consistent with some form of ligature, used to bind his limbs very tightly. There were scraps of black thread between his teeth, suggesting that he had been gagged.

The doctor sent the patient away to be X-rayed. He took a couple of minutes to gather his thoughts. He had a patient who had clearly been the victim of assault and some form of forcible restraint. He had two men who had concocted a patently untrue story to explain their so-called friend's wounds. Something suspicious was going on, but thankfully it was not his job to work out what it was. He walked back to the reception desk.

'Please call the police station, Helga. Ask for the duty officer. Inform him that we have admitted a man who appears to have been the victim of a criminal assault.'

'Is it that Herr Schmidt?' Helga asked.

The doctor nodded.

'I knew it,' she said.

A look of satisfaction crossed her face as she started to dial the number.

Werner woke to discover that, in addition to his broken arm, he had severe contusions to his abdomen, a cracked vertebra in his spine, two fractured ribs and a bruised kidney. The doctor supervising his case told him he would be in hospital for at least three days, should try to get as much rest as possible for at least a week after that, preferably two or three, and should not think of going back to work until medically cleared to do so.

'And you have some visitors,' the doctor added, as he left Werner's bed.

The visitors introduced themselves as police detectives. Their names went in one of Werner's ears and out of the other. He didn't need names because he knew their type right away. One was big with a broken nose like an old prizefighter and had a surly taciturn manner. He was the muscle. The other was more middle-class: neatly dressed, well-spoken and polite. He was the brains.

In a back alley the muscle would be the dangerous one. But in this hospital ward, with the two men pulling up wooden chairs and making themselves comfortable, the brains was the one Werner had to worry about.

'I spoke to the doctor,' Brains said. 'He gave me a list of your injuries. That's quite a beating you took. Must hurt like crazy.'

Werner said nothing. He'd interrogated people for a living. The longer they remained silent, the harder it was for the interrogator. The moment they said anything, no matter how trivial, it gave the man asking questions something to work with. Say one word and chances were, sooner or later, you'd tell them everything.

Brains was smart; he didn't let himself be disturbed in any way. He kept talking.

'If I were in that bed, feeling terrible, knowing someone had put me there, I'd want that person to pay for what he'd done. Don't you want that too?'

Werner gave him nothing: not a word, not a look, not a gesture.

Muscle didn't like it. 'Stop pissing about. Tell us what we need to know,' he growled.

'Now, now, go easy on the poor fellow,' Brains said. 'He's had a bad experience. And he's the victim, not the suspect. We can't force him to say anything.' He looked at Werner. 'I bet you want to tell us. My guess is you're furious about this. A big strong man like you, lying in a hospital bed like a helpless old man. That's got to hurt worse than your bruises . . . no? Come on, who did this?'

Brains was right: a part of Fritz Werner wanted to name von Meerbach and his damned wife. But that would mean explaining what he was doing in the old Zeppelin shed, and on whose orders. And sooner or later it would come out that the woman had been the one who beat him up, and then no one would ever respect him again.

He remained silent.

Brains shrugged. 'Ah well, have it your way. Here, take this . . .' He extracted a card from his pocket and put it on the side table by Werner's bed. 'If you ever change your mind, give me a call, eh?'

The cops got up to leave. Werner slumped back on his bed. The episode had only taken a couple of minutes, but he was exhausted.

Brains walked out of the ward, but the muscle stopped a couple of paces away from the bed, raised his head to the ceiling and sighed, '*Ach!*' as if he'd forgotten something. He turned around and asked, 'What's your name?'

Werner was about to give his real name. He'd opened his mouth to speak. But he stopped himself in time.

Muscle gave him a sly grin. He pushed two fingers together, pointed them at the bed and made a shooting motion. He didn't say 'Got you!' He didn't have to. They both knew it.

The cop was holding his hat in his left hand. He flicked an imaginary speck of dust off the brim, put it on and said, 'We'll be seeing you.'

Heinrich Stark came in later that afternoon. He'd brought a bunch of grapes. As he was looking for somewhere to put them, he noticed the card left by the policeman.

Stark picked it up, looked at it, then sat down on one of the wooden chairs and pulled it to the bedside so he would not have to raise his voice.

'So?' he asked.

'They wanted to know how I got my injuries,' Werner replied.

'I already told that sour-faced old woman on the front desk. You had too much to drink. You fell over.'

'They don't believe you.'

'What did you tell them?'

'Nothing. What did you think? That I'd go blabbing to the first cop I could find? Well, I didn't. I said nothing. Literally . . . not one single word.'

'You talked to someone else though, didn't you? What did you tell them?'

'I gave them a phone number. I didn't say who it belonged to. I didn't say what it had to do with me. Just the number . . . God in heaven, man, they were going to kill me if I didn't give it to them!'

Stark put a finger to his mouth. 'Shh . . .' He leaned forward, his head so close to Werner's that he barely had to whisper. 'Is that how little you think of our cause, that you would betray our secrets to the enemy, to save your skin?'

'Of course not . . . *Ach!*' Werner winced. 'I feel terrible.'

Stark was not sympathetic. 'You'll feel better once you've told me what happened. Maybe you didn't talk to the cops, but you'll damn well talk to me.'

Werner recounted everything that had occurred while he was in the Zeppelin shed. For the sake of his pride, he adapted his account by stating it was Gerhard von Meerbach who had attacked him.

But Werner was unwell and his mind was sluggish. He couldn't keep his story straight as he described what Gerhard had supposedly done and Stark was suspicious.

'You're saying that some pilot, who never had a day's combat training, was able to beat you up?'

Werner shrugged. 'What can I say?'

'Even though you were known for being the meanest, toughest bastard in Smolensk?'

'Must be out of practice.'

'That doesn't sound right to me.'

'What do you want to hear?' Werner asked indignantly. 'The woman did it?'

Stark did not answer. Werner was right. It was crazy to suggest a woman could have beaten him. And yet there was something about the way he had asked the question. Had he inadvertently revealed the truth?

Both men were silent. Then Stark said, 'I'm not happy. And our superiors will be less content with your conduct. When are the medics letting you out of here?'

'Three days.'

'How will you get home?'

'By bus I guess, but . . . Look, I know I messed up. But could you lend me the bus fare? Those bastards took everything.'

Stark didn't hand over the money right away. He made a point of thinking things through before he reached for his wallet and passed over a five-Mark note.

'Buy yourself a meal while you're at it.'

The following morning Stark drove to the abandoned airfield, looking for Ferdinand Posch. The security guard, whom Stark regarded as no better than a drunken tramp, was nowhere to be found. The ashes of the fire outside his filthy, ramshackle hut were stone cold.

He's done a runner, Stark thought. *Presumably von Meerbach assisted him. And why would he do that unless Posch had told him something useful?*

So now Stark knew that Werner had been telling the truth about at least some of what had happened when he had gone to spy on the von Meerbachs. Meanwhile, the von Meerbach traitor was surely now aware that his older brother Konrad had found sanctuary outside the Reich, and was thus almost certainly still alive.

He ordered his men to find out whatever they could about Posch's movements, but was hardly surprised when they drew a blank. The man had been a loner, virtually an outcast. He had no friends. No one ever went out to visit him on that concrete and tarmac wilderness. Why should they know or care where he had gone?

Stark's problem became one of damage control. His superiors would not be pleased by his inability to manage an effective surveillance operation. They would be even more agitated by the breach of the organisation's security and the loose ends that had resulted. He needed to do something to forestall their displeasure and restore their confidence. And it only required a moment's reflection to decide what that should be.

Two days later Werner emerged from hospital. He could walk with the aid of a stick. The bus stop was just across the road. He checked the road was clear and made his slow, shuffling, painful way across.

Fritz Werner saw the car pulling out of the parking space. He heard its tyres squeal and its engine roar as the driver floored the accelerator. He knew at once it was coming for him.

He wanted to run, or even throw himself out of the way. But his body was too weak and his mind too tired. In any case, what was the point? From the moment Stark said he was telling their superiors, Werner had known that his fate was sealed.

He stayed where he was and let the car hit him. And in the second before he died, Werner perceived the irony of his demise. In the war his enemies had never managed to kill him. In peace his friends had done it instead.

Sherlock Holmes was a popular character in Germany, and the young Heinrich Stark had devoured every story he could find about the great detective. He was familiar with Holmes's dictum that, 'When you have eliminated the impossible, whatever remains, however improbable, must be the truth.'

Stark was sure that Werner had been lying when he said that Gerhard von Meerbach had beaten him up. Ferdinand Posch could not have done it because he only had one arm. That left the wife.

It was a wildly improbable proposition, to be sure. But might it be true?

For reasons of operational security, Stark was not privy to the identities of the most senior men in the Nazi veterans' organisation. If ever he had information for his superiors, he passed it on via a contact known to him as 'Braun'. When he delivered his report on the Werner affair, he respectfully suggested investigating Frau von Meerbach to ascertain whether she could have carried out the assault on him. If she had, she might pose as great a potential danger to them as her husband.

Braun dismissed the idea. 'Don't be ridiculous, man. How could a woman overpower a brute like Werner?'

'No, I see, of course you're right,' Stark had replied, not wanting to anger Braun still further. 'It was foolish of me to suggest such a thing.'

But when the meeting was over and both men had risen from the park bench, Braun went to the nearest public telephone and passed on a concise, edited version of his conversation. At the end he had assured the officer to whom he, in turn, reported that, 'Yes, sir, I absolutely do recommend that we follow this up. In my view we should call our London contact as soon as possible . . . Yes, sir, absolutely. I'll get on to it at once.'

When Manyoro wished to celebrate a significant family occasion, he did so at the village, atop Lonsonyo where his beloved mother had lived and practised her powers of healing and prophecy. He had taken the hut where she had lived to be his personal residence, though his decades of contact with the white man's world were evident in the substantial wooden bed, sturdy enough to bear his considerable weight that now stood within the hut, the battery-operated radio that stood on a table beside it, the rattan garden furniture on which he liked to sit while looking out at his private, mountain-top kingdom, and the crates containing bottles of his favourite refreshment: Bass's India Pale Ale.

Manyoro's womenfolk had provided a magnificent feast with which to greet 'Dr Benjamin', as everyone now insisted on calling him. The entire clan basked in the reflected glory of his achievement. But then, when Benjamin and Manyoro sat down upon a pair of rattan chairs for a proper father-and-son conversation, the mood of the day had taken a sudden, drastic turn for the worse.

'You are planning to marry a . . .' Manyoro stopped, barely able to say the word. 'Kikuyu?'

'I am marrying the woman I love,' Benjamin replied. 'She is Kenyan, like me. Her tribe is an irrelevance.'

'An irrelevance?' Manyoro's voice rose in outrage. 'To you, perhaps, boy. But not to me, your mother, or our people. The Maasai people. To them it is an insult. You are slapping them in the face.'

Benjamin took a deep breath. He knew there was no point raising his voice to his father. Not only was that disrespectful, it would ensure that the old man closed his ears to any reasonable arguments.

'Father,' he said. 'You know that I love and respect you. You know that I am proud of my Maasai heritage, proud to call myself a warrior of the tribe.'

'Then why do you betray it?'

'Because we have to move beyond our old tribal conflicts. Don't you see? That is how the white man keeps us down. The English say so themselves – divide and rule. We are so busy arguing between ourselves, we do not notice that the white man has stolen our land, our water, our crops, our animals – he has taken everything from us. And we do not fight him as we are too busy fighting one another.'

If Benjamin thought his words would persuade his father, he was wrong. They made matters worse.

Manyoro's manner switched from heated anger to cold, hard silence. And that, as Benjamin had learned when he was a small boy, was always a danger sign.

'Be careful what you say, boy,' Manyoro warned him in a tone that was all the more intimidating for being quiet and measured. 'You call yourself "Doctor" because of the generosity of a white man. And I owe that same man my life.'

'Yes, of course, Father and I am very grateful, but—'

'There is no "but". Leon Courtney is my brother. We are free to take our cattle across this land as we have always done. When we raise cattle for him, he always pays us a fair price. The Kikuyu who tend their fields for him would say the same thing. You can go from one end of Africa to the other. You will not find anyone who lives better than we do here.'

'Black people, maybe. But what about the whites? You say Leon Courtney is a good man. But he still owns the land and we do not.'

'What is ownership?' Manyoro scoffed. 'Just words on paper. It is still our land in every way that matters. The cattle are still ours. They still eat the same grass and drink the same water. That is how it has always been.'

'But it is not as it must be in the future, Father. That is the point. We have to stand on our own feet and rule our land for ourselves. We must have an independent Kenya. We must be free. And I insist on being free to marry the woman I love.'

*

'I cannot believe it!' Chief Ndiri exclaimed, heaving his corpulent body to its feet to make his point. He placed his hands on the top of his antique mahogany desk and leaned forward, glaring furiously at Wangari. 'My beautiful, brilliant daughter . . . with the whole world at her feet . . . who could have any man she desires . . . and she gives herself to a herder of cattle. Are you mad?'

'He is not a cattle-herder, Father,' Wangari replied. 'He is a doctor.'

'A Maasai doctor,' Ndiri insisted. He sighed and slumped back into his chair, shaking his head sorrowfully. 'I work so hard for so many years. I give you everything any young woman could desire – a fine education, beautiful clothes. How many people in all Kenya, black or white, have been blessed with as much as you?'

It was a fair question. Ndiri was a paramount chief of the Kikuyu, a position created by the colonial administration, for the tribe had traditionally been run by councils of elders. He and his family enjoyed privileges beyond anything his people could hope to attain. The house in which he and Wangari were talking was as substantial as any in the Kiambu district, and the servants were as numerous as those of the richest European families.

The chief had many acres of fertile farmland. From his office in Nairobi he ran a series of companies that dealt in road haulage and wholesale food distribution, and a chain of shops that served the native population. For him, colonisation had not entailed a loss of freedom or independence. Everything he had, he owed to the white man's presence on his land.

'I know that I am blessed. That's why I want to help those who are less fortunate than me,' Wangari replied, doing everything she could to remain calm. She could not allow her emotions to run away with her if she was to have a hope of winning her father over.

He was not impressed by her logic.

'Bah!' He swatted away her arguments with a dismissive flick of his hand. 'Why do you care so much about people you don't even know, but so little about your own family? You've broken your mother's heart. She has dreamed of the day when you would be married. For years she has been talking to the other senior women of our tribe. These are mothers of strong, handsome sons from the best families. She was making sure that you would only be given to the best possible husband.'

Wangari stood tall, holding her head high as she replied, 'I am not going to be given to anyone. I am not an object to be traded. I am a grown woman who will choose the man she wants for herself.'

'Is this what they taught you in London?' Ndiri asked. 'To spit in your mother's face?'

'You were the one who wanted me to go to England. "Learn from the British," you said. What did you expect?'

'I expected that you would learn manners and refinement. You were supposed to become a lady.'

'Oh, really? Are we Africans so lacking in dignity that we have to learn from our masters how to behave?'

'You need to learn from someone, that is clear. How are you going to live when you marry this Maasai doctor? Don't come running to me for money. I'm not paying for you to embarrass me in front of all my people.'

'We don't need your money. Benjamin and I took jobs during our university vacations. We saved our pay. We're going to start a clinic in Eastlands—'

'Eastlands?' her father interrupted, even more scornful than before. 'That's nothing but a slum, a shanty town! It is a den of thieves. How will you heal the sick if the gangsters have stolen all your medicines, eh? Tell me that!'

'Even gangsters need doctors, Father. They have families, too. They will see that Benjamin is helping the people. It will do them no good to harm us.'

'And I suppose you will use that law degree that cost me so much money to help these gangsters stay out of prison.'

'No, I will give the ordinary people of Eastlands advice about their legal and social problems, so that they do not lose out because they are too poor to pay for a normal lawyer.'

Chief Ndiri was barely listening. His head was filled with visions of his beautiful girl surrounded by the scum of the earth.

'My God, is there nothing you will not do to shame your family?' he asked.

Wangari could restrain herself no longer.

'I am not shaming my family by helping those in need,' she snapped back. 'But you are shaming your family, your tribe and your country by licking the backsides of the white colonists. You do Government House's bidding, even if it means hurting our people. You are the one who should be ashamed of himself.'

Chief Ndiri sprang back up again, his eyes bulging, his chest heaving with fury as much as exertion. He pointed at the door to his study.

'Get out!' he snarled. 'Go! Leave this house and never darken its door again. You were the sun in my sky, Wangari. But you are dead to me now.'

The man's passport named him as Michel Schultz. It stated that he had been born locally, and it had been issued by order of a government minister whose loyalty to the cause to which Schultz had dedicated the past quarter of a century was as steadfast and unwavering as his own.

Now, at the end of the working day, Schultz eased the long black snout of his German-made saloon out of the gates of the automotive engineering business that bore his name and into the evening traffic. The car was a new model, powered by an engine that gave it impressive acceleration and speed: qualities that had been enhanced still further by the modifications added by Schultz's own mechanics. One of his most effective sales pitches was to take prospective customers for a drive, floor the accelerator and then shout over the roaring engine, 'We can make your car go as fast as this!'

For now, he was obliged to crawl at walking speed until the car freed itself from the grasp of the rush-hour jams. Schultz drummed his fingers on the steering wheel. He was not a man who liked to be kept waiting. But though it was large and prosperous, the city was a fraction of the size of London, Paris or Berlin, and soon Schultz was driving through rolling foothills, along country roads dappled by the shade of the trees growing on either side and past the gates of country estates blessed with rich pastures and fruitful vineyards.

Schultz could easily have afforded one of those splendid properties, but his ally in high places had advised him to keep a low profile.

'We don't want anyone asking questions about where your money comes from,' he said. 'First, get a nice little business going, eh? That will explain everything.'

Schultz set to work building a new company, just as his forefathers had built the one that he had once ruled. He was confident he would succeed. He knew a great deal about the internal combustion engine. He had enough capital to fund his own enterprise and, if necessary, buy out competitors. Above all, he had a ruthless, domineering, bullying streak, inherited from his father, that made him willing to threaten, blackmail and if necessary destroy anyone who got in his way.

He would have his estate, and even if the mountains here did not soar as high as the ones he had left behind, they were undeniably impressive and the climate was considerably more congenial.

And there was the ocean. The final stretch of Schultz's journey home took him through a seaside town, with fishing boats lined up by the dockside and onto a road that twisted and turned with all the coastline's inlets and promontories. He came to an unmarked turning that seemed to lead nowhere. The view from the road was of nothing but the open sea and the sky.

It was when Schultz turned into the opening and drove down a gravel track that the small headland, barely any bigger than a couple of tennis courts side by side, came into view. When Schultz had acquired the property, paying a pittance for it, all there was on it was a dilapidated hut and a set of stone steps that led down the steep rock face to a crumbling concrete jetty.

Through his friend the government minister, he had found a building company run by a man who could be trusted. The solid rock had been blasted open to create holes in which large tanks for water and generator-fuel could be placed, along with a cesspit. More ground had been levelled for the house where Schultz and his wife Johanne proposed to live. From the rear, as Schultz approached, the walls were unbroken by any windows and the building looked as impregnable as a bunker. The comparison was ironic, given Schultz's personal history, but it also reflected his intentions. If necessary, at a moment of extreme crisis, he needed this place to function as his personal fortress.

Schultz opened the door to his garage, parked his car, and walked into his house.

The woman who now bore the name Johanne Schultz was waiting to greet her husband. Her hair tumbled in golden swirls around her shoulders. Her face was painted with thick black lashes and brazen crimson lips. She was wearing a flimsy, diaphanous gown, tied with a satin bow at her waist and a pair of heels that thrust her body up and out, exaggerating every curve of her buttocks and breasts.

She kissed him lightly on the lips and led him into the main living room. The far wall consisted of floor-to-ceiling windows, fashioned from bulletproof glass that looked over the evening water.

Neither man nor wife were interested in the view. Johanne teetered towards a sideboard on which two drinks were standing: a tall glass, dewy with condensation, filled with ice-cold beer and a shorter one that contained a double shot of schnapps.

She fetched the two glasses as silently and dutifully as a well-trained housemaid and brought them to her master. He took the beer glass, emptied it in one draught and then did the same with the spirit, relishing the way the chill of one was followed by the heat of the other.

She replaced the glasses, knowing that his eyes were following her every step, relishing his ravenous gaze. She came up to him, gently pressing her soft, almost naked body against his massive, fully clothed form.

The fact that she was exposed and vulnerable while he was still hidden behind his clothes excited Johanne.

'Can we play the game?' she asked. 'I've given the servants the night off.'

She ran her hand over his crotch and breathed a little faster as she felt his hardness beneath her palm.

Schultz was breathing heavily too. He pushed his hand between the open folds of Johanne's negligee and cupped her pudenda in his palm. She opened her legs, making it easier for him to slide two fingers inside her to feel her heat and wetness.

'Yes,' he growled. 'We will play. I will ring for you when I am ready.'

She moaned softly and looked up at him. 'Please, I beg you . . . don't be too cruel.'

Schultz's response was instant. He raised his hand as if to strike her. Johanne recoiled, stumbling backwards until her heel caught on the edge of a thick woollen rug and tripped her. There was terror in her eyes as he marched across and glared down at her, his thick neck reddening with fury.

'How dare you tell me what to do?' he shouted. 'By God, I will make you pay for that!'

Schultz turned and stalked away. One of the side walls of the room was lined with bookcases. He pressed a particular point on the wooden panelling. The case opened with the faint hum of an electric motor, to reveal a secret passageway. Schultz stepped into it and disappeared from view as he walked down hidden stairs into a secret cellar.

The cases slid closed behind him.

On the floor of the living room, Johanne Schultz gave a little shiver comprised in equal parts of fear and arousal. She raised a finger to her cheek, imagining how it would be feeling if she had been hit. She pulled herself to her feet. There was no time to lose. The game had begun.

Mr and Mrs Michel Schultz called it 'the game' but it was more of a ritual: an acting out of the shared hate that had first brought them together.

In the early days, their relationship was a sexual version of the old saying that 'my enemy's enemy is my friend'. Yet the bitter intensity of their coupling had awakened something in Johanne, a devilish version of the prince's kiss that rouses a sleeping princess. She had been brought up to be conventionally sweet, a compliant girl. Thanks to Schultz she had become a woman who despised the norms of acceptable bourgeois existence. He had led her into the heart of darkness, and she had found herself at home.

Johanne examined herself in the mirror. She had removed her gown and was naked but for her high heels. At the age of thirty-two she was in her physical prime, a condition she maintained with a programme of diet and exercise as disciplined as any athlete's. Her husband demanded no less and Johanne agreed with him, for her beauty was the source of her power and she had no intention of letting it go.

Johanne trembled with excitement and apprehension. He would hurt her, she knew that, though the methods he chose varied, so that she was never certain what was in store for her. That was part of the thrill.

What she knew for sure, however, was that the more Schultz bound her body, the more he set her spirit and her sexuality free. Every time he hurt her, the brief shock of pain would be followed by a much longer glow of pleasure. And by the time he penetrated her, they would both have been stimulated to levels of arousal that were as addictive as any drug.

Johanne checked that her make-up was perfect and every hair in place. It would not be long now.

She heard it: the ringing of the bell that told her he was ready. She took a deep breath, composed herself and walked to the bookshelf. She pressed the same panel that Schultz had done, waited while the shelf slid to one side and made her way down the stairs, holding on tight to the handrail, for they were steep and made of bare concrete. If she caught a heel and fell it could easily be fatal.

She emerged into the cellar. Schultz was dressed in the uniform he had proudly worn as an *Oberst-Gruppenführer*, or general, in the *Allgemeine-SS*. It was black, with the silver death's head and crossbones badge on the cap and a scarlet, white and black swastika band around the left arm. He styled it with riding breeches and tall, shiny black boots, in the manner beloved by his former boss and hero Reinhard Heydrich, the mastermind of the Final Solution.

Schultz was not a handsome man: his hair was a wiry ginger mat, his facial features were coarse and his smile was invariably malicious. But he possessed an air of raw, brutish power. His brow was heavy and glowering, his neck as thick and pink as a leg of lamb, his shoulders a bullish mass of bone and muscle. Dressed in his uniform, he conveyed an air of hostility, danger and mortal threat.

And all of it was directed at Johanne.

She looked around the room to get some idea of what he had in store for her. Schultz had spent countless hours in the basement cells of the SS headquarters on Prinz-Albrecht-Strasse, Berlin, torturing confessions out of suspects. He knew what he was doing. Her eyes passed over the portrait of the Führer that hung on the wall, past the locked cases in which Schultz kept his equipment – locked so that she would never know the full extent of what was in store for her – and came to rest on a heavy wooden chair, fashioned from solid oak, which had cuffs on each arm and at the bottom of the front two legs.

Beside the chair was a worktable, on which sat a flat wooden paddle and an assortment of chains, gags, masks and blindfolds. Johanne could cope with any of them. And then she saw something that made her belly tighten and her pulse begin to race. It was a simple black box device bearing control dials and output meters, from which snaked a pair of black cables with clamps like metal clothes pegs on the end.

Her husband had only brought the box out once before, but the sense-memory of the unendurable agony it had inflicted was as fresh as ever. This was Johanne's punishment for begging him not to be cruel. Even as she had said the words, she had known there would be a price to pay. Why else say them? But this . . . She raised her right arm across her breasts and flinched at the thought of the clamps.

There was always a moment for Johanne when the acting stopped, the fear became real and her desire to flee was genuine. This was that moment.

'Sit in the chair,' Schultz commanded.

She was his prisoner. She would do what he wanted.

'No!' Johanne gasped. 'No . . . I can't . . . Please . . .'

She took a couple of steps backwards, then turned and dashed for the stairs, her ankles buckling and twisting as the heels scrabbled for purchase on the floor.

But as she ran, Johanne knew that the attempt at escape was futile. Her husband could move much more easily than her and he was stronger. Once he had her in his grasp she would be helpless.

He would place her in the chair. He would lock the cuffs around her wrists and ankles.

He would order her, 'Tell me your name.'

She would refuse at first. She would try with all her might to resist. But once he had applied the clamps and switched on the electric current, there would come a point when she would crack and he would ask her one last time, 'What is your name?'

And she would answer, as she always did, 'Courtney . . . My name is Saffron Courtney.'

Timo Riel was the detective the late Fritz Werner had christened 'the muscle'. As a young uniformed cop he had been the heavyweight boxing champion of the Württemberg police. He'd gone undefeated from 1928 through to '33 before he quit the ring. He wanted to transfer to the Criminal Police, the detective branch of law enforcement, and that meant swapping his boxing gloves for a smart suit.

Almost twenty years later, Riel's imposing bulk and battered face still came in handy. The obvious advantage was that only the cockiest or dumbest criminals considered taking him on in a fight. But the physical threat he posed was so obvious that no one stopped to think that there might be a brain hidden beneath his Neanderthal skull and cauliflower ears.

Riel let his partner, Jaco Maier, ask the questions. He watched and listened while his sharp, intuitive, streetwise mind recorded, sorted and analysed the information provided by the interviewees, and, just as significant, what they left out. He and Maier had come away from their meeting with the so-called Frank Schmidt feeling both intrigued and frustrated. The man was clearly hiding something, but they had no grounds for pursuing it.

Then Schmidt had been killed by a hit-and-run driver as he was leaving the hospital. Both detectives felt certain that it had been a planned execution. Of course, they had no evidence. But it did not matter. The driver of the car had committed a crime by fleeing from the scene of a death he, or she, had caused. Now they had something to investigate.

It took no time to establish that both Schmidt's name and address were false, and the hospital receptionist was quick to confirm that the name had been given, not by 'Schmidt' himself, but by one of the men who had brought him in and subsequently visited him.

So who was he? The dead man had been carrying no identification when he left the hospital, which was both unusual and highly suspicious. But the accident was dramatic enough to make the local papers and the following morning the puzzle was solved.

A woman burst into a police station in Lindau, about twenty minutes' drive down the Bodensee lake shore from Frie-drichshafen, waving a newspaper and wailing, 'That's my Fritzi!'

Her name was Maria Grasse. She was interviewed by local police and she told them that the dead man's name was Fritz Werner, that he worked at the Meerbach Motor Works and that she was his fiancée. The ring on her finger and the pictures in her handbag proved she was telling the truth. When she was taken to the mortuary at Friedrichshafen, Fraülein Grasse was able to identify the mangled remains of her dead lover before fainting.

She wasn't the only one to put a name to the face. Riel and Maier were having a beer after work at a bierkeller known for being a police watering hole when another veteran, smaller than Riel but equally battle-scarred, approached them.

'Willi!' Riel grinned. 'Good to see you. Can I get you a beer? Jaco, this is Willi Roth. When I was winning all my heavy-weight titles, Willi was king of the middleweights.'

'And if I'd been the same size as this old gorilla, I'd have beaten him, believe me,' Roth growled.

The two old friends threw a couple of air punches at one another. Riel ordered more beers. Then Roth's face grew serious.

'I never talk about Russia, the things that happened there. You know that, right?'

'Sure,' Riel said.

He drank some more beer, knowing that his friend had some-thing to get off his chest, letting him do it in his own time. Maier, too, remained silent. Roth pulled out a packet of cigarettes and lit up.

'That man who was run over . . .' he said.

'Fritz Werner?' said Maier.

Roth grunted, blew out a trail of smoke and said, 'His name wasn't Werner. That man was *Kriminaldirektor* Heinrich Schraub and . . .' Roth shook his head. 'I can't tell you the things he did. I mean, I know what they were, but . . .'

Riel reached out his arm and laid a hand on Roth's shoulder. 'I understand, old man. Just tell us what you can.'

'He was a fanatic. Most of us did everything we could to get out of . . . you know, the orders we were given. And if we had to do it, we were drunk . . . I mean, off our heads. It was the only way . . . But Schraub was one of the true believers, a Nazi to the bone. He didn't have to be persuaded. He wanted to do it . . . all of it.'

'Christ . . .' Maier gasped. 'I think I need a schnapps. We all do.'

'Here's the thing, though . . . Schraub didn't come from this part of the world. He was a Dresdener. But somehow he managed to get away from the Ivans in '45 and he escaped the big round-up of SS and Gestapo types by the Tommies and Amis. Someone got him a new name, clean papers. I bet they fixed him up with a decent job, too.'

'Meerbach Motor Works,' Riel said.

Roth gave a shake of the head. '*Ja*, that makes sense. The place was owned by a damn SS general.'

'I wouldn't be surprised if there was a whole nest of them there,' Maier said.

'Maybe,' Riel shrugged. 'But the SS man's brother was sent to the camps for rebelling against Adolf and these days the place is run by the family lawyer. He's a Jew. Can't imagine either of them wanting their business infested by the SS.'

'A Jew and a traitor . . .' Maier mused. 'Listen, I'm no Nazi, but I don't like the sound of that.'

'The Jew won the Blue Max in the first war and the traitor was a fighter ace with more than a hundred kills to his name,' Riel pointed out. 'They did their bit for the Fatherland. And the company always gives generously to the police benevolent fund.'

'You thinking of tipping them off?' Roth asked.

'Might as well,' Riel said. 'You lads know as well as I do that this investigation isn't going to go anywhere officially. This is the new Germany, we're supposed to have put the bad old days behind us. Now one SS veteran turns up murdered by others just like him. Nazis all over the place. No one upstairs wants to know about that.'

sidore Solomons and his wife Claudia lived in a hillside villa close to the Zurich golf and country club. The house had been built in the twenties by a Modernist architect and decorated in the art deco style that was all the rage at the time. The floors were laid with the finest marble and intricately patterned parquet oak floors. The reception rooms were reached through a succession of Chinese lacquer doors. The outer walls were pierced by floor-to-ceiling windows that led onto a terrace from which there were spectacular views across the city towards Lake Zurich.

'You've done well for yourself, Izzy,' Gerhard said as he leaned against the terrace balustrade, taking in the scenery. 'I'm glad it all turned out for the best.'

'Yes, it did,' Isidore agreed. 'But how sad that we had to come here to find peace and prosperity. I should much preferred to have enjoyed those things at home.'

'Hmm . . .' Gerhard nodded. 'I know how you feel. But we are still here when so many are not.'

'Very true. Now, when you called me from St Moritz you said that there had been developments. I have news of my own, but you tell me yours first.'

They sat at a table, shaded by a parasol, where glasses, an ice bucket and a jug of freshly made lemonade were waiting. In these civilised surroundings, Saffron and Gerhard described the grim events on the Meerbach Motor Works airfield. Isidore stopped them occasionally to ask questions that gently obliged them to think harder and provide more detail about exactly what had happened. Every so often he would jot down a short note in a leather-bound book.

When they had finished, Isidore thanked them. He flicked back through his book, found the page and perused its contents.

'Yes, I thought so,' he murmured. To his guests he said, 'That man you . . . ah, incapacitated. The one who'd been spying on you—'

'You mean Werner?'

'Actually his name was . . .' Isidore glanced at his notes again and said, 'Heinrich Schraub. He was a former *Kriminaldirektor* in the Gestapo.'

Saffron frowned. 'You said his name "was" . . . as if he were dead.'

'He is, killed as he was leaving hospital, a hit-and-run attack. The police believe that Schraub-alias-Werner was a member of an SS veterans' gang. Their theory is that he was killed by his comrades as a warning to others that failure would not be tolerated.'

'You'd think they'd have got used to failure by now,' Saffron remarked.

'Indeed. But the question for us now is, how much did Werner tell them before they killed him. Or, more importantly, how much could he have told them?'

'He must have known who we were,' Gerhard said. 'Our visit to the Motor Works was public. He knew where we went, obviously, since he followed us to the airfield.'

'Could he have identified Ferdinand Posch, the man you spoke to out there?'

'Yes, but we got Ferdi to safety. He's not in the area any more.'

'Suppose the SS men have worked out that Posch was working at the airfield when Francesca and Konrad escaped. He might have told you.'

'Only if they knew we were asking him about them,' Saffron said.

'Men like that survive by being paranoid,' Isidore replied. 'They always assume the worst. That way nothing takes them by surprise.'

'Maybe now we should be paranoid,' Gerhard said. 'What is the worst thing that we can assume?'

'That diehard Nazis believe you and Saffron know what happened to Konrad at the end of the war,' Isidore said. 'And that Konrad discovers, through them, that you are looking for him.'

'If I were in his shoes, I'd take that for granted,' Saffron said. 'After all the things he's done to us, he'd expect us to want our revenge.'

'But revenge for what, exactly? We have spoken of the things that you two are supposed to have done to Konrad and Francesca. But what is the worst he has done to you? I mean, the thing he knows would give you a motive for revenge.'

'He had Gerhard arrested, put on trial and sent to Sachsenhausen. Isn't that enough?' Saffron asked.

'Yes . . . but I think there is more than that, something you are not telling me.'

'There is,' Gerhard said. 'He had me tortured.'

'Can you tell me how?' Isidore asked.

'No . . .' Gerhard closed his eyes, bent his head and shook it from side to side, muttering, 'I can't . . . I can't.' Then he straightened his neck, a simple action that seemed to require a huge effort, and said, 'I won't take myself back to that place again.'

Saffron crouched beside Gerhard. 'It's all right,' she told him. 'No one's going to make you say anything.'

But Isidore was not giving up. He took Gerhard's right hand in his own two hands, like a priest giving comfort, and said, 'Try. It's hard. I know. But you have been carrying a terrible burden of pain. Let us share the weight with you.'

Gerhard looked at him. 'I'll need something stronger than lemonade. Vodka would be good, or schnapps. Neat.'

'Of course,' Izzy said.

He went into the house and Saffron asked Gerhard, 'Are you sure about this?'

'I don't know,' Gerhard replied. 'But maybe Izzy's right about sharing the burden. I've been so afraid of telling you – scared of what you might think of me . . .'

'Oh, my darling, there's no need to be afraid,' Saffron said. 'I know you. And I love you.'

'Yes, but you don't know Konrad.'

Isidore returned with a bottle of vodka and a glass. He handed them to Gerhard. He filled the glass, emptied it, then filled it again before he looked at Saffron.

'You remember how cold it was in the first months of '45?'

'Germany was still freezing when I got there in late April,' she replied.

'This would have been March, I suppose – I'd lost any idea of actual dates by then. I was sick, starved, not much better than when you found me. But that was what the camp doctors were looking for. You see, they liked to do experiments to test the limits of human survival and find ways of making our soldiers keep going without sleep or food, but fighting like maniacs, right till the second they died.'

'And I thought the first war was the lowest depth of misery that humans could ever reach,' Isidore said.

'Humans are clever. We find ways to get better at everything, including making life hell.' Gerhard emptied his glass a second time and refilled it again. The alcohol appeared to have had no effect on him. 'The docs wanted to test a new drug, a cocktail of cocaine, amphetamine and an opioid painkiller.'

'So it got you high, it filled you with energy and you never felt a thing,' Saffron observed. 'Any army in the world would buy that.'

'It worked,' Gerhard said. 'All we had to eat every day was a small lump of buckwheat bread. I was so malnourished the doctor could barely find any fat to stick the needle in. But one shot of this drug and I was bouncing around like a spring lamb. They took me and the other test subjects outside and gave us the usual Sachsenhausen treatment, a forced march of forty kilometres around and around that parade ground. On any normal day it was hell from the first step. But this day, with the drug inside me, it was like a Sunday stroll in the park. There was a guy in front of me whistling as he walked. My feet were so blistered my boots were filling with blood. But there was no pain. And then . . .'

Gerhard stopped. He drank more vodka and slammed the glass on the table. He grimaced and went on.

'I saw Konrad. He drove into the camp in a big black staff car, with motorcycle outriders. He got out and was greeted by Kaindl, the camp commandant. The two of them watched us. They were so close I could hear Konrad tell Kaindl, "You must be feeding him too well," as I marched by them. They had a laugh about that and they went off for a tour of the camp.'

'I've heard enough,' Isidore said. 'We can stop now if you like.'

'Stop?' Gerhard replied. 'I haven't even started. You see, the drug only worked for a certain amount of time. And when that time was over, the person who'd taken it had burned up so much energy, there was nothing left. That's what happened to us that day. One minute we were marching, the next . . . bang! It was like a balloon being popped. Some guys' hearts exploded. They died instantly, like they'd been shot. The others took a while longer.

'God knows how, but I survived. I collapsed on the ground, couldn't move a muscle. My mind was as shattered as my body, but somewhere there was this voice telling me to keep going. I started crawling on my hands and knees in the mud. I had no idea where I was heading. I'd lost all sense of where I was, or even who I was – I mean, you had no name in the camp. I was Prisoner No. 57803. I wasn't even human. The guards thought it was great sport. They threw stones at me to make me go faster. They had a dog. They were about to set it on me, just for fun. Then Konrad returned.'

Gerhard gave a mirthless smile and said, 'One more drink,' as he refilled the glass. Saffron and Isidore were silent, appalled and yet, despite themselves, gripped by Gerhard's revelations. Neither dared break the spell that had transported him from this delightful terrace in Switzerland to the unspeakable horror of a concentration camp caught in the death throes of the Third Reich.

'Konrad walked up to me,' he continued. 'I don't know how I remember this because I was barely conscious at the time, and yet I can see his face as clearly as if he were sitting here now. He had a look that was the same as when we were little boys. I used to make little buildings with our toy bricks and he would always have a smile on his face as he got ready to kick them to pieces, because he knew I couldn't stop him . . . That was the smile he had that day.

'He was carrying a riding whip. He flicked the whip across my cheek, cutting it so I bled. I raised a hand to stop the blood, and because I was so weak that made me lose my balance and I fell flat on the ground.

'Konrad burst out laughing. The guards joined in. So now he knew he had an audience, he thought he should put on a show. I got up on to my knees, but I was pointing away from Konrad. So he hit me with his whip, slap-slap-slap, making me crawl around until I was facing him, on my hands and knees, with my head hanging low. And then . . .'

Tears began to stream from Gerhard's eyes, but he seemed unaware of them. His mind was occupied by his memory of that day as he said, 'Konrad told me to lick his boot.'

Saffron gave a little gasp, but Gerhard did not react.

'I tried so hard not to lick Konrad's boot. But he whipped my back, and kept whipping. After a while he stopped and he used the tip of the whip to lift my chin, so that he could look me in the eye. He said it again, "Lick my boot." And . . . and . . . oh, God help me . . . I . . . I licked his boot. And then he patted me on the head, like a dog and said, "Good boy."

'Konrad told the men that even the dumbest animal could be trained to obey a command. He stepped a little way from me and commanded me to crawl to him and lick his boot again – and I did. I couldn't help myself. I guess he was right. He'd trained me. After that Konrad had to go back to Berlin. He ordered the guards to lead me around the parade ground on my knees, licking their boots all the way. And they did . . . and I did.

'So you see, Izzy . . .' Gerhard acknowledged that he had been crying and wiped a hand across his face as he concluded, 'That was how my brother tortured me.'

Silence fell upon the terrace, broken only by birdsong and the distant roar of a passing aeroplane. Saffron was the first to speak. She had not shed a single tear. There was no trace of emotion in her voice.

'I'm going to kill him.' It was a calm statement of fact. 'Tell me where he is and I will terminate his existence.'

Isidore laughed nervously, unable to reconcile the warm, vivacious Saffron Courtney he thought he knew with the cold-faced woman threatening murder. He tried to make light of her words.

'As your lawyer, I certainly couldn't advise such an extreme course of action.'

She fixed her sapphire eyes on him, a look as cold as the deepest ocean.

'Why not? I've done it before.'

'Please, my love, don't lower yourself to his level,' Gerhard said.

He knew that Saffron had been trained to kill. When he saw what she had done to Werner, he had understood her ability to survive a threat to her own life. But never before had he understood her capacity for cold-blooded, calculated violence.

'I wouldn't be lowering myself,' she retorted. 'When I was growing up, my father taught me to love and respect the living creatures around us. But he also taught me that when a lion goes rogue and starts killing cattle, or even people, then it has to be dealt with. What I'm suggesting is no different.'

'Yes it is,' Isidore replied. 'You can't put a lion on trial.'

'Enough!' Gerhard said. 'Konrad is my brother. I was his victim. I have the right to decide how we deal with him.' He looked at the other two. 'Do you agree?'

'Absolutely,' Isidore said.

Saffron hesitated, then sighed, releasing all the tension from her face and shoulders.

'Of course, darling – you're right.'

'Good. Then my decision is that we should try to find a way of bringing Konrad to justice. I want him in a court of law, so that the world can learn what he did. Because it wasn't just me. He was there from the moment his hero Heydrich set up the death camps, right up until the final victims died. I want him to be confronted by his evil. And then, if a judge sentences him to death, yes, by all means let him be killed.'

Isidore nodded in agreement. 'Well said. But you should both be aware that any trial is going to involve allegations about him that might cause embarrassment and even shame for both your families. The prosecution would make terrible accusations against Konrad, but his defence might drag you into this too.'

'That's a risk I'm willing to take,' said Gerhard.

'Even if you have to stand in the dock and tell the world the story you told us today?'

'Even then.'

'Very well, I am in a position to assist this legal process. My son Joshua went out to Israel in '47. A year later he volunteered for service in the war against the Arab League. He works for the government now, in the Central Institute for Coordination.'

Saffron burst out laughing. The change was as drastic and unexpected as the African sun blazing through the clouds after a torrential storm. A puzzled frown crossed Isidore's face.

'I don't understand – why is that so funny?'

'It's just that the Special Operations Executive was officially known in Whitehall as either the Joint Technical Board, or the Inter-Service Research Bureau. The names made a bunch of saboteurs and secret agents sound like pen-pushers. Something tells me the Central Institute for Coordination might be the same kind of outfit.'

Isidore shrugged. 'I cannot say. But you may not be entirely wrong. So, we are agreed that Konrad von Meerbach will be brought to justice. My guess is that he is already on the very long list of men that Israel wishes to punish. To be honest, I don't know whether our infant state yet possesses the means to track down the men who tried to exterminate our race. But I dare say Joshua will have a more informed opinion. I will contact him and explain the situation to him. If you tell me your itinerary, I will ask him to meet you somewhere along the way.

'Let us stop talking business and have lunch. Claudia has been preparing a feast for us. She is longing to hear all your news, Gerhard. And Saffron, I must warn you, my beautiful, sweet wife is one of the world's great interrogators. There is not a scrap of information about your babies she will not soon know.'

'Do you know what I see when I look at you, H-P?' said Sir Jeremy Cummings, MP, turning his head towards the tall, impeccably tailored, blue-eyed man in his early thirties strolling beside him through St James's Park.

Hans-Peter Klammer had been Cummings's guest for lunch at the Carlton Club, at No. 69 St James's Street, the spiritual home of upper-class Conservative politics in London. The two men had got on well. Now Klammer gave the relaxed, confident smile, just one perfectly judged degree short of smugness or arrogance, with which he befriended men and seduced women.

'I dread to think!' He gave a light laugh that put a smile on Cummings's face too. 'Please, enlighten me.'

'I see the future,' Cummings said. 'I see peace between our nations. I see a better, peaceful, prosperous Europe.'

Klammer looked at him quizzically. 'You see all that . . . just by looking at me?'

His English was perfect. His light German accent was as far removed from the harsh guttural tones of all the villainous Nazis in the war films that still filled London's cinemas as a light Strauss waltz from Wagner's 'Ride of the Valkyries'.

'You know perfectly well what I mean,' said Cummings, letting himself be teased. Then his face took on a more serious cast. 'Look here, old boy. Times are changing. Without India, the Empire's a busted flush. Britain's future lies within Europe, a united Europe, run for everyone's good . . .'

'By agreeable fellows like you and me . . .?'

'Precisely. Put the war behind us and work together, that's the way of the future. This new European Coal and Steel Community that just set up shop in Brussels is only the start. We'll be in a United States of Europe soon, mark my words. There are men just like us in Paris and Rome, preparing to lead that union. And you are just the sort of chap we're looking for to join us.'

'A German without any blood on his hands?'

'If you want to put it like that . . . yes.'

'Well, it's an interesting thought, and we must talk about it properly one day. But for now . . .' He glanced at his watch. 'I must get back to work. I can't be late.' He smiled again. 'German punctuality, and all that.'

Klammer thanked Cummings for lunch, bade him goodbye and kept walking past Buckingham Palace to Belgrave Square, where the newly created Federal Republic of Germany, or West Germany as it was commonly known, had recently opened its Consulate-General. His title there was that of Cultural Attaché, and he was charged with using his social skills to remind the British of the civilised values of German culture. Or, as one of his seniors at the Foreign Ministry had dryly remarked, 'Make them forget the Blitz and remember Bach and Beethoven.'

Klammer had given his boss the same delightful smile he had bestowed on Cummings, and regarded him privately with the same emotion: utter, withering contempt.

When he got back to the office, Klammer's secretary, Steffi, handed him a letter, sent from Germany.

'Your mother has written again,' she said. 'I recognise her handwriting. She must be so proud of you. I'd love to meet her.'

'One day, perhaps . . .' Klammer said.

In truth, his mother was dead, her body incinerated in the hellish firestorm created by the Allied bombing of Hamburg in 1943. It was an act of murder that Hans-Peter Klammer would not forgive as long as he had breath in his body.

The letter he held in his hand bore the handwriting of a well-educated woman of a certain age, and was phrased in maternal language, but its intent was very different. So when, among the wittering about Uncle Horst and Auntie Denise, Klammer came across the line, 'An Englishwoman called Saffron Courtney Meerbach has been the centre of attention in our neighbourhood,' his eyes sharpened.

'She's married to Gerhard von Meerbach,' the message went on. 'Do you remember? That fighter ace who was disgraced when he was accused of being a traitor. We're all so curious about her. Since you're in London, you must find out all you can. I want to know everything!'

The men for whom those words had been written commanded Klammer's loyalty now, just as they had through all the years when, as an undercover agent for the Nazi Party's intelligence agency, the SD, he had faithfully reported every scrap of dissent against the Führer that he observed within the Foreign Service, right up to the fall of Berlin.

Klammer got down to work and began by calling a press cuttings agency. He presented his credentials and explained that he was contacting them on behalf of his country's *Stern* magazine.

'They are working on a profile of a German citizen called Gerhard von Meerbach,' Klammer explained. 'He is the heir to one of my country's largest industrial fortunes, and he happens to have married a British lady by the name of Saffron Courtney. Naturally, German readers will be fascinated by this love between two former enemies. So I wonder if you could possibly give me copies of everything you have on her. Bill me privately. *Stern* will reimburse me in due course.'

Within a couple of days, a brown envelope arrived in the post containing carefully labelled and dated cuttings of newspaper and magazine articles in which Saffron Courtney had been mentioned. The majority were dried-out, yellowing snippets that dated back to the pre-war years. Saffron's name appeared in one list after another of Bright Young Things who had attended high society balls and country house parties.

Trivial nonsense, Klammer thought, dismissively. But then he came across an item whose author declared that, 'Not content with dazzling Mayfair and Belgravia, Miss Courtney has been taking Oxford by storm since beginning her studies in Philosophy, Politics and Economics. Those in the know have anointed her the Zuleika Dobson of her generation.'

Ach so, the social butterfly has a brain.

With the outbreak of war, Miss Courtney disappeared from view until her name flickered briefly into view, buried in a long, formal list of recipients of medals for gallantry. She had been awarded the George Medal, the civilian equivalent of the Victoria Cross. It was the last cutting in the file.

That can't be right, Klammer thought. *A beautiful young heroine wins the highest possible civilian award for courage, it should be perfect propaganda. Where are all the front-page headlines? Where are the magazine covers?*

He called the agency to check whether they had missed anything, but was told, 'No, there was nothing else. Not a dicky-bird.'

Sometimes one learns as much from the dog that does not bark as the one that does. The intelligence officer in Hans-Peter Klammer understood that someone had wanted Miss Courtney kept well hidden. And that someone had the power to say 'No' to the press.

So what were you up to, my dear?

Klammer had collected the cuttings, put them into order and was about to replace them in the envelope when he spotted something. The envelope wasn't empty. There was one last cutting, tucked away at the back, that had somehow not come out with the others.

Klammer pulled it out. This piece of paper was not old and yellow. It was dated a couple of weeks earlier. It showed Saffron Courtney Meerbach, as ravishing as ever, leaving a restaurant with her husband and people whom the reporter described as 'old wartime comrades'.

When Klammer read the names of those comrades his face broke into a smile. Now he knew why Saffron Courtney had been kept out of the papers. Hans-Peter Klammer had already informed his handler in Germany that he was making good progress. He confidently expected to compile a thorough dossier on Saffron Courtney Meerbach. Now he had to discover what she had been doing as a British secret agent. And that required a roundabout approach.

There was no point trying to get anything out of the other people in the newspaper photograph. Former SOE operatives were fiercely loyal to their old organisation. They would never tell a stranger, particularly not a German, about a wartime comrade. Any approach to them would lead to Courtney Meerbach being tipped off that someone was investigating her.

But Klammer knew that SOE had not been popular with the rest of the military and intelligence establishment. The professional spies in the Secret Intelligence Service had looked down on the Baker Street crowd as rank amateurs who wasted resources and got in the way of conventional intelligence gathering. The army's senior officers were similarly disdainful about the oddballs and foreigners whom SOE appeared to favour as its recruits, and resented every penny of its budget.

Klammer needed to find someone in the British Ministry of Defence, or the Foreign Office, within which the SIS theoretically operated, who would be willing to pass on gossip from days gone by. His new ally Sir Jeremy Cummings sat on the House of Commons Select Committee for Foreign Affairs. He might know the right person to speak to. But, Klammer thought, he might need a little persuasion to divulge such information.

He thought for a while about Cummings, and then about his wife, Lady Anabel, the daughter of the Marquis of Daventry. She was a plain woman, with the bitter expression of a woman who knew that her husband had only married her for her title, her money and her father's high society connections. Any man who had her for a wife would surely be looking for his amusements elsewhere.

Klammer sent a telegram to Germany:

I HAVE FOUND A SPLENDID AU PAIR JOB IN LONDON FOR COUSIN HEIDI. BUT SHE MUST COME QUICKLY, BEFORE SOMEONE ELSE TAKES IT!

Two days later, Klammer was at London Airport to meet the British European Airways flight from Cologne. A beautiful girl with her hair tied into long, blonde pigtails emerged into the Arrivals area, caught his eye and ran towards him, throwing her arms wide to hug him, squealing, 'Uncle Hans!'

'My dearest Heidi,' he said, catching her and planting a chaste kiss on her forehead. 'How are you?'

'I'm so, so happy to be here!' Heidi exclaimed, her cornflower eyes wide with innocent excitement.

'Well, come with me, and I'll tell you all my news.'

Heidi looked for all the world like a warm-hearted German Mädchen of eighteen or nineteen at most. She was, in fact, a tough, unrepentant, thirty-year-old prostitute, with blood as cold as a viper's. The Führer, it was said, was the only man she had ever loved, and one of the few she had never slept with. In his absence, she had loyally served the Reich as a mistress to a series of high-ranking Nazis. Heidi was even said to have been the last person to have seen Hitler's private secretary Martin Bormann before he disappeared on 1 May 1945, although, as the story went, 'She wasn't looking him in the eye at the time.'

Now she ran a wildly profitable cathouse in Hamburg, but still undertook assignments for the sake of the cause. When Klammer explained the situation, Heidi had shrugged and said, 'If you introduce us on Friday, he'll tell you anything you want by Monday.' Then she'd looked at him and said, 'Come on, Hansi, let's do it for old times' sake. You know we're both as bad as each other.'

Klammer introduced Heidi to Cummings at a performance of *The Marriage of Figaro* at the Royal Opera House. Lady Anabel was there. Before the curtain went up and during the interval, Heidi ignored Cummings completely. Instead she charmed his wife, hanging on her every word and laughing sweetly at her slightest sign of wit. For his part, Cummings could hardly keep himself from drooling, becoming ever more frantic as Heidi ignored his increasingly desperate attempts to catch her attention.

Towards the end of interval, the two women went off to powder their noses. Cummings grabbed Klammer's arm, pulling close like a co-conspirator, and in a low but desperate voice said, 'I'm not going to beat about the bush, old man. That niece of yours, acting like butter wouldn't melt in her mouth. Is she as sweet as she pretends or as randy as she looks?'

'Hmm . . .' Klammer murmured. 'A century ago, a man who asked an uncle such a question about his niece would have found himself fighting a duel.'

'Yes, well, that was then and this is now. So tell me straight, is that little *Fraülein* fair game or not?'

'Well, it is not for me to make decisions on her behalf. I am not her father, and she is twenty-one—'

'Really? Not sure if that's a relief or a disappointment.'

'In any case, she is old enough to make her own decisions . . . And I am old enough to know better than to interfere in another man's marriage.'

'Thanks, old man, much appreciated.'

Cummings made his pass later that evening, as they were all walking between the opera house and the restaurant where they were having a late dinner. As they went to bed that night, he told his wife he would be away all weekend on constituency business, barely bothering to hide his true intentions, which Lady Anabel had plainly worked out for herself. At nine on Saturday morning, he picked up Heidi, who was waiting outside Klammer's flat, and drove her away to a cottage on a friend's country estate.

'How was it?' Klammer asked her, when Heidi reported back on Sunday evening.

'Oh, you know English gentlemen. They're only interested in boys or beatings . . . or both.'

'And Cummings?'

'Beatings. I spent my weekend whipping an Englishman black and blue.' She smiled, kissed Klammer on the cheek and said, 'I can't thank you enough.'

'So, did he tell you anything?'

'Oh yes. He knew exactly who Saffron Courtney was. He'd known her when she was a debutante before the war, and had heard about her during it. His exact description of her was, "Beautiful, deadly, but nothing but ice between her thighs."'

'Charming. Anything more detailed?'

'No, but he said he knew a man who'd be able to help.'

Sir Leonard Minturn was a veteran British diplomat, with strong connections to the intelligence world.

'Happy to help,' he said, when Klammer called him. 'Young Cummings has nothing but good to say about you. Worth keeping in with him, by the way. He'll be Prime Minister one day, you mark my words.'

A little more conversation and a stiff gin later, Minturn got down to business.

'There was an old boy at SIS called Brown, been around since the Stone Age. He'd set up a spy ring in Germany before the first war and he was still going strong when the second show began.'

'They hadn't retired him?' Klammer asked.

His contact shrugged. 'I dare say he'd been taken off the books officially. But one still saw him about the place, and he was said to spend a lot of time at the Cabinet Office, too. Now our Mr Brown was one of those sly old boys who still have an eye for a pretty girl, you know the type, I'm sure.'

'I have every intention of becoming one,' Klammer said.

His contact laughed. 'Don't we all! Anyway, Brown once let it slip to a chum of mine that the two most beautiful women he had ever recruited were a mother and daughter. And I reckon the daughter was this Saffron Courtney woman.'

'Really? What makes you say that?'

'Because we had our eye on her too.'

'On account of her pretty face?'

'That was part of it. The other was her war record.'

'Her George Medal, you mean. I was wondering, what did she do to get it?'

'Manned an ack-ack gun on a sinking ship. The Luftwaffe were bombing the hell out of the ship, strafing it, God knows what. She stayed at her post, blasting away until the water was practically lapping around her ankles.'

'Huh.' Klammer gave an appreciative nod. 'Brave woman.'

'Absolutely, but that wasn't why we were interested. It was what she did next.'

'Which was?'

'Saffron Courtney had an uncle, Francis Courtney. He was the black sheep of the family, bitterly resented his brother Leon, Saffron's father, for his wealth and success. Francis got his own back by getting in touch with the Abwehr and signing on the dotted line.'

'He was a traitor?'

'The worst kind. Luckily for us, it didn't take long before Francis was blown. We were on to him. Difficult position for the Courtneys. They stood to have a family member exposed as a traitor. That sort of thing could have wrecked their business empire. Young Saffron took matters into her own hands.'

The diplomat paused for dramatic effect. He took a long slow drag on his cigarette, stubbed it out, exhaled and then said, 'Uncle Francis was shot dead – by his niece. The official line was self-defence. But that's utter nonsense. Saffron Courtney shot him right between the eyes, cool as you like. She killed him to save her family's reputation.'

'*Mein Gott . . .*' Klammer gasped. 'Now I understand why she was such a valuable commodity.'

'I'll tell you something else, too. In 1943, Miss Courtney was sent into the Low Countries to follow up reports that your chaps had compromised all SOE's networks there. She established, beyond any doubt, that virtually every agent SOE sent into Holland or Belgium had been captured, and either executed or put back in the field as a double agent. She had to be extracted at very short notice—'

'Because her information was so precious?' Klammer asked.

'No – because she'd bumped off an SS officer and was about to be arrested for his murder.'

'Excuse my language, but she sounds like a bloodthirsty bitch.'

'I wouldn't argue with that assessment. But this time it really was self-defence. Apparently the SS chap had tried to rape her. She didn't take kindly to it. Trust me, old boy, Saffron Courtney is not a woman one ever wants to cross.'

'My God! Even our friends in Germany call me Schultz now!' Konrad von Meerbach exploded, ripping off the headphones he wore when taking down the coded messages that were sent from the highest levels of the neo-Nazi apparatus in Germany and received on the powerful short-wave receiver/transmitter he kept in the basement beneath his home. 'It is as if they've forgotten me – the real mc.'

'Hardly, my darling,' Francesca said, handing him a cup of coffee. 'They would not be calling you if they had.'

Von Meerbach grunted non-committally, took out a notepad and began decrypting. The codes they used now were childishly simple, compared to the near-impenetrable sophistication of war-time communications. All the old encryption machines had long since been destroyed, besides which, there were no longer Allied listening stations capturing every dot and dash as it was sent.

Half an hour later he was climbing the stairs back up to the house. Francesca was in the kitchen, preparing supper. She turned to greet him and was about to ask what the message said, when she saw the thunderous expression on her husband's face. Silence was the only option when he was in that mood.

Von Meerbach sat down at the kitchen table, took a second to compose himself and said, 'My brother and the Courtney woman visited Schloss Meerbach and the Motor Works. They met with my mother and the Jew Solomons. There are rumours that they plan to sell everything. The castle, the factory . . . there will be nothing left of my legacy. All my work, my father's, my grandfather's . . . all gone. And there's nothing I can do about it. Nothing!'

Francesca kept a bottle of schnapps in the kitchen, for those times when her husband's behaviour towards her could not be borne without alcohol to dull the physical or emotional pain. She pulled it out of the larder, where she kept it tucked between bottles of vinegar and vegetable oil, poured out a glass and set it before her man.

He grabbed the glass, downed it in one and then slammed it back on the table. Francesca refilled it. Still she had not said a word.

'Apparently the two of them were nosing around the airfield.' Konrad never used his brother's name if he could possibly avoid it, nor Saffron's, come to that, but Francesca knew who he meant. 'They met some man called Posch. The name meant nothing to me but . . .'

'Ferdi,' Francesca said. 'His name was Ferdi. He'd lost an arm in Russia, drank too much. But he was helpful enough.' She paused as the enormity of what she was about to say hit her. 'He loaded the plane when I left for the last time.'

The red flush of rage drained from von Meerbach's face to be replaced by chalk-white horror.

'Then he might have been there . . .' He shook his head, unable to finish.

'They're going to find us.' Francesca looked around frantically, her eyes darting around the kitchen as though its walls were closing in on her as she wailed, 'What are we going to do?'

Von Meerbach was enough of a man to have risen from the table, taken his wife in his arms and told her not to worry. He would make everything all right. But for the next few days a single word echoed around his mind: *How?*

A cornered animal has two basic choices: fight or flight. Von Meerbach was by nature an aggressor. He liked to take the fight to his enemy, but the days when he had the full resources of the SS at his beck and call were long gone. Nor could his old friends help him. Yes, they could gather intelligence on his behalf. They could even carry out the occasional small-scale beating or execution, close to home. But any attempt to kill his brother and sister-in-law would require the deployment of enough men to find them, keep them under surveillance and then eliminate them in potentially hostile circumstances.

Von Meerbach's decades-long hatred for the Courtney clan had begun with Leon, the man who had killed his father. He had even commissioned research into him, searching for any signs of weakness. The man lived in a private kingdom, defended by native warriors. If the traitor and his bitch retreated there, they would be virtually untouchable.

Which left the 'flight' option. Well, it would not be the first time that Konrad and Francesca had moved from one bolthole to another. But that only provoked the inevitable follow-up: where next?

This solitary house on the southern tip of Africa was as safe a hideaway as von Meerbach was likely to find. Moreover, he was a keen hunter, as his father before him had been. He knew that stillness is a hunted animal's best friend. Movement is more likely to catch a predator's eye. And a still, watchful, well-armed predator, who does not seek out their prey, but lets it come to them, can often be the deadliest of all.

Von Meerbach imagined himself as a spider, waiting . . . waiting . . . waiting for the fly to land on his web, or the deadly snake who lies unseen by its prey, right up to the instant when its fangs sink deep into helpless flesh and inject their fatal poison. These images comforted von Meerbach, and enabled him to tell Francesca, with evident sincerity, 'I have my plan. It will work. And we will win, my darling. We will win.'

Now von Meerbach got to work, thankful that he and Francesca had at least taken a sufficient hoard of gold, dollars, bankers' drafts, jewels and paintings with them on their flights from the dying Reich that money would never be any object.

His immediate priority was their physical protection. A steel mesh fence, two metres high, was erected around their property and topped with razor wire. Within it stood a new gate, its posts reinforced to withstand anything short of a tank, that could only be opened by means of a code. A second exit from the property, undetectable to passers-by, was installed, to provide a getaway route by land. And a fast, ocean-going motor boat was purchased and tied up to his private jetty, so that if all else failed they could take to the sea.

Von Meerbach now possessed the means of defence and of escape. If anyone asked, he told them he wasn't letting any black man steal his property and rape his wife. Few people argued with that.

Meanwhile, he instructed his men at the engineering works to reinforce the front bumpers and radiator of his car. He joked with them, 'If I hit anyone, I want to know it'll be them and not me that gets hurt.'

Second, he looked to his local allies for their support. He contacted his government minister friend and passed on the information he had been given. Von Meerbach knew that the man had no love for the Courtneys. The response was immediate.

'If that damned woman ever sets foot in this country, believe me, you will be the first to know.'

Von Meerbach was relieved. Once again he could feel the comfort of having men of power on his side.

Even so, his aggressive instincts were not so easily smothered. As much as he told himself to be patient and wait, another voice was telling him, 'Do something!'

It struck von Meerbach that if he could in some way upset his two enemies, get inside their heads and goad them into rash, precipitate action, well, then he would assert some measure of control over them. Then both their attack and his defence could be conducted on his terms.

But what would it take to knock his enemies off balance? Von Meerbach was not in the habit of asking his wife's advice, but on this occasion he made an exception.

'You know the bitch,' he said. 'What are her weaknesses?'

'The same as any other mother's,' Francesca replied. 'Her children.'

'You think I should kill them?'

'Could you do that without being killed yourself? All the time we were at school she would go on and on about her home, how much land her father had, how devoted the Maasai warriors were to him. If she still lives on that estate, then her children are there also. Could you kill them and get out alive?'

'What do you think?'

The question was a trap. If Francesca answered, 'Yes, you could,' then von Meerbach would know that she was lying, and would punish her for it. If she said, 'No, you couldn't,' then she would have doubted him and again, he would be obliged to chastise her for her disloyalty. Either way, the scrap of power he had ceded to her, by letting her express her view about what he should do, would be ripped away and she would be put back in her place.

From the way Francesca looked at him, head high, eyes raised to his, exuding the haughty dignity that was her birth-right as the precious daughter of a noble family, von Meerbach knew that she understood, and was daring him to do his worst. But then she surprised him, for her answer was neither of the obvious alternatives.

'I think that you do not have to kill them. You simply have to let her know that you have the power to do so. You need to get inside her family estate, their kingdom, within striking distance of her children. Make her feel that nowhere is beyond your reach. Nowhere is safe. Then, believe me, your presence will be like a worm inside her brain, and the only way for her to make it go away will be to kill you before you kill them. If you want to provoke her, that is how to do it.'

Von Meerbach considered what Francesca had said. He could see no fault in her reasoning. He might even act upon her sug-gestion. But that would come uncomfortably close to doing her bidding; it might set an unwelcome precedent. All the more reason to make his retribution even more severe.

And so the game began . . .

In the final months of the war, seeing very clearly that the Reich was doomed, Konrad von Meerbach had commissioned some of the Jewish prisoners at the Sachsenhausen camp who were employed forging high-value British and American banknotes to create a number of false passports for Francesca and himself.

He chose three nations he knew to harbour strong sympathies for the Nazi cause. For all three, the forgers produced two identities each for the von Meerbachs: one to get them in, and another if they had to leave in a hurry.

Now von Meerbach took out one of those passports. It showed him with a moustache, whereas he was currently clean-shaven, but Konrad felt sure that his virility was sufficient to produce the necessary amount of facial hair in the time available.

His plan now fully formed, he sent a radio message to Germany, explaining the sort of thing he had in mind, ending with a phrase he had picked up from his counterparts in the NKVD, the Soviet secret police, during that period at the start of the war when Hitler and Stalin had been allies.

'Find me a useful idiot.'

Saffron and Gerhard spent three days in Athens exploring the city's sights, waiting for word from Joshua Solomons. A decade earlier they had both been in the city within a month of one another: Saffron with the British forces mounting a futile attempt to defend Greece against German invasion, Gerhard as one of the invaders. Now they were together, having their photograph taken arm-in-arm in front of the Acropolis, just as they had done in pre-war days beneath the Eiffel Tower.

One evening, as they were returning from the day's exploring, Saffron found a week-old edition of *The Times* in a kiosk outside their hotel. She bathed, changed for dinner, then sat down to read the paper over a cocktail in the bar, occasionally passing interesting titbits of news on to Gerhard, who was engrossed in James Jones's novel *From Here to Eternity*.

'Oh look, there's a story here about Kenya,' she said.

'What does it say?' Gerhard asked, glancing up from his book.

'Hang on,' Saffron replied, scanning the paper. 'I'll just . . .'

She stopped in her tracks, put the paper down. The blood had drained from her face. She was fighting the urge to scream.

'What's the matter, darling?'

Saffron swallowed and breathed deeply. A wave of maternal guilt swept over her. She said, 'We need to send a telegram to Lusima right now, this minute. I have to know that Zander and Kika are safe.'

'Of course they're safe,' Gerhard said, baffled by the sudden change in Saffron's mood.

'No, they aren't,' she insisted. 'You don't understand. Our babies aren't safe at all.'

Gerhard got up from his chair and crouched beside Saffron. Her shoulders were slumped and her head hung in an attitude of despair.

'What is it?' he asked, stroking her face and pulling back the strands of hair that had fallen across her cheeks. Saffron turned her head and looked at Gerhard. Her expression, usually so fearless and self-confident, was filled with dread.

'It's the Mau Mau,' she said, pushing the paper towards him. 'They've started killing our children.'

Tom Ruddock was a farmer who treated his Kikuyu workers well. His wife Annette was a doctor, who ran a dispensary near their property where local Africans could be prescribed medicines and receive basic everyday care. She was heavily pregnant with their second child, a sibling to their six-year-old son Jamie. The little boy was adored by the family's servants. When he fell off his pony while learning to ride, badly spraining his ankle, the Ruddocks' stable lad, Matu, picked him up and carried him back to the house so that Annette could bandage her boy, give him an aspirin and tuck him up in bed.

Matu's feelings for the Ruddocks were sincere. He loved that little boy. But he had sworn the oath. A short while after Jamie's accident, Matu was spending a day off at a local drinking den that was popular with Kikuyu farmworkers when the menacing form of Wilson Gitiri appeared by his side.

'General Kabaya has need of your services,' he said. 'The Ruddock family are marked for death. You will help us kill them. If you do not, if you break your oath, we will kill you first.'

It was all Matu could do to control his bowels in the face of such a terrifying presence.

'Please, sir, I beg you . . . do not kill them. Bwana Tom is a kind man. Memsahib Annette gives the people good medicine to keep us well. And they have a little boy who has never hurt anyone.'

Gitiri said nothing.

Desperately, Matu tried to offer up alternative sacrifices. 'There are white people round here who deserve to die, many of them. I will lead you to them. Bwana Butcher beats his people all the time. Bwana Henderson takes everything his people try to grow, all of it, so that they have to pay him for every scrap of food. Bwana Jones—'

'Silence,' Gitiri growled.

Matu went from desperate jabbering to total silence as instantly as a switched-off radio.

'Your words only condemn your masters even more,' Gitiri said. 'It is because they are good that they must die. Thus the whites will know that none of them are safe, no matter how they act towards us. And men like you will learn that no white man, or woman, or child can ever be loved. They are all our enemies and our oppressors. We cannot be free until there is no white skin in our land.'

Matu did as he was told. He provided Gitiri with detailed descriptions of the Ruddocks' farm, both the land and the farmhouse itself, and also provided the family's typical daily schedule.

Thanks to the help Matu gave him, and the terrible power of the oath, which made Kikuyu blind and deaf to Mau Mau activities and dumb when asked to give evidence, Kabaya was able to lead thirty men up to the Ruddocks' farmhouse early one evening. They hid among nearby trees and undergrowth and waited for Tom and Annette to come outside for their regular evening stroll in the garden.

When the couple appeared, Kabaya and his men charged. They were not carrying guns on this mission. There was no need. They knew that the Ruddocks were not armed. Pangas were more than sufficient.

The Ruddocks saw the intruders as they emerged from their hiding places. They turned and ran for the shelter of their house. But Annette was slowed by her condition and Tom had no thought of leaving her behind.

The Mau Mau caught them on the verandah. The panga blades glinted in shades of orange and gold as their steel was caught by the last rays of the setting sun. Then they were drenched in crimson and scarlet as they cut into the Ruddocks' limbs and torsos. The couple were butchered, dismembered. Annette's baby was cut from her womb, killed and retained for further use. So were Tom's genitalia. Oathing ceremonies had descended to new levels of depravity and the eating of European flesh was one part of the ritual.

Little Jamie had been put to bed, but he was still awake. He heard his parents' screams and remembered his mummy going to his bedroom cupboard one evening, just before she turned the lights out, and saying, 'If the bad men come, run and hide in here.'

But the cupboard was a dark, scary place, particularly at night, and Jamie was too frightened to go there. So whenever he played hide-and-seek with his parents, or the servants, there was another place in his bedroom where he always went.

Clinging to his teddy bear, Jamie climbed out of bed, then stuffed his pillow under his blankets, making sure that none of it showed. Billy, his best friend at the local primary school, had told him this was a really good trick for making it look as though you were still in bed, when you weren't. Then he crawled beneath the bedsprings and huddled against the wall, as far away from the edge of the bed as he could get.

The next screams Jamie heard were those of the family's cook, who had gone to his employers' aid and met the same fate as them. His eyes stung with hot tears, but he stifled his sobs, knowing that his life depended on his silence.

There were loud shouts, the smashing of glass and crockery, the bangs and crashes of furniture being kicked over and hacked with knives. Through the hubbub he heard a single voice. It was unlike the wild shouts of the other men. The voice was commanding, decisive. Jamie had spent his whole life around Kikuyu people. He understood their language. He was able to understand Kungu Kabaya when he gave his men a single, simple order: 'Find the boy.'

With shock, surprise and bafflement he recognised Matu's voice when he replied, with great eagerness, 'I know where he is, sir. I will find him and bring him to you.'

Jamie heard the footsteps coming down the corridor. They didn't sound as though they belonged to Matu. The stable lad was light on his feet and the only shoes he ever wore were a battered old pair of plimsolls. But the heavy clattering against the floor, coming closer all the time, was the noise of a giant, coming to gobble him up.

The little boy squeezed himself harder against the wall. He clutched his teddy to his chest, listening so hard to what was going on outside his room that he barely even noticed that he had wet himself in terror.

The door opened and the bedroom lights were turned on.

Jamie saw a pair of black legs, in heavy army boots, pass in front of the bed. Then he heard a familiar voice, hissing, 'Jamie, Jamie, where are you? Quick, it's me, Matu!'

Jamie didn't know what to do. He loved Matu. But he didn't dare leave his hiding place. But then Matu got down on his knees and peered under the bed. He saw Jamie, held out his hand and said, 'Quick, now, or you will die!'

Jamie took Matu's hand and was pulled out from under the bed. In the corridor he heard a voice snap, 'He is taking too long! Go after him!'

Another voice answered, 'Yes, sir!'

Matu looked around, saw the chair that Mrs Ruddock sat on when she read Jamie his bedtime story and jammed it against the door. Then he ripped the bedclothes off Jamie's bed and grabbed the bottom sheet.

As Jamie got to his feet, he heard the rattle of the door handle, then saw the door shudder as someone shoved against it, making the chair legs scrape against the bedroom floor. There was a muttered curse and then the words, 'Open up!'

Matu had opened the bedroom window and thrown one end of the sheet out. He was holding on to the other end. He jerked his head towards the open window.

'Climb out!' he shouted.

Jamie went to the window and looked outside. He was only just big enough to see over the window ledge; the ground seemed far below him.

He hesitated.

'Go!' Matu screamed. 'Go!'

Then there was another, much louder crash against the door. The chair gave way and then went flying across the room, kicked by the boot of the man, bigger than anyone Jamie had ever seen. He had the face of a monster and in his hand he carried a long knife, whose blade glinted in the light of the moon, shining through the open window.

Matu had dropped his end of the sheet. He was standing, stock-still, too petrified to move a muscle as the monster's arm swung and the blade flashed. It sliced through the stable lad's throat, sending a great spew of blood, black in the semi-darkness, spattering across the room.

Jamie reached up, grabbed the window frame and tried to haul himself up and out of the window. As his feet scrabbled for purchase, a deep laugh rumbled from the monster's belly.

A massive hand reached down and grabbed Jamie by the ankle.

He screamed and tried to kick, but he was powerless as Wilson Gitiri stood up straight, lifted him up, swung him through the air and smashed him head first against the bedroom wall, again and again.

Gitiri threw Jamie Ruddock's pulped and battered corpse onto the floor, beside Matu. Then four of his comrades, savaging the little body like hyenas ripping at carrion, chopped it to pieces with their pangas.

S affron sent her telegram to Kenya and received a reply the following morning from her father, assuring her that her children were safe and their estate was still untroubled.

CAN'T SAY SAME FOR REST OF COUNTRY,

Leon had added.

PAPERS FULL OF PICS OF DEAD RUDDOCK BOY. GOVT. HOUSE PROPOSING EXTREME MEASURES EG PRISON CAMPS FOR REBELS W/O TRIAL. ARMY AND RAF CALLED IN. KENYA GOING TO HELL IN A BUCKET. THANK GOD WE HAVE LUSIMA.

Saffron and Gerhard checked out of their hotel and boarded a British Overseas Airways Corporation flight to Cairo, travelling on the Comet, the new jet airliner that was the pride of British aviation. On arrival, Gerhard hired a car at the airport.

'There's no point us taking taxis,' Saffron said. 'I spent two years here as a military driver. I know every short-cut in the city.'

The Egyptian capital was sweltering in the blast furnace heat of the midsummer sun. But the streets of the Garden City, where the smartest members of the city's British community had long lived, were lined with trees that cast a dappled shade. Behind high walls, further sheltered by more greenery, lay the mansion that Saffron's grandfather, Ryder Courtney, had bought with the money he'd made as a riverboat trader on the Nile. The lush, immaculately tended gardens surrounding the house ran down to the mighty river.

'We must go to the riverbank at sunset. It's a beautiful sight, very romantic,' Saffron said as she and Gerhard got out of the car.

He smiled and took her arm as they walked towards the house. Saffron's grandmother, after whom she had been named, was waiting for them beneath the portico that sheltered the front door. A gifted artist, whose works had been exhibited all over the world, Grandma Saffron had long ago developed her own personal style based on the practical requirements of living in a desert climate and had kept to it ever since.

She was slim, and closely monitored her weight on the basis that, as she put it, 'A layer of fat is like an overcoat you can't take off.' On the same principle of heat reduction, her silver hair was cut in a short, neat bob. When in Cairo, she invariably wore long, floaty kaftans of linen or fine cotton over harem pants in the same fabrics, enlivened by a selection of her myriad pieces of bold, colourful jewellery.

'Grandma, you don't look a day older than you did the first time I saw you,' Saffron said, after they had kissed hello.

'You're very sweet to say so, though I'm quite sure it's not true.'

Gerhard, whose manners retained the formality and restraint of a well brought-up German, shook her hand and said, 'It is a great pleasure to meet you, Mrs Courtney. Saffron has told me so much about you. All of it complimentary, I must say.'

'Thank you, Gerhard. I think you'd better call me Grandma too. I hope you don't mind, but Mrs Courtney sounds far too formal, and if you call us both Saffron that will drive us all quite mad with confusion.'

'Of course, Grandma, that makes perfect sense.'

'Good. Now, please, do come in. You must be baking after the taxi ride.'

They stepped into the hall, with its cool marble floor, white walls and a high ceiling from which a line of fans was suspended. Gerhard paused for a moment to cast an appreciative eye at the design and decoration. There was greenery everywhere, growing from large copper pots, blurring the distinction between the hall and the garden outside. Every piece of furniture, every picture or mirror on the walls, every one of the objects displayed on table-tops or shelves, reflected the history and culture of Egypt and the Courtneys' place in it. A small, three-thousand-year-old marble bust of Nefertiti sat beneath a vivid watercolour of a modern Cairo street scene with the signature 'S. Courtney', written in pencil, modestly tucked away in one corner.

A console table on one side of the hall bore a pair of photographs of Saffron's grandparents in silver frames, on either side of a telephone. A folded piece of paper had been placed beneath the telephone to keep it from blowing away. Grandma caught sight of the paper and exclaimed 'Aha!' with the relief of someone who has just been reminded of something they might otherwise have forgotten.

'I took a message for you two about an hour ago, from a gentleman who said he was staying at Shepheard's Hotel. I confess it made little sense to me, but he assured me you would understand.'

Saffron took the note, which read, 'I'm in town on business. Papa said I should get in touch with you. He wants me to find some merchandise that you are looking for. Yours, Jonas Stemp.'

She passed it to Gerhard, who remarked, 'So Joshua has finally appeared.' He understood the code name.

Grandma frowned, feeling certain that the name she had written down was not Joshua, but saw that it made sense to her guests.

'Well, I'll leave you two to it,' she said. 'I've put you in Saffy's old room. The boys will have your cases waiting for you. Why don't we all have tea together in the drawing room, once you've got yourselves settled?'

'Thank you, Grandma, that would be lovely,' Saffron said.

She called the hotel and asked for Mr Stemp. She spoke to him in German and, since Joshua had felt it necessary to be discreet, went along with the narrative he had constructed.

'I'm very grateful to you for getting in touch. As your father may have mentioned, my husband and I lost a number of valuable packages in transit from Germany. Perhaps we could meet to discuss the matter.'

'That would be very agreeable. I am free this evening, if that is convenient for you.'

'That would be fine. My husband will send a driver to pick you up. Shall we say, seven this evening?'

'By all means.'

At seven, Saffron called Joshua's room again. She did not give her name to the telephonist.

'Leave the hotel, turn right, walk about two hundred metres,' she said. 'You will see a café called the Maxim Palace. I am waiting outside. The white Austin saloon.'

Joshua made sure he was not being tailed. He spotted the car and got straight in. Saffron drove away, checking the mirror as she went. Joshua looked out of the rear window.

'We're not being followed,' he said.

'I know. I wasn't followed on the way here, either. But one can never be too careful.'

If that remark were not enough to tell Joshua Solomons that he was dealing with a professional, Saffron's driving confirmed it. She sped through the crowded streets with precision, deftness and an insider's knowledge. There was an assurance in the way she cut down narrow side streets, some barely more than alleys, knowing exactly where they would take her.

'It's quicker this way,' she said, as they plunged into yet another cramped, filth-strewn passageway, lined with empty street-traders' carts.

And impossible for anyone to keep up with, Joshua thought.

To his surprise, the next turn took them from the gloomy back alley onto a broad thoroughfare that led to the Garden City. Barely two minutes later they were rolling through a gateway, manned by a servant who saluted as they passed, and up a crunching gravel driveway to Grandma's house.

Joshua gave a soft whistle as he got out of the car. The Garden City was aptly named, for the noise and the pungent smells generated by the cars, the people and the animals – horses, donkeys and camels – that thronged the rest of Cairo, and the baking heat trapped by the closely packed buildings and tarmac roads, were now forgotten as if they had never been. Here there were lush lawns; beds packed with lovingly tended flowers and shrubs chosen with an artist's eye for colour and form; palm trees whose leaves were rustling in the gentle breeze; and all of this was arranged to lead the eye to the end of the garden where the slow brown waters of the Nile made their stately way to the sea.

'Ay-yay-yay,' Joshua sighed. 'Papa said you Courtneys were rich, but this . . .'

Saffron laughed. 'Believe me, we're the poor relations of the family! You should meet my South African cousins. Now, let's go in. Gerhard is looking forward very much to meeting you again. I thought we could talk over supper.'

This was an occasion that required privacy, not luxury. A small, round dining table had been set up in the drawing room. Grandma's cooks had prepared a buffet, so that the diners could select their food and drink without the need for servants.

While Gerhard and Joshua reminisced about the old days – before the Nazis took power, when Isidore Solomons and his family were prosperous, respected members of Munich society – Saffron took the measure of the man that she and Gerhard were counting on to help track down Konrad. Joshua, she reckoned, must be in his mid to late twenties. Old enough to have had youthful idealism and innocence tempered by hard experience, but still at the height of his physical powers. She could see Claudia's influence in the line of her son's mouth and his clear blue eyes. But his physical build and sharp, forensic intelligence came, like his vocal mannerisms, straight from his father Isidore.

Yet while Joshua's parents were true Europeans, steeped in centuries of Germanic culture, he had acquired a toughness that came from living in a small country surrounded by much larger enemies. Saffron knew she could trust him. She also felt sure that he would be less troubled by intellectual niceties and sophisticated scruples than his elders. Other women might have been concerned by this. Saffron was not.

Joshua is Israeli, just as I am African. We'll understand one another just fine.

She tuned back into the conversation. Joshua had spent the first few years of his life in the Solomons' fine house on Königin Strasse, across from the English Garden. Then the Nazis began their assault on the rights of Germany's Jews. By the time Gerhard had managed to find the money to help the Solomons escape the country, they were living in a tiny apartment in one of the roughest areas of the city, close to the railway marshalling yards.

'My family did that to you,' Gerhard said. 'It was unforgivable.'

'You don't need to apologise,' Joshua assured him. 'I am honoured to meet you. To this day, my father always says a prayer for you at Passover.'

'Really?'

'Absolutely. At Passover we Jews celebrate our people's escape from slavery under the Pharaoh. In our family we also celebrate our escape from the Nazis, and we thank the man who made it possible.'

'Thank you, but I don't deserve your prayers. I have seen terrible things, and done nothing to stop them. In Russia, I was present when the SS used a gas van. It was a demonstration for the high-ups . . . Men, women, old folk and children, more and more people were shoved into the back of a van like the ones delivery men use until the bodies were packed so tight they could not move. The SS set up a tube from the exhaust pipe into the back of the van. Then they turned the engine on so that the exhaust fumes went into the truck. They kept going until the fumes – the carbon monoxide in the fumes, to be exact – killed all the people inside.'

'*Oy vey ist mir*,' Joshua murmured, horrified by the picture Gerhard's words painted.

'I stood and watched it and I swore to myself that one day I would bear witness. But I did nothing to prevent it happening. And the truth is, there was nothing I could have done. Those people were going to die, if not then, on that day, then soon afterwards, somewhere else. But that's not the point, is it? I should have tried.'

'The whole world should have tried, Herr Meerbach,' said Joshua. 'You did what you could. You risked your neck to save my family. You went to a concentration camp, rather than pledge allegiance to Hitler. How much more can we ask of any man? You know, we have a phrase in Israel: "Righteous among the nations." It refers to Gentiles who had the humanity and bravery to help their Jewish friends and neighbours, or even complete strangers, in our time of trouble. You are one of the righteous and you deserve justice, too.'

'Thank you,' Gerhard said. 'So, can you help? Your father wasn't sure how far advanced your plans were for dealing with Nazi war criminals.'

Joshua shrugged. 'Well, we've not yet mounted a major operation beyond our borders.' He grinned. 'After all, we only just got borders to go beyond. But we have to start somewhere, and you are giving us an important target. I think I can persuade my bosses to take an interest.'

'And you'll have the assistance of someone with several years' experience of planning, managing and conducting undercover operations in enemy territory,' Saffron observed, matter-of-factly.

Joshua looked at her, grinned and said, 'How can I complain? So . . . let's start by establishing where we are now. My father has given me an account of your investigation. I've done some preliminary follow-ups of my own. But I'd like to hear the story from you, too.'

Gerhard and Saffron outlined everything that they had discovered, while Joshua listened carefully, stopping them from time to time to clarify particular points. When they had finished he said, 'My father has agreed to make discreet inquiries about Countess von Meerbach's possible presence in Switzerland at the end of the war. Now we need to know whether Konrad von Meerbach had any connections with Nazi sympathisers in Spain or Portugal. Did he mention anything of that kind to you, Gerhard?'

'No, but he never trusted me enough to share information like that. The only reason he would offer confidences was either as a boast or a threat, or both.'

'How about your mother?'

'The same – he despised her. He would only ever want to hurt her.'

'In that case, he might just have said something to her, to cause her pain, that gave some kind of clue away. People forget themselves when they're attacking another person. They're so busy thinking about their desire to hurt, they get careless.'

'Very true,' Gerhard agreed. 'I'll send my mother a telegram to ask her.'

Joshua grimaced. 'That could be risky—'

'Do you seriously think that the telegram operators are all Nazi sympathisers?'

'It's possible. Unlikely, but—'

'I'll phone her, then.'

'You'll have to book a call first,' Saffron said. 'International calls to and from Egypt are a nightmare. Not enough lines.'

'In that case, let us reconvene in twenty-four hours,' Joshua asked.

'Same procedure as this evening,' Saffron said. 'But I'll select a different café for the pick-up.'

'Agreed.'

'Excellent. Now, let's have something to eat. Grandma's cook is far too good to let his work go to waste.'

Quentin De Lancey received the best news of his life one evening in the bar of the Muthaiga Hotel. A civil servant from Government House called Ronnie McLaurin had taken the glass of gin and tonic that De Lancey had just bought him, given a quick little nod of thanks, and taken a hefty swig.

'Well?' De Lancey asked, once the drink had been swallowed.

'Good news, old boy,' McLaurin said, reaching inside his jacket for his cigarette case.

He was a thin stick of a man, his skin tanned tobacco-brown by thirty years of service in various tropical outposts of empire, his body as tough and dessicated as a stick of biltong. While De Lancey did his best to restrain the rising tide of impatience coursing through his body, McLaurin took out a cigarette, put it in his mouth, then patted his various jacket and trouser pockets, searching for his lighter.

'Here,' said De Lancey. 'Let me.'

He struck his own lighter under McLaurin's cigarette. McLaurin inhaled and then, finally, he said, 'The job's yours, old boy. Absolutely in the bag. But don't say a dicky-bird until it's confirmed, there's a good man.'

'Quite understood . . . my lips are sealed. Not a dicky-bird to anyone.'

McLaurin nodded, paused for a moment as he exhaled a long, contemplative stream of smoke and then said, 'D'you mind if I ask you a question? Nothing remotely official, you understand, purely my own curiosity.'

De Lancey was feeling a rare sense of bonhomie. 'Not at all,' he said, agreeably. 'Fire away.'

'Well . . .' McLaurin was wondering how best to phrase it, for De Lancey was considerably larger than him and he did not wish to anger him. 'The thing is . . . Well, I've been running the recruitment drive for officer level entries into the

Special Constabulary, and sundry other new units, for the past few months. And we've had no shortage of chaps who want to command constabulary units. They're all tremendously excited by the idea of running round the bush, gun in hand, taking potshots at rebellious Kukes.'

'Not my thing, running around,' said De Lancey, dryly.

'No, quite so . . . absolutely.' McLaurin seemed unsure whether De Lancey was making a joke at his own, very over-weight expense, for the tone of his voice had actually conveyed more of an air of menace than amusement. 'But in any event,' he went on, 'comparable posts in the screening centres have been much harder to fill. Everyone can see the very real need to round up any Kikuyu who may have terrorist sympathies and establish whether or not they pose a danger to public safety.'

'They all do, you mark my words.'

'Well, yes, quite possibly, but the thing is, it's much harder finding chaps who are willing to bear the burden of interrogating endless insolent natives. But it's essential to find out where their loyalty lies, and work out which we should stick in an internment camp, and which we can safely send back home. So I'm both tremendously grateful to you for taking up that burden, but also curious to know why you'd want to do it.'

'Well, let me see . . .' said De Lancey. 'Part of it, naturally, is a matter of one's patriotic sense of duty. We must all do our bit in the defence of the Empire.'

'Oh yes, quite so.'

'But also it's a matter of one's natural aptitudes. I'm no Dead-Eye Dick with a rifle, and I've never known the first thing about bushcraft. But I flatter myself that I do know the black man.'

Entirely indifferent to the presence of the native barman, standing barely three feet away and able to hear every word he was saying, De Lancey added, 'And I dare say he knows me. We have something in common, you see. We're not sentimental. Blacks aren't frightened of inflicting or receiving harsh punishment, and nor am I.

'The Kukes won't dare lie to me, because they'll know I'll thrash the skin from their bones if they play dumb, or tell lies. Believe you me, McLaurin, I may not be much use fighting Johnny Mau Mau in the field. But in the interrogation chamber, I will be in my element.'

'I very much hope that proves to be the case,' McLaurin said. 'And if you can get results, believe me, your efforts will not go unnoticed at Government House.'

De Lancey could not believe his luck. He was about to be paid to bully and abuse people who could not strike back.

Then another benefit of his new position struck him. His wife was always whining at him with one complaint or another. One of her favourite moans, year after year, was that they were never invited to the annual garden party that the governor held for prominent members of Kenya's white community.

I'll have a word with McLaurin, De Lancey thought. *See if he can get me an invitation. Might buy me a moment's peace.*

He glowed with smug satisfaction at his good fortune, and there was more to come.

Just a few nights after his conversation with McLaurin, De Lancey was back at the Muthaiga, when he was approached at the bar by an Austrian businessman called Innerhofer, who said he was in town to buy Kenyan tobacco, for export back to his homeland. He named some mutual acquaintances, said they had spoken highly of De Lancey and asked him if he could do a small favour for 'some friends of mine back home'. It was little more than babysitting, but he would be well rewarded for his time, and if all went well, there could more, equally light, but remunerative jobs to follow.

De Lancey was happy to oblige, which was why he was standing in the arrivals area of the Nairobi Aerodrome, in his Special Constabulary uniform, holding a piece of white cardboard on which the name 'PIETERS' was written in black capital letters.

A man emerged from the customs check, wearing a light-weight grey suit and a black snap-brim fedora hat. He was taller than De Lancey, moustachioed, and although not so obviously overweight, still very heavily built. He took off his hat to wipe his perspiring forehead to reveal a head of bright ginger hair, lightly salted with grey.

The man caught sight of De Lancey's sign, put his hat back on and walked towards him with a strong, determined stride.

'De Lancey?' he asked.

'That's me,' De Lancey said, trying to sound equally assertive, but failing. With the bully's feral instinct for power and weakness, he knew at once that Schultz was not a man to be trifled with.

'I've arranged everything for tomorrow,' he said. 'I trust it will be to your satisfaction.'

Pieters gave a wordless grunt that signalled that he had heard what De Lancey had said, but was waiting to be convinced.

'Take me to my hotel.'

'Absolutely, Mr . . .' De Lancey said. 'Please . . . follow me.'

Twenty-four hours after his first visit to the Courtney mansion in Cairo, Joshua came back again. This time, Saffron suggested that they should take their drinks and walk down the garden to the banks of the Nile. It was a hot, still night and the full moon reflected off the drowsy waters of the great river. A pleasure boat went steaming by.

'We must go on a dinner cruise before we leave,' Saffron said, taking Gerhard's arm.

Aboard the boat, couples were dining beneath an awning, lit by strings of glowing light, while a jazz band played an old Cole Porter song.

'Aah . . . Anything Goes,' Saffron sighed, quietly singing along to the music and thinking back to all the times she'd danced to that tune at debutante balls before the war, and later in cellar nightclubs in London, while bombers flew overhead.

'Did you manage to speak to your mother, Gerhard?' Joshua asked, impatient to get on with their business.

'Yes, as a matter of fact I did.'

'And . . .?'

'She told me that my brother visited Portugal in 1942. It was either March or April. She couldn't remember the exact month, but she did recall Konrad being pleased with himself for spending several days in Lisbon, where the weather was sunny and warm, while it was still chilly for her at home. It was even colder for me on the Russian Front, of course. Konrad made quite a point of that.'

'Did he tell her what he was doing in Lisbon?'

'Not exactly . . . Being Konrad, he couldn't resist telling my mother that he had gone on Himmler's personal orders. It was some kind of an official visit, on behalf of the Reich. But Konrad wouldn't say exactly what the purpose was. He said it was all top secret—'

'Which would have made him feel even more superior,' Joshua pointed out.

'Yes.'

'This is useful information. There has been a thriving Jewish community in Lisbon for well over a century. And more of us fled there during the war. Of course, Portugal was neutral, so the Reich had a presence there, too, as I'm sure you know.'

'I certainly do,' Saffron said. 'I was interrogated by them.'

Both men looked at her quizzically.

'That was how I got into Occupied Europe. I had references from Nazi sympathisers in South Africa, recommending me to their counterparts in Holland and Belgium. I took those references to the Reich consulate in Lisbon, and they gave me the travel permits I needed to get from there to the Low Countries.'

'Hold on.' Joshua raised a hand. 'Talk me through that. Tell me how you put that chain together – I presume you must have sailed to South Africa from England.'

'That's right.'

'Then what?'

Saffron told the full story of how she became Marlize Marais, the fascist daughter of an embittered father, who had blamed the collapse of his business on grasping Jewish bankers. She recounted how Marlize had wormed her way into the Ossewa Brandwag, the organisation that was the fascist heart of Afrikaner politics. She described the night she came within a whisker of being unmasked before she had even left South Africa for Europe. Having landed in Lisbon, she talked her way past the German Deputy Consul General.

'He wasn't a consular official, of course,' Saffron said. 'I could see at once that he was a secret intelligence officer of some kind.'

'How fortunate that he could not see the same about you,' Joshua remarked.

'I'll say . . . Anyway, after that I went by train from Lisbon to Ghent and signed on as a party worker for a ghastly bunch of

Belgian blackshirts called the VNV. Now, tell me, why did you want to know all this?'

'Well, from what I know about your two family histories, your fathers were great enemies, am I right?'

'Absolutely.'

'They had met in Kenya, before the First War.'

'Correct.'

'And Gerhard, your father died on an expedition to Africa?'

'That's also true,' he agreed.

'So we have a connection between the von Meerbach family and Africa . . . and also a strong connection, over two generations, between your two families.'

'Oh . . .' said Saffron. 'Of course – I see where you're going with this.'

Joshua smiled. 'Then please – as the Americans say, "connect the dots".'

'Well, if I could go from Africa to Europe, via Lisbon, why couldn't Konrad make the same journey in the opposite direction?'

'That was what I was asking myself.'

'And that makes even more sense, because some of the Ossewa Brandwag men that I knew during the war are now high up in the South African government, so they might want to help a man like Konrad. I mean, not officially . . . but they'd certainly turn a blind eye.'

'Yes, but there's one more element you should consider. It is true that old Nazis have friends in the government in South Africa. But they do in Argentina, and Brazil, and Chile too. And of course, if Konrad was in Portugal, he could probably have stayed there. The Salazar regime is a right-wing dictatorship, after all. So why go to Africa?'

'Because there was something there for him?' Gerhard suggested.

'Such as . . .?'

'Us,' Saffron said. 'The reason Konrad von Meerbach would go to Africa would be because we are there, and so is my father.'

'And I can tell you for absolute certain,' said Gerhard, 'that he wants to kill us all.'

'In that case,' said Joshua, 'I will put my contacts in Lisbon to work at once. Even if Konrad hasn't made a move yet, you can bet that he has something in mind. We have to find him and take him. Your lives depend upon it.'

f there was one man in the world that Leon Courtney did not want to see turning up outside his front door, it was Quentin De Lancey. It was not just that the man was loathsome and his political views repellent; he also reminded Leon all too painfully of the worst day in his life.

A quarter of a century ago, De Lancey had expounded a series of ill-informed, prejudiced remarks about Kenya's native population, whom he had referred to as 'bone-idle savages' at a dinner party they both attended. Infuriated, Leon challenged him to a wager to demonstrate how wrong he was. He told De Lancey he would pay him five thousand pounds if any three white contenders he selected, going one after the other, could outrun a single Maasai. If De Lancey lost, he would have to run one lap of the track stark naked.

The race was run around the old Wanjohi Country Club polo field. The Maasai won. But De Lancey never had to pay his forfeit because, by then, Leon's first wife Eva was already in her death throes, stricken by eclampsia and bleeding her life away on the dining table in the club's pavilion.

And now, here De Lancey was, following one of the Estate House staff into Leon's office, his grossly corpulent body garbed in khaki shorts, with a matching shirt and peaked cap, holding a clipboard in his right hand. Beside him walked another sizeable individual in a suit and tie, his head covered by a grey snap-brim hat, his eyes concealed behind a pair of metal-framed dark glasses.

'Mr Courtney?' De Lancey enquired, glancing at his clipboard as if he needed to be reminded who he was talking to.

'You know damn well that I am,' Leon replied. 'What are you doing on my property, dressed up like Billy Bunter on a Boy Scouts' outing?'

A flash of anger crossed De Lancey's face. The two constables behind him did their best to suppress their grins. De Lancey did not so much see as sense his men's amusement. He turned his head to glare at them and snapped, 'Outside! Wait by the vehicles!'

When they were gone, his self-importance now somewhat restored, De Lancey introduced the man in the suit, who was removing his sunglasses and tucking them into the breast pocket of his jacket. From the side pocket he was now extracting a small leather-bound notebook and a pencil.

'This is Mr Pieters, from the Reuters press agency,' De Lancey said. 'He is writing an article for global syndication about our response to native insurrection. Naturally, the governor is keen to show the world that we have the whole matter well in hand.'

'Good day, Mr Courtney,' Pieters said. 'Thank you for allowing us on your property.'

'Good day to you too, Mr Pieters,' Leon replied.

Something about the man troubled him. Those beady, porcine eyes reminded him of someone, but before he could work out who, De Lancey was announcing, 'I am here in my role as an officer in the Special Constabulary.'

Leon's loathing of De Lancey drove all other thoughts from his mind.

'Are you now?' he said. 'Well, I have no need of your services. If any man, woman or child living on my estate had done wrong, I'd already know about it and I'd deal with it myself.' He did not try to hide his contempt when he added, 'And not with a horsewhip.'

'That is not the purpose of my visit,' De Lancey added, and the look he gave Leon made it clear that the loathing was mutual. He cleared his throat and began what was clearly a prepared speech. 'As you know, there has been growing unrest within the Kikuyu population, provoked and encouraged by the so-called Mau Mau terrorists—'

'Of course I damn well know,' Leon interrupted him. 'What of it?'

'As you're no doubt aware,' De Lancey continued, 'this unrest is no longer confined to oath-taking ceremonies and actions undertaken by the Mau Mau to enforce their power within their own tribe. We must be ready for the Mau Mau turning their attention to the European population. We have reason to believe that oath-takers are required to swear that they will kill white people. The fate of the poor Ruddock family is a tragedy we do not wish to befall on you or your dependants. For that reason—'

'None of my people have any such intentions,' Leon said.

'For that reason,' De Lancey repeated, ploughing on, 'I have been authorised to conduct inspections of European-owned properties to check that the proper precautions have been taken to render them secure and to keep their owners safe.'

'Are you telling me that you wish to inspect this house?' Leon asked.

'Yes, as well as any other white-owned properties on your estate, and the grounds of the estate itself.'

'You are aware that Lusima covers more than one hundred and eighty square miles?'

'Only the Delamere property is larger, yes. And Lord Delamere has been most cooperative.'

'Is that so . . .?' Leon found it hard to believe that a man as grand as Thomas Cholmondeley, the fourth Baron Delamere and owner of the Soysambu Ranch, would allow anyone like De Lancey to go sticking their nose into his affairs. But he couldn't be bothered to argue with De Lancey. He wanted this whole business done and dusted as quickly as possible.

'Very well then,' Leon said. 'This is what I will allow. You may inspect the exterior of this house and its outbuildings. You may also inspect the ground floor, accompanied by one of my people. You may not inspect my daughter's house, since she is not presently in the country and I will not allow anyone into her home without her consent. And I will absolutely not have you "inspecting" my land.'

'I'm sorry, Mr Courtney, but I must insist.'

'You can insist all you like, but a detailed strategic survey of the Lusima estate would take days, even weeks, and would require airborne reconnaissance. Do you have any aircraft at your disposal?'

'No,' grumped De Lancey.

'Very well then – this is what I am prepared to offer. You may look at my estate maps, which show the topography of the area, plus all significant features, including the various roads, airstrips and so forth that I have put in. As you examine them, you may conclude, as I have done, that it would take a sizeable army to defend the borders of my land, as a result of which, such defensive measures as I have contemplated are centred on this house. The hunting and gamekeeping activity on the estate means that I have a number of guns. You can find the details, I am sure, in my licences, which will be on file at Government House. Satisfied?'

'For the time being,' De Lancey replied. 'Of course, I may well have a number of recommendations to make, in terms of improvements to your security.'

'Put them in writing, I'll read them at my leisure.'

Leon gave a sigh. De Lancey might be both uninvited and unpleasant, but he was still a guest. It would not be in his interests to alienate someone in a position of authority, especially in these febrile times, no matter how detestable. And it was almost lunchtime.

'If you've driven up from Nairobi, I'm sure you could use a bite to eat,' he said. 'We had roast chicken for dinner last night, I dare say there's enough left over for cook to make you a sandwich.'

De Lancey was caught in a bind. The thought of a freshly made chicken sandwich was tempting. But by accepting it he would acknowledge Leon's hospitality, which he hated to do. Greed, however, trumped De Lancey's misgivings.

'That would do nicely,' he said. 'And a cup of coffee, if you please.'

Pieters had been standing to one side, taking in the entire conversation, jotting down the occasional note. From time to time he had glanced out of the open window, through which a gentle breeze was blowing. The view was enough to catch any reporter's eye: a charming English country garden in the foreground, set against the magnificent backdrop of rolling African hills. Now Leon turned to him and asked, 'And a sandwich for you, Mr Pieters?'

Before Pieters could reply, the unmistakable sound of young children laughing drifted in on the wind.

'My grandchildren.' Leon smiled as he thought of the youngsters.

'Charming,' said Pieters, then added, 'I don't think I'll have that sandwich, thank you. But you mentioned we could examine the exterior of your house. Would you mind if I took a little walk around the place, stretch my legs?'

'By all means,' said Leon.

'Thank you.' Pieters put his dark glasses back on. 'I'll find my own way out.'

As von Meerbach was walking out of the house, a middle-aged white woman, informally dressed, carrying a shallow wooden basket containing a bunch of freshly cut roses was coming the other way. This, he realised, was the lady of the house, Harriet Courtney.

He lifted his hat a fraction off his head as he said, 'Good day, ma'am.'

'Oh, yes, absolutely,' she said, giving him the absent-minded smile of a woman whose mind is on other things. By way of explanation, she added, 'Sorry, just got to pop these in some water,' and scurried past him into the house.

Von Meerbach walked out into the sun feeling better than he had done in months. He knew, because he'd spent his entire boyhood being told it, that he had inherited his father's blue eyes, along with his reddish-blond hair. Had he let Courtney see both, the connection would have been too obvious. The eyes alone were not enough to make an immediate connection, or not yet at any rate. Though the thought of Courtney's discomfort when he finally worked out his true identity, put a contented smile on von Meerbach's face. Now all he had to do was to track down those children.

He turned right out of the front door, heading round to the side of the house that the study windows looked out on to. The ground sloped away from the building, and a raised terrace had been constructed beside the house, on which various metal tables and chairs were scattered. All of them, however, were unoccupied.

Below the terrace lay an immaculately mown, weed-free expanse of lawn. Von Meerbach walked downhill and onto the grass. As he turned around the corner of the terrace, he saw something that stopped him dead in his tracks.

Two small children, a boy and a girl, were playing on the grass not far away, watched over by a young native woman in a neat, pale blue cotton dress. The boy, whom von Meerbach estimated to be about five or six, was busily pedalling a red car, making 'vroom-vroom' noises as he went. The little girl, who appeared to be somewhat younger, had assembled a collection of dolls and stuffed animals in a circle around her and was busy serving them tea.

Von Meerbach knew that Saffron was Leon Courtney's only child. These must therefore be her children, staying with their grandparents while their mother and father were away. To chance upon them like this, without even trying was an astonishing stroke of good fortune, like a prospector glancing down into a mountain stream and spotting a nugget of pure gold in among the pebbles. It was all Von Meerbach could do to stop himself cheering and waving his hat in the air.

The boy was wearing a white peaked cap, like a little naval officer. The girl had a pink dress with short, puffed-up sleeves. He had dark hair and brown eyes. She was blonde and blue-eyed. They really were adorable.

The nanny was a pretty thing too, just like her charges. Von Meerbach imagined punching her hard in the face, three or four times, beating her delicate features to a shapeless pulp. He saw himself picking up the boy by the throat in one hand, and grabbing the girl the same way in the other. He would squeeze his fingers tight, throttling the life out of them. Von Meerbach gave a shiver and a silent intake of breath. The image in his mind was so delicious as to be almost sexually thrilling.

On the night when he and Francesca had discussed what he should do, they had specifically rejected the idea of killing the children. But, oh, it was tempting. There was no one else in sight. He could do it and damn the consequences. The pain he would cause his brother and the Courtney whore would be worth it. Then he sighed as he contemplated the hangman's noose and, which was more disturbing, his humiliating helplessness as he was led towards the gallows.

No, I'm not ready for that, he thought.

Von Meerbach said, 'Good morning,' politely to the nanny.

She smiled at him and replied, 'Good morning, bwana,' naturally assuming he must be a friend of the Courtneys'. Deference was ingrained and the white man was above suspicion.

Von Meerbach took off his hat and put it down on the ground, deliberately revealing the colour of the hair that he had kept hidden from Leon Courtney. He turned his attention to the boy and said, 'That's a very fine car.'

The boy grinned proudly. 'It's a Humber,' he said. 'I got it for my birthday.'

'I know how to make cars go very fast. That's my job. I know all about engines. I can make any car go as fast as a rocket.'

'Whoa!' the boy exclaimed, wide-eyed.

'What's your name?'

'My name is Alexander Courtney Meerbach . . . but everyone calls me Zander.'

'And what is your sister's name?'

'Well, we call her Kika, but she's Nichola Courtney Meerbach, really.'

'I see. Well, Zander, I have a question for you . . .'

Von Meerbach reached into his jacket, extracted his wallet and took out a banknote issued by the East Africa Currency

Board. On one side there was a picture of King George VI. On the other was a magnificent lion.

'Do you know what this is?' he asked.

Zander nodded. 'That's a one-shilling note.'

'Would you like it?'

The little boy's eyes lit up. 'Oh, yes please!' he exclaimed.

By now, Kika had got up from her tea party and come over to see what was going on.

'Very well then,' von Meerbach said. 'I will give one of these notes to you, Zander, and another to Kika . . .' The little girl beamed with delight. 'And all you have to do is deliver a message. Can you do that?'

'I think so.' Zander's face screwed up as a worrying thought struck him. 'Is it a difficult message?'

'No, Zander, don't worry. All you have to do is wait until your mummy and daddy get home and tell them, "Uncle Konnie sends his love."' That's not difficult, is it?'

'No, I don't think so.'

'Then say it after me, "Uncle Konnie sends his love."'

Zander repeated the words.

'Good man,' chuckled von Meerbach, patting Zander on the back. 'Now, I am going to give these two notes to your nice nanny . . .'

'She's called Loiyan,' Zander said, helpfully.

'Very well, then, I am sure that Loiyan will remind you to pass the message on to Mummy and Daddy.'

'I will do that, bwana, I promise,' Loiyan said.

'Then I will add another note to you, my dear,' von Meerbach said. 'Oh, and perhaps you could remember to tell your mistress a few words, too. Tell her that I am greatly enjoying my new home, which is so close to her family. I'm sure she will be pleased to hear that.'

'Of course, bwana. You are close to her family. That must be very nice for you.'

'Oh yes . . . very.'

He gave her the money, put his hat back on and then said, 'Goodbye, children, I must be on my way. Goodbye, Loiyan.'

'Goodbye, bwana Konnie,' she replied.

As he walked away, von Meerbach heard Kika's voice declaring, 'He was a nice man.'

'Uncle Konnie can make cars go as fast as rockets!' Zander said.

Then Kika asked, 'Loiyan, why does he have orange hair?'

Von Meerbach smiled to himself as he completed his walk around the house. All things considered, that really could not have gone any better.

He was back home the following day. When he told Francesca what he had done, the look on her face only confirmed his opinion. Von Meerbach had never seen her smile with such joy.

'Oh, you brilliant, brilliant man,' she purred. 'Your plan worked perfectly.'

Von Meerbach noted, with considerable satisfaction, that his wife had praised him for an idea that she had originated.

And now she added, 'It will be just as you predicted. The knowledge that you were there, close enough to touch her children, in the very place where she feels most safe, will drive Saffron mad. That worm will eat away at her, and Gerhard will be furious!'

But then a thought struck her, and a note of concern entered her voice.

'But how will you know that they are coming? What if they take you by surprise?'

Von Meerbach gave a smug smile. 'Ahh . . . I already thought of that.'

'Of course you did, my darling. So what is your solution?'

'I have a spy in the enemy camp. The moment my brother and your old friend arrive in this country, I will know about it. And then we will prepare to give them a suitable greeting when they come knocking on our door.'

Francesca gave a delighted little clap of her hands. They opened a bottle of champagne. For the first time in years, they made love without any games or pain. And as she turned out the light, Francesca whispered, 'Now let them lose sleep.'

S affron and Gerhard landed in Nairobi the day after Von Meerbach left the city. They passed through passport control and customs, then headed to the area of the airport that dealt with private aviation. Earlier in the year they had rolled a flat patch of ground close to Cresta Lodge until it was hard enough to form an airstrip. Gerhard had bought a small, propeller-driven Piper Tri-Pacer aircraft to give himself the pleasure of flying again, and to provide an easy means of crossing the vast Lusima estate, and Kenya as a whole. At the start of their trip he had flown Saffron to Nairobi Aerodrome in the Tri-Pacer and it was waiting for them, fuelled and serviced, when they returned.

Half an hour later they were flying over the Kikuyu farmlands at the southern end of the Lusima estate. These gave way to the open savannah of the game reserve, where the Maasai herded their cattle and the Courtneys had their two homes. The house where Saffron had been raised and Leon and Harriet still lived lay a couple of miles into the reserve. For most of her life, Saffron had simply thought of it as home, but now the family called it the 'Estate House', to distinguish it from the lodge. Seeing it in the distance was enough to bring a lump to her throat.

Leon had installed a landing strip of his own to enable Gerhard to land, and had threatened to buy himself an aircraft to go with it.

'I learned to fly when you were a glint in your father's eye,' he'd told Gerhard. 'I dare say the crates are more complicated since then, but the basic principles must be just the same.'

There was no indication that Leon had acted on the impulse while they were away. The only sign of life was a station wagon waiting to meet them. Gerhard landed safely and taxied the Tri-Pacer under the large, open-sided sun- and rain-shelter that served as a hangar. Their luggage was transferred to the cavernous rear of the station wagon, an American Ford Country

Squire, complete with wooden panelling on its flanks. They set off for the house where their children were waiting for them.

It had been built in the early twenties, when Saffron was still a little girl. Her parents had wanted a property that was British in its layout, but reflected the land in which it was set. The walls were faced in small, irregular blocks of local stone, set into cement like flints, and criss-crossed by sturdy wooden beams, cut from trees that had grown on the estate. The roof was thatched, as a native hut would be, albeit on a greater scale.

The gravel drive that led to the house opened onto a fore-court, ringed by flowering shrubs. Beyond it stood the façade of the house: two gabled ends on either side of a slightly recessed central block. The verandah that ran around three sides of the house deepened into the recess, creating shelter for the front door and a balcony for the master bedroom upstairs. It was a large home, even by the standards of colonial Kenya. There were six bedrooms, all of which had their own bathrooms, a number of spacious living rooms downstairs and a kitchen block at the rear, which opened onto a yard where tradesmen made their deliveries. A garden room, on the left of the house, led to a terrace with spectacular views of the hills that ringed the estate, and stone steps down to a broad flat lawn on which croquet, badminton and even tennis could be played.

These details meant nothing to Saffron, because what she saw as the car rolled to a halt was a building constructed of memories. She recalled the joy of her life with her mother; the awful pain of her loss; the years she and her father had spent, the two of them rattling round a house intended for the bustle of a large, energetic family; and the joy that had returned to the place when Harriet brought love back into Leon's life.

Blinking away a tear, she squeezed Gerhard's hand and said, 'It's good to be here.'

They got out of the car and as they did so, a small, dark, human rocket exploded, piping, 'Mummy! Daddy! Mummy!' at the top of his lungs before hurling himself at Saffron's legs.

'Zander!'

Saffron laughed as his arms wrapped around her thighs. She bent to give her son a kiss and as soon as she had done so he let go, turned to Gerhard and in a calmer, little-manly tone said, 'Hello, Papa.'

'Hello, Alexander,' said Gerhard seriously. 'Have you been good while we were away?'

'Oh yes, Papa . . . almost all the time.'

Gerhard did his best not to laugh. His son was so gleeful, so joyfully determined to have as much fun as he could, every minute of the day, that it was impossible to be cross with him.

'I see,' he said. 'You know, it sounds to me as though you have in fact been very . . . very . . . naughty!'

Gerhard bent down, grabbed Zander under his armpits and lifted him high into the air, shrieking and laughing in excitement. He lowered the boy until they were face to face and said, 'And if you are naughty, then I will have no choice but to punish you . . .'

'No!' Zander cried, squirming in Gerhard's hands.

'. . . with the most awful, terrible, horrible punishment . . .'

'No, please, please!'

'. . . known to mankind, the dreaded, unbearable torment . . .'

Zander was wriggling like a fish in a net.

' . . . of tickling!'

Gerhard tapped his fingers into the side of Zander's body, under his arms and down his ribcage, inducing fits of helpless, hysterical laughter, which persisted until he was lowered to the ground, where he lay for a few seconds, gathering his breath.

'We are going to have one very overexcited boy on our hands,' Saffron said. 'And guess who's going to be left to look after him . . .'

Gerhard was saved from having to answer her by the arrival of another character on the scene, making her golden-haired way across the gravel with a determined stride, crying, 'Daddy, Daddy, lift me too! Lift me, lift me!'

Gerhard glanced at Saffron, who shook her head with a sign of resignation and said, 'Oh, all right, then.'

'Come here, *liebchen*,' Gerhard said, holding out his arms for the plump apple of his eye.

He took Kika in his hands and she beamed happily as he lifted her gently up and down and then, on the third time, surprised her by throwing her up in the air and catching her.

'Again, again!' she cried.

'One more time . . .' Gerhard said, throwing her again. 'And one for luck.'

Kika was still giggling happily as he replaced her on the ground and let her run to Saffron.

Gerhard found that he was breathing quite heavily from the exertion. He was only in his early forties, but the suffering he had endured in the last months of the war could still leave him feeling like an old man. He looked at his family, at the landscape around them and the sky above and thought, *Damn, it's good to be alive!*

Leon and Harriet were coming to join them.

'Hello, my darlings,' Harriet said, hugging Saffron and exchanging kisses. 'We thought we should let you have some time with your children before we barged in.'

'Welcome back, Gerhard,' said Leon, shaking his hand. 'Good to have you.'

'Thank you, Leon, it's wonderful to be home again.'

'You must tell me about your trip in due course. But I dare say you could use a drink.'

'A cool beer would be very agreeable.'

'Then you shall have it. Let me say hello to my little girl.'

Leon hugged Saffron with a most un-English display of affection, to which she responded in kind. They talked for a few moments, while Gerhard and Harriet greeted one another less exuberantly but with warmth.

Leon said, 'Right, time we went in. I promised Gerhard a beer, and how about a stiff g-and-t for you, Saffy?'

'I would absolutely say, yes,' she replied.
'Well, let's go and get them.'

The hall and staircase of the Estate House were both a celebration of the Courtneys' lives in Kenya and a tribute to Harriet's personality, in which common sense and emotional sensitivity were almost perfectly balanced.

When Harriet had first arrived at the house as Leon's second wife, the presence of her predecessor Eva was everywhere, from the worn and fading curtains and seat covers of rooms untouched since her death a decade earlier, to the large portrait of Eva which hung over the fireplace in Leon's study. Some women might have been frightened to change a thing. Others would have insisted on sweeping away all trace of Eva's existence. Harriet chose a dignified compromise.

She redecorated the house, bringing colour, light and life back into the building. But while she was doing this, she was in touch with Leon's mother, his cousins in South Africa and Britain, and his friends in Kenya. Harriet obtained a gallery of photographs, drawings and paintings from every stage of Leon's life, including his first marriage and Saffron's childhood. She added her own images of the time that she had spent with him, including their wedding and honeymoon. She took the portrait of Eva down from Leon's study, but commissioned the artist who had painted it to produce a smaller copy, which she placed among the other pictures, in a position which neither hid Eva away, nor gave her undue prominence.

Saffron had liked Harriet from the day they first met. She was thirteen, about to begin her first term at Roedean girls' school in Johannesburg, when Leon took her to an outfitter to get her school uniform. Harriet was the saleswoman who served them. Saffron noticed right away that her father had become a happier, lighter spirit in Harriet's company, but it had taken a few more years and a chance meeting in London to bring them together as lovers and then man and wife.

Saffron was delighted by the marriage, but in the back of her mind there had always lurked the worry of what would happen when Harriet became mistress of the Lusima estate. She wanted her father and his new wife to be happy, but she could not bear the thought of her mother being forgotten. The moment she had seen the way Harriet had put up those pictures, she knew that the present had made peace with the past, and she loved Harriet for that.

'I have a special treat for the children,' Harriet announced as they made their way into the house. 'You can have lunch with the grown-ups today.'

Amid high-pitched cries of 'Hooray!' and 'Yippee!', Zander and Kika were placed at one end of the table under the watchful eye of their nanny Loiyan, who was one of Manyoro's myriad grandchildren. The cook, Mpishi, who had worked at the house for as long as Saffron could remember, outdid himself and the meal ended with cups of heavenly coffee made from beans grown on the Lusima estate.

For Gerhard, that coffee was almost the greatest of all the many wonders that this private paradise had to offer. He had spent six years drinking the ersatz coffee, made from chicory and brown boot polish, with which Germans in wartime had been forced to make do.

'Ah, what a fine end to a delicious meal,' he sighed. 'Thank you, Leon, for your hospitality. Thank you, Harriet, for running your beautiful house with such admirable efficiency.'

'Coming from a German, I take that as quite a compliment,' she said.

'*Ach*, but it's true. Mpishi is a great chef. Your staff all work hard. But it would not happen without you. I am sure you chose the food for our meal, as you had these beautiful flowers placed in that particular vase on the table in front of us. So, you see, out of efficiency comes beauty and love . . . and all because of you.'

'That's very sweet of you, dear,' said Harriet.

'He never thanks me like that,' Saffron said, with a smile.

'I thank you in other ways,' Gerhard replied.

'Honestly, darling, really! *Pas devant les enfants . . .*'

Leon looked on, pleased to see his daughter and son-in-law flirting. It showed him that they were still interested in one another as lovers as well as spouses. And that, as his own experience had twice taught him, was one of the most important keys to a happy marriage. *Actually liking one another helps too, of course, which those two patently do.*

Leon proposed to reward his son-in-law for his kindness to Harriet with a small, postprandial expedition.

'You know, Gerhard, it occurred to me the other day that in all the years you've been living at Lusima, I've never shown you my gunroom,' Leon said.

'Oh, this is a rare honour, darling,' Saffron said. 'Only Father's most valued guests are shown the gunroom. I'm not sure I've ever been allowed down there.'

'Strictly gentlemen only, my dear,' Leon said. 'Not even a markswoman as fine as you may set foot in there. Has to be somewhere a chap can have a brandy and a cigar without any danger of the ladies barging in.'

'Meet my father, Gerhard,' said Saffron. 'Still not entirely reconciled to women having the vote or the right to wear trousers. Isn't that right, Papa?'

As Leon harrumphed, Harriet played the diplomat.

'To be fair, Saffron, I wouldn't like a man, your father included, coming into my dressing room. I'd feel like a magician letting the audience see how his tricks were performed.'

'I would be delighted to see your gunroom, Leon,' Gerhard said.

'Thank God for that. Pour yourself a drink on the way.'

Leaving the women to look after Zander and Kika, Leon led Gerhard along the hall to a door under the stairs which opened onto stone steps that led down into the basement. The walls were unplastered brick, covered by dirty white paint that was littered with marks, scratches and pockmarks of various kinds. A corridor ran the full length of the house, with a number of open storage bays and locked rooms on either side. A further set of steps led up to a wooden hatch that could be opened to provide access to the outside of the house.

'That's the wine cellar,' Leon said, pointing to a final door that faced back down the corridor at the far end of the basement. 'Take a look in there, too, if you like, once we've given the guns the once-over. Picked up some pretty decent vintages over the years.'

'I'd like that very much,' Gerhard replied.

Leon opened a door to the right of the corridor and led Gerhard into the gunroom. Suddenly, the scruffy practicality of the rest of the basement gave way to décor worthy of a gentleman's club. The weapons were stored in glass-fronted cabinets that stood against wood-panelled walls. There were Turkish rugs underfoot, a leather Chesterfield sofa and a large mahogany table on which to lay out the weapons for inspection.

Beneath the gun cabinets were drawers for ammunition, spare parts and other accessories. Cartridge-belts hung from hooks on the wall. And then there were the guns.

'You've got quite an arsenal,' Gerhard said, running his eyes along the neatly racked weapons.

'I suppose it built up over the years,' Leon said, gently swirling the glass of brandy in his hand. 'I led hunting parties, back in my youth. That's how I met your father.'

'And Eva?' Gerhard asked.

'Yah . . .' Leon gave a sigh that seemed to express both his wonder at his good fortune and deep sorrow at his loss. 'I still remember the first time I laid eyes on her, can picture the scene as if it happened yesterday. My God, what a woman . . . Words can't describe how lovely she was.'

'I understand . . . I felt like that when I saw Saffron for the first time.'

'Mind you, I thank my lucky stars every day for giving me Harriet.' Leon studied his brandy in the glass, and said, 'I was a goner, you know. I got through every day – had to, for Saffy's sake – but I was dead inside. Then Hatty brought me back to life, made a new man of me. God alone knows what I did to deserve such good fortune.'

'I'm sure she feels the same about you. Think of everything you've given her, the life you have here. Who wouldn't feel blessed by that?'

'I suppose. But do you know, Gerhard, in all the time that Harriet and I have been together, I have never for a single second thought that my money, or my land, had the slightest thing to do with why she wanted to be with me. And I'm sure I don't have to tell you, with your background, what a rare and marvellous thing that is.'

'Quite so,' Gerhard agreed, thinking of the girls he had known in the past for whom the name von Meerbach, with the wealth and prestige it conveyed, had been such a powerful aphrodisiac. 'But about the guns,' he said, changing the subject. 'Tell me about this one . . .'

He pointed to a gun that appeared older than the rest. It was a stunning example of the gunsmith's art, a double-barrelled rifle with a walnut butt. Leon smiled as if he'd bumped into an old friend.

'Ah, that takes us back to the subject of beautiful women.' He opened a glass door and removed the rifle from its mounting. 'It's a Holland and Holland Royal .470 Nitro Express, fifty years old but still as good a hunting rifle as any on the planet.' He tilted the rifle to show Gerhard a gold oval inlay set into the end of the butt. 'D'you see those initials, "PO'H"? They stand for Patrick O'Hearne. He was a coffee farmer, in the Ngong hills. He was killed by a lion, poor beggar, leaving a very beautiful, very lonely widow called Verity. I got to know her when I was a foolish, headstrong, randy young subaltern of nineteen and, God bless her, she gave me a much-needed education in the art of pleasing a woman. They ran her out of town, of course—'

'Who did?'

'The usual gang of hypocrites and bullies. There was one particularly nasty piece of work, a major by the name of Snell. He'd got the wife he deserved, a haggard old shrew, and I've always believed he was jealous of me for succeeding with Verity where he had not. He got his revenge on me by having me court-martialled for desertion. Totally trumped-up charge, I might add. Anyway, I was in my quarters, feeling damn sorry for myself, when this gun appeared, out of the blue, in a very fine, but much used case. Inside was a note from Verity, testifying to the receipt of £25 from me for the purchase of the gun. Of course, I'd never paid her a penny, I'd never seen the damn thing in my life before that day. It was just her parting gift.'

Leon picked up the gun and swung it up to his right shoulder with a relaxed, easy grace that made him look like a man half his age.

'Bang!' he said, aiming at an imaginary target. 'You could say it made my fortune, this .470,' he said, bringing the gun down. 'Without it, I could never have started my hunting business.'

'Do you miss it?'

'I miss being young. God, what it was to be fit, strong, with so much energy. I miss the innocence of it all. Africa was wilder in those days. One felt as free as a bird. I think it was the war – the first show, I mean – that changed everything for me. I saw some pretty hard fighting, chasing von Lettow-Vorbeck and his forces across East Africa. You know how war is, you can't help seeing a bellyful of death. And afterwards, Kenya seemed to attract every ne'er-do-well, chancer and remittance man that Blighty had to offer. I'm lucky I've got enough land that none of that sort come anywhere near me.'

'Lusima is its own, private world. I love that about it,' Gerhard said. 'But I know what you mean about war. I shot down over one hundred enemy aircraft. That was enough killing for me. I haven't fired a gun since my last flying mission.'

'You take one with you when you're out in the bush, I trust. You never know when there might be a dangerous animal about. Look at poor Paddy O'Hearne.'

'Yes, I do, but I've not had to use it yet. I would do to protect myself and certainly to protect my family. I just can't shoot for sport.'

'Well, that's your prerogative,' Leon said. 'I take a slightly different view. The grimness of war made me appreciate the nobility of hunting. It's the oldest battle of all, man against beast. There's a purity to it, if you ask me, a nobility, even. Mind you, I can't spend days on end trekking across country in pursuit of a lion or a bull elephant, the way I used to. Getting shot up by your Luftwaffe chums when they sank the *Star of Khartoum* put paid to that.' Leon took a swig of brandy that injected some fire into his belly. 'Bloody Stukas!' he hissed. 'Damn near lost my right leg. One smug so-and-so even gave us a fly-past, when we were sitting in the lifeboat, just to have a good gloat.'

Gerhard wondered whether there would ever come a day when he could reveal that he had been that 'smug so-and-so', and he had not flown over the lifeboat to gloat, but to catch sight of Saffron.

'For a man who's not the huntsman he once was, you're not doing badly when it comes to weaponry,' he said.

'That comes with running a hundred thousand acres of nature reserve,' Leon replied. My boys have to be armed if they're out in the bush with half-a-dozen tourists. Our standard rifle here is the Winchester 70, chambered for the .300 Holland and Holland Magnum cartridge, though I've got a couple of H&H double-barrelled rifles for my own use.'

'And Saffron's use too – I've seen her shoot one of those rifles.'

'Always had an eye like a hawk, that girl,' said Leon, with the pride of a doting father. He gave a grin and added, 'Even if I don't let her down in the gunroom, eh?'

'And the shotguns?'

'They're for duck shoots on our lakes. I've got half a dozen 12-bores of various makes.'

'I pity the man who tries to attack you here, that's for sure.'

'I sincerely hope that never happens. I constantly get people calling me a black-lover because I treat the Africans on my land fairly. But it's a matter of self-preservation. I keep my people contented because I don't want any of them trying to bump me off in the night. But, one can't be too careful. And, as you say, anyone who tries is in for a nasty surprise.'

There was a knocking on the door. Before Leon could say a word, Harriet walked in, her eyes twinkling as she wagged a finger at the two men and said, 'That's enough gun talk. It's time you two came upstairs. Zander and Kika have something to say and they're adamant that their father has to hear it.'

Harriet led Leon and Gerhard to the garden room, where Saffron was waiting for them. Zander and Kika were standing opposite her with Loiyan beside them. Saffron smiled as she saw her husband come in.

'Apparently our son and daughter are about to deliver their first public speech.'

'Is that so?' Gerhard replied. He looked at the two children, who were practically bouncing up and down with pent-up excitement, barely restrained by Loiyan's attempts to calm them. 'Well, in that case we had all better listen, because I'm sure they have something very important to say.'

'We do!' Zander piped up.

The adults stood in a row and assumed suitably serious expressions as Loiyan said, 'Now then, children, remember your message. You won't be getting your shillings unless you do.'

Kika looked at her nervously, so Loiyan got down on her haunches and whispered in the little girl's ear.

'While you were away . . .' Kika began, before stopping and looking at Loiyan for help.

'A nice man . . .' Loiyan whispered.

'A nice man came to see us . . .'

Harriet and Leon looked at one another, as if asking themselves who Kika was talking about.

'And he had orange hair,' Kika continued, 'like . . . like . . . like an orange!'

Saffron laughed and applauded. With her concentration entirely on her children, she didn't notice the frown that briefly fell upon Gerhard's face, nor the tension in his body. Leon too, had failed to join in the fun. His expression was frozen in shock, the colour draining from his skin.

'Are you all right, Daddy?' Saffron asked.

'Did you say "orange", child?' Leon growled, frowning at Kika.

She could tell that he was angry with her, but didn't know why.

'Yes, Grandpa,' she said, and then looked at her mother.

Saffron was still no wiser as to why her menfolk were so upset.

'Come here,' she said to Kika, who ran across and buried her head in Saffron's skirt.

Zander was oblivious to all the undercurrents in the room. He just wanted to take up the story, making it plain that he needed no help from his nanny.

'This man said he knew all about cars and engines and could make cars go really, really fast, like rockets.'

'What a remarkable gentleman.'

Harriet was beginning to think that this was a story the children had made up. Saffron, however, was looking at Gerhard. When the children had been talking about orange hair, the image was so clown-like that it hadn't occurred to her to be suspicious. But now a sickening feeling of utter horror was forming like a cold, dead weight in her belly.

'And he told us to give you a message,' Zander continued. 'And the message was . . .'

He looked at his sister and whispered, 'You say it with me.'

Kika lifted her head, let go of Saffron and took a deep breath.

Both the children chorused, 'Uncle Konnie sends his love.'

They stood there proudly as Loiyan clapped. Harriet joined in, like a good grandmother should. But Leon was staring thunderously at the children, and Saffron was hissing at Gerhard in German, '*Sag nichts!*' – meaning, 'Don't say a thing.'

Now it was Zander who looked from one grown-up to another with worried eyes.

'Did we say something wrong?' he asked.

Saffron went to him. 'No, darling, you did very well. It's just that, well . . . we didn't know that Uncle Konnie was going to pay you a visit.'

'Memsahib, bwana Konnie had a message for me also,' Loiyan said, now visibly nervous herself.

'It's all right.' Saffron's voice was tense. Loiyan's wide eyes made it clear that she knew it was very much not all right. Saffron told herself that none of this was the poor girl's fault, and did her very best to sound calm as she added, 'Go ahead, you can tell me.'

'Bwana Konnie said I should tell you that he was greatly enjoying his new house, living near your family.'

'My family?' Saffron said. 'He didn't mention Bwana Gerhard?'

'No, memsahib. My message was for you.'

'Thank you, Loiyan. You have done nothing wrong. But please, tell me, when did this happen?'

'A few days ago,' she replied. 'The day the policeman came to look at the house.'

'Quentin bloody De Lancey!' Leon hissed.

Harriet opened her mouth, about to suggest to her husband that he shouldn't swear in front of the children, but thought better of it.

'What was that man doing here?' Saffron asked.

'Conducting some damn-fool security inspection to keep us safe from the Mau Mau. As if I need a lecture from that fat buffoon.' Leon paused, not wanting to tell Saffron the worst of it, then said, 'There was a man with him, said his name was Pieters, some kind of journalist.' Leon screwed up his face in frustration, furious with himself as he added, 'Dammit! I knew there was something fishy about him. But that blackguard De Lancey distracted me.'

'Loiyan,' said Gerhard, 'please take the children to play outside. We need to talk in private.'

'Can we have our shilling now, please?' Zander asked. 'Uncle Konnie left one note each for Loiyan, Kika and me.'

'No, you may not have a single penny from Uncle Konnie,' Gerhard replied.

'But, Daddy—!' Zander protested.

'But . . .' Gerhard interrupted him. 'But you can each have a five-shilling note from me instead.'

'Five shillings . . .' Zander gasped, awed by the very idea of such a vast sum. 'Thank you, Daddy! Thank you very, very much!'

As Loiyan led him away, Zander took his sister's hand and said, 'Did you hear that, Kika? Daddy said we can have five shillings instead of one.'

Saffron waited until the children were outside before she turned towards her father and bluntly asked him, 'How the hell did that happen? How did Konrad von Meerbach, a Nazi war criminal who is supposed to be a fugitive from justice, just saunter into our estate and go right up to my children without so much as a by-your-leave? You told me my children were safe, Daddy. And you left them at the mercy of the SS. Does that sound safe to you? Does it?'

Leon had never been spoken to like that by his daughter. But his only response was a sad shake of the head and a heartfelt apology.

'I'm so sorry. I had no idea. I'd have bloody well shot him if I'd known, same as I shot his damn father.'

'Or maybe we should have shot Werner, when we had the chance,' Gerhard said.

'Who's Werner?' Leon asked.

'A low-level thug who's part of some sort of Nazi organisation that helps old SS men. He spied on us. Saffron took him prisoner, but we let him go. My guess is that his bosses tipped off my brother that we were after him, and Konrad decided to demonstrate that he could get to us as easily as we could get to him.'

'Good God,' Leon gasped. 'Do you really think your brother could mount some kind of attack upon us, here at Lusima?'

'Hmm . . .' Gerhard considered the question. 'I don't think so. For a start, where would he find the manpower? There are a lot of people in the European community here whose racial prejudice verges on Nazism, but they're mostly just drunks in country club bars. You'd need harder men than that to attack Lusima.'

Leon shrugged. 'I know the type and I think you're right. Even so, one can't be too careful. I'll have a word with Manyoro, get him to make sure that Cresta's got eyes on it at all times.'

'Thank you, Daddy.' Saffron walked across to give her father a peck on the cheek. 'I'm sorry I was cross with you.'

'Not at all, just a lioness defending her cubs, perfectly natural. And I asked for it, allowing that man in here.'

'You weren't to know.'

'That's no excuse. At times like these one can't afford to be lax.'

'You're right,' Saffron said, straightening her back and squaring her shoulders. 'It's time to get a grip and sort this mess out once and for all. So . . . Konrad said he was living near my family. Well, we have Courtney and Ballantyne relatives in the UK, but I hardly think that he and Chessi have settled down there. And even he wouldn't have the brass nerve to live in Kenya, right under our noses.'

'If he'd found himself a cushy billet here, he'd have made his presence felt long before now,' said Leon. 'The Barons von Meerbach aren't exactly shy and retiring in my experience. And just look at this one, marching in here, bold as bloody brass.'

'I agree,' Gerhard nodded.

'So that just leaves Cairo and Cape Town,' Saffron continued. 'And Egypt is a definite possibility. There were certainly plenty of people there during the war who would have been only too happy to see Rommel's tanks conducting a victory parade through the streets.'

'I think it's South Africa, my darling,' Gerhard said. 'After all, you've often told me about all the Afrikaner politicians who were Nazi sympathisers. And those people were originally Dutch, first cousins to us Germans, correct? Lots of big, blue-eyed men with red or blond hair, who want to keep lesser races in their place?'

'Absolutely.'

'Then Konrad will feel right at home. Tell me, Leon, do you have a Telex machine, by any chance.'

'In my study, you're welcome to use it.'

'Thank you. I think Joshua needs to know about these latest developments.' He looked at Saffron. 'Konrad wants us to find him. Very well, let us grant him his wish.'

Two weeks later a small Israeli cargo vessel docked at the port of Mombasa, on Kenya's Indian Ocean coast. Joshua slipped ashore and proceeded to a small café-restaurant a few blocks inland from the harbour. At the front, there were a dozen or so tables, in the shade of a grubby white canvas awning. Joshua sat at one of them and ordered a cup of coffee.

A few minutes later, Saffron and Gerhard joined him.

'I was very sorry to hear about von Meerbach's little visit,' Joshua said.

'He talked to our children, Joshua – our children!' Saffron exclaimed, still unable to think of what had happened without feeling a surge of bitter emotion.

'Well, if it's any consolation, he really helped our people in Portugal. Focusing on possible connections with Egypt or South Africa gave them something to work with. They had a lot of leads to check, a lot of people to talk to. Government officials, concierges, café owners, caterers, domestic servants . . . and some of them needed persuading before they talked. The Reich still casts a long shadow, you know?'

'But you got something in the end?' Gerhard asked.

'Oh yes. We got it all.'

'And?'

'And I think we should order more coffee. This will take a while to tell . . .'

K onrad, Count von Meerbach had never in his life been obliged to undertake domestic tasks. There had always been servants to make his bed, launder his clothes, cook his food and keep his properties and possessions in order. But on this particular spring day in 1942, in Lisbon, he had decided to make an exception. He wanted no witnesses to the meeting that was about to take place and so he made his own coffee and put out a cup, milk and sugar for his guest, just as a lesser mortal might do.

He checked his watch. There were three minutes to go before his appointment. The man would be on time; von Meerbach was sure about that, because precision was in his nature and because no one with a shred of intelligence would be anything other than punctual for a meeting with a senior officer of the *Schutzstaffel*. To pass the time, von Meerbach took his cup of coffee and walked out onto the balcony of the rented apartment.

The view across the Sea of Straw, the sheltered waterway into which the River Tagus flowed before it reached the sea, was breathtaking. The warm sun on his face was a delight after the bleak chill of Berlin, and the coffee tasted even better than it smelled. Yet von Meerbach had nothing in his heart but hate, nothing on his mind but the longing for revenge.

He heard a sharp tap of a knock on the door and glanced at his watch: as expected, almost to the second. He walked back into the apartment, placed his cup on a table, and picked up the pistol that was waiting there, a Walther *Polizeipistole Kriminal*, otherwise known as the PPK. When meeting a dangerous man, it was only sensible to take precautions.

Von Meerbach opened the door, then stepped back, pointing the gun towards the doorway, waist high as his guest walked in.

The man who came into the apartment, closing the door behind him, was neatly dressed in a jacket and tie. But the clothes were of inferior quality to von Meerbach's tailored suit. They were creased, in need of laundering and worn with overuse. De La Rey looked around with an air of suspicion that was not just due to the gun pointed at him. Von Meerbach had an acute, feral instinct for the strengths and weaknesses of the people he encountered. He saw before him a man simmering with resentment.

He feels betrayed and abandoned by the people he trusted, von Meerbach thought. *His hurt feelings make him vulnerable. Prey on them.*

And yet De La Rey still conveyed an air of the wildness and savagery of the Africa in which he had been born and raised. His eyes now looked directly at von Meerbach, who was struck by their colour, the pale, tawny topaz of a lion's irises. Between them stood a broken nose that was the result of a boxing career that had gone all the way to a final at the Berlin Olympics of 1936. The body beneath the shabby suit had not put on an ounce of fat or lost any of its power. For all that he had fallen on hard times, this was a real man.

'Manfred De La Rey?' von Meerbach asked.

'Yes.'

'Turn around and place your hands on the door, above your head.'

De La Rey did as he was told. His movements were calm and measured. He stood still as von Meerbach frisked him. He knew that these were the formalities of a meeting such as this, just as a handshake might be in other circumstances.

Von Meerbach was unruffled. His status and his gun were not his only protections. Though he was not as fit as he had been in his youth and the years of desk work had softened his heavy, muscular frame, he still possessed an imposing, even intimidating physical presence. The two men were well matched.

'Please, come in, take a seat,' von Meerbach said, pointing to two dining chairs that he had arranged with a small side table between them. There were armchairs in the room. They would undoubtedly be more comfortable. But comfort was not what von Meerbach had in mind. He put the gun down. 'Coffee?'

'Black.'

'Help yourself,' said von Meerbach.

De La Rey filled his cup. Then he asked, 'What do you want from me?'

'Nothing . . . nothing at all. Or not now, at any rate. I have asked you here, Herr De La Rey, because I believe that we share a common interest and that there may come a time, once the Reich's inevitable victory has been won, when we may find it mutually beneficial to pursue this interest as – how can I put it? – a joint venture.'

'You mean a business of some sort?'

'Let us just say a matter of common interest. I will explain everything very soon. But first, tell me, how would you describe your personal circumstances at the present time?'

De La Rey gave a snort of contemptuous disgust. 'How do you think they are? Your friends in the Abwehr have turned their backs on me. They won't even let me back to the Reich . . .'

'They are hardly our friends. But perhaps they feel you let them down. You were sent to South Africa to assassinate Prime Minister Smuts. You failed.'

'It's not my fault that bastard Smuts is still alive. Here I am, rotting away in this godforsaken place. My country, South Africa, is still ruled by the damned British and I haven't seen my wife or my boy since I left Germany for South Africa more than a year ago.'

'What are their names?' von Meerbach asked, taking a Mont-blanc fountain pen and a slender notebook from his suit pocket.

'Heidi and Lothar De La Rey.'

'I will make inquiries, you have my word on it,' von Meerbach said. 'Do you have the last address at which they were living?'

He wrote down the details De La Rey provided, though he knew that they were out of date. Heidi De La Rey was currently to be found in the home, and bed, of her former boss, *SS-Oberst* Sigmund Bolt. Lothar was being raised to think of Bolt as his real father. It was only a chance conversation with Bolt, during which the latter had boasted about cuckolding an Olympic boxer, that had led von Meerbach to look at Manfred De La Rey's official files. It had occurred to him that an angry, pugnacious husband might prove a useful weapon against Bolt in the Darwinian war for survival that raged between rival SS officers. But the more he read about De La Rey, including Heidi's lengthy, detailed reports on everything he had told her about himself, the more von Meerbach realised that he could be used as an even more effective weapon against a far more valuable target.

'You said we shared a common interest. What is it?' De La Rey asked.

'The Courtney family.'

A jolt went through Manfred De La Rey as if he had been touched by a live electric wire. He clenched his fists as he leaned towards von Meerbach.

'Is this some kind of joke?'

'On the contrary, my hatred of that family is something I take very seriously indeed.'

'Hate? You don't know what the word means,' De La Rey snarled. 'Look at you, with your fat face and your fancy suit. I'll bet you've never known a day's hunger, or poverty, or suffering in your whole life. Well, I've seen my father's life destroyed and mine too. And it was that bitch Centaine Courtney who did it.'

'You mean, the Centaine Courtney who was born New Year's Day, 1900, whose principal residence is the Weltevreden Estate, near Cape Town, South Africa and whose fortune derives principally from the H'ani diamond mine? Her only child, Shasa Courtney, lost an eye last year while serving as a fighter pilot in the South African Air Force.' Von Meerbach paused for a second and then added, 'As you can see, I am very familiar with the woman in question.'

'Why?'

'Because she's a cousin of Leon Courtney, date of birth 6 August 1887, and of his daughter, Saffron Courtney. He is the owner of the Lusima Estate in Kenya and the principal shareholder in the Courtney Trading Company, based in Cairo. She was the personal driver to a British Army general in North Africa, Greece and the Middle East. Her present movements are unknown, although I have reason to believe that she has returned to Britain.'

Von Meerbach paused to savour some coffee. De La Rey said nothing.

'So, why do I know so much about both these people? They are of no interest to the Reich, although you may be sure that when we win this war and our Führer's vision becomes reality, there will be no place for British imperialism and all their property will be confiscated.'

De La Rey gave a grunt as he nodded at those words. At last he had heard something that pleased him.

'But for me that is just the start,' von Meerbach went on. 'I do not want the Courtney family's money. I am hugely rich. But you were wrong to suppose that I have not suffered. When I was ten, my father was killed, shot by Leon Courtney. The murderer's accomplice was my father's mistress, a woman called Eva von Wellberg, though she was in fact a British spy – her real name was Eva Barry. She was seduced by Courtney and is mother to his daughter.'

Von Meerbach leaned forward, and he let De La Rey see the cold-blooded torturer and murderer who hid behind an impeccable façade as he added, 'I will not rest until I have repaid Leon Courtney for destroying my family. I want him to understand death, intimately and slowly and as painfully as possible at my hands, and believe me, De La Rey, I am deeply familiar with the contortions of an agonising death. And when he is dying and pleading for mercy from whichever God he worships, his cries filling the air, I want Courtney to know that his darling daughter Saffron, the apple of his eye, has gone before him, and has experienced the brutal horrors of her own passing just as keenly.'

'That is how I feel about Centaine Courtney and her bastard son Shasa,' De La Rey said, his voice constricted by the intensity of his feelings.

'Quite so . . . and thus, as I told you, we have interests in common. So I am here today to register that interest with you and to assure you that there will be a time when I call on you again. That we will win this war is not in doubt. The Führer has planned a summer campaign that will destroy the Communists and leave the Reich with an eastern border that stretches from Leningrad in the north, past Moscow, to the oilfields of the Caucasus in the south. With Russia neutralised, and the Americans fully occupied in the Pacific, the British will be forced to sue for peace and we will dictate the terms.'

'I yearn for that day . . .'

'It will not be long in coming, that I can promise you. And when it does, then I will have the time to pursue my, ah . . . personal interests, while you will be free to return to a South Africa that is no longer part of any British Empire. At that point I will come to you and offer you the chance to work with me to destroy the Courtneys – and not just them. There is another enemy, much closer to my own home. He has betrayed our family. He must be punished too.'

A smile crossed Manfred De La Rey's face.

'You can count on me, von Meerbach. You have my word on it.'

'Good man, I felt sure that you would not let me down.'

'You know that I have the technical skills required for acts of reconnaissance, espionage, kidnap and assassination?'

'Of course . . . You are a trained radio operator, pilot and parachutist, an expert in small arms and explosives, a crack shot with rifle or pistol, deadly in all forms of unarmed combat and can send and decipher messages in code. Have I left anything out?'

'I have a Master's degree in Law, but I don't think we'll be needing that.'

Von Meerbach gave an appreciative grunt. 'Then we are agreed,' he said. 'When the war is won, I will return here and we will start a private war of our own. Excuse me one moment . . .'

He walked to a sideboard and returned carrying a bottle of cognac and two glasses, which he placed on the side table. He poured a generous measure into each glass and passed one to De La Rey.

'Please stand,' von Meerbach said. 'I wish to propose a toast . . . To the Courtneys! May they lose all that they possess. May they die at our hands and be crushed beneath our feet. And may the pain they have brought us be repaid a thousand-fold.'

'The destruction of the Courtneys,' De La Rey replied.

They downed their drinks in one and replaced the glasses on the table.

Von Meerbach clicked his heels, flung out his right arm and cried, 'Heil Hitler!'

'Heil Hitler!' De La Rey responded with equal enthusiasm.

'Thank you,' said von Meerbach as he showed De La Rey to the door. 'That was most satisfactory.'

'I've heard that name, Manfred De La Rey, before,' Saffron said. 'It must have been one of the times I was in South Africa, staying with my cousins. I don't think they liked him much, that's for sure.'

'Well, that could be a good thing for us,' Joshua replied. 'I'm sure your family would want to help you anyway. But if they don't like De La Rey, that could be the icing on the cake.'

'How so?' Gerhard asked.

'Well, let me tell you what happened after the war, when your brother got to Lisbon.'

A year had passed since Konrad von Meerbach had climbed aboard the futuristic jet plane that had provided his escape from the dying Reich, and a great deal had changed. He was now called Bruno Heizmann and his wife Francesca went by the name of Magda. The Heizmanns led a comfortable enough existence, thanks to the wealth that they had taken with them on their respective flights from Germany. They were able to rent a charming villa in the seaside village of Cascais, a few kilometres west of Lisbon, with a housekeeper, maid and handyman-cum-gardener to look after them. It was not a bad life. Unless, of course, one was accustomed to having power.

Von Meerbach had once been able to have a man executed, tortured or sent to the Russian Front with a flick of his fingers. Now he was just another ordinary man, and his unaccustomed impotence was driving him mad with frustration.

When he had come to Lisbon in '42, the Nazi empire was at its zenith. He had treated Portuguese government ministers with lofty condescension. He had walked into the casino at Estoril, with his gold Nazi Party badge pinned to the lapel of his dinner jacket, and everyone had stepped aside to let him pass. The waitresses had fought for his patronage. The croupiers had granted him respect worthy of royalty.

No one reacted that way to Bruno Heizmann.

When he had taken private meetings with government officials who knew of his true identity, the humiliations visited upon him were even worse. When the Reich was riding high, the Portuguese needed and feared him. Now that it was in ruins, he needed them to keep him safe from Allied prosecutors, looking for more famous names to parade at their damned Nuremberg trials. A man so accustomed to throwing his weight around and gloating at others' misfortune found himself pleading to men who now gloated over him.

'We've got to get out of this pathetic backwater,' he raged at Francesca one night. 'I'll go mad if we have to stay here another day longer.'

'It's not all bad,' she replied, trying to calm him. 'We lead a good life, and we should be thankful for being alive at all. The Führer, Himmler, Bormann, Heydrich – all of them are dead. Goering, Hess and Speer are on trial for their lives, along with half the High Command.'

'That's their lookout. They should have had the good sense to see which way the wind was blowing and make their preparations accordingly.'

'But where would we go, my darling? After all, wherever we went, we would still have to live as we do now.'

Von Meerbach did not reply. He knew Francesca was right, and in due course he would punish her for that. But in the days that followed, he set his mind to the problem. He happened to be sitting in a café he frequented, by the marina, when the solution came to him.

The café owner kept a selection of foreign newspapers. He knew they attracted the many prosperous citizens of other European nations, who had swapped their cold, war-ravaged homelands for Portugal, where the sun was warm and property, servants and wine were cheap. Von Meerbach had started taking a daily coffee and pastry there so that he could catch up with the *Frankfurter Allgemeine Zeitung*. More recently, however, he had taken to reading *The Times*.

It pleased him to learn how the poverty-stricken British were beset by austerity and rationing while their great empire collapsed before their eyes. It was only a matter of time before Gandhi won independence for India. They were the supposed winners of the war, yet they could barely have suffered more had they lost.

On this occasion, the *Times*'s attention had shifted to South Africa. It seemed that there was a real prospect of the National Party taking control of the nation's parliament at the next election. This would, the writer noted, mean victory for the Afrikaner element of the white population, over those who considered themselves to be British. The descendants of the Boers were about to overturn their Anglo-Saxon masters. Furthermore, he added, the policy of apartheid – or separation of the black and white races – that the Nationalists advocated, had disturbing echoes of the Nazis' racial programme. Many of the most prominent Nationalists had supported Hitler during the war and even been interned as dangers to the state. Soon they might be running the very country that had once imprisoned them.

It struck von Meerbach that he knew just such an Afrikaner: Manfred De La Rey. And from what he remembered of De La Rey's files, he had possessed close links to senior figures in the Nationalist movement.

The man is a sporting hero, von Meerbach thought as he swilled the dregs of coffee around his cup. *Idiot voters love that sort of thing. And he's not stupid. He wouldn't have got that law degree if he was. If I back him, so that he has the means to buy his way into power, he will become my creature. And then there will be a place on earth where I will have real protection. A place where I can actually live again.*

He explained his idea to Francesca when he got home.

'I'll write to Heidi De La Rey,' she said. 'We've both been meaning to get together.'

'I had no idea you were in contact with that woman,' von Meerbach said.

'Well, of course I am. We knew each other in Berlin.'

'When she was Bolt's tart?'

'What was Heidi to do? Her husband was in another country. She had a child to look after. She found a man who could help her. When he was no longer able to do that, she got out while she could, just as we did. Anyway, she's here now and it's only natural for us to keep in touch, being in the same country.'

'It's not her I'm interested in. It's her husband,' von Meerbach said.

'I know, my darling,' Francesca replied, in the sweetly patronising voice wives reserve for patiently explaining the obvious to a wilfully obtuse husband. 'But if she tells him to come to dinner with us, he's hardly going to say no.'

Von Meerbach exhaled crossly. He was irritated enough that women seemed to possess a private intelligence network exclusive to their species. It made matters worse that the meeting was more likely to happen if the men were ordered to attend by their wives than if he had tried to set it up directly.

Even so, he would have the opportunity to sit down with Manfred De La Rey and put his offer to him directly. That was the main thing.

The women, in due course, agreed on a date for dinner at the von Meerbachs' villa. Francesca pulled out all the stops. She bought new silver cutlery and ordered vases of fresh flowers that lit up the reception rooms with their brilliant colours and filled the air with their scent. She hired a caterer to provide the food, ordered a new gown from her dressmaker and took herself off for a full day of beauty treatments and hair styling.

'I don't think De La Rey is the kind of man who gives a damn what a woman looks like,' von Meerbach said.

'I'm not doing any of this for you men,' Francesca replied. 'It's Heidi I need to impress.'

Von Meerbach was not a man to beat about the bush. Before dinner, as Heidi and Francesca reminisced about the good old days in Berlin, he came straight to the point.

'I think we can help one another,' he told De La Rey. 'I need protection. You may soon be in a position to provide it. Very well, then, I will give you a nice sum of money, and all you have to do is make sure I'm safe in your country.'

De La Rey burst out laughing. 'I don't need your money, man! I've got plenty of my own. I may have left South Africa in a hurry, but I didn't leave it poor.'

'Then why did you look so down-at-heel the last time we met?'

De La Rey grinned and there was something approaching a twinkle in those feline eyes.

'I was not exactly persona grata with your people,' he said. 'How do you think they would have reacted if the man who had let them down was living like a king in the sunshine, while they were stuck in Berlin, being bombed to hell and back?'

It sickened von Meerbach to admit it, but he was dealing with a different man from the one he had first met a decade earlier. De La Rey's shabby suit had given way to sober but elegant clothes, befitting a man who was a devout Calvinist and also prosperous. He wore grey lightweight wool trousers and a black sports jacket, cut to emphasise the width of his shoulders and slenderness of his belly and waist. His plain white shirt was made of fine cotton and was open enough to reveal the top of his tanned chest and a hint of tawny hair.

His wife Heidi was an equally impressive specimen. A close-fitting silk dress in a bold floral print showed off a tall, hourglass figure that, von Meerbach was certain, would look as magnificently female without a stitch of clothing to support it. Yet for all her femininity, there was nothing yielding or vulnerable about this woman. Her smile revealed perfect white teeth. But her eyes were as cold and hard as the gemstones about which her man had been boasting.

'When we go back to Africa, Heidi's going to live like a queen,' De La Rey boasted. 'Isn't that right, *mein Schatz*?'

'So, you have cash. But it's one thing paying for a wife, it's quite another paying for power. What about your party, the Nationalists?' he asked. 'Do they have money? I mean, big money?'

De La Rey did not answer at once. He was giving the question serious consideration.

'No,' he said. 'They do not. And they have a general election to fight in two years' time.'

'Suppose you arrived back in South Africa with cash for that campaign, money provided by me. That would make you a very popular man in the party, a man of great influence.'

'Uh-uh . . .' De La Rey nodded in acknowledgement.

'In that case,' said von Meerbach, 'I believe we have a deal. And now that we have agreed that, there is one other thing to discuss.'

'The Courtney family?'

'Yes, them, but also my brother.'

'Even now, after all this time, when so much has changed, you have not forgotten your grievances, eh?'

'Have you forgotten yours?'

De La Rey smiled. 'No, man, I have not.'

'Then we understand one another on this matter, too.'

Joshua Solomons finished his story. Their coffee cups were empty. A handful of cigarette stubs lay in the ashtray that sat on the table in front of Joshua's chair.

'Are you sure Konrad went to South Africa?' Saffron asked.

'Yes,' Joshua replied. 'And we're certain he's still there . . .' He gave a grimace of embarrassment. 'Except when he's in Kenya . . . Anyway, we haven't found him yet.'

'I thought you knew he was living under the name of Heizmann,' said Gerhard.

'In Portugal, yes. But we have checked out a great many people called Heizmann in South Africa and none of them fit the descriptions of Konrad and Francesca von Meerbach. I would have been here a lot sooner if they had. We have to assume that they have new identities.'

Gerhard nodded. 'That would make sense. There was a special unit at Sachsenhausen when I got there. The SS had rounded up Jews with particular skills – artists, engravers, even criminal forgers – to produce false banknotes and documents. Those guys were brilliant. They turned out perfect passports in their sleep. Konrad could have any number of false identities.'

'Maybe it's time we used my connections in South Africa,' Saffron said. 'Let's pay my cousins a visit. I know Centaine's dying to meet you, darling. And Shasa was a fighter pilot, so you two would have lots to talk about.'

'Be careful in South Africa,' Joshua said. 'Your enemy has friends in high places there. So be discreet.'

'Point taken.'

'And speaking of identities, do you remember that ID you told me about, the one you used to get into Occupied Europe?'

'Marlize Marais?'

'That's the one. Do you still have any of her papers?'

'I think I do. No one at SOE asked me for the passport back, because it wasn't one of theirs to begin with. Shasa got it for me.

And I certainly had it with me when I got out of Belgium. It's probably in a trunk somewhere. Do you want me to dig it up?'

'Yes please.'

'What do you have in mind?' Gerhard asked. 'I mean, for my brother.'

'Well, my bosses have come to the same conclusion as you and my father did. They want Konrad von Meerbach to be located, captured and brought back to Israel to be tried for his crimes against our people. Will you want to participate in that operation?'

'Yes,' said Saffron.

'I assumed so. That is why I want as much as you have on Marlize Marais. When the time comes, you will have to approach this like an SOE operation, with total security and false identities. I take it a full legend was created for this Marais woman – birth certificate, school records and so on.'

'Yes.'

'Then why create another one? Marlize Marais brought you luck once. Let's hope she brings us all good fortune.'

The sound of twin Rolls-Royce Merlin engines echoed around the hills of the Lusima Estate, both mellifluous and powerful, like the purring of a lion god.

'There,' said Gerhard, pointing his finger at a dot in the clear, late afternoon sky. 'That's your cousin Shasa's Mosquito.'

Saffron raised the binoculars. 'Got it,' she said. 'I hope the landing strip's long enough.'

'It should be. I had it lengthened specially.'

Saffron needed to speak to Shasa and his mother Centaine about the hunt for Konrad von Meerbach. Shasa was a member of the South African parliament. Centaine had limitless financial resources. Their help would be invaluable.

Ten years earlier, Shasa had worked with Saffron to use South Africa as a route into Occupied Europe, and he had taken great pleasure in the friendship she had formed with his wife

Tara. Saffron had no doubt that he would be willing to help her again, likewise Centaine, who had also shown her nothing but kindness.

Her initial instinct had been to pay a visit to Weltevreden, the beautiful estate on the outskirts of Cape Town that Centaine had bought and remodelled, before handing it over to Shasa and Tara. Joshua, however, had been adamant that she could not go to South Africa until they launched the mission to capture von Meerbach.

'And then you will go as Marlize Doll, née Marais, and Gerhard will be your husband Herman Doll,' Joshua said. 'The documents are being prepared. Your story will be that you met in Belgium during the war, when your husband was part of the German occupation. If you go back before then, under your own identity, how could you then return as someone else?'

Saffron had accepted the logic. Since she could not go to her cousins, she invited them to stay at Cresta Lodge.

It had not been easy. Shasa juggled his role as an MP with his business career. Centaine was the owner of the Courtney Mining and Finance Corporation, but Shasa ran the company. He took all the key investment decisions, though not without running them past his mother first, for there was no one whose judgement and business acumen he respected more.

'Nothing would please me more than seeing you again, Saffy,' Shasa had said when she called his Cape Town office, a couple of minutes' walk from the parliament building. 'But I've got the minor matter of a new goldmine to think about. It's only going to cost ten million pounds, nothing serious. But still, I need to spare it a moment or two of my time.'

Saffron had laughed. She and Shasa had a teasing, bantering way of talking that was more like brother and sister than two distant cousins. Both were the only children of their parents, and he was two years her senior, so they were close enough in birth to be siblings. They had similar features: the dark hair, blue eyes and tall, athletic physiques. Above all, they shared an

essential identity that came from their shared Courtney heritage. They were passionate in their enthusiasms, intense in their
hungers, but capable of cold, calculating ruthlessness in pursuit
of their ends, or defence of their loved ones.

'You'd better spare me more time than that, Shasa, dearest,'
Saffron replied. 'And I'm sure you'll be delighted to meet
Gerhard. He can show you what a real pilot looks like.'

As the line fell silent, Saffron wondered whether she'd pushed
it too far. Shasa had been forced to leave the Royal South African
Air Force early in the war, having lost an eye during the Abys-
sinian campaign. The feeling of uselessness, when he could no
longer fight for his country, had all but broken him. Perhaps
those mental scars had never quite healed.

But Shasa laughed and said, 'Only you could get away with
that! But I'll have my own back. I'll show that Hun of yours
what a proper fighting aircraft looks like. Mater and I will fly
up to see you in my Mozzie. She's quite a special crate, I can tell
you. Had her restored myself.'

'What, Mater or the Mosquito?'

'Oh, you are really going to regret that comment when the
Mater hears about it.'

'I was trained to withstand torture by the Gestapo, I can cope.'

'The Gestapo have got nothing on my mother when she's on
the warpath.'

'Hmm . . . you may have a point. I'll keep a bodyguard of
Maasai warriors with me at all times.'

'You'll need more than that, cuz . . . Listen, I've got things to
do. But I'll get my mechanic Dickie to liaise with my personal
assistant Janet, who runs the whole show around here. She'll
get in touch with you, with a date when Mater and I can come
up to see you and the specifications of the landing strip we'll
need. And, seriously now, I'm really looking forward to seeing
you again, Saffy. It's been far too long.'

Saffron put the phone down and jotted a couple of notes for
Gerhard. He would probably know what needed to be done

to make their small private landing strip suitable for a twin-engined RAF fighter-bomber without any of Shasa's people having to tell him.

As she was putting her notebook away in her handbag it occurred to her: *Shasa didn't say a word about Tara. I wonder why not.*

The Mosquito pulled to a halt, the engines died and the propellers stilled. The canopy slid open and Shasa emerged in his flying suit. He jumped to the ground, then turned to help his mother get out. Saffron and Gerhard walked across the rock-hard surface of the rolled, compacted earth strip to greet them.

'Shasa looks as piratical as ever,' Saffron said as her cousin, who wore a black patch over his missing eye, came towards them.

Centaine shook out her hair, which had been pinned up inside her helmet for the flight. Like her son, she was wearing a khaki flying suit. But hers appeared to have been cut by a Paris couturier, for it skimmed every curve of her slender body and a diamond brooch glinted from her left breast.

'Mein Gott, she is magnificent,' Gerhard said. 'Can she really be more than fifty?'

'I told you, she was born on the first day of the twentieth century. That's why her parents called her Centaine.'

'I know you did. I just can't believe it.'

'Watch it, mister!' Saffron warned him. 'I don't mind you saying flattering things about my family members. But don't go too far.'

Gerhard laughed. 'You needn't worry. Yes, she is magnificent. But no one could ever be as magnificent as you.'

'That's better! Come on, let's say hello.'

Introductions were made in a flurry of handshakes and kisses. Saffron and Gerhard had arrived at the airstrip in a Land Rover, with another identical vehicle behind them, driven by their senior houseboy, Wajid, to pick up their guests' luggage. While Saffron and Centaine complimented one another on their ability to survive childbirth and passing time with their beauty unscathed, Shasa showed Gerhard and Wajid how to open the hold that now replaced the bomb bay with which the Mosquito had originally been fitted.

'She's a fine aircraft,' Gerhard said, casting an eye over the sleek lines of the fuselage. 'I never saw one in action, though of course we'd all heard about the Mosquito. Goering himself said he was yellow and green with jealousy at the British for having such an aircraft.'

'You chaps didn't have anything that could catch it. Not until you put jet fighters in the air.'

Gerhard shrugged. 'I'm not sure about that. The Focke-Wulf was as fast, I think, and some of the later models of the 109. It all depended on altitude, fuel load – you know the kind of thing. Willy Messerschmitt's jets were much faster, of course, but less manoeuvrable. They could go very fast indeed, but if they over-shot their target, they had the devil of a time turning round and coming back again!'

'You said "Willy Messerschmitt". Did you know him?'

'Oh yes, in fact he let me fly an early 109 prototype.'

It was not often that Shasa Courtney was genuinely awe-struck. But now he felt as a Renaissance artist might if a fellow painter had revealed that he had seen the Sistine Chapel while Michelangelo was working on it.

'No, really?' he gasped.

'Absolutely,' Gerhard replied. 'My family made aviation engines, you see, and his factory in Augsburg was not far from our motor works, maybe two hours' drive. Less by air.'

'You must tell me about it over a drink or two. Hell of a plane, the 109. Even as an enemy, one can't deny that.'

'We felt the same about the Spitfire.'

'I don't think we need worry about the men getting on with one another,' Centaine said, as she and Saffron watched the two former fighter pilots set off on a detailed inspection of the Mosquito. 'And to think they would have been trying to kill one another if they'd ever met in the war.'

The word *ever* was pronounced *evair*. Her *the*s came out as *ze*. Even now, thirty-five years after she had left her childhood home in northern France, Centaine still spoke with a French accent.

'Gerhard says that fighter pilots have a different attitude to their enemies than soldiers do,' Saffron replied. 'He has a story about a dogfight he once had with an American. They tried as hard as they could to shoot one another down, but both ran out of ammunition. Gerhard was running low on fuel, so he turned to go back to base and suddenly he saw the American plane, I think it was a Mustang, flying alongside him. The American looked at him with a grin, waved and flew away.'

'They love the flying itself, more than anything – maybe even more than they love us. Michael, Shasa's father, was the same. It was like a drug to him.' Centaine had met Michael in France when he was stationed there with the Royal Flying Corps during the First World War. Michael was a fighter pilot. Centaine patted Saffron's arm. 'You were lucky, you know, to be parted from your man all through the war. You did not know what he was doing. I used to watch Michael fly away on his missions. Every morning I would ride out on my horse to wave to him. He said I was his lucky mascot.

'One day I was not there, and that was the day he died. Shot down by the Germans. I have never told Shasa this, but when I heard that Shasa had been injured and could never fly in combat again, I thanked God for delivering him from evil. It meant I would not have to go to his grave to visit him. An eye was a small price to pay.'

Saffron nodded, understandingly. 'The day I found Gerhard, in a hotel, of all crazy places, by a beautiful lake in the Tyrol, he was so thin it almost makes me cry just thinking about it. Skin stretched tight over a skeleton, covered in red sores. He had typhus. The doctors told me that he was about to die and I should accept the inevitable. But I wouldn't. I knew he was going to live, I refused to let him die.'

'Look at them, like a couple of schoolboys,' Centaine said as the two men emerged from behind the Mosquito.

Shasa was describing a dogfight he'd been in, using his hands to demonstrate the relative positions of his Hurricane fighter and his opponent's aircraft, while Gerhard looked on in rapt concentration.

'They have no idea how it is for us, do they?' Saffron said.

'No, my dear, no idea at all,' Centaine replied. 'But perhaps that is as well, because if they did, no man would dare risk his neck to do anything. And then where would we be?'

Hannes de Koch was a mechanic at Weltevreden, employed to look after the family's cars, as well as all the trucks and machinery. Whenever any of the cars needed work that required either more skill or better equipment than he had at his disposal, he took them to Schultz's garage. It was the best place in town for high quality repairs and services, particularly for the fancy, money-no-object motors that the Courtneys liked to drive. Schultz himself was a sound man, too, in de Koch's estimation.

They'd got talking one day when de Koch had brought Shasa Courtney's latest toy, a Bristol 402 cabriolet sports car, in for a tune-up. It was an elegant, powerful-looking machine and Schultz had come over to take a closer look at it.

'I've not seen one of these before,' Schultz remarked.

'That's because it's the only one in South Africa. The boss had it shipped out from England. The company that makes it used to make aeroplanes. The boss was a pilot, right? Couldn't resist it.'

'So, what's he like, this Courtney fellow? I hear he's made of money.'

'Oh, *ja* . . . Mummy owns a damn diamond mine – not that you'd know it from what he pays me.'

'Tight with the cash, eh? Well, that's how the rich stay rich, never spend a single penny that they don't have to.'

'That's the truth, all right. But it's not just that, it's the man himself.'

'Is that so?' Schultz had said. 'But, say, it's going to take my boys a while to work out what needs doing on that car, what with it being so unusual. Why don't I get my girl to make us some coffee? We can sit in my office and talk in comfort.'

'Are you sure?' de Koch had asked, taken aback by Schultz's hospitality.

'*Ja*, of course. Hell, man, you're an important customer. You bring me all that Courtney business. A cup of coffee is the least I can do.'

So they had talked and de Koch had told Schultz about his boss.

'Look, you know what those English bastards are like, particularly the rich ones. Real plum-in-mouth types who think all Afrikaners are second-class citizens. But Courtney was all right, not a bad man to work for.'

'Was?' Schultz asked.

'*Ja*, "was", because he's damn well not like that now, I can tell you. His lot have been kicked out of government and his wife is screwing a black man.'

'Ha!' Schultz had let out a great bellow of laughter. When he'd recovered he said, 'Are you sure you're not joking?'

'Hell, no. I heard it from one of the housemaids when I was screwing her!'

'So who's tupping the missus, one of the farm workers?'

'No, man, a damn Commie! One of those black rights boys!'

Schultz had guffawed again. 'That is the funniest thing I've heard in years! God in heaven, no wonder Courtney's sick as a pig. Here, let me put some schnapps in your coffee.'

They'd talked a bit more, mostly swapping stories about cars, and then Schultz had said, 'Listen, can you do me a favour?'

'Sure,' de Koch had replied. 'What do you want?'

'Well, a man I knew years ago, before the war, a German fellow, Gerhard, married a Courtney girl, just as rich as her cousins.' He smiled at the memory. 'Good old Gerdi, he always was a lucky bastard. Now what was that woman's name? Rosemary? Ginger? Some kind of spice . . .'

De Koch thought about it for a moment, his mind a blank, and then he suddenly made the connection and said, 'Saffron!'

'*Ja*, that's the one.'

'Hell, man, she's a fine-looking piece. Came out here during the war, when I first started working up at Weltevreden.' He let out a low, appreciative whistle. 'What I'd give for a ride in that little beauty.'

'Well, I tell you what,' Schultz said. 'If she ever comes down to see her cousins again, you tell me, all right? If my pal Gerdi's in town, I'd like to look him up. You know, have a drink and talk about the old days.' He grinned. 'Maybe I could take a good look at that wife of his too, eh? See if she's as easy on the eye as you claim.'

De Koch laughed. 'Oh, she's that all right!'

'So you'll help me out, then?'

'Sure, no trouble, I can do that.'

'Good man. And hey, I'll tell you what,' Schultz had added. 'If my pal and his missus come to stay with your boss, you let me know . . . and the next time you bring a car in, I'll put a hundred pounds in your back pocket. How does that sound?'

It sounded like more than de Koch earned in a month. He shook hands with Schultz and hoped to God that the Courtney family would have a nice reunion in Cape Town. But of all the rotten luck, he had been the man who drove Shasa Courtney and his mother Centaine out to the airfield where he kept his beloved Mosquito. Overhearing his passengers' conversation on the way, he realised that they were going to Kenya to visit Saffron.

De Koch had wondered whether to tell Schultz. But what was the point? The man wanted to have a drink with his old mate. It was no use to him if his mate was five thousand kilometres away to the north.

Just as they were getting to the airfield, Centaine had said, 'You know, while we're there, we must make arrangements for them to come and see us.'

Fine, thought de Koch. *I'll tell Schultz to expect a visit soon. Maybe he'll give me a tenner, just to keep me sweet.*

De Koch had dropped by the garage to pass the news on to Schultz, who had seemed very interested indeed.

'Could you advance me some money?' he'd asked. 'Ten pounds, maybe?'

Schultz had beamed. 'Tell you what, let's make it twenty. And you make damn sure you let me know, the second they arrive.'

Saffron had given great thought to Shasa's and Centaine's visit and how best to prepare them for its true purpose. Her guests were staying at Cresta Lodge for three nights. But having arrived late one afternoon, they would leave early on the third morning, meaning that there would only be two full days to play with.

The first day began before dawn, when they walked in silence to a hide to watch the game come down to the waterhole. A small herd of buffalo, no more than twenty strong, was standing in the water like bathers at a municipal pool. As the sun rose above the trees a line of elephants appeared, backlit by the morning light.

Led by a mighty bull, with mothers and their young following in his wake, they stopped at the water's edge, sucked up the water in their trunks and deposited it in their mouths to drink or sprayed it over their dusty grey hides. Beside them, giraffe stood spay-legged so that their necks could reach low enough to drink.

A pair of black rhinos sauntered through the long grass with ponderous, bleary-eyed deliberation, their oddly porcine ears constantly twitching from side to side. A young buffalo led astray by curiosity wandered towards them, to be greeted by a lunging horn as one of the rhinos reacted with typical irascibility. As the buffalo hastily retreated the two rhinos found a quiet spot and stood knee-deep in the water to slake their thirst.

'Look, over there!' Shasa whispered. 'Leopard. Beneath the acacia.'

Sure enough a leopard was waiting in the shaded grass, observing like a hungry diner at a delicatessen counter, who hasn't got the price of a meal. Shasa gave a soft chuckle.

'He won't move, doesn't fancy the odds.'

It was only when the buffalo and elephants had moved on that the leopard padded down to lap at the water. They looked at one another with silent, knowing smiles, acknowledgements that the magic of African wildlife had not dimmed, but deepened with the years that they had spent among it.

The children joined the party for breakfast. Zander had seen the arrival of Shasa's Mosquito from the playroom window, been awestruck by such a magnificent machine and could not hide his admiration for Shasa as he besieged him with questions about his aircraft and his piratical eyepatch, and begged him for a ride in the wonder-machine.

'I'd be delighted to give you a ride, dear boy,' Shasa told Zander, 'but I'm afraid your mater and pater have other plans for me.'

The grown-ups were soon setting off to drive to the foot of Lonsonyo Mountain, followed by a walk to the top for an audience with Manyoro. As he entered old age, the Maasai chief spent ever more of his time there, where his mother had lived, as if preparing for the day when their souls, parted in life, would be reunited by death. Manyoro's love for Saffron, as well as the dignity he displayed as the leader of his tribe, were undimmed, and Saffron could see that Shasa and Centaine came away from Lonsonyo understanding why it was an important, magical place for her.

They returned to Cresta, freshened up and were flown by Gerhard to the Lusima Estate House for lunch with Leon and Harriet.

The meal was a convivial one, for Centaine and Leon were cousins as well as old friends and Harriet, as always, made an occasion planned with military precision seem effortless. Mpishi excelled himself and was summoned from the kitchen to accept the diners' congratulations. It was shortly before three in the afternoon when they finally got down from the table. Saffron, Gerhard, Centaine and Shasa had been on the go for more than nine hours; the two South African members of the party were recovering from a day and a half in the air and Leon had served a succession of excellent wines with the meal. A number of loungers had been set up on the terrace, shaded by a large umbrella, and soon four contented guests were snoozing the afternoon away. Gerhard flew them back to Cresta in time for Shasa to take him up for a quick joyride in the Mosquito, with the promise that he would let Gerhard have a go in the pilot's seat the following afternoon.

After a light supper, followed by a few hands of bridge, they retired to bed. As she lay next to Gerhard, on the point of falling asleep, Saffron murmured, 'I think that went well, don't you?'

'Uh-huh,' Gerhard agreed.

'Now, if all goes according to plan in Nairobi tomorrow, we should be set to get down to business over dinner tomorrow.'

'Uh,' Gerhard grunted.

Saffron took that as a 'yes', rolled over and was out within seconds.

The following morning, the weather was perfect: cloudless skies with a warm sun. On the flight from the Cresta airstrip to Nairobi, Gerhard took the scenic route, flying parallel to the western escarpment of the Rift Valley and then the unique double crater, one ring within another, of Mount Suswa. They landed at Nairobi aerodrome to find a car and driver waiting for them, as Saffron had planned. Her intention was to show her guests the poverty of the Kikuyu people living in the city, and the work being done to improve the lives of humble folk by two young Kenyans of noble birth.

'Play your cards right and I wouldn't be surprised if cousin Centaine makes a donation on the spot,' Saffron had told Benjamin and Wangari when she was arranging the visit. 'She can afford it.'

She was only in her early thirties, but the drive to the clinic made Saffron feel ancient. She could remember the days, in the twenties, when Nairobi had been no bigger than a provincial English market town and felt like one too. The streets bore British names, the municipal buildings were constructed as if they were in Essex, rather than East Africa, and the only black faces on the streets belonged to the servants of the white population.

Over the past quarter century, more and more black Kenyans had been forced off their land, or been unable to get work in the ever-diminishing areas of the country that were still assigned to the native population. They had moved to the city in search of employment and established a swathe of shanty towns to the east of colonial Nairobi.

The roads were unpaved, there were no proper drains, let alone sewers, and the people lived in an urban equivalent of the huts they had left behind. Mud and thatch were replaced by seemingly random combinations of wooden planks, corrugated iron, steel scaffolding tubes and canvas sheeting. Women walked the streets carrying their possessions, or the goods they hoped to sell at market, on their heads.

The clinic was near the Burma Market, a place most white people regarded as a den of thieves, ruled by gangsters and terrorists. As Saffron drove past the market, she saw stallholders standing guard over great haunches of beef, goat and wild game-meat that hung from the wooden frameworks of their stalls. Small children played on the dusty, filthy paths that ran between the houses and the market stalls. Tradesmen and their customers haggled over piles of fruit and vegetables, fresh from Kikuyu farms, or bolts of brightly patterned cotton, or strings of glittering beads.

The driver pulled up outside one of the few solid buildings in the area, a bungalow surrounded by a verandah. In the days when this was open country, some settler had built it as his farmhouse. Benjamin and Wangari had bought it, with help from Saffron. She had also agreed to contribute around half the clinic's monthly running costs, and persuaded Gerhard and Leon to provide additional funds.

The farmhouse had been converted to provide a waiting room, a medical dispensary and consulting rooms for Benjamin and Wangari at the front of the building. One of the former bedrooms had been turned into a three-bed inpatients' ward; another served as the office from which the operation was run. A few rooms at the back of the house had become the cramped, but clean and serviceable apartment in which they lived.

It was obvious at once that the services Benjamin and Wangari were providing were desperately needed. A line of people ran the length of the verandah as Saffron led the others into the building, and the waiting room was packed. Benjamin poked his head around the door of his consulting room to summon his next patient, saw Saffron, said, 'Hello, with you in a minute,' and disappeared again as his next patient went in to see him.

Saffron waved a greeting to the Indian pharmacist, his wife and daughter, who ran the dispensary that doled out the medicines prescribed by Benjamin and paid for largely by the Courtney family. She knocked on the door of Wangari's office.

Wangari emerged, closing the door behind her. Her belted, khaki linen shirt dress was freshly laundered, crisply ironed and had clearly been an expensive purchase. But Saffron saw that the colour was faded and some of the buttons that ran from the neckline down to the hem of the skirt were mismatches: replacements for originals lost along the way. In days gone by, her father would have long since bought her a new dress. But the last time they had spoken, Wangari had made it plain that, with his opposition to her marriage to a Maasai as strong as ever, there was no chance of help of any kind from him. She was therefore obliged to make do and mend. Her hair, likewise, was no longer straightened and styled in Nairobi's finest salons, but simply gathered up in a brightly coloured cotton scarf. But as Wangari had said to Saffron, 'I don't care a bit about the money. It's my daddy that I miss.'

The two women exchanged kisses. Gerhard said, 'It's good to see you again, Wangari,' and then Saffron introduced Centaine and Shasa.

'Benjamin's with a patient,' she added. 'He said he'd be out in a mo. Why don't you tell us about your legal work, while we're waiting?'

'Of course,' Wangari replied. 'Let's go into my office, it's a little quieter.' As they followed her in, she added, 'I wish I could offer you all a cup of coffee, but I'm afraid we don't have that sort of thing. Every single penny we have goes on essential supplies. I don't even have enough chairs for you all. But I'd be happy to get some water, if anyone would like.'

'Please, don't go to any trouble,' said Centaine. 'I can see that you are busy enough as it is. Tell me, what do your clients need from you?'

'Well, it used to be mostly about resolving disputes. For example, neighbours fighting over a boundary would come here and I'd try to help them broker an agreement. Or if people came with legal problems, I'd explain their rights and, if needs be, put them in touch with solicitors' practices that could pursue legal action, because I'm not yet qualified to represent them in court myself. But recently . . . Well, it's very different now . . .'

'How so?' Centaine asked.

'It's the uprising . . . The people who come to me are caught in the crossfire between the Mau Mau and the government. The terrorists will stop at nothing to keep ordinary Kikuyu men and women under their control. And the authorities have thrown away every principle of British justice. Habeas corpus, the right to a fair trial, freedom from police brutality – absolutely everything's been ditched in their determination to lock up anyone they suspect of the slightest contact with the Mau Mau.'

'I'm sorry, but that's just absurd!' Shasa objected, and Saffron was surprised, even shocked by the anger in his voice. 'This is just propaganda, put about by Commie agitators.'

'Shasa!' Saffron exclaimed. 'Really!'

'No, I understand. No one likes to hear the truth about their own people,' Wangari replied.

Shasa ignored her. He had turned his fire elsewhere.

'And you're involved in this, are you, Saffron? Spending hard-earned Courtney money?'

'And von Meerbach money,' Gerhard pointed out, with studied amiability. 'Worth every penny, too.'

Before Shasa could reply, Benjamin came in through the office door. Saffron saw Wangari flash him a quick look, at which Benjamin cleared his throat to get everyone's attention and said, 'I hope I'm not interrupting. But I've only got a few spare minutes. Perhaps I could give everyone a guided tour of our medical facilities?'

'Excellent idea!' Saffron was grateful for the interruption. 'I'm so sorry,' she whispered to Wangari as they walked back out into the waiting room. 'But is it true, then . . . are things that bad?'

'Yes, but you have to see for yourself. Come back another day, and I will prove it to you.'

They had just entered the inpatients' room. Benjamin spoke to each of the patients in Swahili, for, as a Maasai, he was far from fluent in Kikuyu dialects. Saffron, Centaine and Shasa could understand every word, and even Gerhard had by now learned enough to be able to get the gist of what Benjamin was saying.

In truth, though, it really wasn't necessary to know that Mrs Kiprono was recovering from a severe bout of dysentery, or that Mr Cheruiyot had a heart condition, or that Benjamin had arranged for little Mary Jermutai to have her tonsils out at the Native Civil Hospital, to understand that Benjamin was born to be a doctor. He remembered everyone's names without needing to check their notes, was entirely genuine in his concern for them, but was also quite firm in his instructions.

'You take your pills, like you're supposed to,' he told Mr Cheruiyot. 'Or the next time you have a heart attack, it will be your last.'

The scepticism on Cheruiyot's wrinkled old face suggested that he was not entirely convinced, and Benjamin knew it.

'I'm sure that Germans believe their doctors,' he said to Gerhard, as they left the room. 'But a lot of my patients, the old ones particularly, still cling to the old superstitions. He'd rather be seeing a witch doctor to get rid of the demon in his chest than take a white man's medicine.'

'Well, this man needs his lunch,' said Shasa, making it only too plain that his interest in the clinic was at an end.

'Darling, could you take everyone out to the car?' Saffron said to Gerhard. Then she went back to Benjamin and Wangari.

'What was all that about?' Benjamin asked.

'God knows,' Saffron said. 'But don't worry, my faith in you is as strong as ever, and I know Gerhard feels the same. Now, Wangari, I'm going to be a little busy for a while. There's a family matter to attend to. But when that's done, I'll come back and you can tell me the truth about what's really going on. And I swear I will believe you.'

They went into the centre of Nairobi for lunch, and it was not until Saffron and Centaine left the table to powder their noses in the privacy of the ladies' room that Saffron was able to ask, 'Why was Shasa like that at the clinic?'

'Like what?' Centaine replied.

'You know what I mean. He was downright rude to me, and Wangari too. I've never known him like that.'

Centaine sighed. 'Tara has a clinic just like that one in a township near Cape Town.'

'I know she does. That's one of the reasons I thought you might be interested to see something like it here.'

'You don't understand, my dear. Shasa's marriage is falling apart. Tara has become a Communist revolutionary.'

'Surely not! I mean, I know she's a bit of a lefty, but she's not taking up arms against the capitalist state.'

'I'm afraid that's exactly what she's doing. The police have a file on her that contains enough allegations to get anyone less well-connected locked up in prison. She is very close to the most radical wing of the black freedom movement in South Africa.' Centaine gave Saffron a meaningful look and repeated the words, 'Very close.'

'Oh . . .' said Saffron. 'You mean . . .?'

'Yes. I believe so. I have my own intelligence network. A woman in my position, with so many native workers, needs to know what the black leaders are thinking and doing. I haven't discussed Tara's activities with Shasa. He may not be aware of everything himself. But he must have his suspicions.'

'It all makes sense now. Oh, hell! Today's outing was the worst thing I could have thought of.'

'You weren't to know, my dear. Your intentions were good.'

'I hope he doesn't think I'm really a Communist too. Or that I'm disloyal to my husband.'

'I'm sure he doesn't. You're liberal in your opinions, but you're not a Communist. You're too much of a Courtney for that! And you and Gerhard are either the world's greatest actors or as happily married as any couple could be.'

'The latter, thank God. But I suppose, from Shasa's point of view, that makes matters worse. I mean, we remind him of what he doesn't have.'

'Yes, *chérie*, I dare say you do. But that is hardly your fault. Now, let's rejoin the men before they think we've run away.'

'Ah, there you are, my darling!' Gerhard exclaimed when Saffron and Centaine returned to their table. 'We were beginning to wonder what had happened to you.'

'We thought we'd let you two have some man-talk,' said Centaine.

'About aeroplanes,' added Saffron.

'How did you guess?' asked Shasa.

He laughed and it was such a natural expression of amusement, and so much like the boy she had first met nearly twenty years ago, that Saffron almost believed everything was all right again.

'Do you know, Saffron, I've a mind to hate your husband,' Shasa said that evening, before dinner at Cresta Lodge. 'I mean, he seems like a nice enough fellow. He's as good a German as they come. But I detest the bounder, and do you know why?'

'No,' said Saffron, not certain after the day's events whether Shasa was being serious or not. He still wasn't calling her 'Saffy'. So she was nervous, asking him, 'Why?'

'Because he's too good a pilot.'

Thank God, nothing to worry about, Saffron thought, doing her best to muster a laugh.

'Let me tell you,' Shasa went on, 'the Mosquito is known for being tricky to fly. She's like a high-bred racehorse – goes like the wind, but bloody temperamental. She's particularly dicey if you're not used to twin-engined planes. They're not the same as single-engined ones, you see, a whole other kettle of fish.

'Gerhard has spent his life flying planes with one engine. For all I know, he can't even count to two. That made me a little edgy letting him sit in the pilot's seat. Wasn't sure whether I was risking my aircraft and my neck, both of which I value highly. I gave him a few words of advice, as an experienced Mosquito pilot to a novice.'

'Much appreciated, old man,' Gerhard interrupted.

'We head down the runway. Gerhard takes off and, stone me, it was like he had been flying Mozzies all his life. Five minutes in, he turns to me and says, "Do you mind if I see how she manoeuvres?" "Be my guest," I say. The next thing he's flinging my poor crate around the sky like he's got the Red air force on his tail. I mean, barrel-rolls, Immelmann turns, a split-S, a pitchback, high and low yo-yos . . . This may sound like gibberish to you ladies, but, Saffron, your husband is the best damn pilot I have ever encountered. Now I feel like I did the day you first arrived at Weltevreden and you went down the throat at me.'

'I have no idea what you are talking about,' said Gerhard.

'It's a polo expression,' said Saffron. 'It means charging at your opponent and daring them not to turn away before you do. Playing chicken.'

'I was almost sixteen,' Shasa continued. 'Three years later I was playing polo for South Africa in the Berlin Olympics. And I'd gone down the throat once in my life, to score a goal that won a tournament. But for a thirteen-year-old girl to do it to me—'

'And you pulled away,' said Saffron, only too happy to rub it in, twenty years later.

'I did, because I didn't want to kill you,' said Shasa, not willing to concede a thing. 'I was a well brought-up boy. I knew that killing one's guests was bad form, particularly if they were younger and female.

'My point is, I was furious at you for doing that to me, Saffy, but damn, I admired your guts and I've respected you ever since. Now your man has let me know that anything I can do in a plane, he can do better. I don't like that. I am not a man who appreciates being beaten at anything, ever. But even so, I can't deny it, Gerhard. You're a hell of a pilot.' Shasa raised his glass. 'I salute you.'

Oh, well done, my darling, Saffron thought. *It was you that got Shasa back on side.*

There was a knock on the door and Wajid came in.

'Cook is ready to serve, memsahib,' he said.

'Thank you, Wajid,' Saffron replied. She took her cousin's arm. 'Would you be kind enough to lead me in?'

Shasa smiled. 'My great pleasure.'

Gerhard took Centaine's arm and in they went to eat.

The two couples chatted for a while about their respective homes, in a light-hearted competition to determine which branch of the Courtney family had the most desirable residence. In the end it was agreed that the house at Weltevreden made the Lusima Estate House look like a humble cottage and Cresta a mere shack. Furthermore, the Kenyan Courtneys could not begin to compete with the Old Master paintings and museum-worthy antique furniture with which Centaine had decorated her home.

On the other hand, the South African Courtneys could not match the size, beauty and fertility of Lusima's land. Weltevreden's fields, vineyards and pastures were beautifully maintained, but they could fit into Lusima several hundred times over. A draw was therefore declared, to everyone's satisfaction.

The last dishes were being cleared away. They settled down to glasses of cognac and coffee from Lusima's own plantation. The gentlemen lit cigars rolled from estate tobacco.

Saffron said, 'I think it's time I told you why I invited you both here.'

'I was beginning to wonder when you would get around to it,' Centaine remarked.

'And there I was thinking it was for the pleasure of our company,' said Shasa, his good humour apparently restored.

'It has to do with my brother, Konrad von Meerbach,' Gerhard said.

Together they told the whole story, from Count Otto's death at Leon Courtney's hands, to Konrad's encounter with their children.

'*Mon Dieu*,' Centaine gasped when Saffron described how 'Uncle Konnie' had used the children to send a message to their parents.

'And we're the family he was talking about?' Shasa asked.

'We think so, yes,' Saffron replied.

'The man's got some cheek, hasn't he?'

'Well, we're planning to make him pay for it.'

Saffron was about to tell the story of their meetings with Joshua Solomons and the Israelis' efforts on their behalf, but then a memory of her days at SOE came to mind. When an operation was being planned, sending agents into Occupied Europe, absolutely no one was told about it, except for the people directly involved and the senior officers who sanctioned it. Joshua worked for an equally secretive organisation.

Yes, but I can trust my own family. And then the voice in her head insisted: *absolutely no one.*

'We've been doing some sleuthing and we've worked out Konrad's movements after the War.' Saffron looked at her husband, hoping that he would spot what she was doing, as she went on, 'Gerhard's ma has been incredibly helpful. She was able to tell us that Konrad went to Lisbon in '42. Anyway, to cut a long story short, we then linked him to a South African, Manfred De La Rey. It seems they initially met in Lisbon on Konrad's first visit, then again when Konrad escaped there after the war.'

At the mention of De La Rey's name, both Centaine and Shasa had visibly tensed.

'I remember from the old days that he was someone you didn't get on with,' Saffron added.

'That is one possible interpretation,' Centaine replied, but there was something about the way she said the words that seemed to Saffron to hint at a whole other story, as complicated as the one that she and Gerhard had just told, of which she had no knowledge.

Saffron had the worrying sense that the visit into which she had put so much thought and effort was not panning out as she had expected. When she described Konrad's appearance at the Estate House, Centaine was appalled by the vision of this monster playing with Zander and Kika, but Shasa tried to play it down.

'I wouldn't worry about it too much, old girl,' he said. 'After all, the children came to no harm. I see this as a sign of weakness, actually.'

Saffron bit back the words 'Well, I bloody well don't!', and instead composed herself and calmly asked, 'How so?'

'Well, it's a gesture, a diversionary tactic, isn't it? He must have known that if he touched a hair on those kiddies' heads, he'd never have left Lusima alive. All he could do was try to get under your skin, which he apparently did quite successfully.'

Again, Saffron had to take a breath and count to ten, and she could see Gerhard's jaw tighten. They glanced at one another, as if to say: *stay calm.*

'The thing is,' Saffron said, trying to get the conversation back on track, 'we could use your help. I'm sure I don't have to tell you why tracking down a Nazi war criminal is a good thing, in itself. And this particular Nazi is a danger to us, your family. Plus, he is an ally of someone who is, I think, your enemy. It just seemed to me to make sense for us to work together on this.'

When she had been imagining the way these days with her cousins would go, this was the moment when Saffron had seen Centaine and Shasa reacting as they always had done in the past, with an immediate, unquestioning eagerness to help her. Instead her words were met with indifference. Centaine offered no encouragement, either by words or in her facial expression. Instead, she focused on Shasa, who took a thoughtful pull on his cigar, looking up at the ceiling as he blew out a long stream of smoke.

'I'd like to help,' he eventually said.

But . . . Saffron thought, suddenly very glad that she had not told him everything.

'But things are a little complicated these days. You're right, of course, De La Rey and I have cordially loathed one another from the day we first met. You're also correct in describing De La Rey as a man of great influence. He's a senior minister and the youngest member of the National government's cabinet. That makes him the coming man in South African politics, particularly if, like me, you think that the Nationals are in power for the long haul. They're the Afrikaner party. Afrikaners make up the majority of the white population and the blacks don't have votes.'

'Yet,' Saffron said.

'You sound like someone I know. Take it from me, they won't have the vote in our lifetime.'

'That's what people here say about blacks in Kenya. I think they're wrong.'

'*Ja*, they may be. The British aren't as single-minded as the Afrikaners. In the end, there are too many people in London who regard the Empire as evil. They will support the blacks in Africa, even against their own people. They even teach the blacks to rise up against their white masters. Kenyatta, here in Kenya . . . Julius Nyerere in Tanganyika . . . hell, Gandhi in India . . . Men bent on destroying the British Empire and all of them educated in Britain. Look at that young man we met today, Benjamin. Had all sorts of ideas put into his head by studying in London. I dare say he can't wait to end the empire, either.'

'He can't, you're right. But then again, neither could Benjamin Franklin, Thomas Jefferson and George Washington. They fought for the right to govern themselves. Black Africans will do the same thing, unless we accept the inevitable and find a peaceful way to give them the same freedom we take for granted.'

'Well, you may think that, Saffron, but I can assure you that the National government doesn't. And they are the people who are determining the future of South Africa.'

Saffron felt a sickly pall of disappointment. She didn't need to hear another word from Shasa. It was obvious he was going to refuse to help her. She told herself that she should have seen this coming.

The way Shasa behaved at the clinic, the things Centaine said about him and Tara . . . Why didn't I understand how much he's changed?

The idea that Shasa might not stand by his own family, that he would put politics ahead of blood, was a bitter, dispiriting blow.

'Excuse me for intruding,' Gerhard said. 'I have picked up a little understanding of African politics in the last few years, but of course I know less than all three of you. But I can't help noticing something, Shasa. I'm right in thinking that you are an MP for the opposition party?'

'The United Party, that's right.'

'The National Party is your opponent. But forgive me, you don't speak like a man who is opposing his country's government. You sound more as though you agree with the Nationals.'

'Well, I wouldn't go that far,' Shasa said, sounding like a politician. 'I don't approve of the way they keep the black population in poverty. As a businessman, of course I want to control workers' wages, but wasn't it Henry Ford who said he wanted his workers to afford the cars they made? Makes no sense to keep millions of people too poor to buy the products business has to sell.'

'But you agree with the Nationals about denying the blacks a vote?'

'Yes . . . yes I do. And I'm damned if I should apologise for that.'

'No, of course not. Every man should be entitled to his opinion. But what I am getting at is I sense you no longer see Manfred De La Rey as an enemy. Maybe he is now an ally.'

Shasa gave another few seconds' attention to his cigar, then he gave a dry smile and said, 'You're a shrewd bastard, aren't you? I mean, you present yourself as the good brother, nothing like the other one. But you're as tough as old boots. You'd have to be, I suppose, to survive what you've been through. I say that as a compliment, by the way . . . sincerely.'

'I take it as one,' Gerhard replied.

It occurred to Saffron that Gerhard had quietly sidelined her. *He's taking charge of the negotiation*, she thought.

This was not the kind of treatment to which she was accustomed. She should have been infuriated. And yet, to her surprise, she was intrigued, and a little attracted by her husband's unexpected assertiveness.

She glanced across the table at Centaine and saw that she, too, was fascinated by this new side to Gerhard's character. He had let Shasa know that there were two alpha males in the room. Shasa had acknowledged him as an equal. How would the contest between them be resolved?

'Now,' said Gerhard, 'I feel that I have responsibility here, since this is my brother we are talking about. And I, like you, Shasa, have found myself responsible for a large family business.

So let us be frank. I do not think you are going to give us the help for which we are asking. Correct?'

'Correct.'

'But equally, I know that you and Saffron are close and that you would never wish to hurt her, or set her interests aside in favour of someone who was not a family member.'

'Also correct.'

The two men were focusing their attention on one another. But Saffron happened to have her eyes on Centaine when Gerhard used the words 'not a family member' and Shasa answered in the affirmative. She saw Centaine give a tiny, involuntary shake of the head, so barely perceptible that she may not have been aware of it herself.

But she shook her head. She disagreed. Does that mean that she . . . No, that can't be possible! Is Manfred De La Rey part of this family?

'Very well then, I have a proposition, or perhaps it is a request,' Gerhard said. 'We will demand nothing of you. You need not lift a finger to help us catch my brother. All I ask in return is that you do not lift a finger to stop us, either. Does that sound fair to you?'

Shasa made them wait before he replied, 'Yes, I believe I can live with that. And because, as you say, I love Saffron dearly – and also because I like the cut of your jib and would rather have you as a friend than an enemy – I will do you both one small, but possibly significant favour.'

'Might I ask what?'

'You might, Gerhard, but I can't tell you. Let's say that I'm still British enough to believe in fair play.'

'That is part of your national character that we Germans have always admired.'

The two women glanced at one another, both relieved by the way their men had found a way not to fight, without either losing face.

'In that case,' said Shasa, 'why don't you open another bottle and we'll drink a toast . . . to our family and fair play.'

Manfred De La Rey drove his modest private car through the tradesman's entrance to the Weltevreden Estate and up to the house, where he was greeted by Shasa.

'We've got the place to ourselves,' Shasa said. 'The children are asleep in bed and my wife is off at one of her damn political meetings.'

'I know,' said De La Rey. 'I can tell you the address of the house where she has gone and the names of the other people she is meeting.'

Shasa gave a humourless chuckle and said, 'One day she will go too far. I know that.'

'And you will have to deal with it, if you want to be part of our government.'

'I know that too. But that's not all I, or you, for that matter, have to deal with. Drink?'

'Water is fine for me.'

'I'll get you a glass. Excuse me while I pour myself some Scotch.'

'As you please, this is your house. Why did you ask me here?'

'Because we need to make an agreement . . . as well as our other agreement.'

De La Rey fixed Shasa with his eerie, feline eyes. 'Go on . . .'

'You know a man called Konrad von Meerbach. You met him in Lisbon during the war when he was a senior SS officer, and then again in Lisbon when he was in exile, living under an assumed name. You helped him come here to South Africa.'

De La Rey's eyes narrowed, making him look even more like a leopard waiting to pounce.

'Don't worry,' Shasa assured him. 'I have no intention of using that information against you. Not that it would count against you in your party. It's riddled with Nazi sympathisers from the top down.'

'Man, have you dragged me all the way here for a lecture about Nazism?'

'No, I'm here to tell you that there are people hunting your man von Meerbach.'

'I know . . . and those people include a certain Saffron Meerbach, née Saffron Courtney, who, I presume, is a family member.'

'Then you will understand that this puts us in a delicate situation, now that we are burying the hatchet and becoming political allies. We might find ourselves on opposite sides in someone else's private battle. That could be bad for our future relationship – and our ambitions. We are both young men, younger than the men currently leading this country. The future is ours for the taking.'

'So why risk it now, eh? Is that what you're saying?'

'Got it in one. I have told my cousin and her husband that I will neither help them, nor hinder them, in their search for Konrad von Meerbach, or whatever he calls himself these days. I can tell you that at the moment they know neither his name, nor his whereabouts.'

'He will be relieved to hear that.'

'If you tell him. But I would rather you did not. The way I see it, we should both take a step back, so that neither of us has anything at stake in this fight. I will give you my word that I will do nothing to help my cousin and her husband, if you give me your word that you will not help von Meerbach. Furthermore, neither of us will step in when it is over, no matter what the result.'

'What, precisely, do you mean by that?'

'Well, suppose von Meerbach should happen to be killed, and suppose that my cousin is arrested for his murder. This is not impossible, I might add. You presumably know that she has killed before.'

De La Rey nodded.

'In those circumstances,' Shasa continued, 'I will do nothing to influence the course of justice or public opinion in any way. I may visit her privately in prison, but that is all. By the same token, let us suppose that von Meerbach is captured and taken away for trial in another country. Neither you nor this country's government will express support for him, nor make any attempt to apprehend the people who abducted him.'

'So we are reduced to the role of spectators?'

'Interested spectators is how I would put it, but yes, we will observe without interfering. That way, however this turns out, and whoever wins or is defeated, neither of us will gain or lose a thing.'

'Thus our political agreement is not compromised.'

'Exactly.'

De La Rey's eyes lost their killer intensity. His body relaxed.

'Yes,' he said, 'that is an arrangement I can accept.' He held out his hand. 'I give you my word on it.'

'I give you mine,' Shasa said, taking the proffered hand and shaking it.

'And now,' said Manfred De La Rey, 'let the contest begin.'

In his role as the businessman Michel Schultz, von Meerbach did not turn away customers he suspected of being Jewish. That would only arouse suspicion. But he made a point of not dealing with them personally. When he heard that a Dr Jonathan Goldsmith had brought a Jaguar XK120 drophead coupé in for a tune-up and had asked to speak to him personally about improvements that might be made to the car's performance, von Meerbach was cautious. 'Goldsmith' was an English word. But it could easily be an Anglicisation of the Jewish surname 'Goldschmidt'.

'Where is he?' he asked the mechanic who had delivered the message.

The mechanic led von Meerbach to the window, from which his upstairs office looked down on his works' shop floor. He pointed and said, 'That one.'

Von Meerbach saw a tall blond man in his early thirties, wearing flannel trousers and a tweed jacket, with a silk cravat around his neck, tucked into a pale blue shirt. He was standing beside a long, low, open-topped sports car, painted in British racing green. He did not look like any Jew von Meerbach had ever met. But he did look exactly like an English gentleman.

'Very well,' he said. 'Tell him I will be down in two minutes.'

Von Meerbach was correct in part of his assessment. Jonathan Goldsmith carried a British passport. He spoke the King's English in the manner he had acquired at Rugby, one of the country's most eminent public boarding schools, where the game of rugby football, so beloved by South Africa's Afrikaner populations, had been invented. He had studied medicine at Cambridge University before qualifying as a doctor at Barts Hospital and had come to work as a surgeon at Cape Town's Groote Schuur Hospital because, as he blithely put it, 'I thought I'd work better with a bit of sunshine on my skin and some decent food inside me.'

The SS, as an institution, had regarded the British as racial equals, even if they had made the regrettable decision to be enemies of the Reich. The Führer greatly admired the way the British Empire had been won and maintained, despite its masters being outnumbered by the lesser races they ruled. Von Meerbach was therefore content to introduce himself to Dr Goldsmith and have an agreeable conversation with him about the various enhancements that could be made to the Jaguar's engine, suspension and brakes to improve its already impressive capabilities.

What von Meerbach did not know was that his fears were justified. Dr Goldsmith had indeed been born Yonatan Goldschmidt in Vienna. His family, like many upper-class Austrian Jews, had intermarried with their Christian equivalents over the centuries, which accounted for Yonatan's colouring. His father, who was a psychiatrist, had seen which way the wind was blowing and in 1932 had taken his family from Vienna to London, swiftly establishing a successful practice in the North London suburb of Hampstead. The family had made both their family and given names more English. The children were sent to good schools and emerged entirely assimilated into the culture of their new land.

Jonathan was at university when the war broke out. He qualified as a doctor in 1943 and joined the Royal Army Medical Corps, serving with distinction on the Italian front. He had become a proud, patriotic Briton, and intended to return home in due course to work in the newly formed National Health Service. And yet, he was equally proud of his Jewish heritage and played an active role in the Jewish community in Cape Town.

He was one of a small number of trusted men who had been summoned to a private meeting and informed that the Israeli government had reason to believe that a former high-ranking SS officer called Konrad von Meerbach, who had taken an active part in the creation of the Reich's death camps, was living under an alias in South Africa. They were also informed that von Meerbach might have chosen to settle in the Cape, to be under the wing of a prominent National Party politician, with whom he was known to have a connection. A detailed description of von Meerbach was provided, along with a short background briefing of his life and personal characteristics.

The man they were looking for was distinguished by a powerful, thick-necked physique, possibly now running to fat, and red hair, which would be turning grey. He was a man accustomed to power, a bully who enjoyed the ability to intimidate and belittle.

As a qualified doctor, who was also the son of an eminent psychiatrist, Jonathan Goldsmith saw these traits displayed in Michel Schultz. And as Schultz gave an expert, albeit boastful account of the transformation his company could work on the Jaguar, Goldsmith noticed he spoke with an upper-class Munich accent and recalled that the briefing on von Meerbach had included the information that his family owned a company that specialised in engine manufacturing.

Having concluded that he might be dealing with a man who had helped the Third Reich murder six million of his co-religionists, Jonathan Goldsmith found it hard to keep smiling and conclude his business. He held his nerve, agreed to the work and cost suggested by 'Michel Schultz', and handed over his car.

Mr Schultz graciously rang for a taxi. When it arrived, Goldsmith bade Schultz farewell and told the driver to take him to Groote Schuur Hospital. A minute later, as they were driving away, Goldsmith informed his cabbie that he wished to be taken to the offices of the Carmel Shipping Company in the Port of Cape Town. There he met with the company's proprietor, Manny Ishmael, who had invited him to the meeting at which the von Meerbach manhunt had been discussed.

'I think I found him,' he said.

Ishmael was seventy-three years old. He was still as sharp as a tack, but experience had taught him not to rush to hasty conclusions.

'You walk into a garage and meet a fat goy with red hair and a German accent . . . and this makes him von Meerbach?' He gave a world-weary sigh. 'We should all be so lucky.'

Goldsmith gave his reasoning in more detail. Ishmael conceded a little ground.

'You may be right. My father was a baker from Slutsk, Byelorussia. I don't know from Munich accents. If you tell me this man had one, why should I argue? I will call my contact in Pretoria. Let him decide.'

Manny Ishmael's contact was nominally a First Secretary at the Israeli Embassy. Like Joshua Solomons, he was an officer of the Central Institute for Coordination. The Hebrew word for 'Institute' is 'Mossad', the name by which the organisation would come to be known. When word was passed on to the institute's headquarters in Tel Aviv, its director, Reuven Shiloah, determined that this lead was worth following up.

Joshua Solomons considered sending a team to Cape Town to photograph Michel Schultz, so that a definitive identification could be made. But he realised there was an easier solution. He contacted Jonathan Goldsmith and asked him to undertake a simple task.

'You may find this sickening. But if it helps get justice for the dead . . .'

'Don't worry,' Goldsmith replied. 'I spent two years practising battlefield surgery. It takes a lot to sicken me.'

A few days later, Goldsmith went to collect his car. Michel Schultz offered to accompany his customer while he took the Jaguar for a spin, just to check that everything was in order. When they returned to Schultz Engineering, Goldsmith thanked Schultz for doing such a fine job, praising him, sincerely, for the improvement in the Jag's performance. He opened his medical briefcase, took out a Leica IIIf camera and took a couple of pics of the car, which had also been cleaned and polished to a dazzling sheen. He handed the camera to one of the mechanics and invited Schultz to join him beside the car.

Schultz hesitated. 'I do not like to have my photograph taken,' he said. 'The camera is not my friend.'

'Oh, don't be shy, old boy!' Goldsmith said with public school heartiness. 'Tell you what, let's make it a team photo, get all the chaps who worked on her into the picture, eh?'

The mechanic holding the camera thought this was a splendid idea. He waved to three of his colleagues, and they hurried over with such eagerness that Schultz could hardly refuse to oblige them.

He stood next to Goldsmith with his employees on either side, resplendent in their Schultz Engineering boiler suits. As the man holding the camera was about to shoot, Schultz turned his head away from the lens, then back again when he heard the click. The mechanics gave a ragged cheer, grinned at one another and the group by the car broke up.

'I took three,' the man with the camera said, handing it back to Goldsmith. 'Just to be safe.'

Schultz was already walking back to his office. He did not hear the photographer's words, any more than he had heard the camera's clicking, for the noise his men were making had drowned it out.

Goldsmith took the undeveloped Kodachrome film to Manny Ishmael. He had it couriered to Pretoria. There it was placed in the diplomatic bag to Tel Aviv.

Before he left Ishmael's office, Goldsmith said, 'Word of advice for your people. If Mr Schultz really is Konrad von Meerbach, he drives an exceptionally fast car. If he tries to make a run for it, they'll have a hell of a job trying to catch him. But thanks to the efforts of Schultz himself, my Jag is one of the few jalopies in Cape Town that's powerful enough to keep up with him. If you think it might come in handy, please don't hesitate to ask.'

Ishmael grasped his hand and said, '*Sheynem dank*, Yonatan. I will make sure that whatever happens, you will get it back again as good as new.'

Four days after the pictures were taken, Joshua Solomons had three colour transparencies sitting on his desk. He took them to a briefing room equipped with a projector and a screen. In the first image, most of the men were looking directly at the lens. Only Schultz's face was too blurred to make any identification.

Joshua swore under his breath. But it occurred to him that a man who did not want to be identified might turn his head when he knew a picture was being taken.

But you didn't know about these, did you? Joshua thought as the second and third shots flashed up on the screen. These were less formal. Some of the men were laughing. Others had turned to one another. Their faces were less clear. But Schultz, believing the threat had passed, had relaxed. He had turned his head so that he was looking straight into the camera.

'That's him!' Joshua exulted.

He had prints made from the transparencies and took them to Reuven Shiloah, with other, historical pictures of Konrad von Meerbach as comparison. Shiloah agreed that the resemblance was pronounced.

'But we need to know for sure. Ask the brother.'

Joshua and Gerhard met at the same café in Mombasa. They talked for almost an hour, but the key business took no more than a few seconds. Joshua opened a brown paper envelope, extracted the two images and handed them over.

Gerhard grimaced. He leaned back and looked up at the sky as he recovered from the shock of what he had seen. He pushed the prints across the table, face down. He turned away again, fighting to control a storm of emotions.

Joshua had seen other men and women react this way: concentration camp survivors who gazed again on the faces of their tormentors.

'My father told me what your brother did to you,' he said. 'I'm sorry to make you look at him again.'

Gradually Gerhard relaxed. He drank some coffee, watched the world walk past the café.

Finally he said, 'It's all right. You had to show me. Now tell me, how we are going to get him.'

'I have your papers,' Joshua said. 'Marlize married Herman Doll, an architectural draughtsman who visited Belgium to work on the Atlantic Wall defences.'

'So not a man that the Allies would have been interested in.'

'No, just a guy in an office drawing plans of gun emplacements. He went home to Friedrichshafen after the war. You notice I am giving you a job and a home that you can talk about convincingly, if required.'

'Yes . . . thank you.'

'Marlize lives with you now in Germany. You have been saving up for years. Now you can finally afford to visit her homeland, South Africa. It is, of course, unlikely that you will ever have to answer any questions. There is no reason for you to be stopped by the immigration officials, since your wife has dual nationality and your visa is in order. South Africa is not a nation in which citizens are arbitrarily stopped and forced to account for themselves—'

'Unless they are black.'

Joshua gave a nod of the head to acknowledge the point, then continued, 'The only circumstances in which this might become an issue would arise from something going wrong. If the operation is blown, or your brother is harmed or even dies, the police might take an interest. If they do, say as little as possible. Ideally say nothing at all. If you are forced to talk, stick to the story of an innocent German tourist caught up in something of which he knows nothing.'

'Have you worked out how the operation will proceed?' Gerhard asked.

'Yes.'

'Can you tell me about it?'

'Not yet. At this stage, the less you know the better. But you will be briefed when you get to South Africa.'

'And how would you rate our chances of success?'

Joshua gave a wry smile. 'Don't worry. Gerhard. We are not going to fail. We are going to get your brother, take him back to Israel and make him pay for his crimes.'

'It sounds like Herr Doll is going to have a very exciting holiday in South Africa.'

'I'm certain he will.'

K onrad von Meerbach did not ask a great deal of Manfred
De La Rey. It did neither of them any good to draw attention to their relationship. Nevertheless, he took it for
granted that if he contacted De La Rey's office, his call would
be returned.

Von Meerbach had found himself feeling uncharacteristi-
cally edgy and insecure. His encounter with his young niece
and nephew had made him feel better than at any time since
the collapse of the Reich. The news that Shasa and Centaine
Courtney had flown to Kenya had filled him with a tension
that was almost pleasurable. His plan was working. He'd provoked a reaction. Now it was just a matter of De Koch telling
him that Gerhard and Saffron had arrived in Cape Town. Von
Meerbach's staff at the garage were all good men, whose skill
as mechanics was matched by their sound views on racial matters and their physical toughness. He therefore felt confident
that when the time came, he would not only have news of his
enemies' presence, but also enough men to keep an eye on
them, guard his own home and finally overpower them.

Whether Gerhard and Saffron came to his house of their
own accord, or he found a means of abducting them while they
were out and about in Cape Town, they would end up in the
same place: von Meerbach's cellar. It was hidden from public
view, soundproof and equipped with everything he needed to
help him finish the job. And, oh, how he relished the thought of
the suffering he would inflict before he finally finished Gerhard
and Saffron off for good, took their bodies down to his boat and
then went out to sea to feed them to the great white sharks who
patrolled the waters around the Cape.

But the days and weeks went by, and they didn't arrive. Von
Meerbach was certain that they must be up to something. But
what? He could hazard plenty of guesses. Gerhard had displayed Jew-loving tendencies when he helped the Solomons to

leave for Switzerland. It was possible, even likely, that he kept in contact with that family. Isidore Solomons, in von Meerbach's estimation, was the kind of Jew who involved himself in his race's unending efforts to bend the world to their will, conspiring to bring down great Christian nations and profiting from others' misfortunes. He would surely be in contact with other high-ranking Jews willing to track down a man who, like von Meerbach, understood their true intentions and thereby threatened the success of their wicked schemes.

Von Meerbach wanted to discuss the matter with De La Rey. He had always been sound on the Jewish Question and, with his political allies, was applying the same principles to the subjugation of the Negro race in South Africa. And yet, when von Meerbach rang De La Rey's office and left a message with his secretary, there was no response.

Von Meerbach left another message, doing his best to sound casual: this was a minor matter that could easily slip the mind of a government minister with many other more important issues to worry about. Privately, however, von Meerbach was becoming more anxious. Having been in De La Rey's position himself, as a company boss and senior SS officer, he was accustomed to cutting his ties with underlings who had outlived their usefulness. He found himself on the receiving end and, like any other loyal retainer who has lost their master's favour, he asked the same questions again and again.

Why is this happening? What went wrong? What can I do about it?

His desperation became so apparent that Francesca offered to call Heidi De La Rey to see if she could shed light on her husband's change of behaviour.

When the two women spoke, Heidi insisted, 'Honestly, darling, Manfred's not said a word to me about Konrad. I'm sure there's nothing to worry about.'

Francesca tried to persuade her husband to believe Heidi's words but he refused.

'Are you so stupid that you can't see that she's lying to you? De La Rey dotes on that woman. She knows exactly what he thinks about everything.'

Von Meerbach had one last opportunity to discover what lay behind his sudden relegation to non-person status. The National Party was holding a fund-raising dinner that week, an all-male affair for prominent members of the local business community. Von Meerbach despised the kind of men who attended these events as jumped-up shopkeepers and factory owners, giving themselves airs of importance. But he bought a table for himself and a few of his staff, gritted his teeth and went along to pick up the latest political gossip in the hope he might just hear something of use.

After three hours of bad food, worse wine and endless sounding off about the inferiority of the blacks, von Meerbach had learned nothing. He was on the point of leaving when a garage owner called Piet Kronje, with whom Schultz Engineering did a fair amount of business, came up to him. Kronje sidled up close and, exuding a malodorous blend of cigar smoke and pungent fumes of *mampoer*, the local peach brandy, furtively asked, 'Hey, Schultz, have you heard the latest news from parliament, eh?'

'What news is that, then?' von Meerbach replied, wondering how long he would have to endure Kronje's company.

'One of the top men in the United Party is coming over to our side. It's all been agreed, they're just waiting to announce it.'

'How do you know this?'

'Let's say a little birdie told me. A birdie who was sitting on his branch by the table when the deal was done.'

'And who is this top man?'

Kronje looked around to check that no one could overhear him, lowered his voice and said, 'Courtney . . . you know, the fellow with that eyepatch, makes him look like a *verdoem* pirate.'

Suddenly von Meerbach did not have to feign his interest.

'Are you sure?' he asked. 'Courtney is the stepson of Blaine Malcomess, United's deputy leader. That won't go down well the next time they meet for Sunday lunch.'

'Maybe not, but he's joining us anyway. I can tell you who brokered the deal – Manfred De La Rey.'

Now it all made sense. But von Meerbach gave nothing away to Kronje.

'That's a good story, Piet,' he said, slapping him good-humouredly on the back. 'Who knows, it may even be half-true.'

Von Meerbach did not bother calling De La Rey's office the following day. He went there himself, at a time when Manfred was likely to be present, barged past the secretary and kicked open the door. Ignoring the shocked expressions of the civil servants gathered to receive their minister's instructions, von Meerbach jabbed a finger at De La Rey and snarled, 'I know why you've been avoiding me. And I swear to God, I'll have it all over Cape Town by sunset if you don't tell me, man to man, what the hell you're up to.'

De La Rey looked at him with an intensity that made von Meerbach glad he had never had to face him in the boxing ring. Keeping his unblinking gaze fixed on this intruder into his private space, he said, 'Please leave the room, everybody. This will only take two minutes.'

When the office had been cleared, De La Rey said, 'What's the meaning of this?'

'You made a deal with Courtney. I know it.'

De La Rey's face betrayed no sign of reaction.

'Did you hand me over to him and his family?' von Meerbach asked. 'Was that the little sweetener that made him say yes?'

'I have no comment to make about wild, unfounded accusations made by an uninvited intruder into my office,' De La Rey replied. 'Look at yourself, man. Have you no pride, no dignity?'

'You don't know what it's like to be a fugitive.' Von Meerbach could not keep a plaintive note of self-pity out of his voice.

'On the contrary, I know exactly what it's like. But I have not handed you over to anyone. No one has asked me to help them find you. I haven't told anyone that you are in South Africa, what name you are using or where you live. I have done nothing, absolutely nothing, to threaten your security.'

Von Meerbach felt the merest scintilla of relief, but he wanted confirmation.

'So no one is coming for me?'

'How would I know? But I can tell you this – there are fifteen million people in this country and they are scattered across more than one million square kilometres. That is a very big haystack and you are one small needle. There is no reason to believe that anyone will ever find you.'

Von Meerbach was about to speak, but De Lay Rey raised his hand.

'Enough. Leave this office. I have work to do. And I do not wish to speak to you again.'

Saffron ran the final twenty-five yards to the far end of her training circuit. *Okay . . . ten more burpees*, she told herself. *Hit them hard. No slacking.*

She stood up straight, then dropped into a squatting position with her hands on the ground in front of her. She thrust her legs out behind her, brought them back in again to the squatting position and jumped into the air. One burpee down, nine to go.

She was breathing hard. This was her third rotation. She turned right, sprinted another fifty yards and turned right again. Ahead of her was a crude tunnel, formed by a ditch covered by a series of concrete slabs. She dived into the ditch, ignoring the scraping of her elbows and knees against the hard, stony earth, cursing beneath her breath when she banged her head on the concrete.

Saffron emerged from the ditch and sprinted another twenty-five yards, jogged twenty-five, then sprinted another twenty-five to the scramble net hung from an eight-foot-high wooden frame. Up the net she went, rolled over the top, dropped to the ground then sprinted again to the shooting range.

Her Beretta 418 pistol, the weapon that had seen her through the war, was sitting on a stool, fully loaded, with Wajid waiting, ready to reload it once Saffron had emptied its eight-round magazine. The gun was not the most powerful available, but it was small, light and could easily be tucked into the canvas shoulder-bag Saffron carried in wartime, a civilian handbag or even a pocket. It was known as the Italian 'pocket pistol'. It had fixed iron sights: a rear notch and front blade.

Joshua had specified that she and Gerhard would only take part in the mission as advisors and observers. Still, she had no intention of taking any chances. She was determined to be fighting fit by the time the call came to say that the ship carrying the Israelis was on its way to Cape Town.

If she had to use her gun, she anticipated it would be defensive and at close quarters. The range had been set up as a rough copy of the killing house that had been created for SOE trainees near their base at Arisaig on the west coast of Scotland. A week earlier, Saffron had bought a dozen tailor's dummies: stuffed, fabric-covered male torsos on wooden stands. Red circles were painted on the centre of their chests, above their imaginary hearts. Six of the dummies were mounted on wooden poles that were rammed into the ground, deep enough to remain upright despite a bullet's impact, in a line across the range, at distances of between ten and twenty yards from her firing position and numbered, from left to right.

The drill was always the same. Saffron picked up the gun, still out of breath, pulse racing, muscles protesting. She stood with her back to the range. The moment she got into position, Wajid shouted, 'Turn!'

She spun round and immediately Wajid shouted four numbers in quick succession, giving her no time to rest. This time his sequence went, 'Four! One! Six! Three!'

Saffron shot the way she had been taught at Arisaig. She didn't take aim in the conventional manner. SOE training doctrine considered that too slow and ineffective in close-quarters combat. She simply looked at the target, let her hand follow her eye and shot on instinct. She fired two rounds in quick succession: the double-tap technique that was another SOE innovation. She looked at the next target and did exactly the same thing.

Her groupings weren't perfect. Barely half her rounds hit the red circle. But they all hit the dummies somewhere, and if things got messy, a man with two bullets in him would pose a drastically reduced threat. Not that Saffron was satisfied.

'Useless!' she gasped as she turned to run back up the circuit to do the next set of burpees, while Wajid watched her and shook his head in bafflement at his mistress's bizarre behaviour.

When she completed her fifth and final rotation, Saffron sprinted to the finishing line and collapsed on the ground, her chest heaving until she recovered enough to get back on her feet, wipe the sweat from her face and accept the water-bottle Wajid handed to her. He would rather have prepared a jug of fresh orange juice or lemonade, properly iced and served in frosted glasses. But the memsahib had insisted: plain water, served in her old military canteen.

Gerhard, watching to one side, walked over and said, 'Well done. That was very impressive.'

Saffron shook her head. 'Not really. I should be able to do ten circuits. And my shooting was rubbish.'

'It can't have been too bad. Those dummies have been shot to bits. You'd better put the next six up. Anyway, I couldn't do a single circuit. Five sounds pretty good to me.'

'I don't expect you to do any.'

Saffron managed an exhausted smile. She saw it was difficult for Gerhard, seeing her do this when his health, though good enough for everyday life, was not up to the strain of high-intensity training. His doctors would never allow it.

'You're alive,' she said, taking his hand. 'That's a miracle in itself. I don't care about anything else.'

He kissed Saffron, whispered, 'I love you,' in her ear, then said, 'I've been thinking, maybe I should do some shooting, in case.'

'Now that's the most sensible thing I've heard you say in ages,' she replied. 'Wajid, please reload the gun for Bwana Meerbach.'

'Yes, memsahib.' He did as he'd been bidden, handed the loaded gun to Gerhard and asked, 'Will Bwana be shooting like the memsahib?'

Gerhard considered for a moment and said, 'Yes, why not?'

He took up his position with his back to the ragged targets.

'Turn!' Wajid shouted. 'Two! . . . Three! . . . Six! . . . One!'

Gerhard fired a faster series of double-taps than Saffron had managed. Seven of his shots were inside the red circles. The eighth missed by a whisker.

Saffron could hardly believe what she had witnessed.

'Good Lord . . . I had no idea. You're . . . You're actually better than me.'

'Yes, but you were out of breath, so your hand was bound to shake. It's not a fair comparison.'

'But even so . . . for a man who doesn't want anything to do with guns, you're a hell of a shot.'

Gerhard put his hands on Saffron's shoulders and looked into her eyes.

'My darling, I was one of the highest-scoring fighter aces of the war. I was not standing at a range. I had to shoot from an aircraft travelling at five hundred kilometres an hour, sometimes more, while turning, climbing, rolling or diving. And my targets were doing the same thing. Yes, I had three heavy machine guns to play with, not one pistol or rifle, but even so . . .'

Saffron said nothing.

Gerhard frowned. 'What is it?'

'Not only was that the first time I have seen you fire a gun, it's also the first time I've heard you talking about your war service with anything close to pride.' She gave a smile which turned into a blown kiss and added, 'Not to mention a little arrogance.'

'Is that a problem for you?'

Saffron shook her head. 'Not at all . . . In fact, I like it. Does me good to be reminded that I'm not the only warrior in the family.'

Gerhard laughed softly. 'Yes,' he said, 'it does me good, too.'

They drove back to the lodge. Saffron had a long shower to wash away the sweat, the dirt and the lingering smell of cordite. She changed and came downstairs to find Gerhard waiting for her. He was holding a telex.

'One of your father's boys drove this over from the Estate House.' He read it out: "*I'm expecting to arrive Cape Town within the next three days. Looking forward to our safari! Send your ETA and I'll pick you up at the airport: J*".'

'We'd better sort out tickets first thing tomorrow morning.'

'I'll do it,' Gerhard said. 'I'll fly to Nairobi as soon as the sun is up and be at the travel agents when they open.' He smiled. 'You can do another training session.'

'I'll do two,' Saffron said. 'And another two the day after tomorrow.'

'On the day after that we take the plane to Cape Town. And then we get my brother.'

Kungu Kabaya strolled into the Mighty Lion Taxi Company garage in Nairobi, looked at its ranks of Ford Consul saloons, and summoned the company's owner, Javinder Singh.

'Which is the best?' he asked, nodding at the assembled vehicles.

Singh paid a substantial chunk of his income to Kabaya, to ensure his protection from other gang leaders, who in turn extorted other taxi firms.

'That one, sahib,' he said, pointing to a car whose bodywork was somewhat less dented and paint a fraction fresher than the rest. 'She is a real beauty. One of my drivers will be happy to take you wherever you wish to go.'

But Kabaya was not interested in a taxi ride.

'Give me the keys,' he said.

Singh rushed back to his office to grab the keys from their hook.

'Give them to him,' Kabaya said, indicating Wilson Gitiri, who climbed into the car and started the engine.

Before he got in, Kabaya looked at his watch. It was five past eleven in the morning. He told Singh, 'At midday you will call the police and report this car as stolen. Not before. Not after. At midday. Do you understand?'

Singh nodded nervously. 'Oh yes, sahib. I understand very well. I will call the police at twelve o'clock, on the dot.'

'That's good,' Kabaya said. Then he added, 'You know what will happen if you do not.'

He slipped into the taxi.

As Gitiri drove away he asked his boss, 'Do you want me to get any of the others?'

'No,' Kabaya said. 'They would only get in the way. I can handle this myself.'

'What do you mean, our retail turnover is down by thirty per cent?' Chief Ndiri raged, while his bookkeeper quailed at his boss's fury. 'People have to eat. How can they not buy food? Tell me that, eh? How . . . can . . . they . . . not . . . buy food?'

'Because they have no money, sir,' the bookkeeper said, blinking nervously behind his thick spectacles. 'The terrorists raid the farms on which they work. They force workers in businesses to come out on strike. We have had six stoppages in the past months in our own enterprises – our wholesale food shop in Nyeri, the vegetable canning plant in Nakuru, the—'

'But I told the cannery workers to go back to work! I am their chief. How dare they disobey me?'

'They love you, sir, and respect you . . . but they fear the Mau Mau more. And that is not all. Thousands of our people have been placed in the British internment camps. That means they are not working, so their families have no money and—'

'Enough! I will arrange a meeting with Governor Baring. We will talk man to man and I will tell him that more must be done to end this nonsense. These Mau Mau are no better than rats that eat a farmer's crop, and they must be exterminated like rats, too.'

'That is very wise, sir. Surely the governor will listen to a man of your eminence, for he trusts you above all our people.'

The bookkeeper's flattery served its purpose. Chief Ndiri called their meeting to an end without any further reprimands. He went back to his desk and collapsed into his chair.

Ndiri, meanwhile, thanked his lucky stars for the sizeable fortune that he had salted away in Switzerland, where neither the Mau Mau, nor the British, nor anyone else but him could touch it. He looked at the gold Audemars Piguet watch that he had bought for himself on his last visit to his bankers. It was time for lunch, which he would take at home, as was his daily custom. His temper somewhat restored by the thought of the excellent meal that would soon be laid before him, he left his Nairobi office building and settled into the back of his splendid Hudson Commodore Super Six saloon.

This car epitomised everything for which Chief Ndiri had strived. He had imported it from the United States and he loved everything about it. The nose of the bonnet rose from the gleaming chrome of the front bumper and radiator, tall and pointed like the prow of a great ocean liner. The wheel arches on either side were splendidly wide and muscular. The body of the car, painted a rich chocolate brown, was magnificently American in its length, breadth and strident assertion of power and might. The whitewall tyres were the proof of Ndiri's wealth, for in a country of red earth roads, they could only be kept clean by means of constant labour by his garage hands.

Ndiri sank into the cream leather expanse of the rear passenger seat with a contented sigh.

'Drive on,' he commanded his chauffeur as he lit one of the cigars, made specially for him from the finest Rhodesian tobacco. A bodyguard occupied the other front seat. His name was Mathu and he was a former soldier, tough and well-trained, twice decorated for acts of valour during the war. He was armed with a Colt revolver. Whatever wickedness the Mau Mau might have in mind, Mathu could deal with it.

Ndiri puffed away, looking out at the world passing by as the Hudson sped up the Limuru road, on the western outskirts of the city. A splendid lunch was waiting for him at home. His fields were fertile. His cattle were fat. The Mau Mau be damned, his life was as good as it could be.

There was little traffic on the road. But just then a car came speeding by. It was smaller than the Hudson, but it churned up a thick cloud of dust as its driver overtook around the outside of a blind bend, heedless of the risk of oncoming traffic.

'Bloody fool!' Ndiri snapped.

'It's a taxi,' Mathu replied, leaning his head to talk over his shoulder. 'They drive like madmen.'

There was no other car in Nairobi like Chief Ndiri's Hudson, but Kabaya wanted to make sure that the chief was aboard.

'Well?' Gitiri asked as the taxi raced away up the road.

'He was there, sitting in the back like a big fat pig, puffing on his cigar.'

Gitiri laughed. 'Now you will slaughter the pig!'

Kabaya made no reply. He was concentrating on the road ahead.

'There,' he said. 'Do you see it?'

About two hundred yards away was a turning to the left, at a point where the Limuru road curved uphill to the right.

'I see it,' Gitiri said. 'I know what to do.'

He waited a few seconds, then drifted across to the right-hand side of the road before turning the steering wheel hard to the left. At the same time, he jammed on the brakes.

The Ford Consul swerved and skidded until it came to a halt, side-on across the road at the point where it forked, blocking both the main road and the turning.

Kabaya reached inside his pocket and took out a Luger 9mm revolver of the type used by the Wehrmacht. It had been retrieved from the body of a dead German soldier by a farmer who was, like many emigrants to Kenya, a former soldier. Now Kabaya had taken it from him.

Earlier that morning, before setting off for the taxi garage, he had stripped the gun, cleaned and oiled its parts, reassembled it and loaded it. He pulled back the cocking mechanism to put a round into the chamber.

'Let's go,' he said.

'Why are we slowing?' Chief Ndiri asked.

'That madman in the taxi, sir,' Mathu said. 'Do you see . . .?'

Ndiri peered through the windscreen. The taxi driver had obviously lost control of his vehicle. Now he and his passenger were standing in the middle of the road, looking down at the front tyre. The passenger was pointing at his watch, then jabbing it in the driver's face. Ndiri could not see the tyre. He did not need to. The tyre had burst. The passenger wasn't happy about the delay.

Nor, for that matter, was Ndiri. He took a mental note of the name, Mighty Lion, written on the side of the cab.

The taxi passenger had noticed the Hudson's arrival. He turned away from the taxi, leaving the driver crouched by the damaged wheel, and walked towards the Hudson, arms raised to either side and shrugging as if to say, 'I'm sorry, but it's not my fault.'

'I'll deal with this, sir,' Mathu said, getting out of the car.

Ndiri relaxed as the chauffeur turned off the engine. This was a nuisance, but no more than that. Mathu would have everything sorted soon enough. He took a puff on his cigar as Mathu walked towards the taxi.

The passenger kept walking towards Mathu. He lowered his hands. He reached inside his jacket. He pulled out a gun and before Mathu could react, the passenger fired.

Mathu fell to the ground. He did not move.

Ndiri choked on his tobacco smoke. His protector was dead.

'Get out of here!' he screamed at his chauffeur. 'Move! Move!'

Kungu Kabaya did not glance at the man he had shot. As the Hudson's engine coughed and spluttered back to life, he kept walking at a steady pace until he was no more than ten feet from the car, then he paused long enough to put two rounds into the nearest tyre. He saw the driver let go of the wheel and stare at him with eyes so wide the whites were visible. Kabaya ignored him.

He opened the rear passenger door. Ndiri was sprawled across the back seat, his fingers frantically scrabbling at the handle of the opposite door.

'Chief Ndiri,' Kabaya said. 'Look at me.'

His voice was so commanding that Ndiri, praying that there might be hope of mercy, sat up.

Kabaya shot Ndiri four times, rapid fire at point-blank range, punching a fist-sized hole in his chest and killing him instantly. His body slumped back onto the seats, his blood spreading in a rich crimson stain across his beloved creamy upholstery.

Kabaya turned to the chauffeur and said, 'You have a wife and three children.'

The chauffeur nodded.

'Think of them now . . . You saw nothing. You can't remember what happened. Here, this will help you with the police.'

Kabaya whipped his pistol across the chauffeur's face, then hit him again, harder. The chauffeur slumped forward in his seat, barely conscious, with his head in his hands. Blood was seeping between his fingers.

Kabaya walked away. As he passed Mathu's body, he paused, looked back at the car and saw that the chauffeur was still hunched over, oblivious to anything but his own pain.

'Get up,' he said.

Mathu got to his feet, untouched. He dusted himself down and walked with Kabaya to the taxi. Gitiri was already behind the wheel with the engine running. They were on the move again within a few seconds.

'You did well,' Kabaya told Mathu. 'All your information was accurate. You did as you were ordered today. Lucky I'm a bad shot at close range.' He smiled.

'I took the oath,' Mathu replied. 'What else could I do?'

Wangari heard the news of her father's assassination on the radio news. The realisation that he was dead was bad enough. But the fact that he was gone before they had had the chance to be reconciled deepened the wound still further. Wangari called her family home from the clinic, only to be told that her mother would not speak to her. She and Benjamin had no car, but she took a bus out to the suburb where her family lived and walked a mile from the nearest stop to their house.

She was turned away at the gates. One of the staff, whom Wangari had known since she was a little girl, and who was in tears herself, both because her master was dead and because she could not bear to see the pain on Wangari's face, informed her that, 'Your mother has given orders that you are not to be admitted . . . Forgive me, Miss Wangari, I am so, so sorry. But I also have to tell you, you will not be welcome at the funeral.'

The combination of grief and humiliation overwhelmed Wangari. The agony was replaced by a sort of semi-conscious daze. When she finally arrived back at the clinic, she was hardly conscious of how she had got there. In desperation, she called the estate house at Lusima.

'You poor thing,' said Harriet Courtney. 'You have my deepest condolences. And, please, don't take your mother's behaviour to heart. I'm sure she's in shock. She doesn't know what she's doing. She'll come back to you in time, I know she will.'

'Maybe,' said Wangari, though she didn't for a moment believe it. Her mother was not the kind of woman to change her mind about anything. Then she said, 'Can you get a message to Saffron, please? I'd really love to see her.'

'I know she'd feel just the same. She'll be devastated when she hears about this. But I'm afraid she's not here. She and Gerhard left this morning. They're on their way to South Africa.'

'God in Heaven! Now I know how the Führer felt, those last days in the bunker!' shouted Konrad von Meerbach as he paced across the living room, again and again, heedless of the panoramic views of the Indian Ocean revealed by the wall of glass to his side. 'My enemies are everywhere! My friends have deserted me – friends I trusted and rewarded, yet they repay me with nothing but scorn!'

He had been like this since he returned from his meeting with Manfred De La Rey, five days earlier. The following day he announced he would not be going into work. Francesca had to call his secretary and explain that her husband had come down with a bad case of food poisoning, while Konrad howled at his enemies, real and imagined.

Along with the ranting came wild schemes to make their property even more impregnable. Konrad decided he would replace their fence with solid walls, three metres high and topped with razor wire. He planned to install invisible trip-wires, formed by beams of infrared light that would set off alarms if intruders crossed into their property. He dreamed of packs of killer dogs that would sniff out and savage anyone who dared to approach them.

Francesca did not suggest there could be flaws in any of these ideas. Konrad did not take well to criticism. She gently reminded him what De La Rey had said. There was little chance of them being found. They had done as much as they could to protect themselves without drawing attention. The best thing to do was to carry on with their lives as normally as possible.

Konrad had screamed at Francesca for joining the ranks of traitors. She offered herself up to play 'our little game', knowing that she would pay the price for displeasing him, but hoping it might help him let off steam. Yet though Francesca endured punishments worse than any he had ever inflicted on her, Konrad awoke the next morning as bad-tempered as ever.

Now here he was again, restless and resentful, pacing and shouting, while she was bruised and battered, hardly able to move for all her aches and pains.

Francesca cracked. She walked across the living room and stood in her husband's path.

'Enough!' she screamed. 'I'm sick of this! You are nothing like the Führer! He was a greater man than you could ever be! And he really was surrounded by enemies. The Red Army were in Berlin. The only safe place was the bunker. But where are your enemies? Show me!' She swept an arm across the expanse of the windows. 'Can you see any enemies?'

Von Meerbach had stopped in his tracks when Francesca started shouting at him. He took three paces towards her. She did not flinch. He had slapped her across the face so many times that she had lost her fear.

But this time he did not slap her.

He clenched his right fist and punched her with all his strength, smashing her in the side of her face.

It felt as if a bomb had gone off inside her head. Her eyes saw flickering dots and flashes of light. Her ears were ringing. There was so much pain from so many places as she fell to the floor, barely conscious, dizzy, nauseous, unable to move or speak.

Francesca had no idea how long it took for her to push herself onto her elbows and look around. Her mouth was filled with blood. She spat it out and saw a tooth lying there, a flash of white amid the crimson mess on the cold marble floor.

She ran her tongue across her lips, feeling the swelling and tasting more blood from a surface cut, then felt around the inside of her mouth. Another of her teeth was loose. She raised a hand to her jaw and pressed it gently. The pain caused by the slightest touch was enough to tell her the bone was broken.

Konrad was looking down on her. She could tell that he knew he had gone too far. What he had done could never be undone, let alone forgiven.

'You coward,' she mumbled. 'You stinking, rotten, gutless coward.'

He stepped closer to her, near enough to kick her defenceless body.

'Go on then,' Francesca said. 'I can't stop you.'

Konrad glared at her. He turned away and stalked towards the windows, his back to her.

Now he looks at the view, she thought. *If it stops him having to look at me.*

She crawled to the nearest bathroom. She locked the door. In time she would gather the strength to stand up straight enough to look in the mirror and see what he had done to her.

Until then she would lie on the cold, unforgiving marble and wonder what had happened to her life to lead her to a fate as miserable as this.

From the moment they walked up to the check-in desk at the Nairobi Aerodrome, Saffron and Gerhard became Marlize and Herman. They spoke to one another in German and continued to do so in the departure lounge, on the flight via Johannesburg to Cape Town and through the customs and immigration process. Even when they first saw Joshua, they stayed in character. Only once they were in his car taking them into the city did they revert to their true identities and speak English again.

'I have a nice surprise for you, Gerhard,' Joshua said. 'I know how much you enjoy speed, what with being a pilot. And my father was telling me the other day how you still have the Mercedes sports car you drove as a young man.'

'He still drives it just as fast, too,' said Saffron.

'Then you'll appreciate the car I have procured for your use tonight.'

Joshua drove them to the modest hotel where Mr and Mrs Doll were booked in for the night. They checked in, took their luggage to their room and then went outside to meet Joshua. He drove them to one of Manny Ishmael's many properties, which the Israelis were using as their base and safe house.

Gerhard spotted the Jaguar as soon as they pulled up outside the safe house.

'Is that the one?' he asked as they stepped onto the pavement.

Joshua grinned. 'She's yours for the night.'

Gerhard ran his hands over the bodywork as he looked the car up and down. Had Saffron not been long used to her man's passion for machines that went fast, she might have been jealous.

'I have no interest in automobiles,' said Joshua. 'But this one's owner asked me to inform you that she – apparently his car is a female . . .'

'Of course,' Gerhard murmured.

'She is a 1950 Jaguar XK120, with handmade bodywork and a . . . let me get this right . . . A dual overhead-cam 3.4 litre XK engine, originally developing 160 horsepower, but subsequently modified – by your brother's garage, ironically – to more than 200 horsepower.'

'Racing specifications,' Gerhard nodded.

'If you say so. You are also invited to observe the chrome-plated wire wheels and Pirelli Cinturato radial tyres. Apparently both are the latest innovations.'

'They are. I'd like to meet the man who loaned you this. I think we'd get along.'

'As long as you return his car in one piece, I'm sure you would. But he also asked me to say, if you crash it, you'll have to buy him a new one.'

Gerhard laughed. 'I'd make the same demand if this was my car.'

'If it's so fast, don't you chaps want it?' Saffron asked Joshua.

'Very much, but there are six of us and this car only has two seats. But don't worry, our own vehicles are certainly not slow. In any case, if all goes well, we won't be needing to drive anywhere.'

'Why on earth not?'

Joshua smiled. 'Come inside, and all will be revealed.'

This is like the old days, Saffron thought, as she joined the seven men clustered round the dining-room table. A map had been spread on the table, marked with an assortment of arrows and crosses to show salient points and lines of movement.

Joshua stood at the head of the table. 'Listen up,' he said. 'We'll start with Konrad von Meerbach's present location.

'This map shows the city of Cape Town, and the Cape of Good Hope peninsula, to the south of the city. As you can see, it extends like a long, thin hook for about fifty kilometres from the city to its southernmost point at the Cape of Good Hope itself. To the west of the peninsula lie the waters of the Atlantic Ocean and to the east is False Bay, which is part of the Indian Ocean.'

Joshua had found a stick of bamboo that was being used to support a plant in the safe house garden. He used it as a pointer.

'Here,' he said, stabbing at an *X* marked on the map, about a quarter of the way up the eastern, False Bay side of the peninsula, 'is the property where Konrad and Francesca von Meerbach have lived for the past six or seven years.

'As you can see, it sits on the coast, south of Simon's Town. The property occupies a small parcel of land between the coast road and the seashore, with no other properties nearby. This provides von Meerbach with privacy, but it also means we can operate without fear of being overheard. It is worth noting that the coast road runs north-south for several kilometres in either direction without any turn-offs. Traffic on this stretch of road is not heavy, and virtually non-existent at night. Again, we are unlikely to be disturbed.

'The property is approximately twenty metres above the level of the sea, with a sheer rock face down to the water. Steps lead down to a jetty, where von Meerbach keeps a fast motor-boat. Clearly this boat is intended as a means of escape in case of emergency. Our first move, therefore, will be to secure the boat, cutting off that escape route.'

Saffron knew that all the Israelis in the room must have heard this account before, several times. She also knew that Joshua would be going over it, yet again, even if she and Gerhard were not there. The briefing had to be ingrained so deep into the minds of the mission personnel that every detail was locked into their brains.

Joshua continued. 'A few of our friends from our embassy have come down from Pretoria to keep an eye on the property over the past three days. The von Meerbachs have not left the place. He's not gone to work. She's not gone out to do any shopping or visit friends. There's no reason to believe they know we're here. But something's clearly not right.

'But let them worry about that. We will concentrate on our mission. Our mother ship is taking up a position six kilometres offshore, outside the three-mile limit of South African waters. At 02.30 tomorrow morning, the ship's cutter will be launched, with one crewman and two of our agents aboard.

At approximately one kilometre from the shore, our men will disembark from the cutter and paddle towards the shore, using a small, collapsible kayak.

'The moon is almost clear tonight. The weather forecast is good. There is only one jetty in the area. Our guys are confident that they can get to the jetty shortly before 03.00 and secure von Meerbach's boat. When they reach the house they will send a radio signal to us. The only way from the house to the jetty is down a set of stone steps. If the von Meerbachs try to make for the boat, they will be completely exposed on those steps. However, I have ordered the men not to shoot to kill. We want von Meerbach alive.

'Now to the land assault . . .'

The other men had been paying attention before, but now their concentration noticeably increased.

'We will work as two three-man teams, with Gerhard and Saffron as guides, observers and backup. To remind you, gentlemen, Saffron Courtney Meerbach has more than four years of wartime experience of commando and espionage operations. Anything we can do, she can do too.'

'It's all right, ma'am,' one of Joshua's men said. 'We've had women in the Defence Force since the day the state of Israel was formed. And these women . . . ay-yay-yay!'

Saffron joined in the laughter. Joshua continued.

'We will approach the target property from the north and south. Two vehicles, three men in each, cutting von Meerbach's escape route in either direction. I will come in from the north. Chaim –' Joshua glanced up at the man standing to his right – 'you bring your boys in from the south. Gerhard and Saffron, follow me. We will lay up a few hundred metres from our target and wait for the signal that the boys in the kayak have arrived safely before we move in.

'Let's assume we get to the property without incident . . .'

Joshua reached for a cardboard tube from which he extracted a rolled-up sheet of blue-grey paper. He spread it across the map and held the corners down with coffee cups.

'This is a copy of the master site-plan submitted to the planning authorities by Michel Schultz, alias Konrad von Meerbach. Note, there is one entrance from the road to the property, here . . .' He tapped at the gate. 'The fence and gate are constructed of steel supports holding steel wire mesh, topped with barbed wire. The gate is secured by means of a heavy chain, held by a padlock with a combination lock. We will cut the chain and enter through the gate.

'There are three ways in and out of the house. A front door, here, a back door which opens into the garage, here, and through the sliding windows that form the wall of the living room, here. We remain as silent as possible until we get to the house. I will take the front door with my team. Chaim, you and your men go in the back. Saffron and Gerhard, you stay on the road. We'll pick the locks if we can. But if the doors are bolted, we'll have to smash our way in with our battering rams.'

'Is the house alarmed?' Gerhard asked.

'Not that we know of. There's no sign of an alarm in the plans, no box on the outside of the house.'

'Hmm . . .' Gerhard murmured. 'My brother sees enemies everywhere. He'll want to know if anyone gets into his house, and he'll have a plan for when they do.'

'Including another way out,' Saffron said. 'I'm bothered by that gate. It's just . . . I don't know . . . too obvious.'

'Maybe,' Joshua conceded. 'But he can't have planned for what we are going to throw at him. You are the only people outside Israel who know that this unit even exists.'

'And we haven't told anyone,' said Saffron.

'Then we will have the element of surprise. But we have to move fast.' Joshua turned back to the contractors' plan. 'The master bedroom is on the first floor. We'll converge on that as quickly as we can. Ideally, I want to take them in the bedroom. Failing that, we'll flush them out and drive them towards the sea, where the boys at the boat will apprehend them.

'In either scenario, we will extract the von Meerbachs by sea. We use their boat to get them and us to the mother ship.

Once we cast off from shore, we fire a single red flare to indicate that we are on our way.'

'And what do Gerhard and I do under these circumstances?'

'When you see the flare, drive back here to the safe house and get some rest. In the morning, you will receive a telegram informing you that Herman's elderly mother has died. You will therefore have no option but to cut short your holidays and return home. Place the keys to the Jaguar in an envelope, addressed to "Mr Ishmael", and give that to the concierge. Then take a taxi to the airport and fly away.'

'That sounds fine,' Saffron said. 'But what are your contingency plans, in case you do not capture the targets?'

Joshua smiled. 'I was coming to that.'

He rolled the plan back up and returned it to the tube, so that the map was visible again.

'First scenario,' Joshua said. 'We get into the house, the von Meerbachs are there, but they fight it out to the end, or take the Adolf and Eva way out. In that case, if they die, we take photographs establishing their identities and deaths, then we leave exactly as before. This time, however, we will fire two flares in quick succession. We go back to the ship, you two drive to the hotel. Everything proceeds as before.

'But there is another possibility . . .' Joshua looked at the faces watching him. 'What if, by some chance, the von Meerbachs attempt to escape by land, rather than sea. Either they somehow get wind that we are coming, before we arrive, or they manage to evade us after we have entered their property. Konrad von Meerbach is a wealthy man. He may have made modifications to his property that do not appear on the official plans. He can certainly afford to do so.

'Let us suppose he somehow gets wind of our approach before we arrive. Our cars will be in radio contact with one another and with the boat team. If we're lucky, the boat boys will already be on site when the von Meerbachs break out. They will hear the noise of a car leaving the property and alert us. But they may not be there, so from the moment we get on the coast road, we have to be alert to any traffic on the road. There should be very little. Von Meerbach drives a black Mercedes, whose performance has been significantly upgraded. We do not want to get into a chase with it. Therefore, we will use our vehicles to block the road if possible. If not, Gerhard, we will be counting on you.'

'Don't worry. The day my brother drives faster than me will be the day I hand in my licence.'

'Why even worry about Konrad's Mercedes?' Saffron asked. 'Can't you just disable it, so he can't go anywhere?'

'I thought about that,' Joshua replied. 'But the car is in the garage, behind a locked door. The only way to get past that lock, from the outside of the building, would be to shoot it.'

'And that would wake up Konrad . . .'

'Exactly. But by the same token, that locked door makes it harder for Konrad to escape. Even if he has the key, it takes several seconds to unlock it before he can get in his car and start driving.'

Saffron nodded. 'That all makes sense.'

'Thank you, ma'am,' Joshua said, getting a chuckle from a couple of his men. 'But still, it's a risk. God knows how, but von Meerbach and his wife may just get to the car, and open the door, and get out, in which case, Gerhard, you have to catch him quickly, because the longer he stays away from us, the more choices he has. Let me show you on the map.'

Picking up his pointer again, he said, 'Coming out of his property, von Meerbach only has two options – right, or left. If he goes right, that takes him north to the city, via the coastal towns of Simon's Town and Fish Hoek, here, and the vineyards of Constantia, here. If he turns left, it's the scenic route. See how the road goes south along the coast to . . . ah . . .' Joshua peered at a name on the map and then said, 'Smitswinkel Bay, then turns back on itself, here.'

They followed Joshua's directions as the road took a hard right turn and continued across the tip of the peninsula, following the boundary of the Cape of Good Hope Nature Reserve and on up the Atlantic coast towards Cape Town.

'But remember,' Joshua concluded, 'it doesn't matter which route von Meerbach takes. The sooner we can get him, the better. We cannot let him get to the city. If he does, we've lost.'

'Message received and understood,' said Gerhard.

'Good . . . Okay everyone, make sure to eat and rest well over the remainder of the day. You won't be sleeping or eating tonight, that's for sure.'

As everyone went their separate ways, Saffron tapped Joshua's arm.

'Can I have a quick word?'

'Sure . . . Is there a problem?'

She shrugged, 'No . . . not yet. Your plan is fine. You've thought it through and dealt with every conceivable contingency. But one thing I learned in those years you were talking about – things always happen that no one had ever imagined.'

He frowned. 'Are you saying we should think of something better?'

'No. I'm saying that it doesn't matter what you think of, things will always go wrong. That's normal . . . and it needn't be the end of the world.'

Joshua nodded, thoughtfully. 'Thank you. You've told me the whole operation is likely to blow up in my face, and yet I somehow find that oddly reassuring.'

'Good. Now let's get some rest.'

Gerhard and Saffron were tired from their flight. They each got around three hours of deep sleep, enough to keep them awake and alert through the night. Joshua woke them shortly after seven in the evening. He seemed tense.

'Anything the matter?' Saffron asked.

'I'll let you know in an hour,' he replied.

Saffron had brought a small haversack containing all she'd need for the night's mission. She removed the clothes she'd worn as the tourist Marlize Doll and put on garments more suited to an undercover operation on a South African winter's night: a lightweight merino vest under a slim-fitting black polo neck jumper. Her trousers, also black, were made for a man. They possessed long legs so that her ankles were not bare, and pockets in which she could store essential items, rather than the useless, postage-stamp-sized excuses for pockets deemed sufficient for women's needs.

Her hair was pinned back and held in place by a black silk scarf. Her Beretta fitted neatly into one of the trouser pockets. Her black kidskin gloves were so fine that they did not impede her trigger finger. Gerhard was very similarly dressed, with the addition of a black woollen bomber jacket over his jumper.

'I'm getting old,' he'd grinned when they'd packed for the trip. 'I feel the cold more than I used to.'

Chaim whistled softly as Saffron and Gerhard joined the others for a light meal.

'Now why don't our Defence Force girls look that good?' he sighed.

Saffron smiled, taking the compliment. But her eyes were taking a good look at the men with whom she was about to go to work. They were all plainly in excellent physical condition, without a scrap of excess flesh on any of them. They were keyed up, as was only natural before the start of an operation, but she was pleased to see that the nerves were of the positive kind that heightens the competence of well-trained operatives, rather than the fear that induces panic and loss of discipline.

But, oh, they're all just boys, Saffron thought, for Joshua's men looked, if anything, even younger than him. But then she reminded herself that she had barely reached her twenties when she saw her first wartime action. *They're all old enough to have fought in the war against the Arabs*, she told herself. *Their commanders think they're competent to do the job. So let them do it.*

Joshua himself was doing his best to radiate an air of confidence and control, but Saffron could detect an undercurrent of restlessness and anxiety. Something was not going to plan. But what?

The phone in the property, fixed to the wall of the entrance hall, rang. He dashed to answer it. By the time he returned to the main room, no more than two minutes later, Joshua was a changed man.

'We're cleared to go,' he said. 'That was the guys watching the von Meerbach property. Shortly before five this afternoon, the count and his wife left the house and drove north on the Simon's Town road to Cape Town. That's why I've been jumpy. I thought they'd made a run for it and we'd missed them. But they're back on site. And we're going to get them.'

Von Meerbach had initially refused to let Francesca get any treatment for the jaw he'd broken. Sure, he'd say it was an accident and she would back him up. But it would only take one do-gooding doctor to call the police and God only knew what might happen after that, particularly now that De La Rey didn't have his back. Eventually, however, the swelling, bleeding and pain had become so severe that there was no alternative. Konrad called a fellow National Party member, who ran his own dental practice, promising him a new car if he treated Francesca out of hours and in complete secrecy.

'She fell and hit her head as she was stepping off our boat,' Konrad explained.

It was plainly a lie, and both men knew it, but it gave the dentist an excuse not to ask any more questions. He took an X-ray of her jaw and declared she had a single, clean break.

'It should heal itself,' the dentist said. 'I'll wire the jaw shut, so that the bone is not disturbed, and give you a prescription for some liquid codeine to sort out the acute pain, but you don't want to take it for more than three days. After that you can make do with paracetamol, taken either in liquid form or . . . ah . . . up the back passage.

'I'm afraid you won't be able to eat solid food for at least a month, Mrs Schultz. I would say a liquid diet will be very good for your figure, but you look delightful as you are. The good news for you, Mr Schultz, is that you can look forward to a period of peace and quiet. A wife who can't talk is every man's dream woman, a-ha-ha-ha!'

Francesca had returned home, dosed herself with codeine and taken to bed. But sleep would not come. Despite the painkiller, her jaw hurt if she lay in any position other than flat on her back. The inability to open her mouth was not just a discomfort; it made her feel nervous, even panicky. The dentist had advised her to keep a pair of small, sharp scissors in reach at all times, in case her nose became blocked and she had to open her mouth to breathe. And there were other bruises all over her body, constantly reminding her of Konrad's brutality.

Konrad had come up to bed at about midnight and amused himself by telling Francesca what a frigid, unattractive, stupid bitch she was, revelling in the fact that she could not answer back. He had then fallen fast asleep, leaving Francesca staring at the ceiling.

She started hearing noises. There was a ship out at sea. She looked at her bedside clock, which told her it was half-past two. Twenty minutes later there was a banging down by the jetty. As she was finally drifting off to sleep, there came a rattling at the gate.

It was three o'clock.

Francesca shook Konrad's shoulder and tried to express her alarm.

He growled, 'Shut your face, woman, or I'll break your nose.' He rolled over.

And then all hell broke loose.

The front door wasn't bolted. Joshua had no trouble forcing the lock. He stepped into the hallway. Suddenly his head was filled with the high-pitched ringing of an alarm bell, loud enough to wake the dead, let alone two people sleeping upstairs.

'Move! Move!' he shouted to his men as they raced into the living room. Chaim and his team arrived at the same time, coming in from the kitchen.

'Secure the ground floor!' Joshua shouted over the din of the alarm. 'We're going upstairs!'

Joshua didn't have a second to waste. He hurtled up the steps, two at a time. He reached the top, looked around to get his bearings and relate what he could make out in the near darkness to what he had seen on the plans.

The bedroom door was at the end of the corridor spread across the width of the house, taking full advantage of the sea view. Joshua ran down the corridor. He stopped at the door, long enough for his two men to catch up. He kicked open the door and charged in.

The room was empty, but the bed had been slept in. Joshua reached his hand under the blankets and could feel residual warmth. Someone had been sleeping there, only minutes, per-haps even seconds earlier.

But where have they gone?

'Check the wardrobes!' Joshua ordered his men.

He went to look in the en suite bathroom.

There was no one there. The wardrobes were clear.

'Check the other rooms,' Joshua said, leading his men into the corridor.

There were two more bedrooms and a large bathroom. Joshua took the nearest bedroom and directed one of his men to each of the other two rooms.

'Clear!' he shouted.

'Clear! . . . Clear!' came the other men's voices.

Joshua led his men downstairs. Chaim was standing in the middle of the living room.

'Any sign of them?' he asked his boss.

'They were here,' Joshua said. 'The bed was warm. But they weren't upstairs when we got there. Dammit! The bastard's vanished into thin air!'

Joshua slammed his fist into his palm in frustration. Some-where close by an engine started up with a growl of raw power, the brake was loosed and Konrad von Meerbach's Mercedes went roaring into the night.

*

Gerhard had been right about his brother. The same hidden staircase that ran downstairs from the living room to the cellar ran upstairs to the bedroom as well. Just as the door from the living room was concealed behind a bookcase, the one from the bedroom lay behind one of the wardrobes.

Konrad had time to get through it, dragging Francesca along, closing the wardrobe and stairway doors as he went. He wrapped one arm around Francesca's slender frame and carried her down the stairs to his dungeon.

Francesca punched and kicked out, but her blows bounced off her husband or hit the rough concrete walls, adding to her injuries.

'Listen to me,' Konrad hissed, when they reached the bottom. 'You have a choice. Either you come with me, no fuss, no complaints. Or I leave you here and you starve to death because no one will ever know this place exists and they'll never find you.'

Francesca was tempted. Death seemed preferable to one more minute with Konrad. But not starving to death, alone in this concrete dungeon.

'Get dressed,' Konrad said.

He had thought of everything. Years earlier, anticipating that they might one day have to get out at night, straight from their beds, he had told Francesca to put out two sets of clothes in zipped plastic bags: a pair of slip-on loafers, trousers and a pullover for each of them. There were also two getaway bags. One was a small, light holdall containing washkits and underwear. The other was a briefcase, heavy with gold coins hidden in its base, which also contained two more sets of passports, a bag of uncut diamonds, five thousand dollars in cash and bearer bonds to the value of a further half-million dollars. They could get anywhere in the world and live in comfort for the rest of their lives.

Konrad had made them practise their quick-change routines. They could do it in seconds. Francesca put on her clothes, wincing as she pulled the sweater down over her battered face. She took the light holdall. Konrad held on to the money bag. He retrieved a loaded Browning Hi-Power pistol, and four more of its 13-round clips. Those extra bullets allowed the Hi-Power to keep firing after an opponent wielding almost any other pistol had stopped to reload. And there was nothing Konrad liked better in a fight than an unfair advantage.

He ran to the end of the cellar, past his cabinets of memorabilia and the instruments whose capacity to hurt Francesca had brought him so much pleasure. And her, Konrad thought as he left them behind. She'd wanted it too.

He reached up towards the ceiling and pulled down an extendable metal ladder.

'Climb!' he told Francesca, pointing the way up the ladder with his gun.

This, too, had been rehearsed on countless occasions. Francesca dropped the bag and went up the ladder. There was a hatch at the top. She opened it.

Konrad had sent her first because if anyone was up there when the hatch opened, Francesca would be the one who got shot.

The hatch was a simple piece of wood that fitted into the escape hole. A hinged door would have been much easier to move. But it would also be easier to slam back down, and Konrad had not wanted that temptation in Francesca's way.

He was glad of his foresight as he passed the two bags to her, for she would have shut him in if she could have done so. He raced up the ladder, carrying the money bag, and ran for the car.

Heedless of her discomfort, Konrad shoved Francesca into the passenger seat and slammed the door. He ran to the other side of the car, got in and retrieved the set of keys he kept attached to a magnet on the side of the driver's footwell. He turned the ignition. The engine started up first time, as always. He let off the handbrake, engaged the gear, flattened the accelerator and sent the Mercedes roaring straight at the door of the garage.

The reinforced radiator smashed into what appeared to be solid wood, but was actually just a sheet of ply, fitted to a pine frame. As the Mercedes went through it like a cannonball, von Meerbach's face split into a triumphant grin. Once again, his world had fallen apart around him. And once again he'd escaped.

'Damn!' Saffron had muttered as the six Israelis made their way through the gate towards the house. 'Joshua's made a mistake. I should have spotted it from the start.'

'How so?' Gerhard asked.

'He's not left anyone covering the gate.'

'Isn't that why we're here?'

'Yes, but there should be at least two more men on the ground, to stop an escape before Konrad and Francesca even leave the property.'

'I thought they had every exit covered.'

'Yes, every exit they know about. But what if there are others?'

'Well, in that case, let's do something about that,' Gerhard said.

He drove the Jaguar across the road so that it covered the gate, with the passenger seat closest to the house.

'Now you can fire at them if they try to get out this way,' he told Saffron.

'Yes, and they'll run straight into me.'

'Then I'll get out of the way. I do know about evasive manoeuvres.'

'Let's hope so.'

Saffron watched Joshua go up to the front door. She saw him open it. And then she and Gerhard heard the alarm sound.

'Oh hell!' Saffron muttered. 'Here we go.'

She got out her Beretta and wound down the window. Ten seconds went by and nothing happened. The ten seconds became thirty . . . almost a minute. The chill of the night made Saffron give a little shiver.

'Would you like—' Gerhard began, reaching into his jacket, but then the door of the garage seemed to explode. The sound of a high-powered engine roared like a lion in the night and headlights cut through the blackness.

Saffron felt her stomach tense. It could only be Konrad's car, and it was coming straight for them. The rounds from her small-calibre revolver would bounce off its bodywork like peas off an elephant. She'd have to aim for the lights or the tyres.

The Merc was seconds away. The lights were shining in her eyes, almost blinding her.

Gerhard had turned on the engine of the Jaguar, ready to get out of the way.

Suddenly, the headlights weren't shining in Saffron's eyes. They'd vanished. Dazzled, she tried to make out what was happening.

She heard a clanging sound. A section of the fence had disappeared and two beams of white light, followed by a huge black shadow, passed across her field of vision. The Mercedes raced through the hole that had appeared in front of it. There was more clattering as the Mercedes drove over the fencing that had fallen to the ground.

The beams turned ninety degrees until they faced back down the road, towards the Jaguar. They started moving closer and as they passed, Gerhard slammed the Jaguar into gear, raced forward and immediately wrenched the car around, with the tyres screeching and smoking in a one-eighty-degree turn.

He too was facing down the road, pointing south, in the same direction as the Mercedes.

Gerhard turned to Saffron and she saw a predatory grin.

'Right,' he said, 'let's see how fast this car is.'

The Jaguar hurtled down the road. Every time Gerhard changed gear, Saffron felt a punch in the back as another surge of power was engaged. The speedometer moved from zero to sixty miles an hour in the blink of an eye, and it kept moving until it passed a hundred. Gerhard never seemed rushed; his handling of the car was smooth and controlled.

They were gaining on their quarry. Saffron could see the red pinpricks of the rear lights on Konrad's Mercedes and the beam of his headlights on the road ahead. The Merc turned hard right and then vanished.

'That's the hairpin bend where the road turns back up towards the Atlantic coast,' she said. 'You'll need to watch out.'

Gerhard waited until the turn was almost upon them. He braked a lot later, harder and for a shorter time than Saffron would have done. Then he started accelerating again, even as he was pulling the car round a bend so tight they almost doubled back on themselves.

The Jaguar was rapidly picking up speed when Saffron shouted 'Slow down!' to make herself heard over the roar of the engine and the rushing of the wind.

Gerhard looked at her, shrugged, and did as he was told. Then he understood.

The road ahead was empty. There were no lights anywhere.

'They've disappeared,' Saffron said.

V on Meerbach had considered every permutation of available routes away from his property. He knew where opportunities to lose a pursuer could be found. And one of them came after the switchback bend at Smitswinkel Bay. A left-hand turning led onto a dirt track that ran across the nature reserve to Cape Point. The track was more than four miles long, but von Meerbach had no intention of going further down it than was necessary.

He turned as quickly and sharply as he dared. The Mercedes slewed from side to side as the tyres fought for grip on the dusty, pebble-strewn surface. Francesca was taken by surprise. The car had no safety belts. She was thrown hard against her husband's shoulder, then back again towards the door, banging her head.

The pain of the impact against her broken jaw was excruciating, a lightning bolt of agony inside her head worse than anything she had ever known. It took her a few seconds to realise that the pain now had a second source, for her nose was in agony too. As new wounds were added to the old, blood was pouring into her mouth and down the back of her throat. Francesca started to cry. She tried to sniff. And nothing happened.

'Stop snivelling,' Konrad snapped, unaware of the look of panic that had just flashed across his wife's face.

He had turned off the headlights. His mind was fixed on getting the car to a point he knew: a slight turn that passed behind a bush that would be more than adequate to hide a black car at night.

He would wait until his pursuers had gone by, then sneak back onto the main road and head in the opposite direction, past his house and on to Simon's Town, Fish Hoek and the city.

First von Meerbach had to find the bush.

It was somewhere close by. He knew it was. He had scouted the area in daylight and made a mental note of its position. But in the early hours of the morning, with dawn almost three hours away, he could not find the damn thing.

Francesca started coughing, the sound muffled by her closed and blood-filled mouth, like a trumpet by a mute. Still, it was enough to infuriate her husband.

'Shut up!' von Meerbach shouted. 'Can't you see I'm trying to concentrate!'

She paid no attention and gave a few feeble punches against his arm.

Von Meerbach swatted her away with his left hand. He could not see the damn bush.

Francesca threw herself at her husband, jolting him so hard that he wrenched the steering wheel to the right. The car ran across the road and onto the surrounding earth before Konrad braked and it came to a stop.

He grabbed Francesca and threw her away from him, slamming her into the door frame. Only then, as he looked at her for the first time and saw her frantically clawing at her mouth, did he get the message she'd been desperately trying to convey.

Her nose was blocked. Her mouth was wired shut. Von Meerbach saw blood, as black as oil in the near-darkness, seeping between her lips. She could not breathe. She was choking to death.

Von Meerbach's planning had allowed for every contingency. But he had not anticipated a wife who could not breathe unless her jaw wires were cut by a pair of nail scissors. Nor had Francesca thought to grab the pair lying on her bedside table as von Meerbach manhandled her towards the secret escape-door in the back of the wardrobe.

So now she was suffocating. And there was nothing anyone could do about it.

Frantically, von Meerbach grabbed hold of his wife's face and tried to wrench her jaws apart by sheer brute force, but as her limbs thrashed wildly in response to the excruciating torture he was inflicting on her, the dentist's wiring remained as firm as ever.

Von Meerbach felt helpless, impotent. That made him angry. And his fury was directed at Francesca because this was her fault. She was wrecking his getaway, thrashing around and dying when he wanted to be hiding the car and waiting for the chance to escape.

She was grabbing him, glaring at him with terrified eyes, making feeble, wordless mewling sounds, knowing that her life was coming to an end.

Her death could only be a minute away, a couple at most, but von Meerbach couldn't wait. He had placed his gun in the map pocket attached to the door beside him, in case he had to fire at his pursuers.

He reached inside, pulled out the gun and placed it on Francesca's forehead. Her eyes widened, pleading. She tried to scrabble backwards, away from the gun.

Von Meerbach fired.

The bullet entered the middle of Francesca's forehead, blowing out the back of her skull and smashing a hole in the window behind her.

Konrad von Meerbach had played a hand in the deaths of countless thousands of innocent people. He had been present when hundreds more, including his own brother, were tortured. But he had never spent a day on a front line. He had never killed another human being in cold blood.

Now he had murdered his own wife.

Von Meerbach opened his door and flopped out of it, onto his knees on the russet earth of the nature reserve, and threw up. He was kneeling there, his hands on the ground, his head hung low, when he heard the sound of a highly tuned sports car engine.

It was coming closer.

Von Meerbach saw the lights coming towards him and realised that the plan he had worked on for years, and honed over countless hours, was falling apart by the second.

Saffron had thought about the empty road. She considered what von Meerbach might have done. She pictured the map that Joshua had laid out on the dining table. She remembered a dotted line running down from the road. And then, approximately ten seconds after Gerhard had brought the Jaguar to a halt, she said, 'Turn the car around.'

Gerhard executed a swift three-point turn.

'Now what?' he asked.

'Go back. But slowly. Look for a turn on the right. It'll probably be unmarked.'

They found the turn.

'I think he's down there,' Saffron said. 'Waiting for us to get far enough away that he can sneak out again and go back the way we came.'

'But Joshua and his guys will still be there, blocking his route,' Gerhard said.

'Not if he hangs around long enough to let them follow us and go by.'

'Okay, let's try it. All or nothing . . . Lights out?'

Saffron nodded.

Gerhard rolled the Jaguar onto the dirt track and drove forward slowly. A minute went by as they crawled along. Gerhard began to increase the pace as his eyes adjusted to the absence of the lights and his night vision improved. But there was no sign of Konrad's car.

They heard a single sharp, explosive crack.

Gerhard stopped the car. 'Gunfire?' he asked.

'Yes, but not at us,' Saffron replied. She thought for a second and realised there was only one possibility. 'Oh, Jesus . . . has he killed Chessi?'

Gerhard waited a few more seconds, but there was no second shot.

'Lights on,' said Saffron. 'Let's go.'

They saw the car barely fifteen seconds later, and the figure on his knees beside it.

They saw Konrad realise that they were almost on him and leap back into his car. They were no more than twenty yards away when the Mercedes started moving, and almost on its bumpers before Konrad could pick up speed. And then they were off.

The two cars sped down the single-lane track. Konrad could see the road ahead of him, and he knew it well enough to feel confident about the twists and turns as it crossed the bush towards the cape. Gerhard could only react to the movement of the car ahead, and the task was made harder by the dust churned up by the Mercedes' wheels, which blinded and choked him and Saffron in their open-top car.

'Back up!' Saffron shouted over the roar of the Jag's engine and the clattering of the tyres and suspension over the rough track surface.

Gerhard glanced at her as if to ask why.

'It's all right,' Saffron assured him. 'He's trapped. This is where Africa ends.'

Joshua Solomons and his men had run to their cars and set off on the road heading south. Their saloons were not as fast as the customised machines they were chasing. They were half a minute behind the two von Meerbach brothers when their own pursuit got underway, and lost another fifteen by the time they reached the turn at Smitswinkel Bay. As they took the hairpin bend and looked at the long, straight stretch of road ahead of them, the Mercedes and Jaguar had disappeared.

Joshua brought his two cars to rest, just as Saffron and Gerhard had done. He had a smaller pocket map in his car and was trying to work out what had happened when he heard the gunshot. It came from the nature reserve, to the south of the road. There was nothing there but open country, all the way to the Cape of Good Hope, and beyond it open sea to Antarctica. But someone was firing a gun at a quarter past three in the morning.

'They're in that direction, somewhere.' He looked at the map. He too saw the dotted line that marked the dirt road. 'There,' he said, stabbing at the paper. 'That's where we go.'

'I know where Konrad's going,' Saffron said. 'There's a disused lighthouse on Cape Point, at the top of the cliff. Perfect place for a final stand. Anyone trying to get there has to go along a causeway, uphill. It can't be much more than six feet wide, eight at most. They're sitting ducks for anyone who's already at the top.'

Gerhard asked. 'Is there a drop off the side of the cliff?'

'Eight hundred and fifty feet, straight down to the sea.'

'If he thinks he's losing, Konrad will jump. So how do you get to this lighthouse?'

'There's a bus called the Flying Dutchman that gets you part of the way in the daytime, but at night you have to climb.'

'Eight hundred and fifty feet uphill . . . huh!'

'There are steps to make it a little easier.'

Ahead of them the ground rose to a sharp, triangular hill that looked like a miniature alpine peak, more than a thousand feet high.

'Where's the lighthouse?' Gerhard asked.

'The other side of that hill,' Saffron said. 'Look where Konrad's going . . .'

Gerhard saw the Mercedes following the road as it curved around the base of the hill.

'There's a car park below Cape Point where you can catch the bus or start up the steps. It's uphill from there,' Saffron told him.

'My doctor wouldn't like me chasing Konrad up those steps,' Gerhard replied. A mischievous smile crossed his face as he said, 'Hold on tight when I tell you to. And when I say jump, get out fast, and run like hell. I'll be right behind you.'

The Jaguar picked up speed. Saffron liked the idea of going into battle, side by side with her man. And she had absolute confidence that he could deliver the plan that he had in mind, whatever it might be.

The Jaguar steadily caught up with the Mercedes. Konrad must have spotted the headlights looming in his rear-view mirror because he sped up. The two cars were racing across the bumpy surface of the track and, as they rounded the pointed hill, Konrad's destination became visible.

Cape Point lay ahead of them, a black shadow rising into the deep purple sky, and at its top the stubby tower of the old lighthouse. The open expanse of the car park came into view. At the far end of it stood the restaurant that catered to tourists visiting the lighthouse, boarded up for the night. To the right of the restaurant were the steps at the foot of the climb.

Konrad turned the Mercedes towards the steps.

The instant Gerhard spotted the change of course, he flattened the accelerator and sent the Jaguar shooting forward, coming up behind the Mercedes, then swinging out and pulling alongside it.

Konrad didn't slow down.

Gerhard was going faster.

The two brothers were playing chicken, heading for a wall of solid rock, neither willing to give way.

But Gerhard was the faster driver in the better car. He overtook the Mercedes, passing by its passenger side. Saffron glanced across, and saw the blown-out window.

The Jaguar was past the Mercedes, and the hill was so close it filled her entire field of vision.

'Hold on!' Gerhard yelled.

He pulled the handbrake hard with his left hand and yanked the wheel clockwise with his right. The Jaguar screamed in protest as it turned in an instant through ninety degrees. Saffron was buffeted from side to side, but clung on for dear life.

Gerhard stamped on the brake pedal, bringing the car to an emergency stop in front of the onrushing radiator grille of Konrad's Mercedes.

'Jump!' Gerhard shouted, but Saffron was already head first over the passenger door and scrabbling up the first step.

Gerhard grabbed hold of the top of the windscreen, vaulted over it and onto the car's bonnet.

Konrad made a desperate attempt to brake.

Gerhard leaped again, over the nose of the Jaguar. He stumbled as he landed, hitting the ground hard and winding himself.

The Mercedes slowed down, but Konrad had left it too late. With a deafening, screeching bombardment of steel against steel, his car piledrived into the side of the Jaguar, almost snapping it in two. Konrad's body was thrown against the steering wheel, then slumped back against his seat.

'Run like hell,' Gerhard had said, and for once, Saffron was following his orders, racing up the steps, not looking behind her. Maybe he'd be behind her. Maybe he had another plan. Sometimes you just had to trust that the other person knew what they were doing.

Konrad survived the impact, but at the cost of a punctured lung and half a dozen fractured ribs. To his right, through a gaping hole in the shattered windscreen, he could make out the dark mass of his brother's body, still flat out on the ground. He was no threat in his physical state. But his wife was lethal and out there somewhere. And she was a highly trained operative. Konrad decided to concentrate on her.

His nose was broken, and blood was streaming from a deep cut on his forehead. Yet brute strength and willpower, fuelled by furious hatred, gave Konrad the energy to punch open the door and pull himself out of the car. He got to his feet, his gun in his right hand, resting his left for support on the side of the car and looked around in the gloom.

Up the hillside, Konrad could hear the sound of the woman's breathing and her feet on the steps as she ran away up the hill. Then he saw his brother move. Suddenly the woman could wait. As Konrad lifted his gun he had a closer, better target.

Gerhard got to his knees, gasping for breath. He'd been planning to follow Saffron up the steps. Now here he was in the dirt, facing up the hill, parallel to the crashed Mercedes to his left. He glanced across at the car and saw the door burst open, saw Konrad emerge holding a gun, less than ten metres away, and knew at once that he'd been spotted.

Dragging oxygen into his lungs, Gerhard lifted his knees off the ground, like a sprinter getting set for a race.

Saffron was concentrating on putting distance between her and Konrad's gun. She was counting in her head. When she got to ten, she'd stop and look around. '*Seven . . .*'

Konrad lifted his arm and, as he twisted his head to look at him, Gerhard could see the gun in his brother's hand, like a deadly starter's pistol. He could see his brother's face twist into a hellish grimace. But it was one of triumph, not agony.

Gerhard sprang forward.

Konrad fired. At that range he couldn't miss. His first shot hit his brother in the chest, spinning his body round and leaving him flat out on the ground, unmoving. He was dead, but Konrad wanted to make sure. He wanted to grind Gerhard's head into the ground. He took aim again and . . .

Saffron heard the sound of the bullet. Only one man could have fired it. Only one man could be the target. Without thinking, without letting herself feel a thing, she spun around, raised her gun and pulled the trigger.

Konrad heard the crack of a small-calibre pistol and in the same instant the clang of a bullet hitting the crumpled bodywork of the Mercedes. The vibration of the impact was barely a centimetre away from his hand.

Konrad ducked down behind the open car door, wincing at the shocks of pain that the sudden movement sent through his shattered ribcage as another round fizzed overhead, smashing through glass where he had been standing. He took a couple of painful breaths, calming himself. The Browning's unusually large magazine gave him the advantage. She had already used two rounds. He still had all but two of his.

Sooner or later, though, the men who had broken into his house would work out where he had gone. It was imperative to deal with the traitor and his whore as fast as possible, so he could get away before the others arrived. That meant taking a risk, leaving the shelter of the car to gain the offensive.

He ran towards the back of the Mercedes, crouched as low as he could manage, agonised by every step, but ignoring the pain. Saffron fired twice more, again coming within a whisker of hitting him. But she was having to shoot downhill, with the moonlight to provide visibility. His body would be a shadow moving alongside another. And she had spent four shots discovering how hard a target he was.

Konrad wanted to get around the back of the Mercedes, then dash for the shelter of the Jaguar, which lay side-on to the hill from which the Courtney woman was shooting. He hid behind the boot of the Mercedes, and steeled himself for the sprint. It was no more than three or four paces, but he would be out in the open. He had no choice; he had to do it.

Konrad ran. There was no sound of gunfire. He'd left himself exposed, but she did not shoot at him.

The silence unnerved Konrad almost more than the bullets that had narrowly missed him. *What is she playing at? Why didn't she open fire?*

Saffron had carried her Beretta through six years of war and it had never let her down. She had fired hundreds of rounds on her training range at Cresta Lodge. She had stripped it, checked it, oiled it and reassembled it before she left for South Africa, as she had done before other potentially dangerous missions.

But now, when she needed it most, when Gerhard was lying dead on the ground and his killer was on the loose, her beloved little pistol jammed.

Saffron fought back the emotions that beat at her mind like storm waves against the shore. She couldn't give in to the grief of losing Gerhard. She couldn't let her concentration be distracted by the anger and frustration of being left without a weapon at the precise moment she needed it most. All that mattered was making Konrad pay for what he had done. She just had to think. Fast.

She had four rounds left in her magazine, but they were of no use to her now. And Konrad von Meerbach had a gun in his hand that he had not fired once in her direction.

Somehow she had to deal with him. And that meant getting close enough for unarmed combat. As close as she had been to Werner. With Konrad's gun in the small of her back, if needs be. In the distance, Saffron could hear the engines of approaching cars. The Israelis were on their way.

If she could hear them, so could Konrad. She knew he was not in the business of taking prisoners. But he might at least stop and think about taking a hostage. In his eyes, she might yet be his ticket out of here. *Fine then, give him that ticket . . .*

Saffron put her gun back in her trouser pocket and crept down the hillside itself rather than the steps, until she found a scrap of cover behind a small bush, no more than fifteen paces away from Konrad.

She called out, 'My gun has jammed. I can't shoot. I surrender.'

As if to prove her helplessness, she threw the useless gun through the air towards him.

Konrad was not in the hostage business either. He fired in the direction the gun had come from.

Saffron leaped to one side. She landed awkwardly, lost her footing and twisted her right ankle. The sudden pain made her cry out, a stifled yelp.

Konrad knew exactly where Saffron was. She was hobbled, on her knees, unable to put any weight on her injured foot.

She tried to crawl away, but Konrad came after her. His luck had suddenly changed. His brother was dead and the pride of the Courtney family was at his mercy. For years he had dreamed of this moment, imagining the insults with which he would humiliate Saffron before he killed her. But now that the moment had come, he had no breath to spare for speeches. His movements were awkward. The pain from his injuries was unceasing. He had to wipe away the blood that was streaming down his forehead into his eyes. But his purpose was merciless.

He was going to get close enough to his brother's wife that he could not miss, and then he was going to put enough bullets in her to make sure that she was a pulverised mess.

Saffron saw the lumbering bulk coming towards her like a wounded bear. Konrad was breathing heavily and with difficulty, but he had a weapon in his hand. She suddenly realised that she was terrified, mortally petrified in a way that she had not been since she was a seven-year-old girl, watching her mother dying. Then she had been horrified by her mother's death. Now it was the prospect of her own demise that was sending Saffron's pulse racing and convulsing her guts.

Konrad raised the gun and aimed at her. Saffron threw dust at his face, but the dirt blew away as Konrad twisted from it.

Konrad returned his aim. The mask of blood across his face was split by a spiteful smile as he prepared for the kill.

Then, out of nowhere, there came a scuffling sound and a sudden shout that made Konrad turn to his right. He fired the gun, but not in Saffron's direction.

A body came flying through the air and hit the side of Konrad's legs above the knees.

Konrad crashed to the ground. Saffron caught a glimpse of Gerhard's face as he scrabbled to his feet and dropped astride Konrad's body, pinning him down.

Her mind was spinning. She had barely let herself feel any grief for Gerhard's death, and now he was here, looking her in the eye for an instant, then turning his attention back to his brother.

Konrad had bullied and humiliated Gerhard when they were boys. He had done everything in his power to ruin his life as an adult. He had caused him to be imprisoned and watched with delight as he had been tortured and degraded in the filth of Sachsenhausen. And now Gerhard was letting four decades of pent-up rage loose on his tormentor, hitting him again and again.

Finally, the storm of rage blew itself out. Gerhard sat up, his chest heaving. Konrad lay beneath him, battered into submission. His eyes were swollen shut, his nose shattered, his mouth a shapeless pulp. One of his puffed-up eyelids opened a fraction. He turned his head and spat a gob of saliva and blood onto the dirt.

'Is that the best you can do, little brother?' he croaked.

Gerhard smiled. 'No,' he said, calmly. He looked at Konrad, took aim and hit him one last time. 'That is.'

But Konrad could not hear him. He was out cold.

Gerhard rolled Konrad's body over until he was face down.

'Saffron, are you all right?'

'I think I may have broken my ankle, but what about you? I thought—'

'Yes, me too . . . Let's deal with Konrad and then I'll explain.' Gerhard helped her up.

'Take my scarf,' Saffron said, removing it from her head and shaking her hair free. 'Silk is very strong, ideal for tying up a prisoner's wrists. Your belt will do for his ankles.'

Gerhard trussed Konrad up, then went back to Saffron, draped her right arm across his shoulder and helped her down the hill.

'So?' she asked when they got to the bottom. 'Why aren't you dead?'

Gerhard smiled and reached up to the left-hand chest pocket of his blouson. Now that she looked closely, Saffron could see that there was a ragged tear in the fabric, running right across the pocket. Gerhard pulled out the metal flask he'd been given at Schloss Meerbach.

'Say a prayer of thanks to Herr Schinkel and his boys – and to the finest von Meerbach steel.'

They both looked at the flask. There was a long dent, exactly comparable to the tear in the fabric.

'The round must have hit me at an angle and deflected off the metal,' Gerhard said.

'It wouldn't have deflected off your ribs,' Saffron said quietly. 'It would have gone straight through your chest.'

'I thought it had, to be honest. The impact sent me flying. Then I realised I was alive, and I heard you calling out to Konrad.' He gave Saffron a light kiss on the cheek. 'Sorry I took so long.'

'No need to apologise. Your timing was perfect. But where's Francesca?' She remembered the sound of the single shot. 'Oh Jesus, what has he done to her?'

They made their way to the crashed cars. They found Francesca inside the Mercedes.

'That filthy bastard shot his own wife,' Gerhard said.

Saffron looked at the gruesome ruins of Francesca's face and thought of the sweet, rather nervous girl she had met on the first train journey to boarding school. 'Oh, Chessi, I'm sorry . . .' She turned her despairing eyes towards Gerhard. 'It's our fault, you know, all of this. None of it would have happened without us.'

Gerhard took her in his arms. He didn't say anything. He knew how Saffron was feeling. Chessi von Schöndorf had been his fiancée and Saffron's friend. Saffron should have been maid of honour at their wedding. He thought of the Francesca he had loved, and the way her now unseeing eyes had lit up with joy at the sight of him. And then he and Saffron had met, neither knowing the other's connection to Francesca. They had fallen in love and, with true love's unblinking ruthlessness, had put their need for one another ahead of their duty to her.

The consequences of that decision had played out over the years since, and now they had reached their conclusion.

'It's not all our fault, my darling,' Gerhard murmured. 'She chose to be with Konrad. He was the devil who took her to hell . . . But yes, we started it, and we have to live with that.'

Joshua Solomons and his men arrived less than two minutes later. Joshua dealt with the situation with a calm authority that belied his youth.

'We'll take your brother with us to the ship, as we planned. We anticipated that he might be wounded. There's a military doctor on board, he's used to dealing with badly injured men.'

He looked at Saffron. 'He can check out your leg, too.'

'Aren't we going back to Cape Town?' she asked.

'No, it's an unnecessary risk. We'll go up the coast and put you ashore in Mombasa. Don't worry about the chaos here. We've got a few hours before anyone arrives in the morning, and our friends in Cape Town can tidy everything away.'

'Can your friends see to it that the countess's body is well treated and returned to her family in Germany, please?' Gerhard asked. 'I can give them the necessary details. They can send me the bill.'

'Of course. But your brother can pay for his wife's funeral. My men found this in the car.'

Joshua handed Gerhard the briefcase. There was a spattering of blood across its black leather surface: Francesca's blood, Gerhard realised.

'My father told me that your brother had stolen a great deal from your family firm,' Joshua said. 'I think we may have recovered some of that money. Several hundred thousand US dollars, by my rough estimate.'

'I don't want it – it's not right.' Gerhard managed a weak smile. 'You can spend some of it to buy your friend a new Jaguar. I made a mess of that one. As for the rest, I would like it to go to any organisation that helps Jewish victims of the Nazis, and their families. I will leave it to your government to select them.'

'You don't have to do this, Gerhard.'

'Yes, I do. My family has a debt to honour. But can you do one thing for me in return?'

'It would be my honour.'

'Make sure that when my brother is tried, there is one more charge added to the list. He murdered his wife and he should pay for it.'

G erhard and Saffron were home within the week. A few days later, the Israelis formally announced the capture of the former SS general Count Konrad von Meerbach, who was accused of crimes against humanity and the murder of his wife. The minister who provided this information to Israel's parliament, the Knesset, revealed that the prosecution would be presenting detailed documentary evidence that would establish the prominent role the accused had played in the planning, construction and management of the Nazi death camps, and the personal delight he had taken in torturing individual victims. Nevertheless, he added, the accused would receive the kind of scrupulous, unbiased trial that he had denied his own victims and would, of course, be allowed to mount his own defence.

The same announcement expressed the government's profound gratitude for the help provided by the accused's brother, Gerhard Meerbach, who would be giving his own testimony for the prosecution. Herr Meerbach, the minister said, had risked his life to help a Jewish family escape Nazi Germany. He was to be given the formal title of 'Righteous among the nations' and placed on the roll of honour at Israel's newly opened Yad Vashem memorial to the murdered six million.

The story of the evil brother and the good, a tale as old as Cain and Abel, sparked the imagination of the world's news media. That Gerhard should be praised for his humanity, even as Konrad languished in a prison cell, was seen as a symbol of the possibility of redemption and goodness, even in the midst of unspeakable evil.

Gerhard regarded the attention as entirely undeserved and retreated to Lusima, happy to hide away in the Courtney kingdom, without a telephone to connect Cresta Lodge with the outside world.

He, Saffron and the children were living in a private paradise. But even there, the war intruded in the deep rumble that echoed across the savannah and against the hillsides as the RAF's four-engined Lincoln bombers flew overhead, and the distant sound of man-made thunder as their bombs rained down on the Mau Mau's positions in the forested hills of the Aberdare range.

'I hate it!' said Saffron to Gerhard one day, as they stood side by side, his arm around her shoulder, hers around his waist, watching half a dozen bombers fly over Lusima, their silhouettes black against the sun like grotesque birds of prey. 'Just think of the money those raids cost. Father was telling me the other day that the government is currently spending ten thousand pounds for every terrorist killed.'

'Why don't they just spend the money on the Kikuyu?' Gerhard asked. 'It would be a cheaper way of winning them over, and more effective too.'

'Instead we're sticking tens of thousands of Kikuyu in detention camps. I mean, really, what the hell are we doing, locking people up because they belong to a particular tribe?'

'Ah, yes . . . I do know about that.'

'Exactly! And that's what drives me mad. We fought a war to rid the world of tyranny and now look at us. And did you see the story in the *Standard* this morning? Apparently, Government House is about to announce a new anti-crime initiative. From now on there doesn't have to be a proper signed, written record of an accused man's confession. If a police officer testifies that he has confessed, that's good enough. But it's not just that. We're censoring the African newspapers, banning the native population from driving at night, punishing whole villages because one man has been accused of a crime. What does that remind you of?'

There was no need for Gerhard to answer the question.

'I can't bear to see this being done by my country, in my name,' Saffron said, sounding almost more sorrowful than angry. 'It's the camps I can't stand. The idea that we might be creating more Dachaus, more Sachsenhausens . . .'

'It's unspeakable. But what do you want to do about it?'

'I don't know.'

'Because you know what the answer will be if you go to Government House and start arguing with the governor and his staff . . .'

'Apart from, "Calm down, you silly, hysterical woman"?'

'They'll point out that they didn't start it. They'll say, "The Mau Mau have created an emergency and we're trying to deal with it." If you want to make an effective protest, you need facts – and an ally inside the governor's staff would help.'

'A friend at court . . .'

'Exactly.'

'I think my pa may know someone . . . He mentioned a young man he met at some cricket match he and Harriet went to. I'll look him up. And in the meantime, I promised Wangari I'd go and see her at the clinic. She wants to show me proof of what our people have been up to in the screening centres. It's about time I made good on that promise.'

'Good idea. Make sure to tell her that I'm thinking of her, and her loss. I know we both wrote, but it still needs to be said.'

'Of course.'

'Will you want a lift in the plane?'

Saffron smiled and squeezed him tight. 'Any excuse to fly will do, won't it? But I'm sorry, darling, I think I'm going to drive. I can stay overnight in town and do a little shopping in the morning. Zander's grown out of half his clothes and Kika needs a dress for her birthday party.'

'Life goes on, eh?'

Saffron looked up at Gerhard. Time, suffering and African sun had etched lines in his skin, but the soul that she saw when she looked in his eyes was still just the same after all these years, and the sight of him was still enough to make her heart constrict with the sheer force of her love.

'You know, it's very annoying, the way you're always so calm and sensible,' she said, not sounding in the very least annoyed.

He grinned. 'And always so right, too.'

'That just makes it worse.'

The two women exchanged kisses and Saffron said, 'I'm so sorry to disturb you, but I had to come down here . . . I need your help.'

'Really?' Wangari smiled. 'It's usually us asking you. But please, tell me what you need. If I can help you in any way, of course I will.'

'It's about the screening centres and the camps. One hears such terrible rumours about what goes on in those places. Of course the governor and his people deny everything. I thought maybe you might have heard something, or spoken to someone who could provide some evidence, one way or the other.'

Wangari's face fell. 'It's not just rumours,' she said. 'In fact . . .' She stopped, thought for a second and then said, 'Wait a moment.'

Wangari returned to her office. A couple of minutes went by and Saffron was starting to wonder whether she should find somewhere to sit down when Wangari re-emerged and said, 'Come in.'

She showed Saffron to a plain wooden seat opposite her desk. The client she had been seeing was sitting next to Saffron on an identical chair.

'This is Mrs . . . Otieno,' Wangari said, and by the slight pause Saffron sensed that this was an alias, rather than a real name. 'I have told her you can be trusted.'

'Hello, my name is Saffron Courtney,' she said, speaking Swahili. 'Please, call me Saffron.'

Mrs Otieno was a young woman, still in her twenties by Saffron's estimation, but she sat hunched in a chair like a woman three times her age. She had an air about her that Saffron had only encountered once before, during her journey across Germany at the end of the war. It was the desolation of someone who has been utterly defeated, whose soul has been crushed, and whose body has been abused.

'Please, tell Saffron why you are here,' Wangari said.

'I want to know what has happened to my husband,' she said.

'When did you see him last?' Saffron asked.

'At the screening camp.'

'So you were there with him?'

'Yes, we were both taken there. The police said it was because we had taken the oath.'

'And had you?'

'Yes – but we had no choice. They said they would kill us if we did not. We said that to the police, but they did not believe us.'

'I see . . . Did they question you at the screening centre?'

'Yes, but not together.'

Wangari gently said, 'Tell Saffron about the man who questioned you.'

Mrs Otieno grimaced. She wrapped her arms around herself and curled her torso into a ball, as if she were at any moment expecting to be beaten.

My God, the poor woman is petrified, Saffron thought.

'It's all right. No one can hurt you here,' Wangari said.

Mrs Otieno looked at Saffron with the sorrowful, liquid eyes of a beaten dog.

'It was Nguuo,' she said. 'The torturer.'

Saffron recognised the word: *nguuo* was the Kiyuku term for hippopotamus.

'Is he very fat?' she asked.

Mrs Otieno nodded.

'And is he as deadly as the hippopotamus?'

Another nod.

Saffron was going to ask Mrs Otieno another question, but decided it would be cruel to force her to relive her torment a second time, if she had already done so for Wangari. She asked Wangari, in English, 'What did he do to her?'

'He punched her, slapped her and hit her with a *kiboko*. His men kicked her, repeatedly, while she was on the ground.'

'That's awful . . . shameful,' Saffron said.

'No, that's normal – but Nguuo did more than that. He took nettles, which had been bound together to form stiff bunches, and he shoved them up her anus and her vagina.'

'Oh, dear God . . .' Saffron gasped.

'She can count herself lucky. Other women have suffered the same torture, with thorn branches.'

Saffron shook her head in disbelief. 'I thought it might be bad . . . but this . . . It makes me think of the things the Gestapo did to our captured agents. Have you been able to find out anything at all about what happened to Mr Otieno, Wangari?'

'A little. I've been pestering the authorities for months, and I've confirmed that Mrs Otieno's account of their arrest is accurate. They were taken to the screening centre. They were interrogated. Mrs Otieno was released when it was clear she knew nothing about the Mau Mau's activities. As for Mr Otieno, he is no longer listed as an inmate at the screening centre, but I have not been able to find any record of him at any of the detention camps.'

'What do you think?'

'That he died under questioning. We've had reports of electric shocks, eyes being gouged out, men being castrated—'

'Why do men do this?' Saffron asked, and her eyes were full of tears. 'How can they do it . . . now . . . when they know what this leads to?'

'I don't know,' Wangari replied. 'Perhaps mankind is doomed never to learn from its past. Perhaps we will always repeat the same mistakes, the same evils forever.'

'No, we can't . . . we mustn't.'

Saffron looked at Mrs Otieno. She was cowering in her chair, paying no attention to their conversation, lost in her own world of grief and desolation.

'Gerhard was like her, you know,' Saffron told Wangari. 'When I found him at the end of the war, after he'd been in the Nazis' camps, he was lying in bed, so ill, so starved, I actually thought he was dead. As time went by, his body started to recover, but not his mind. He was frightened all the time. He recoiled if I reached out to touch him. He was still in shock, I suppose. It took a long time, but we got there in the end.'

Saffron looked at Mrs Otieno.

'I know what it is to be beaten,' she said. 'I know what it is to suffer. But you will get better, I promise. I will find you a home where you can be safe. I give you my word.'

Mrs Otieno was uncertain how she should react to this unexpected kindness, unable to believe it could be true.

'You can trust Saffron,' Wangari said.

Mrs Otieno burst out crying. Saffron knelt by her chair to comfort her.

'This man, Nguoo,' Saffron said to Wangari. 'Do you have his real name?'

Wangari looked through her papers and said, 'De Lancey . . . Quentin De Lancey. Apparently he's some kind of auxiliary policeman.' Wangari caught the reaction on Saffron's face when she heard the name. 'Do you know him?'

'Oh yes,' said Saffron. 'My family is all too familiar with Quentin bloody De Lancey.'

Wangari got up from her chair and walked towards the door. She gestured to Saffron to join her.

'When are you going home?' she asked, in a low voice, not wanting Mrs Otieno to overhear them.

'I was planning to drive back this afternoon.'

'Could you stay in Nairobi tonight?'

'I suppose so – why?'

'There's someone I want you to meet. He might be able to give you hope that people can learn from their experiences.'

Saffron knew better than to ask who that 'someone' was. If Wangari had felt able to give his name, she would already have done so.

'Then tell me where I have to be, and when, and I will be there.'

'Good evening,' said the tall, thin, bespectacled man who greeted Saffron when she rang his front doorbell. 'Do come in. Would you like a glass of sherry?'

The Reverend Jasper Plaister was a Church of England vicar in his late sixties, who worked as the chaplain and Latin master at the Prince of Wales school, less than half a mile away. He possessed a thin sprinkling of unkempt grey hair around a bald spot whose skin was mottled by decades of exposure to the African sun. He wore a grey wool cardigan, fraying at the hem, with leather patches at the elbow. The front garden of his modest villa in the western suburbs of Nairobi was small, but well-tended. The car outside was an Austin 7, at least fifteen years old and battered around the edges.

Plaister led Saffron into the hall and she smelled cooking as he called out, 'Agatha, dearest, Mrs Courtney Meerbach is here.'

A door opened and a plump woman with a smiling face, topped by a silver bun that was gradually escaping from the hairpins keeping it in place, appeared.

'So good of you to come,' she said, wiping her hands on her apron before she greeted Saffron with a firm handshake. 'I'll be with you in a second, just preparing some nibbles.'

Like her husband, Agatha Plaister worked at the Prince of Wales School, where she was the matron of one of the houses. The school was a fee-paying, all-white boarding establishment for boys, proudly modelled on the great English public schools.

The Plaisters were dedicated to their jobs and the boys they taught and cared for. But they were equally passionate in their commitment to the ideal of African independence. For the past twenty years, the couple had been staunch supporters of political organisations like the Kikuyu Central Association and the Kenya African Union that were set up by the colony's native population.

For years, their beliefs had been regarded by the school's headmaster and governors as unfortunate but essentially harmless. They were the kind of woolly-minded do-gooding one might expect from a vicar and his wife. Now the stakes were higher and the Plaisters' views were more controversial.

'Jumbo,' Plaister said cheerfully as he led Saffron into the living room, where she spotted Wangari and Benjamin sitting side by side on a sofa. 'Here's our final guest.'

From the way the Plaisters spoke, it was as if Saffron was joining them for tea at a country vicarage. Yet the middle-aged African in a checked shirt and leather jacket who rose to his feet to greet her was regarded as a dangerous menace to society by the majority of white Kenyans.

'Mr Kenyatta,' Saffron said, recognising the colony's leading black politician.

She was taken by surprise. She had no idea that Jomo Kenyatta was the person Wangari had wanted her to meet, nor that he was the kind of man who wore a leather jacket when not undertaking public engagements, still less that anyone would call him 'Jumbo'.

'It's a pleasure to meet you,' she said, shaking his hand.

'The pleasure is mine,' Kenyatta replied. 'I am no admirer of the seizure of land by white settlers. But I do acknowledge the efforts your father has made on behalf of the workers on his estate. He shows them great respect and consideration. I wish there were more like him.'

'He will be pleased to hear that,' Saffron said, taking a chair that stood at one end of the settee. Kenyatta sat down opposite her.

'Your father sounds like a true Christian, Mrs Courtney Meerbach,' Plaister said. 'All God's children are equal in His sight. Once one accepts that, then it is simply unacceptable, indeed impossible, to discriminate on the grounds of race.'

'I'm afraid religion doesn't play much part in my father's thinking, Reverend,' Saffron replied. 'He'd say he was being practical and businesslike. His view is simple. Africa will gain its freedom, just as India has done. It is therefore in everyone's interests, not least for families like ours, to let that process happen peacefully. The last thing we want is a violent revolution. We all have too much at stake.'

The chaplain handed Saffron the glass of sherry he had promised her with a kindly smile on his face. But his eyes were disconcertingly sharp.

'Not every man who does God's work is aware that the Lord is working through him,' he said.

'I will point that out to my pa. I'm curious to hear what his answer will be. But can I ask you, Reverend, why did you call Mr Kenyatta "Jumbo"?'

The two men laughed.

'I'll answer that, Jasper,' Kenyatta said. 'It was a nickname I acquired in England during the war. As you may know, I spent the years from '39 to '45 working on a farm near a place called Storrington, in Sussex, a beautiful part of the country. My friends at the local pub, where I was a regular, used to call me Jumbo. I told Jasper about it once and he seemed tickled by the name. I said he was free to use it too, since he is also a dear friend.'

'It's a pity more people don't know that story,' Saffron observed. 'They might not be so convinced that you are a dangerous Communist revolutionary if they thought of you drinking a pint in a country pub, surrounded by English friends who'd given you a jolly nickname.'

Kenyatta gave a long, sad sigh. 'That misconception is the bane of my life. It is true that I went to university in Moscow, just as I also studied in London. But studying in Russia does not make me a Communist, any more than wanting freedom and justice for my people makes me a revolutionary. What could be more British than the idea of one man, one vote? All I am seeking is the same rights for my people as you take for granted for yours. But for some reason, the colonial authorities are convinced that I am behind what you whites call the Mau Mau. I can assure you, nothing could be further from the truth.'

Wangari leaned forward. 'This is why I wanted you to be here tonight, Saffron. Your family is influential in the white community. If it can work with those of us seeking peaceful change, maybe we could create something new, something better, instead of repeating all the old mistakes.'

Before Saffron could answer, there was a hammering on the front door.

Plaister got to his feet, saying, 'I'll see to that,' and left the room.

Saffron felt a sudden jolt of alarm. Throughout her time in Occupied Europe, a knock on the door had been the sound she dreaded most, for it would mean that the Gestapo had come for her. In the atmosphere of fear and suppression that was settling over Kenya, her first thought was, *it's the police come to break up our meeting*.

She heard Plaister say, 'I'm sorry, but you can't come in,' followed by the sound of a brief scuffle and heavy footsteps down the hall. Kenyatta rose and Saffron did the same, steeling herself to stand up for everyone against the accusations of sedition and conspiracy she felt certain were about to be thrown at them.

But the men who barged into the room, with Plaister trailing behind them, were not policemen.

They were both black and, Saffron guessed, Kikuyu. The first was tall and handsome. The other embodied the Mau Mau, as portrayed by white politicians and journalists: a savagely scarred African with a panga in his hand. The good-looking one stared at her. Saffron was well accustomed to men examining her from head to toe, whether to satisfy their sexual interest, or to judge whether she could be trusted. But never in her life had she been confronted by a gaze as hard and implacable as this.

'What is this woman doing here?' the man asked.

'She's my guest, which you are not,' Plaister said, as forcefully as he could, though there was a reedy, trembling edge to his voice. 'I'll thank you to leave.'

The intruder ignored him. Instead he addressed Kenyatta.

'She leaves, now. The old man and his wife wait outside until we are done.'

'No, it is you and your tame ape who must leave,' Kenyatta said.

'I don't think so.' The man pulled a gun from his jacket. He looked at Benjamin and Wangari. 'I know you,' he said, frowning as he tried to place them, and added, 'You run the clinic.' He looked at Wangari. 'Your father is the traitor, Ndiri, who grows fat on his people's suffering.'

Neither she nor Benjamin said a word, though both looked at the man with unflinching eyes.

'You leave too,' he said. 'Or you and your white friends die.'

Saffron was studying the two armed men, assessing the threat they posed. They carried themselves with assuredness and alertness that suggested they were well trained and battle hardened: war veterans, most likely. There was no bluster in the death threat. It was a statement of fact: 'I get what I want or people will be killed.'

I could probably deal with them if I had to, but there would be blood, Saffron concluded.

Kenyatta turned to his friends. 'Go,' he said. 'I will deal with this warmonger myself.'

'No, old man. I will tell you how things are, and you will accept it, or . . .'

There was no need to repeat himself. It was obvious what alternative was being offered.

'Go,' Kenyatta repeated.

The Plaisters, Saffron, Benjamin and Wangari went outside and stood in a cluster on the immaculately mown front lawn, like evacuees from a fire drill.

'It's probably best for you to leave,' Plaister said. 'I fear for your safety if those murdering hooligans find you here when they leave.'

'I take it they're Mau Mau,' Saffron said.

'Oh yes. The chap with the gun is one of their most senior men.'

'He looked like a man who was used to being in charge. But what about you and Agatha? Will you be all right?'

'Oh, we'll manage, dear,' Agatha said. 'We've been here for more than forty years, Jasper and I. We began as missionaries, way out in the bush. Life was much wilder and more dangerous then, I can assure you. We can look after ourselves.'

'Then I'll take my leave,' Saffron said. 'Can I give you two a lift?' she asked Benjamin and Wangari.

'It's all right,' Benjamin said. 'We came here on our bicycles. We'll ride back to the clinic.'

Saffron kissed Wangari goodbye and shook hands with all the others. She got back into her car and drove towards the Muthaiga Club, where she was spending the night. Her mind was trying to make sense of everything that had happened at the Plaisters' house.

She didn't notice the black saloon that pulled out into the road, about fifty yards behind her and followed her all the way to the club.

When she got back to Lusima the following day, Saffron asked her father for the name of the Government House official he had met at the Wanjohi Country Club cricket match.

'Stannard,' Leon replied. 'Ronald Stannard ... He was an interesting young man. Looks like a total wet blanket, and he let himself down badly in the eyes of the Wanjo mob by being filthy sick at the sight of a club servant getting whipped for stealing.'

'I don't blame him. It's a hateful punishment.'

'Then you two will get on splendidly. There's more to young Stannard than meets the eye. He's a damn fine cricketer, and a brave one, too. It takes real guts to hold one's nerve when a fast bowler's chucking it down, but Stannard stood his ground then and he did it again when we talked about the political situation. He's got a sight more sense than some of his masters at Government House.'

'In that case I shall write to him at once.'

Gerhard had left for Germany on business, tying up the sales of the Meerbach family's various assets, so Saffron was staying at Lusima for a week or so. Leon and Harriet loved having the grandchildren to stay, and it was more sociable for Saffron than rattling around her own house without anyone to talk to.

She wrote her letter to Stannard and drove into Nakuru, the nearest town of any size, to be sure of getting it in the afternoon mail to Nairobi. Two days later, she was in her father's study, talking over the latest accounts for Courtney Trading, the Cairo-based company founded by her grandfather Ryder Courtney, when two visitors arrived at the house.

The first was a middle-aged man in a stone-coloured suit, with a crisp white shirt, a regimental tie and a steel-grey moustache to match his short, neat hair. He carried a black leather briefcase with the royal crest stamped in gold below the handle. Beside him stood an unprepossessing young man, with prematurely thinning hair and the kind of milky white skin that burns at the first glimpse of the sun.

'Hello, Henderson,' Leon said, shaking the older man's hand. He turned to address Saffron. 'Mr Henderson and I met at the very cricket match where Stannard here distinguished himself, my dear.'

'I was Stannard's captain,' Henderson explained, while his companion gave an embarrassed nod of greeting.

'I must say, I hadn't expected to see you so soon, Mr Stannard,' Saffron said, shaking his hand. 'I only posted the letter the other day.'

'What letter's that?' Henderson asked.

'I wrote to Mr Stannard on the subject of the treatment of Kikuyu men and women at the screening centres.'

'I, ah . . . Well, I don't think . . . No, I'm certain I haven't received that letter,' Stannard said.

'So why are you here?'

Henderson ignored Saffron. He addressed Leon.

'I'm sorry to say that we are here to speak to your daughter, Mrs Courtney Meerbach. It's an extremely serious matter that might have grave consequences for her.'

'In that case, Henderson, why don't you address your remarks to her. My daughter is a grown woman. She's perfectly capable of looking after herself.'

'This is your house, Courtney,' Henderson said. 'You have a right to know why we're here. Now I must ask you, is there anywhere that Stannard and I can interview Mrs Courtney Meerbach in peace?'

'My study will do.' Leon looked at Saffron and quietly added, 'I suggest you sit behind the desk. Remind them who's boss, eh?'

'Follow me,' Saffron said.

It was clear to her that, the Kenyan situation being what it was, the words 'extremely serious matter' were bound to have something to do with the Mau Mau. But what had she done that could have grave consequences?

Saffron had no intention of waiting for them to get to the point. She wanted to take back the initiative.

'Tell me exactly what this is all about,' she said, as soon as Henderson and Stannard had taken their places opposite the desk. Stannard had produced a notebook and pen, ready to make a record of the conversation.

'It's about your association with Jomo Kenyatta, the leader of the Mau Mau movement. Specifically we are investigating your meeting with him at the home of two known terrorist sympathisers, the Reverend Jasper Plaister and his wife, Mrs Agatha Plaister, at their property, Morningside, last Wednesday night. Do you deny that you attended that meeting?'

Saffron saw Stannard tense slightly in his seat, suddenly sharp-eyed and alert, giving a glimpse of his sporting self as he waited to discover how she would respond.

'I do not deny that I was at a meeting with Mr Kenyatta at the Plaisters' home,' she said. 'But I certainly don't believe that Mr Kenyatta is a leader of the Mau Mau, or that the Plaisters have any sympathy for terrorists.'

Stannard gave a barely perceptible nod. Saffron spotted it, but Henderson was too busy forcing home his attack to notice.

'With the greatest respects, Mrs Courtney Meerbach, a wealthy housewife, not even one with your reputation for gallantry, cannot possibly be in possession of the kind of intelligence available to Government House, nor possess the specialist knowledge required to make that kind of assessment.'

Saffron burst out laughing. Stannard looked up from his notebook in surprise. Henderson was furious.

'I'm sorry, but I do not see anything remotely amusing about any of this. You are in very serious trouble, ma'am, and—'

'No, Mr Henderson, you are the one in trouble,' Saffron interrupted as Stannard scribbled down his verbatim notes. 'You're slandering me and making an enormous fool of yourself. You must know that I have considerable experience in intelligence work, and I can assure you that I am very well equipped to spot a terrorist.'

'I was referring to specialist knowledge of the situation in Kenya.'

'Were you born here, Mr Henderson?'

'No, but I don't see what—'

'Do you speak Swahili or Kikuyu?'

'A fair amount of Swahili, but none of the tribal dialects.'

'Have you ever met Jomo Kenyatta?'

'Good Lord, no, why would I want to sit down with a terrorist?'

'Well, I was born here. I speak fluent Swahili and a smattering of Kikuyu.' She shrugged. 'Maasai is more my language. But in any event, I have met Jomo Kenyatta. And I can tell you categorically that he is not a terrorist and wants nothing to do with the Mau Mau.'

Ronald Stannard looked like he wanted to jump up off his chair and applaud, but he clearly recognised the gravity of the situation.

'Then why did two known Mau Mau operatives also attend that meeting?' Henderson asked.

Saffron looked at him coldly. 'So Morningside was being watched, that night?'

Henderson said nothing. Saffron went back over the evening in her head. She took herself through the sequence of events: arriving, the meeting, the intrusion of the Mau Mau, the five of them standing out on the lawn, driving away . . .

Damn! she cursed herself. *How could I have missed it? The headlights in my rear-view mirror, on the drive to the Muthaiga Club. They must have followed me from the house.*

'Right,' Saffron said. 'I'm going to assume you are aware of what went on. A group of people meet at a house owned by known liberals. They are joined by two terrorists. Therefore they and the terrorists are on the same side. You put two and two together and think you've got four. But you haven't.'

'Why should we doubt our evidence?'

'Because you've failed to analyse it correctly. They key question is – why did the Plaisters leave their own home, in the

middle of the meeting, along with three other people, of whom
I was one?'

'But that's obvious,' Henderson said. 'In order to allow Kenyatta and his men to hatch their plans in secret.'

'It's obvious if you've already decided that Kenyatta is a
terrorist. In actual fact, the two men arrived uninvited. They
verbally insulted Kenyatta, precisely because he opposes their
violent methods. They threatened the rest of us with death if
we did not leave the house. And I imagine they used their time
alone with Mr Kenyatta to put the fear of God into him too,
though he did not strike me as a man who scares easily. Tell me,
where did the other two men go after they left Morningside?'

'I'm not at liberty to say,' Henderson replied.

'We don't know,' Stannard added, getting a furious glare
from his boss.

'You lost them. Well, I'm not surprised. The men you are
looking for, whom I will happily describe, if you like, struck me
as knowing their business. I assumed they were army veterans.
Is that right?'

'I'm not at liberty to say.'

'Well, I am at liberty, so I will say this. If you persist in treating
Kenyatta as the Mau Mau leader, you will be making an enormous, amateurish mistake. The wrong man will be arrested, the
right man will go scot-free. If you take any action against me, or
the Plaisters, or Benjamin and Wangari Ndiri, you will be fighting a lost cause. And you'll be doubting not only my word but
those of a qualified doctor and the holder of a master's degree
in law, who are both the children of tribal chieftains. It won't
go down well.'

'Mrs Ndiri is known to be estranged from her father. Her
actions are clearly intended to repudiate and shock him.'

'She had a row with him because she married a Maasai boy.
Her actions are that she and her husband run a charitable centre –
funded by my family, I might add – that provides medical care and
legal advice to the poor. Who on earth would find that shocking?'

'It would be shocking in the extreme if that centre was a front for terrorist activities.'

'Oh, for heaven's sake, don't be ridiculous. They are kind, decent, highly intelligent young people who want to help those less fortunate than themselves – as the eminent London barrister whom I will personally hire, should any accusations be made against them, will certainly observe.'

'There's no need to make threats, Mrs Courtney Meerbach.'

'Then why did you come here with the express intention of threatening me? But if it's threats you want, I'll make a proper one. I have heard the first-hand testimony of a woman who was brutally maltreated by her interrogators at one of your screening centres. It would be very easy to gather further evidence of a kind so shocking that it would, if published in the global press, make the British government's conduct in Kenya a topic of worldwide condemnation.'

'How dare you drag our nation's reputation through the dirt!'

'How dare I what?' Saffron fixed Henderson with a stare that Brigadier Gubbins himself would have envied. 'Did you fight in the war?'

'I served my country in an official capacity.'

She gave a snort of amusement. 'Behind a desk, in other words. Well, as you may have heard, I risked my neck for my country and I did it gladly, because I believed in our cause. We were fighting against dictatorship, and that's why it breaks my bloody heart to see us behaving in such a shamefully dictatorial way now. The only reason I have not already made my views public is that, contrary to your accusations, I do not want to help the Mau Mau in any way, but . . .'

Saffron left the word hanging before she added, 'If you should even think of pressing trumped-up charges against me, or my friends, or my hosts at Morningside, I will make sure that the world hears the truth about Britain's campaign against the Kikuyu people of Kenya. And before you suggest that I'm being a traitor, look in the mirror and ask yourself who's really betraying their nation. I love Britain and the values for which we stand,

and I cannot bear to see those values trampled in the dirt by grubby, time-serving, paper-chasing little bureaucrats like you.'

Stannard was gazing at Saffron with something that seemed like worship, but Henderson had adopted a mask of glacial indifference to her insults.

'I notice you left Mr Kenyatta off your list of the people you were planning to defend.'

'I would not presume to protect him,' Saffron said. 'He can look after himself.'

'Well, he'll need to. He was arrested this morning and will be kept in custody somewhere even you can't reach him, until his trial. He will then be charged with masterminding the Mau Mau, which is a proscribed, illegal group. And he will, I assure you, be found guilty.'

'So was Gandhi,' Saffron replied. 'Repeatedly. And look what happened to him. Now, shall I see you out?'

When she returned to the office, she saw that Stannard had left his notebook and pen on the chair. *Clever boy*, she thought.

Sure enough, he appeared a few seconds later.

'I think you're looking for these,' Saffron said, handing them to him.

'I just wanted to say, Mrs Courtney Meerbach, I agreed with every word you said. What we're doing is a disgrace, and the way we're going after Kenyatta is completely wrong and stupid. It will all blow up in our faces, I'm sure of it.'

'Me too,' Saffron agreed. 'Look, could I ask you a favour?'

'Anything.'

'I have the name of the man who tortured the woman I mentioned at the screening centre. I'm pretty sure he may have killed her husband too, though I can't prove it.'

'What's he called?' Stannard asked, opening up his notebook.

'Quentin De Lancey.'

Stannard grimaced. 'I know him. He's a vile man.'

'Yes, he is, but as long as there are people at Government House willing to turn a blind eye to what he's doing, he's going to get away with it. But if there was anything you could do . . .'

'I quite understand,' said Stannard. 'There's a few at Government House who share the same views as you and I. We can't bring Mr De Lancey to justice. But we may be able to make his life a bit more miserable. You know, let him know that some of us don't feel he has any place in civilised society.'

'Good man,' said Saffron. 'Now, you'd better run before Henderson blows his top.'

'How was your meeting?' Leon asked, when Saffron emerged from the office and joined him in the garden room.

'It was rather fun, in an odd sort of way.'

'Really? It didn't seem like a social visit.'

'It wasn't. That fool Henderson wanted to make out that I'd been consorting with the Mau Mau.'

'Never nice to be falsely accused,' said Leon. 'I speak from personal experience.'

'Absolutely not. But always a pleasure to fight back.'

Leon Courtney had dropped into the Muthaiga Club for a quiet drink with a couple of old friends, only to find Quentin De Lancey leaning against the bar and, as was his habit, letting the men around him have the benefit of his opinion on the issues of the day.

'Of course the governor's garden party should go ahead,' he declared.

Leon's friends had not arrived, so he took a seat at a table behind De Lancey, where he would not have to make eye contact with the man. It was impossible not to hear what he was saying, so Leon decided he would pay attention. He thought of it as a form of intelligence gathering. De Lancey epitomised the kind of white settler that Leon had always cordially loathed. So if one wanted to know what those people were thinking, his opinions were as good a guide as any.

'Of course, I can't abide that kind of affair – nothing stronger than tea to drink, stale cucumber sandwiches, endless boring conversations with people one has never met before,'

De Lancey went on, causing Leon to laugh so hard he almost sprayed a mouthful of whisky across the room. He'd bet the entire Lusima estate against a single shilling that De Lancey had never been near a garden party in his life.

'Of course, the memsahib loves the whole show. Well, they do, don't they, the little darlings? Nothing they like more than putting on a new dress and a smart hat and spending the afternoon gossiping away to their empty-headed friends. But that's not the point . . .'

'So what is, old boy?' piped up another drinker, a little further down the bar from De Lancey, an old boy called Major Percy Nicholson, who, it was said, had attended the Muthaiga's opening party on New Year's Eve, taken a seat at the bar and sat in the exact same place, virtually every evening ever since.

'The point, Major, is that whether one likes these events or not, it is the governor's duty to have a garden party, and our duty, as Englishmen, to attend. Just because there's a war on, that doesn't mean that we should start cancelling our social events. Quite the contrary. This year, of all years, there's all the more reason to show that we are not going to be deterred or cowed by a bunch of monkeys dressed up as terrorists.'

'Fair point,' murmured Major Nicholson, nodding his head in agreement.

'And if I am invited – or perhaps I should say when –' De Lancey gave a knowing smirk – 'I will make a point of attending.'

Oh Lord, I hope not, Leon said to himself, even though he had to admit that he was no great lover of the governor's overgrown tea-party himself. He was just considering the unwelcome discovery that he and De Lancey might share an opinion when his friends arrived.

'Why don't we take a table on the verandah,' he said. 'It's getting a bit loud in here.'

The governor's 'stiffies', as the English upper-class called formal invitation cards, arrived at both the Lusima Estate House and Cresta Lodge.

'I see that my marriage to you has made me an honorary Englishman,' Gerhard remarked, as he saw his name on the cream-coloured envelope, embossed with the royal seal of the United Kingdom.

'You don't have to come, darling,' Saffron said, as she pulled out the governor's invitation. 'I'm sure it will be the most frightful bore. Huh . . . It says, "*Gentlemen may wear medals*." Nothing about ladies wearing theirs. Still, mine wouldn't go with the dress I'm planning to wear.'

'I'll go as a simple civilian, all things considered,' Gerhard remarked.

'Probably just as well.' Saffron opened another letter, addressed solely to her, looked at it for a few seconds and then said, 'Well now, what have we here . . .?'

They were sitting at their breakfast table on the verandah, overlooking the watering hole. Gerhard was about to refill his cup of coffee. He paused and looked inquiringly at Saffron.

'Ronald Stannard has written to me,' she said. 'His letter goes as follows. "Dear Mrs Courtney Meerbach . . ." God, I wish he'd stop being so formal and just call me Saffron. I know he's being polite, but . . .'

She gave a sigh.

'"I believe I mentioned that there are a few of us here, mostly the younger types, who agree with you about the need to do something about the way the campaign against the Mau Mau is being conducted. But we also want the Mau Mau to be defeated, and we certainly don't want to do anything that might look like a betrayal of our country. So how to do one thing, without the other?"'

'That's a very fair question,' said Gerhard, stirring some milk into the cup he had just filled with coffee. 'And I know exactly how Stannard and his young friends must feel. It's exactly how any decent German felt, too. And, my darling, you must be careful, too. If you are seen to be going to war against your own community, it won't do you any good, and it won't help your cause either, no matter how just it is.' He sipped his drink and asked, 'How do you think this will end?'

'You mean the fight against the Mau Mau? We'll win, of course. It'll take a while, but in the end, we'll just have too much power for them to have any chance of beating us.'

'Yes, but after that . . . What happens then?'

'Oh, that's obvious, isn't it? Kenya will get its independence. It has to. Once the people have made it clear that they won't put up with being ruled by us, the game's up. And the silly thing is, deep down, everyone knows it. I mean, once India proved that it's possible to leave the empire, well, it was only a matter of time.'

'And if the country gains its independence, who will lead it?'

'Kenyatta, I think, if we haven't killed him first.'

'And will he be a good leader?'

'Who knows? But he's certainly clever, and quite wise, too, I think, which is a different thing. Put it this way, Kenya could do a lot worse.'

'And he has some respect for your family, right?'

'I think so.'

'Then here is my advice. Do nothing now. Let history take its course. And when a new Kenya is born, then you, with all the wealth and status of your family behind you, can serve this country best, by putting that privilege to good use.'

'If I do, will you help me?'

'Of course.'

'Then I'll think about it, though I warn you now that "do nothing" has never been my style. But anyway, can I finish poor Stannard's letter?

'"We have at least done our best to make De Lancey's life as miserable as possible, though it sadly won't do anything to rescue the people he mistreats. But, on a brighter note, I do hope you will come to the governor's garden party. There is someone I would very much like you to meet. I believe he is the single most interesting and impressive individual on our side in the war, and I know for a fact that he's eager to meet you and pick your brains. Until then, Yours sincerely, R. Stannard.'"

'Well, that's intriguing,' said Gerhard. 'We should certainly attend the party.'

'Will you mind if I desert you in favour of Kenya's finest cricketer?'

'Not at all. Will you mind if I bask in the adoration of women who find fighter pilots devilishly attractive, even enemy ones?'

'Pah! They wouldn't dare go near you. They're all terrified of making me angry.'

'I know how they feel,' replied Gerhard, laughing.

Saffron threw a bread roll at him. Gerhard caught it one-handed.

'Pass me the butter,' he said calmly, as if she had been politely handing the roll to him. 'And the honey, please.'

'You really are the most awful, beastly Hun,' Saffron said, though her tone was as much an invitation as an accusation. 'Come here.'

She walked around the table and sat on Gerhard's lap. He wrapped his arm around her.

'Why don't we go to Nairobi the night before the reception?' he said. 'Leave the children here with Nanny.'

'Mmmm . . .' she purred.

'Let's stay at the New Stanley, the best suite – it will be quieter than the Muthaiga.'

'And more private.'

'By the time we go to the reception, we'll know why nobody else could ever tempt us.'

'I take it back,' Saffron said, giving Gerhard a quick kiss. 'You're quite a sweet old Hun, really.'

Prudence De Lancey was furious.

'You promised me we were going to the governor's garden party!' she shouted, her voice rising in pitch. She was pacing up and down the floor of their cramped kitchen, on the very edge of bursting into tears. 'You said it was absolutely a done deal. Those were your exact words – weren't they?'

De Lancey was sitting at the kitchen table. He had been expecting his wife to serve his supper. Instead, he was having to put up with this hysterical tirade. He said nothing.

'Didn't you?' Prudence repeated. 'Answer me, damn it!'

'Yes, dear,' he said, only able to restrain the urge to hit her because he was so exhausted by a twelve-hour day of non-stop interrogations. Now he was the one getting the third degree.

'Well, why haven't we got an invitation, then? Tell me that. The Murchisons have got theirs – I know because Bella told me. And the Stanley-Wrights. Oh God, now I'm going to have to put up with another bloody year of that stuck-up cow Muriel lording it over me.'

'It's only a party . . .'

Prudence came up to the table, directly opposite her husband, put her arms down on its surface and leaned forward.

'No, it's not "just a party".' Her voice was quieter now, absolutely controlled, and that unsettled De Lancey far more than the screaming had done. 'Don't you see? That bloody party is one day in my stinking, godforsaken life when I can forget that I live in this ghastly, godforsaken flea-bitten corner of Africa and actually behave like a civilised human being. I know you don't understand why it matters to me to have my hair done, and put on a nice dress and make civilised conversation. I know you think it's just me being a stupid empty-headed woman . . .'

De Lancey was quite shocked to discover how completely his wife understood the way his mind worked.

'. . . but it's not that at all. It's me trying to live like a civilised human being for one short afternoon. Just one time when I don't spend every minute of every hour wondering how I can get back home.' She let out an exasperated sigh. 'I thought Bexhill-on-Sea was a boring little provincial backwater. I thought I wanted to see the world. What a silly fool I was.'

Prudence reached into the oven and pulled out a plate on which lay a leathery piece of liver, two boiled potatoes and a spoonful of canned peas.

'There's your supper,' she said. 'I'm going for a walk. With any luck I'll run into the Mau Mau and they can put me out of my misery.'

'Let's hope so,' De Lancey muttered under his breath.

The whole miserable scene had been typical of his wife. All that bloody woman cared about was herself, with never a thought for him. And it wasn't as if he hadn't tried.

When the other chaps at the Muthaiga started joking about how excited their memsahibs were over the little bits of cardboard now proudly displayed on their mantelpieces, De Lancey had realised he'd missed out.

He'd telephoned McLaurin, not once but three times. On the first call, McLaurin had told him there was nothing to worry about, it would all be sorted out. On the second, he'd said that he couldn't help: 'Not my line of country, old boy.' And on the third, he'd slammed the door for good.

'Look here,' McLaurin had said. 'I've had just about enough of this nonsense. So I'll tell you the state of play. You're not on the invitation list, and that's final. As it happens, we senior chaps are all supposed to submit the names of people we think deserve an invitation, and your name was among those I submitted. I did my bit, though precious little thanks I'm getting for it. But someone saw fit to blackball you. From what I can gather, you've upset certain . . . how can one put this? . . . influential members of our community. They feel that you're just a bit too robust in your approach to interrogating the darkies.'

'It's that bastard Courtney, isn't it?' De Lancey snapped. 'Arrogant shit. He's been trying to do me down for more than twenty years.'

'I'm afraid I couldn't possibly comment. Now, this conversation is over and this subject is closed. Good day, De Lancey.'

McLaurin had hung up, leaving De Lancey feeling utterly deflated. In the past few weeks he had increasingly felt as though he had done something to offend someone. But he didn't know who that might be, or what he had done. Two of his colleagues, who certainly delivered fewer confessions than he did, had received promotions, pay rises and commendations, while he got nothing. Out of the blue, he'd been getting endless forms from Government House, each to be completed in triplicate, followed by a request to detail every piece of expenditure that his unit had generated for the past two years, with full receipts. As if these hellish, Herculean labours were not enough to deal with, De Lancey had just been informed that he was to be transferred, without the slightest explanation, to a different screening centre, far from home.

All in all, things were not going well for Quentin De Lancey. As he sat disconsolately at the kitchen table, trying to separate the few bits of edible liver from the excessive amount of gristly veins, he searched for someone to blame for his misfortune. And the answer came soon enough. Hell, McLaurin had as good as given it to De Lancey himself.

On their way from London to Schloss Meerbach, a few months earlier, Saffron and Gerhard had stopped off in Paris, to relive the memory of their first visit in April 1939, when they were young and first in love.

Lying in bed one morning Saffron had said, 'You know how I've always hated the idea of being a spoiled little rich girl . . .?'

'Uh-huh,' Gerhard had grunted, rubbing his eyes and, as he did so, feeling his stubble rasp against his palms. He tried to focus on the bedside clock, saw it was half-past eight and groaned softly. He and Saffron had celebrated their return to the City of Light with a splendid dinner, washed down by champagne, fine wine and more than one postprandial cognac. Various after-dinner activities had then kept them both wide awake into the early hours. Gerhard was feeling the after-effects and suspected that he looked as rough as he felt. His wife, on the other hand, looked as fresh and bright-eyed as a teetotaller after twelve hours' sleep.

'Well,' she said, 'I have a confession to make. I'm about to do something very spoiled and self-indulgent.'

'Really?' Gerhard said, reaching for the bedside phone and dialling room service. He needed coffee, fast.

'Yes, really . . . I made an appointment to see Monsieur Dior this afternoon. He's going to make me some dresses. Do you mind?'

'*Deux pots de café, s'il vous plaît, avec du lait chaud et du sucre . . . merci,*' Gerhard said, speaking into the phone. He put the handset back onto the receiver and looked back at Saffron. 'Why would I mind? If there's one thing in the world I know about, it's good design. Dior is a genius. You deserve to wear his clothes.'

So, while Gerhard went on a tour of his favourite pieces of Parisian architecture, Saffron had spent the afternoon having every inch of her body measured, examining one beautiful fabric after another and, above all, talking to Christian Dior about the clothes that he was going to create for her.

'Ahh, it will be my pleasure, Madame Meerbach,' he had sighed, looking her up and down. 'Such perfect, long limbs, such a slender waist, such an adorable bosom . . . and eyes the colour of an African sky. What beauty!'

Three months later a package had arrived at Nairobi airport. It contained three outfits: a black silk cocktail dress, a charcoal grey woollen skirt suit ('Just in case I ever have to attend another board meeting,' Saffron had told Gerhard), and the dress she was wearing to the governor's garden party.

It was an apparently simple, almost girlish design: fitted over the bust and torso, then flowing out into a gathered skirt that was long enough to cover Saffron's knees, while still revealing her coltish calves and slender ankles to their very best advantage. But the white silk chiffon fabric, printed with big, pink watercolour roses, was so fine that it felt weightless, and the cutting was so precise that the dress fitted Saffron like a second skin, without constricting her in the slightest.

'I've never seen you look more beautiful,' Gerhard said, as Saffron placed a little straw boater coquettishly on the back of her head. Its band was made of the same fabric as the dress, tied in a little bow. Her gloves were white. Her shoes were a very pale pink, picking up the colour of the roses.

She looked at her man, in his pale grey bespoke suit, sky-blue shirt and dark blue knitted silk tie and smiled.

'You're a handsome devil, yourself . . . Now, let's stop fancying ourselves and get to that bloody party.'

'Here we go, darling. Wish me luck,' Saffron said to Gerhard as she spotted Ronald Stannard waving to her across the giant marquee that had been erected on the lawn of Government House. She smiled back and the young colonial official took this as a signal to make his way to them.

'How good of you to come, Mrs Courtney Meerbach.' Stannard looked at Gerhard and added, 'Mr Meerbach.'

'Good to see you, Stannard,' Gerhard replied, shaking Stannard's hand. 'I'll leave you both to it.'

Saffron blew Gerhard a kiss, then turned her attention to Stannard. He looked, as ever, like a man not cut out for life in the tropics. His linen suit was crumpled, his face was glowing pink in the heat of the crowded tent and thin, damp strands of hair lay pasted across the crown of his head.

'I'm so glad you came. There's a chap I'd like you to meet. He knows more about the Mau Mau than any white man in Kenya.'

Stannard looked around the marquee, spotted his target and gave another wave, this time of summons. A man about twenty yards away grinned in acknowledgement and began making his way through the crowd, smiling politely as he cut a path between one little knot of guests and another, ignoring the looks he was getting, which ranged from startled surprise to undisguised hostility, as he passed.

Saffron knew that it was rude, not to mention undignified, to stare, but she couldn't take her eyes off the man. For one thing, he was almost the only black man in the entire marquee who wasn't one of the servants. And for another, he was one of the most beautiful human beings she had ever seen in her life.

He was tall, an inch or two over six feet, by Saffron's estimation, dressed in the police uniform of khaki shirt, shorts and socks, with brown lace-up shoes. It was an outfit that made even the most handsome white man look like an overgrown Boy Scout. Yet on this African paragon it seemed as elegant as the finest Savile Row tailoring, perfectly designed to set off his broad shoulders, deep chest, lean abdomen and long, well-muscled legs. The sergeant's stripes on his sleeves and the long line of medals across his left breast only added to the effect.

If Michelangelo had ever seen you, Saffron thought, *he'd have told David to hop it, your services are no longer required.*

The man's face was worthy of his body. His skin was a rich coffee brown and his head was shaved, emphasising the elegance of his forehead, which was smooth and lustrous, unsullied by the slightest furrow or wrinkle. He had high cheekbones which seemed to angle across his face in perfect parallel with the clean-cut line of his jaw. His nose was straight, its nostrils slightly flared above a mouth whose lower lip was full, while the upper was shaped like a wide, shallow bow.

At rest these lips looked sensual, brooding, almost pouting, and his dark eyes had a slightly narrowed, penetrating gaze. But when he smiled, revealing a set of perfect white teeth, his eyes lit up, creasing to either side and a youthful, almost cheeky side to his character revealed itself.

Saffron seldom felt vulnerable, let alone helpless, but she was suddenly very aware of the delicate femininity of her dress, the frivolity of her little hat and the very obvious vigour and strength of the man walking towards her.

Get a grip, girl, she told herself, feeling her pulse racing as his eyes met hers and began their own examination. *You could get yourself into serious trouble here.*

Stannard knew a great deal more about cricket than he did about sex, and seemed entirely oblivious to the electricity crackling in the air.

'Mrs Courtney Meerbach, may I introduce Sergeant Maku Makori of the Kenyan Police? Sergeant, this is Saffron Courtney Meerbach.'

They shook hands. 'It is a pleasure to meet you, ma'am.' Makori's handshake was confident and his good manners contained no shred of servility, nor any hint of inequality. This was plainly a man of dignity and self-respect. 'Mr Stannard has told me something about you,' he added. 'It made me curious to know more.'

Saffron gave a little laugh, which, she realised, sounded a lot more nervous than she had intended.

'Goodness, Ronald, what have you been saying?'

'Oh, well, ah . . .'

Stannard was blushing furiously and Saffron had to suppress a giggle when she caught Makori's eye and spotted his evident amusement at the other man's floundering.

'Mr Stannard was kind enough to tell me a little about your war work,' Makori said, rescuing the situation. 'It sounded very impressive.'

'No more so than yours, Sergeant,' Saffron said, feeling more at ease now. 'Am I right in thinking that I can see a Distinguished Conduct Medal among your gongs?'

Makori nodded. 'That is correct.'

'And a bar to it, too . . .'

The DCM was the second-highest award for gallantry that a soldier below officer rank could win, only bettered by the Victoria Cross, and Makori had won it twice over.

'Might I ask how you came by them?'

Makori gave a modest shrug. 'I was in the King's African Rifles during the East Africa Campaign – that was where I got the medal. They gave me the bar in the Far East. By then I'd been transferred to the Chindits. I'd served under Wingate in Abyssinia and he took me with him.'

Makori hadn't given any details of what he'd actually done. Perhaps he was too modest to brag about himself, or he just didn't want to relive painful memories. Either way, Saffron knew enough not to press him any further.

'Well, now I'm the one who's impressed,' she said.

She was beginning to get an idea now of why Stannard had wanted to introduce the two of them. The Chindits, or Long Range Penetration Groups, went deep behind Japanese lines to carry out surprise attacks and sabotage the enemy's lines of communication. Though they were uniformed soldiers, rather than spies, the Chindits were not entirely unlike the Special Operations Executive, just as Brigadier Orde Wingate, their unconventional – sometimes controversial – commanding officer, was cut from a similar cloth to Brigadier Gubbins.

'You know it's a rare treat to see Sergeant Makori here in Nairobi. Most of the time he's up country,' Stannard said, as if reading Saffron's mind. 'I wanted to introduce the two of you, thought you might be interested in having a chinwag, as it were, because although you come from very different . . . ah, backgrounds, you share a similar sort of . . . how can one put it? . . . professional expertise.'

Saffron couldn't resist a little gentle teasing.

'Really? I'm sure I don't know the slightest thing about being a policeman.'

'Well, no, dare say you don't . . . quite so,' Stannard floundered.

Makori stepped smoothly into the breach.

'What Mr Stannard means, Mrs Courtney Meerbach, is that you are a legend in this country for your mission into Occupied Europe during the war and I . . .' He paused. 'I have to be careful what I say . . .'

'I'm familiar with the need for security,' Saffron assured him.

'Then I will say that I too work in enemy territory, but nothing compared to what you have done.'

'Now, now, Sergeant, you're selling yourself short.' Stannard looked around to make sure that none of the waiters were in the vicinity, then in a low voice said, 'He's the absolute scourge of the Mau Mau, Mrs Courtney Meerbach. Goes deep into the forest, walks right into their camps, cool as you like, acting like he's one of them, and comes back with extraordinarily useful intelligence material.'

'I must say, you don't look much like an evil terrorist, Sergeant,' Saffron said. 'I'm amazed that the Mau Mau don't take one look at a clean-cut chap like you and say, "Now there's a copper."'

Makori laughed. 'Oh, believe me, ma'am, I look very different when I work undercover. You would not recognise me.'

'He's absolutely serious, Mrs—' Stannard began.

'Oh, for God's sake, Ronald, do call me Saffron.'

'Ah, yes, quite . . . Well . . . Saffron . . . Makori's exploits really are remarkable. He and his people are known as the pseudos, because they pretend to be Mau Maus. A few of them actually were the real thing, but they've come over to our side.'

'Really? What makes them change sides?'

'Discovering that they've been lied to,' Makori said. 'It takes time to win them over. Many remain loyal. But some, often those who were the most fanatical before, realise that they were misled. Their cause is not invincible. Their god is not on their side. And once that happens, they feel anger towards those who misled them. Then they are great fighters for our cause.'

'And you are the one who turns them?' Saffron asked.

'I have to be, or else they would not follow me.'

'I must say, I'm very glad that Ronald introduced us, Sergeant. I can see why Wingate regarded you so highly.'

'I can assure you that the governor feels the same way,' Stannard said. 'One of those gongs on Sergeant Makori's shirt is the Colonial Police Medal for Gallantry. And I've heard whispers that the governor has put his name forward for the George Medal, which would give you both another common denominator.'

'Please, Mr Stannard, that really is going too far!' Makori protested.

'It may be indiscreet, I grant you, but you've got a damn good chance and no one would deserve it more. Anyway, I think I'll leave you two to it,' Stannard concluded, dabbing his glistening face with a white handkerchief. 'Henderson won't be happy if I'm not seen to be mingling.'

'Of course, Ronald, that's quite all right,' Saffron said. 'We can look after ourselves, can't we, Sergeant?'

'Oh yes, ma'am, we certainly can.'

Lady Virginia Osterley was the young, blonde, very beautiful and very, very frustrated wife of a wealthy peer whose family required him to produce an heir, but who was not, by choice, a lover of women. When the inactivity on her wedding night made it plain that she was never going to get any more marital sex than the bare minimum required to produce a male baby, she and her husband had come to a very secret agreement. Since each provided something that the other needed, and they got on perfectly well in every respect other than sex, they would remain married. They would both turn blind eyes to one another's private activities, provided that they remained private.

'And if someone else can give you a boy,' Lord Leggett had added, 'I have no objection, so long as he can plausibly be raised as my son, and neither he, nor anyone else ever, ever discovers that I am not the father.'

'Agreed,' Virginia had replied, before setting off on a discreet, but determined hunt for lovers who might also be suitable sires for her child. With that in mind, she had fallen on Gerhard like a hungry lioness on a lone wildebeest.

'Has anyone ever told you that you have the most amazing eyes?' she asked, gazing at him adoringly. 'I think they're sort of grey, like a pebble, but sometimes they look blue, or even green, depending on the light. They're quite extraordinary.'

'Thank you,' Gerhard replied. 'People have said that, yes . . . about the changing colour, I mean.'

'And is it really true that you were a Luftwaffe ace?'

'Yes,' he said, a little curtly this time, because as much as he might joke about his past with Saffron, this really wasn't a subject he regarded as suitable tea-party chit-chat.

'And that you rebelled against Hitler and were sent to one of those beastly camps?'

He nodded. The only thing he liked to relive less than his combat missions on the Russian Front was his time at Sachsenhausen and Dachau.

'I'm sorry,' Virginia said, showing more perceptiveness than he'd given her credit for. 'I'm sure these aren't subjects you like to discuss. I don't blame you really. Must have been utterly beastly.'

Gerhard softened a little. Here was a young woman, plainly desperate for the company of a real man, for all Kenya knew her husband's so-called secret. She meant no harm.

'Utterly,' he said, with a wry smile. 'So hellish, in fact, that I very much hope that you could not even imagine the things that I have seen . . . and endured.'

'Oh . . .' she said, taken aback by the fact that he so obviously meant what he said.

'Which is why that is the very last thing we should talk about.'

The crowd behind Virginia parted for a moment. Across the other side of the marquee, Gerhard spotted Saffron, deep in conversation with a man in a police uniform – a tall, very handsome, Kenyan man with whom, Gerhard knew, just by the posture of her body and the angle of her head, his wife was very taken indeed.

For the first time in his married life, Gerhard felt a sudden sharp shock of jealousy. For an instant he felt like striding across to the two of them and letting them know what he thought of their little display. But he knew right away that he would only be making a fool of himself. And while Saffron might be attracted to another man, particularly when he was so plainly attractive, Gerhard had faith that she would not act upon that feeling.

'Gerhard?' Virginia said, dragging him back to his immediate surroundings. 'Are you all right?'

He held his hands up in apology. 'I'm so sorry, I was miles away.'

'Is it my fault, for bringing back terrible memories?'

'Not at all . . . I'm entirely to blame.'

And, Gerhard decided, *I'm entirely within my rights to enjoy a little flirtation of my own.*

'Come now,' he said, linking his arm with Virginia's. 'Let's go and find champagne to drink, and cake to eat. And let's only talk about things that are cheerful, and bring pleasure into our lives. For example, that is a very pretty dress that you are wearing.'

Virginia smiled happily, and pulled her body a little closer to Gerhard's. She was wearing a heady oriental scent that reminded him of a girl called Helene, whom he'd loved very much when he was a student at the Bauhaus.

My God, that was almost twenty years ago!

He remembered the name now: Shalimar by Guerlain – he'd bought her a bottle for Christmas.

'Oh, this little thing,' Virginia said. 'It was made for me in London by Norman Hartnell. He's such a sweet old thing.' She fixed her big baby-blue eyes on his and added, 'But honestly, Gerhard, I'm sure there are simply oodles of things that are much more interesting, and much, much more fun to talk about than that . . .'

Makori had waited a moment or two, to let Stannard get away and then, as if making idle cocktail party conversation, said, 'I believe we have acquaintances in common. From the clinic at the Burma Market.'

As casually as the line was delivered, Saffron sensed that there was a deeper purpose behind the question.

'You mean, Benjamin and Wangari?' she replied.

Makori nodded.

Saffron smiled. 'They're hardly acquaintances! Benjamin's part of the family.' She caught the puzzled frown on Makori's face and said, 'His father, Chief Manyoro, is my father's blood brother, his oldest, dearest friend. They've been as close as two horns on the same buffalo for the past thirty-five years.'

'A white man . . . and a Maasai?'

'Why not? Isn't that how the world should be – people being friends without worrying what races they come from?'

'Yes, it should be,' Makori agreed, with a sad smile. 'But it very seldom is.'

'Well, be that as it may, my father thinks of Benjamin as his nephew. He put him through medical school in England.'

'So, your father is Leon Courtney, from Lusima?'

'Yes.'

'Hmm . . .' Makori gave a thoughtful nod of the head. 'In Abyssinia, there were men in my unit who came from Lusima. They used to boast about how good life was under Bwana Courtney, how he let them make lots of money and gave them land for their sons, so that they could start their own families. I remember how I wished other white bwanas could be like that. But now I think that even though the people of Lusima have roofs over their heads and food in their bellies—'

Saffron finished the sentence. 'My father still owns the land, and they do not.'

Makori shrugged in acknowledgement. For all his bravery, all his service to the Crown, still he had to be careful before expressing an opinion that many white people would consider grossly impertinent. Saffron, however, was not one of those people.

'That's Benjamin's argument, too,' she said. 'No amount of prosperity means anything if the people aren't masters of their own land, their own destiny.'

'And what do you say?'

'I think you're both right. I never used to. I don't suppose I thought about it, to be honest. I mean, all the people who worked for us seemed to be happy, and I knew that Father really cared for them, so I couldn't see anything wrong with it.'

'And what changed your mind?'

'Well, this rebellion for a start. I can't abide the things we're doing to the Kikuyu. And, well, the whole idea of the empire seems to belong to another age . . .' Saffron stopped as a thought occurred to her. 'Does Benjamin know what you do? Does he know you work for us against the Mau Mau?'

'Yes – and so does a man that he and I both admire . . .' Makori looked right at her. 'Perhaps we should continue this conversation outside, where we can be more private?'

In other circumstances, Saffron would have taken that as a pass, been very tempted to say 'Yes,' but then have made herself decline the offer. But she knew full well that there was no sexual intent in the invitation. Still she hesitated. She didn't want Gerhard to see her with the ultimate tall, dark, handsome stranger and be needlessly concerned. Although, come to think of it, where was Gerhard? Saffron scanned the marquee, but instead of spotting her husband, her eyes alighted on Henderson. He was talking to Stannard, or rather, at him, angrily.

As if sensing her gaze, Henderson turned and glared at Saffron. That made up her mind. She wasn't in the least bothered about upsetting him.

'Good idea,' she said, with a happy smile on her face. 'It would be nice to get a breath of fresh air.'

The lawns of Government House were much less crowded than the marquee. Makori led Saffron to a spot beneath the branches of a Meru oak tree, which was private enough to allow them to talk, and yet sufficiently visible to ensure that there could be no malicious gossip about them disappearing into the bushes.

'I presume you were referring to Kenyatta?' Saffron said. Makori nodded. 'Well, there's another reason I think our time here will soon be up. I mean, carting him off to some sort of jumped-up kangaroo court to denounce him as the leader of the Mau Mau rebellion. It's such an obviously desperate, stupid thing to do, when he is patently no such thing.'

Makori smiled. 'You should lead his defence. What court could resist you?'

Saffron laughed. 'Sorry, I get a bit carried away sometimes. But here's what I don't understand. You plainly believe in Kenyan independence. But you're risking your life in the service of the people who are trying to prevent it, and horribly mistreating your own people while they're at it. It doesn't make sense – unless you're a plant, I suppose, Kenyatta's inside man . . . But you'd hardly tell me if you were.'

'I will do better than that. I will tell you the truth.'

'That, of course, is the very first thing a liar would say,' said Saffron, in a tone that, she realised, was altogether too close to flirtatious, for try as she might, she could not help the fact that Maku Makori was a man who made her feel very, very much like a woman. Once again, she controlled herself and much more matter-of-factly added, 'But I will give you the benefit of the doubt. Tell me your truth.'

'It's very simple. First, I am not a Kikuyu. I am a Kisii. So I am as different from a Kikuyu as a Scotsman is from an English-man. But I am also Kenyan and, most of all, I am a policeman.

'I believe in the rule of law, Mrs Courtney Meerbach. I believe that people should be able to live their lives in peace, knowing that the law protects them from violence, intimidation and coercion. And, yes, it distresses me, as it does you, to see the way that the British Empire is treating its subjects. But I am even more disgusted to see the way that these gangsters who say they are freedom fighters treat their Kenyan brothers and sisters. And it makes me angry, because I have fought with the British and I know what they are like. The more they are attacked, the more they refuse to be defeated. So the more this rebellion goes on, the further away we get from the day when Kenya is free to govern itself. It is a stupid fight, for it achieves the very opposite of what it intends.'

'Well said . . . and truthfully said, too.'

'Thank you, ma'am.'

'But a lot of the Mau Mau fought in Burma, like you did, isn't that right?'

'Yes.'

'So why did you come back from the war with such different ideas to them?'

'Because I was lucky. When I was a small boy, one of the teachers at the mission school . . .' He smiled fondly. 'Mrs Parker . . . She saw that I found the work easier than the others and she made a special effort with me. She gave me books, played me records with beautiful music, showed me pictures of great works of art. She used to say, "A man is never so old or so wise that he should ever stop learning."

'So, during the war, I kept learning. When we were on leave in India, while the other men were off wasting their money on bad women with nasty diseases, I was paying attention to a little man called Gandhi, asking myself, "How can such a weak old man defeat such a great empire without firing a single shot?" For surely such a man had a lot to teach me.'

'Were you really not at all interested in those bad women?' Saffron asked, smiling. 'The other men must have thought you were very odd.'

Makori's face split into a broad smile and he laughed. 'Not when I showed them pictures of my wife!'

Saffron felt a sudden jolt of disappointment, followed by a terrible feeling that she'd made a fool of herself. Why did married men not have to wear rings when women did? It was so unfair.

'It's getting on a bit,' she said. 'Perhaps we should go back to the tent. My husband will be wondering what's become of me.'

'Wait!' Makori said. 'There is something else. Is it true that you went into Europe, undercover, and lived among the enemy for months?'

'Yes.'

'Then I really would like to talk about this with you.'

'I'm not sure what I could tell you. I mean, you fought with the Chindits. And I don't know anything about jungle or forest warfare – let alone about the Mau Mau.'

'Yes, but you know about disguising yourself as someone – and something – you are not. You know how it feels to be alone, surrounded by your foes. No one else in Kenya knows these things, and maybe you know things that I do not . . . things that might keep me alive.' He paused. 'I have a son, Jacob. I want him to have a father when he grows up.'

Saffron smiled. 'Of course – I'd be happy to help in any way I can.'

'Then start by coming on a patrol with me and my unit. Just a routine sweep through the woods.'

'Ahh . . . I thought you were just asking for advice.'

Saffron sighed, frowning. Her instant, unthinking reaction to Makori's suggestion had been an adrenalised shot of excitement. And now she was wrestling with something that she had been troubled by, ever since the showdown with Konrad: the realisation that the thrill of the chase and the danger to her life had excited, as much as scared her. Gerhard had emerged from the war with no desire to fight anyone ever again, until necessity had forced him to do so. But Saffron was different: the nearness of death made her feel all the more alive. She was addicted to that danger, she could no longer deny it. But her life was no longer the only one at risk.

'I don't know,' she said. 'I have a son, too, and a daughter. And I don't want them to grow up without their mother, the way I had to do.'

'I understand, Mrs Courtney Meerbach. It will just be a routine patrol, like a policeman on his beat. I will make sure you are kept safe, and I tell you this. Even if we never see a single Mau Mau, even if no guns are ever fired, you will learn more about what the war is really like than all these people at this party will ever know.'

Saffron knew that for all his good intentions, Makori could not guarantee that she would be completely safe. And even if he was married, she could not promise herself that she would never be tempted. She could just imagine what her father would call the notion of going on patrol into enemy territory with this man: 'a bloody damn-fool idea'.

So she looked at Makori and said, 'Well then, how can I refuse?'

Makori and Saffron went their separate ways. As she was setting out across the lawn, en route to the marquee, she saw Gerhard walking arm in arm with a blonde woman who, on closer examination, she identified as Virginia Osterley.

'God, that woman's a menace,' Saffron muttered under her breath.

Her ladyship detached herself from Gerhard's arm, gave him a peck on the cheek and trotted off towards the house, presumably in search of the ladies' room, which was located there.

Gerhard pulled down the sleeves of his jacket, adjusted his tie and, when he finally looked up, spotted Saffron coming towards him. He smiled broadly, but, she thought, a little sheepishly, knowing that she must have seen Virginia's fond farewell.

'Ah, there you are!' Gerhard said, striding towards her.

Saffron waited until he was a little closer and said, 'Did you have a lovely time with Ginnie Osterley? She's a pretty little thing, isn't she?'

'Very,' he said.

He did not seem remotely flustered. Gerhard's ability to remain cool under pressure was one of the things about him that Saffron found most admirable, but also, at times, most infuriating.

'Did she lead you into temptation? I can't say I blame her. The poor girl must be desperate for a proper seeing-to. She certainly isn't getting it at home.'

Gerhard smiled. 'It's not like you to be catty, darling . . . but yes, since you ask, I was tempted.'

'And?'

'And I thought about it and realised that I was very happily married. So I politely declined the offer. How about you and that policeman? From what I could see, he looked like a tall, fit, handsome sort of fellow.'

'Oh, he is, yes, very handsome. Very tempting too.'

'And?' Gerhard echoed her earlier question.

Saffron gave a teasing little half-smile. 'Well, I thought about it and realised that he was very happily married.'

Gerhard laughed. '*You* are a very wicked woman, Saffron Courtney.'

She laughed, too, pleased by Gerhard's faith in her, and also by his self-confidence. He backed himself against the other man, just as she would absolutely have backed herself in any contest with Virginia Osterley. That was a good sign.

All the same, she did not feel like telling Gerhard about the forest patrol with Makori. Not yet, at any rate.

Leon Courtney had tolerated, rather than enjoyed, the governor's garden party. But the following afternoon's social activity was far more to his liking. Leon was sitting on the stone steps that led from the terrace of the Lusima Estate House down to the garden, drinking a chilled bottle of Bass Pale Ale. A cool box beside him contained a further five bottles, for this was Manyoro's favourite tipple and today the two men would share the drinks and talk, just as they had been doing for nigh-on fifty years.

Leon lifted the bottle in salute as he saw Manyoro walking across the grass towards him, and grinned as his Maasai brother waved back.

His smile faded. Manyoro was not well. It was obvious from the way he walked. His stride had lost its energy, his back was not straight, nor was his head held high as befitted a great chief.

It had been a couple of months since the two of them had spent any time together. Manyoro had complained of having a stomach ache that wouldn't go away. His normally ravenous appetite had all but disappeared. He found himself getting tired much more easily.

Leon had put it down to the inevitable effects of the ageing process.

He must be almost eighty by now. He has to show it eventually.

But as Leon got to his feet to shake hands, he saw that this was more than passing time taking its toll.

Manyoro's body seemed diminished. He had never looked so thin. The muscles and fat were wasting away from his frame; his cheeks were sunken, his mouth downcast. His skin seemed sallow, unnaturally pale and tinged with a yellowish hue.

'I see you, my brother,' Leon said, taking Manyoro's bony hand.

'And I you, Mbogo,' came the reply, but the words lacked their usual booming volume.

Manyoro took the bottle that Leon held out to him.

They drank in companionable silence and then Leon asked, 'What ails you, brother?'

Manyoro shrugged, grimaced dismissively and then said, 'It is nothing. It will soon pass.'

'Have you consulted a doctor?'

Manyoro emitted a laugh that turned into a dry hacking cough.

'You know me better than that! I am never ill. And if I were, I would summon the *Makunga* and he would see to me.'

Leon did not want to insult his friend, but the *Makunga* was nothing but a witch doctor, and whatever disease had Manyoro in its grasp, herbs and spells would not suffice to cure it. He had to try to get him proper help, his conscience demanded it, but it would take diplomacy and tact.

And even my dearest friends would not list those two qualities as my strong suits.

'You are the son of a great healer . . .' Leon began.

'We are both Lusima's sons,' Manyoro pointed out.

'Indeed – and we both had cause to thank her for her skills, for she healed us both. I know that Africans have ancient knowledge that my people do not comprehend. But Europeans have modern science, and this enables us to know the world in a different way and find cures that may help when the old ways are not enough.'

'Are you suggesting that I go to the hospital in Nairobi? You know that the hospital for black men and women is not like the one for you whites.'

'I know,' Leon admitted. 'And I can only hope that in time, justice and fairness will demand equal treatment for everyone. But for now, all I care about is you. I will get you the finest doctors in Kenya. Once they determine what is wrong with you, I will fly in the top specialists from Johannesburg or Cape Town. Nothing will be too good for you.'

Manyoro sipped some beer, then gave Leon a feeble pat on the back.

'You are a good friend, Mbogo. You love me and you reach out your hand to help. I thank you for that. But maybe there is no need for help. What if this is just my time? Death comes to all of us in the end.'

Leon felt a sudden, primal shock of fear, less like one grown man facing the loss of another than a child discovering that their father will soon be gone forever.

'No! Don't say that! There must be something . . .' He cast around for what that might be. But only one possibility crossed his mind. 'What about Benjamin? He is a doctor. Surely he can help you.'

Manyoro's face tightened with barely suppressed anger. 'I told you – never mention that name to me again. He is no longer my son. I do not wish to see him. And he will not come to me . . .'

As Manyoro said those last words, they seemed to be laden with the pain and desperation that lay beneath his anger.

Leon said, 'My father and I were enemies. He died before we could reconcile. But I would give everything I own – all this land, my businesses, every penny in the bank – to be able to see him again and tell him that even when I hated him, I loved him too. And I'm sure that the old bastard would say the same.'

Manyoro did not reply. Leon pulled out two more bottles of beer from the wicker hamper. He passed one to his friend and let him drink almost all of it before he said, 'So, tell me, you mighty chief . . . I know you Maasai own all the cattle in the world. But how many head do you want to give me to take to market?'

The old man grinned and they settled into a conversation about livestock that kept them both happily occupied until the hamper was empty.

That night, lying next to Harriet, Leon said, 'We have to do something to bring Benjamin and his father back together, before it's too late.'

'You're right, darling, that has to happen,' his wife replied. 'But we aren't the ones to do it. And we both know who is.'

'No, I won't,' Benjamin said. 'I can't. He won't see me. He said that and he meant it. Now, I know you meant well, but I have patients to attend to—'

'Wait,' Saffron said. 'Hear me out. Please, Benjy . . . for old times' sake.'

He turned, unable to look her in the eye, and stared at the framed medical certificates on the walls of his consulting room.

'Please, my darling,' Wangari said, 'listen to what Saffron has to say.'

'Very well then, go ahead.'

'I'll keep it brief,' Saffron said. 'Think about this as a doctor. You know someone is sick. How can you refuse them treatment?'

'What if they refuse to let me treat them? I can't force them.'

'All right then, think about this as a son . . . My father told yours how much he regretted never being reconciled to his own father. Now look at me. I lost my mother when I was a little girl. I never had the chance to say goodbye to her. Not a day goes by that I don't think of her and wish I could see her again . . . just once.'

'I feel the same,' said Wangari. 'Please, Benjamin . . . You know I didn't make peace with my father. I still dream about him all the time. We are together again as father and daughter, like the old days. Then I wake up and he has gone and I know that I will never, ever be able to tell him that I love him, or hear him say that he loves me, and it breaks my heart. You have that chance . . .' She took her husband's hand and there were tears in her eyes. 'I'm begging you . . . go to your father.'

Benjamin lowered his head. 'He won't see me.'

'Oh, for heaven's sake, Benjamin!' Saffron exclaimed. 'Grow up. Be a man. If Manyoro goes to his grave and you didn't try to see him, you will not forgive yourself. And I won't forgive you, either!'

'Well?' said Saffron, when Benjamin and Wangari were led into the drawing room at the Estate House, where she, Gerhard, Leon and Harriet were waiting. 'What happened?'

Benjamin's eyes were like two pools of sorrow. Wangari was clinging to him as if he might collapse. Finally he spoke.

'My father saw me.'

'Oh, thank God!' Saffron exclaimed, and moved towards Benjamin to embrace him.

He lifted a hand. 'Wait, that's not all . . .'

Saffron held back.

'I examined my father,' Benjamin continued. 'I was able to make a preliminary diagnosis. Ideally one would follow it up with blood tests and X-rays. But I can say with a fair degree of certainty that the patient – my father – has liver cancer. The disease seems advanced, to the point where a cure . . .' He shook his head. 'Ahh, what am I saying? There is no cure for liver cancer.'

'How long . . .?' asked Saffron.

'I don't know. It could be a few months, it could be days.' Benjamin looked at Leon. 'Could I have a glass of whisky, please?'

'My dear boy, of course,' Leon said. 'I should have had one waiting for you.'

He poured a generous measure, added ice and handed Benjamin the glass. Benjamin downed half the drink and let it calm his nerves.

'My father wants to go back to Lonsonyo Mountain, to be close to my grandmother's spirit. I will be going with him.'

'Oh, I'm so glad,' Saffron said, and it was the good news, rather than the bad, that made her cry.

'My father will only have his wives and offspring with him on the mountain, but he'd like to see you – all of you – before he goes . . . You most of all, sir.'

'Of course,' Leon said. 'Shall we go to him now?'

'No, he's sleeping. But in the morning—'

'Absolutely, we'll do that. And perhaps we can see him more than once, you know . . . before he sets off.'

'I'm sure that will be possible.'

Leon saw it as his duty to keep a calm, unruffled demeanour, even in the face of bad news. He maintained the façade through dinner. Afterwards, he was the attentive host as he suggested to Benjamin and Wangari that they should stay the night.

'Harriet, darling, could you ask Tabitha to make up one of the spare rooms?'

'No need, darling,' Harriet replied. 'Tabitha keeps them all in a perfect state of readiness, just in case.'

'Excellent. How about you, Saffy? Bit late for you and Gerhard to head off to Cresta now.'

'It's all right, Daddy, the children and staff were told we might not be back till tomorrow.'

'Then I suggest we turn in. We can reconvene at breakfast and make a plan for the day.'

Leon went upstairs, washed, undressed and got into bed. He laid his head on Harriet's breast and let her wrap her arms around him as he sobbed uncontrollably at the thought of losing the brother he loved.

S pecial Constable Quentin De Lancey owned a farm near Nyeri, to the east of the Aberdares, the hills where the bulk of Mau Mau forces were based. But the screening centre to which he had been transferred lay on the lower slopes on the far side of the hills, to the west. It was a long way to go home every evening, so for the first few months of the emergency, he had no option but to spend every weeknight in the white officers' quarters at a police station near the centre.

His room was small, poorly ventilated and furnished with a bed, a table and a chamber pot. This meagre accommodation added to De Lancey's sense of injustice. It proved that, after all he had done, the men who ran Kenya treated people like him as if they were no better than blacks. Resentment ate away at his soul. He lay awake at night, while insects buzzed and fluttered around the tiny bedchamber, dreaming up ways to get his own back on those who had looked down on him.

To compound De Lancey's belief that he had been hard done by, there was nowhere for his loyal houseboy, Josiah Ethigiri, to sleep, so that for the first time in thirty years, he had no personal servant to see to his needs. Josiah remained at the farm with De Lancey's wife, Prudence. She was terrified, living up country without her husband to protect her from the savages she imagined to be hiding behind every bush. Soon she was threatening to leave Kenya and return to England to stay with her aged mother.

De Lancey solved his problems by requisitioning a farmhouse about a mile from the camp, where he and Prudence could live.

'It's close enough to our chaps to be safe, but far enough away that I can't smell the blacks,' he told his like-minded pals, when he found the time to visit the Muthaiga Club.

Knowing that he would be a target for the Mau Mau, De Lancey had a stockade of thick, sharpened logs, eight feet high, erected around the house. A gate formed of the same logs was secured at night with a heavy wooden bar.

'A battering ram couldn't budge that, my dear,' he told Prudence. 'We'll be safe, I assure you. But just to be certain, I've arranged for armed police officers to stand guard, round the clock. These are good, loyal men. They know which side their bread is buttered, you mark my words.'

If an intruder managed to scale the stockade and evade the guards, they would confront De Lancey's three Rhodesian ridgebacks: large, pale brown hunting dogs who had been given a cruel, abusive upbringing, calculated to make them hate and distrust human beings.

When at home, De Lancey made sure to have his revolver within reach at all times.

'Purely precautionary,' he said. 'One can't be too careful.'

Prudence, however, saw this as a worrying sign that the Mau Mau could still get into the house.

He went through his elaborate precautions for the umpteenth time, telling Prudence every detail of the lines of defence.

'You are perfectly safe. And the Joneses are only a hundred yards away. Gareth's a sound chap. He'd come running at the first hint of trouble.'

The months went by. De Lancey returned from work every day to find that Josiah already had a fire going beneath the boiler, so that he could scrub the sweat and dirt from his exertions in the interrogation chamber. Josiah would gather up his uniform to take to the laundry room and wash away the blood of his own tribespeople.

The dogs frequently barked in the night, but only at other animals. The guards never reported anything suspicious. The fence was never climbed, the gate was never breached.

One night, De Lancey and Prudence were reading in their small drawing room after dinner when there was a brief flurry of barking, which died away in a matter of seconds.

'Josiah!' De Lancey called out.

The houseboy appeared in the drawing room doorway.

'Yes, bwana.'

'See if you can find out why the hounds were making that racket.'

'Yes, bwana.'

'And pour me another whisky when you're done.'

'Yes, bwana.'

Josiah disappeared. A few moments later the house lights went out.

'Damn and blast!' De Lancey exclaimed. 'Bloody generator.'

He made his way in the darkness to the doorway. His revolver was lying on the table beside his chair, next to his empty glass of whisky.

'Josiah!' De Lancey bellowed.

'I'm here, bwana. But please, bwana, come with me. One of the dogs is sick.'

'Oh, for hell's sake.'

He stepped down the hall in the direction of Josiah's voice. Only then did he notice that the front door was open, and smell the sweat in the air and see the black shadowy outlines around him.

De Lancey opened his mouth to cry for help, but before he could make a sound, a hand was clamped across his face. His arms were grabbed and forced behind his back and suddenly he was being frogmarched to the door.

Behind him he heard his wife's call. 'Quentin . . . Quentin . . . Where are you?'

The nightwatchman was due to be relieved at dawn. In the first chill light of the new day, his replacement arrived to find the gate open. Clutching his rifle, for fear was already spreading like poison through his body, the policeman made his way into the compound.

There was no sign of the guard.

The policeman went into the compound and walked towards the house.

The front door was open too.

The policeman was approaching the verandah and about to enter the De Lanceys' house when something caught his eye. He moved to the side of the building and saw three dark mounds.

The Rhodesian ridgebacks had been skewered on the needle-sharp logs like chunks of meat on a kebab.

The policeman considered running for help, but told himself that if anyone was still in the house they would already have killed him.

He stepped inside, calling 'Hello? Hello?' But there was no answer.

He looked in the study and the dining room. Both rooms were empty, as was the downstairs cloakroom.

He came to the drawing room.

Prudence De Lancey's body was lying naked across the sofa. Her throat had been cut so deeply by a Mau Mau panga that she had almost been decapitated, and her head was lying at a grotesque angle to her body with a huge, gaping wound that seemed to laugh at the policeman.

Blood had sprayed across the wall behind the sofa, and onto the furniture and carpet.

There was more blood that had seeped from the pulpy red mess between Mrs De Lancey's legs. The Mau Mau must have raped and tortured her before she died.

The policeman felt dizzy. He went outside and threw up.

He wiped his mouth and ran from the charnel house, shouting frantically for help as he went.

S affron waited a couple of weeks before telling Gerhard about her plan to go on patrol with Sergeant Makori and his gang of pseudo-terrorists. But then a letter arrived, giving the place, date and time for her rendezvous with Makori. It was only three days away. She had no alternative but to come clean.

It was half past ten at night, and they were both getting ready for bed. Gerhard was sitting on the edge of their bed, in his shirt and underpants, pulling off his socks.

'Was this what you two were talking about, when you spent most of the garden party with your handsome police sergeant?' he asked.

'You weren't exactly unoccupied, as I recall,' Saffron snapped back. 'Bravely fighting off sexy Ginnie Osterley.'

She was standing in the doorway that led to their bathroom in her dressing gown and nightie, her face covered in night cream.

We both look ridiculous, she thought. *Why in God's name did I choose to pick a fight now?*

'But I'm not making appointments with her, am I?' Gerhard barked back, pulling off his second sock and throwing it onto the floor.

'I don't know – maybe you are. Many a bored husband would.'

'Is that what you think I am?'

Saffron said nothing, just glared at Gerhard in miserable, guilty anger as he looked back at her across the room.

'Well, I'm not,' he said. 'And what's much more important, I'm not planning to risk my life chasing after the Mau Mau. For God's sake, what about our family? How can you risk that?'

Gerhard was right, but that only made Saffron defend her position all the more bitterly.

'You didn't seem to mind me taking risks when we were chasing your bloody brother.'

'That was different, and you know it. Konrad had come right into our world. He was threatening us and the children. We had to deal with him, we had no choice. But this is different. The Mau Mau pose no threat to us here. Our children are safe. For God's sake, why can't you be happy with that?'

'Because I have to know what's really happening?'

'Why? Why do you have to know? What difference will it make to you, to us, to anyone, what you know?'

'I just have to . . .' Saffron's voice died away. She shook her head, looking down at the floor.

Gerhard got up from the bed, walked across to her and put his hands on her shoulders, gently, showing no aggression. Then he quietly said, 'Look at me.'

Saffron raised her head. Her anger had ebbed away. All that was left was her unhappiness at the fight that they had just had.

'I need to ask you a question, and you must promise to answer truthfully. During the war you went into the Low Countries . . . but were there other missions as well, ones you've never talked about?'

Saffron took a deep breath, exhaled, then nodded and mumbled, rather than said, 'Yes.'

'Dangerous . . . even deadly missions?'

She nodded again.

'Were you obliged to undertake these missions, or did you volunteer?'

She shrugged. 'Both . . . I mean, sometimes I was ordered to go somewhere that didn't seem like a dangerous mission, but—'

'You found a way to make it one?'

'I suppose.'

'Because once you've been in danger, life without danger feels a little boring, no?'

Saffron's eyes widened. There was more energy in her voice as she said, 'You mean, you felt that too? I always thought—'

'What? That I was always the reluctant warrior? That I never wanted anything more to do with any of it? Well, in some ways, yes. But I flew hundreds of missions, three whole years on the Eastern Front – and survived. I shot down more than one hundred planes and never lost one, never even had a single flesh wound.

You think a man can do that if all the fighting, and killing, and risking his life doesn't thrill him at some level? I could have had a desk job. I could have spent my entire time touring the Reich, playing the great war hero. But when I went home on leave, I'd find myself drinking too much, driving too fast—'

'Screwing too many women?'

Now it was Gerhard's turn to shrug. 'I'm not proud of any of it. But I was addicted, like some of my friends were addicted to the drugs that woke them up in the morning and sent them to sleep at night. Even just now, when I finally had the chance to fight my brother . . . Well, you saw me – I was loving it. So, what I am saying is, I understand how you feel.'

'Thank you,' Saffron said, putting her arms around him and holding him tight. 'I'd been feeling so guilty, so ashamed of how I am . . .' Then she smiled and glanced up, looking him in the eye. 'I wasn't an entirely good girl, myself.'

He gave an affectionate little laugh and used his forefinger to scrape some of the cream off her cheek. Then he kissed her there and said, 'We were apart for six years – and you are not a nun. None of that matters now . . . But, darling, we have to grow up now and think of our children. They need us.'

'I'll write back to Makori and tell him I can't come on his patrol.'

Saffron looked very closely at Gerhard, wanting to see his reaction, because she wanted him to be pleased that she had made this choice for him, and for the children, rather than for herself.

He nodded and was about to speak, but then stopped himself, paused for a moment and said, 'No . . . go on the patrol. Get the drug out of your system. And then you must promise me . . . never again.'

'I promise,' Saffron said. 'Never again.'

And she swore to herself that she meant it.

'Stay out of trouble,' Gerhard said, halfway between a command and a plea.

It was three mornings after their argument, and he was lying in bed as the very first rays of morning light shone through the bedroom windows at Cresta Lodge, painting the bedroom with glowing orange and gold.

'Yes,' said Saffron, a little irritably, pulling on her trousers.

Their argument the other night had ended peacefully enough, but the memory of it clung to them both and the tension between them was still unresolved. Gerhard might have said she should go on the patrol, but he plainly would prefer that the subject had never been raised at all.

'And if trouble comes looking for you,' he added, 'please, try for once to run away and avoid it.'

There was no sound of argument in his voice, just genuine concern for Saffron's safety.

She came back to the bed, and sat down beside him, softening her tone as she said, 'There won't be any trouble, but if there is, I really will do my absolute best to stay out of it. Even if I'm tempted.'

'Huh!' Gerhard gave a rueful smile. 'As if you could . . .' He reached across and put his hand on hers. 'Go,' he said. 'And come back safely.'

'I will,' Saffron replied.

But when she closed the door behind her, she realised that neither of them had said, 'I love you.' For a second she hesitated, wondering whether to go back to Gerhard. But then she thought, *I'll make it up to him this evening*, and went instead to the bedroom that Zander and Kika shared.

The children were both asleep, but Saffron kissed their foreheads and whispered, 'Mummy loves you,' to them both.

Then she ate a hearty breakfast, for there was no telling when her next meal might be, and filled the small, battered canvas shoulder bag that she had carried throughout the war with everything she might need. She set off from Cresta Lodge in one of the Land Rovers that she and Gerhard kept there.

Makori had told her to meet him at half past eight. She had five minutes to spare as she drove through the gates of the police headquarters in Molo, a small town about fifteen miles from the northernmost point of the Lusima estate. The town lay at an altitude of over 8,000 feet, and there was still a sharp chill in the air.

Up ahead lay the police station, a single-storey, L-shaped building. Beyond it, dotted across the hillside that rose behind the station, were the men's living quarters: huts for the Africans, bungalows for their white officers. Uniformed men were scurrying to and fro. To an untrained eye they might have looked like efficient, well-drilled men going about their business. But Saffron had six years of wartime service and she knew what she was seeing.

Something had gone wrong. Or, as the forces saying went, 'There's a bit of a flap on.'

She parked her Land Rover and walked towards the main entrance.

Amid the uniforms, a solitary black man was squatting by the entrance, smoking a hand-rolled cigarette as he rolled dice along the ground in front of him. His tufted hair and beard were equally scraggly and unkempt. The whites of his eyes had the discoloured, jaundiced look that came from a lifetime of disease and poor nutrition. He scratched himself contemplatively, then picked the dice up and rolled again.

As Saffron came closer, she saw that his clothes were unwashed and he stank of sweat and filth. His tattered old trousers had gaping holes at the knee and were held up, like a tramp's, with knotted brown twine. She walked past him and was about to push on the door to the police station when she heard a voice she recognised say, 'Good morning, Mrs Courtney Meerbach. I do hope you are well today.'

She spun round to find the African was standing up, holding out a grimy, calloused hand. It was only when he smiled that the penny dropped.

'Sergeant Makori!' Saffron exclaimed. 'You fooled me.'

'Meet Sungura,' Makori said. 'That's the name I go by, when I'm undercover.'

'*Sungura* means rabbit,' Saffron said. 'Doesn't sound right for a commanding officer.'

'The pseudos gave it to me because I'm the most nimble runner in the group. I don't object. If I'm walking into a Mau Mau camp, I don't want any of them seeing me as a threat. So far as they're concerned, my number two, Thiga, is our leader. He used to lead one of the biggest rebel gangs, over by Meru. No one knows he's been turned. They think he's still General Thiga, the famous terrorist. And I am just his rabbit.'

'Well, it's an excellent disguise,' Saffron said. 'Though I pity your poor wife having to put up with you being quite so dirty.'

And there's no danger of me fancying you either, thank God!

Makori gave a sad smile. 'She never sees me like this. When I am working undercover, I have to stay away from my family, for their sake.'

'I understand, I know just how tough that part of the job is. But there's one thing I have to know – how did you get your eyes to go that colour?'

'Potassium permanganate solution,' Makori said, and added with a proud smile, 'I have a Higher School Certificate in Chemistry!'

'A man with your intelligence should have gone to university,' Saffron said.

'I wanted to, but then the war came. And afterwards, I had a wife and a baby on the way. I had to get a proper job. But one day, maybe . . .'

'When this awful bloody mess is over, and we can lead normal lives again, you and your wife must come to dinner with my husband Gerhard and me. And we will talk about how we're going to get you a damn good degree. I mean it.'

'I know you do, Mrs Courtney Meerbach,' Makori replied, with a quiet intensity. 'And I hear you.' He paused, then snapped back into policeman mode. 'Now, it seems that I have picked quite a day for our patrol. When I tell you why, you may wish to come back another day.'

'I doubt that,' Saffron said.

She had promised Gerhard she would stay out of trouble. But now, at the very suggestion of its presence, she sensed her pulse quicken and her senses come alive, like a gundog pricking up its ears at the sound of the first shot.

'Very well,' Makori said. 'Do you know of a man called Quentin De Lancey?'

'Oh yes,' Saffron replied, not bothering to keep the loathing out of her voice.

Makori frowned before he went on. 'Well, he has disappeared, presumed kidnapped by the Mau Mau. The officer guarding the gate of his house has gone, too, and also the houseboy. His guard dogs were killed and his wife . . .' He paused, unsure how much detail to give.

'I get the picture,' Saffron said. 'Do you have any leads?

Makori shrugged. 'Nothing definite. The local police are handling the investigation, but we have been ordered to keep a sharp eye out for anything that suggests he has been taken to this area. We're heading out on patrol in ten minutes. May I ask – how would you describe your competence as a driver?'

'Well, I served in the Western Desert as General Maitland Wilson's driver, if that's any guide.'

'Did you ever come under fire?'

'We bumped into an Italian patrol once, behind the front line in Libya. They pursued us at high speed.'

'And you escaped . . .?'

'Yes, but I had to shoot their driver first.' Saffron reached inside her bag, pulled out her Beretta, rigorously serviced since her mishap in South Africa, and added, 'With this.'

A sardonic smile spread across Makori's face.

'That will do . . . Please follow us in your vehicle. I will give you one of my best people to go with you and I will keep you posted on what's going on whenever I get the chance.'

'Thank you.'

'There is one other thing. I am in command of this patrol. My orders must be obeyed by everyone. You must therefore obey them too.'

'I understand,' said Saffron. 'I wouldn't expect anything else.'

When Makori told her that he was sending her one of his best people, Saffron had expected a man. Instead she received her second shock of the day when a woman, dressed in a thick coat over a brightly printed cotton dress came up to the Land Rover and said, 'My name is Wambui, Sergeant Makori told me to ride with you.'

'Good morning, Wambui,' Saffron replied. 'My name is Saffron.' She patted the seat beside her. 'Please, get in.'

Wambui paused while she considered the fluency of Saffron's Swahili, her good manners, and her willingness to allow Wambui to sit beside her and use her first name. No white person had ever shown her such respect, and it was clear that this one's actions had been automatic, as if they were entirely normal. She therefore deserved equal respect in return.

Wambui climbed in. She was carrying one of the straight, double-sided short swords that Kikuyu people called a *simi*.

'Do you fight alongside the men?' Saffron asked, starting the engine.

'Oh yes,' Wambui replied. 'Always.'

'Yet you do not carry a gun.'

'The men would not allow it. They would be insulted if a woman was as well armed as them.'

'Men can be very stupid sometimes.'

Wambui burst out laughing and gave a clap of her hands. 'Yes, they are no better than baboons!'

Up ahead, there were two more Land Rovers, both pockmarked by dents and rust patches. They did not look like properly maintained police vehicles, which was intentional. Makori was at the wheel of the lead vehicle, with one of the pseudos driving the one behind him.

'That is General Thiga,' Wambui said, when Saffron asked her to identify the second driver. 'He is Sergeant Makori's deputy.'

'But he is Sungura's commander.'

'Oh yes,' Wambui said, with another beaming smile. 'That is also true.'

The column rolled out of the police compound and turned onto a road, little more than a dirt track signposted, 'To Keringet'. This was a farming district, and every so often signs could be seen, on one side or other of the road, indicating the way to individual properties and bearing the names of their owners: Barrett, McEwan, Jarvis.

All British, Saffron thought. *And scared stiff that their own workers have taken the Mau Mau oath.*

'How did you come to serve under Sergeant Makori?' she asked Wambui. 'What were you doing before?'

'I was with Major Jimmy.'

'Is he another rebel?'

'He was. I was his woman. But Sergeant Makori killed him.'

'Are there many women among the rebels?'

'Yes . . . wherever there is a camp, there will be at least one woman.'

'Does she belong to the leader?'

'Yes, but she can go with the other men, too.'

Saffron knew that the Kikuyu, like the Maasai, had a different attitude to sexual morality than Europeans, particularly where women were concerned.

'But she chooses which man to go with?' she asked.

'Oh yes,' Wambui replied. 'It is a great honour for a man to go with the chief's woman.'

'And Sergeant Makori took you prisoner?'

'Yes. I was taken to a screening camp, with those of Major Jimmy's men who were not killed.'

At last Saffron had the chance to hear a first-hand account of life in the internment camps. Makori had been right. She would never get a better chance to understand what the rebellion and the fight against it were really like.

'Was Sergeant Makori with you at the camp?' she asked.

'Oh yes.'

'Did he hurt you at all? I have heard that many Kikuyu have been badly hurt in the camps.'

Wambui nodded. 'I have heard that too, such terrible stories. But Sergeant Makori did not hurt us. He showed us that it was better for us to go with him.'

'How did he do this?'

'He told us, "If your leaders were truly powerful, they would not have let me kill them. If they truly cared about you, they would not have let me kill your brothers and capture you. But I am powerful, and I will care for you."'

'And you believed him?'

'Not right away. But I considered what he had said over many days. And I saw the truth of his words. Also, he gave me food and found me new shoes, for I had none. My dress was torn, so he gave me a new dress. So I thought, "This is a powerful man, and a good man. I will follow him."'

'He is a good man,' Saffron agreed, considering how much more effective Makori's policy of persuasion, time and patience was than the aggression and brutality that was so common elsewhere. 'And a wise one, too.'

If only I could say the same about the others.

They drove through the small hamlet of Keringet. By now they were approaching the edge of a forest that rose up through the surrounding hills, as far as the eye could see. Makori turned off the dirt road and onto a narrower, more pitted track that bumped and twisted uphill until it reached a small glade, barely bigger than a tennis court.

The lead Land Rover came to a halt; the other two vehicles pulled up beside it and everyone got out.

Saffron counted nine male pseudos, including Thiga, all of them armed with rifles. Makori was carrying an army-issue Sterling sub-machine gun. A fighting knife in a battered leather sheath was now tucked into the belt of string around his waist. With her and Wambui, there were a dozen people in all: a decent fighting force in a guerrilla campaign.

Makori approached her, with a pseudo by his side. Saffron could see at once that he was not a Kikuyu. His skin was darker than theirs and his hair was not cut tight to the scalp, but stuck up around his head in a wiry frizz.

'This is our tracker, Wando. He's an Okiek.'

Saffron and Wando shook hands. She knew that the Okiek were a forest-dwelling tribe, famed for their hunting and tracking skills. If De Lancey really had been brought through this forest, Wando would find his trail.

'The plan is as follows,' Makori continued. 'If De Lancey has been captured, and if any of the rebels around were involved, then we know the general direction of their route between the Aberdares and here. We will therefore march in a south-south-easterly direction, hoping to cross the path of the kidnappers – if there is any path to cross. Please do not take this the wrong way, ma'am, but purely for your safety, I am hoping we do not find anything.'

There are times when a wife finds herself talking to her husband like a mother to a child.

'No,' Harriet told Leon, 'we can't cancel everything. It's too late. Dorian and Sophie are arriving from Cairo today, expecting to have a lovely relaxing break with us, and you simply can't cancel your own brother and sister-in-law. In any case, they'll be in the air by now so there's no way of turning them back. The Sharpes and the Finneys are coming to dinner and I've asked them to stay on for a couple of nights. We'll have a proper house party. It will do us both good to see other people and have a jolly time.'

'But Manyoro—'

'Would not want you to be moping around feeling miserable on his account. No one has taken more pleasure out of life than him.'

'Well, that's certainly true,' Leon admitted with a sad, affectionate smile. 'As his many, many wives could testify.'

'And this one and only wife is telling you that the best way to honour your dearest friend is to enjoy yourself and be happy.'

Leon gave a sigh of surrender. 'You're right, as always, my love. We'll drink a toast to Manyoro tonight. Several toasts, in fact. I'll tell Mpishi to put some champagne on ice. Let's do the job properly, finish off the last of the Krug '45.'

'Now that's more like it,' Harriet said.

Saffron had been marching for more than three hours, uphill and down without a break, when Wando, who was a few yards up the road, suddenly stopped dead. The column immediately did likewise.

Wando looked down, took a couple of paces to either side and contemplated the ground. He asked Makori to join him.

Saffron watched as Wando and Makori stood huddled over whatever it was that had attracted Wando's attention: footprints, she presumed. Wando squatted down, picked up a twig and pointed it at a spot on the forest floor. Makori got down on his haunches beside the tracker and the two of them had a lively debate, while the others waited.

Makori walked back to his team and said, 'Wando has found several sets of footprints. He is sure that one of them belongs to a white man. He says this man is heavy and that he is stumbling and scuffling his feet as if he is very tired, or injured, though there are no signs of blood anywhere.'

'That sounds like De Lancey,' said Saffron. 'But how is Wando sure that the prints were made by a European?'

'They are much clumsier, more obvious than the others. Forgive me, but Wando says an elephant could move through the forest with more grace than a white man.'

As the pseudos chuckled, Saffron added, 'De Lancey's a blundering great oaf all right. So, are we going after him?'

'Yes, but if we find the camp, the rest of you will have to take cover, while Thiga and I go in and try to find De Lancey.'

'Do we have to rescue him? He's a vile man. He's tortured hundreds of people.'

'I have heard that too. But that is not our business now. All we know is that the rebels have committed the crimes of murder and kidnap. It's our job to free their victim.'

Makori looked hard at Saffron, while the pseudos watched on, fascinated, but also confused by this conversation between a white woman and a black man who treated one another as equals. How could this be? White men did not consider black people their equals. Women were certainly not men's equals. And yet, here they were.

'Do I have to remind you of the terms of our agreement?' Makori asked.

'Of course not,' Saffron replied. 'You're in command.'

The men nodded, relieved that the rightful order of things had been restored, not noticing the little roll of the eyes that Wambui had directed at Saffron.

Makori gave a curt nod. 'Good.' He turned to the Okiek tracker and, switching into Swahili, said, 'Wando, lead the way.'

For two hours they marched in silence through the forest. In the shade of the trees, with the only sounds coming from the songs of the birds up above and the rustle of animals through the undergrowth, it was hard to believe that this was a place where a war was being fought and blood being shed. From time to time, Wando would stop and whisper to Makori. Following close behind him, Saffron learned that the white man's footprints were telling Wando that his physical condition was worsening. If his captors did not arrive at their destination soon, they would be forced to stop if they wished to keep their prisoner alive.

With every step, the tension grew as the inevitable contact with the enemy drew closer. Saffron's belly clenched a little tighter as she thought about what would happen if the men they were hunting discovered that they were being followed.

All they have to do is double back, set up an ambush and we'll be goners.

She dragged a hand across her face to wipe the sweat away from her eyes, and gave a wry, exhausted smile as another thought occurred to her. She was now safer here, with the others, than if she tried to make it back to the cars by herself. That meant she could no longer run from trouble, even if she wanted to.

The forest seemed to have quietened, as though the birds and animals were retreating to nests, hides and burrows in anticipation of a storm to come. The air was growing heavy, electric with anticipation.

Wando held up a hand and Makori mimicked the gesture, bringing the column to a halt. They conferred once again and Wando stepped off the path, into the forest and disappeared. Houdini himself could not have performed a more magical trick.

'Wando has seen signs of other men in this area,' Makori told Saffron. 'He believes we may be approaching a camp, so he's going to see for himself.'

Makori posted two lookouts, then told the others to fall out. The pseudos had been marching for hours, and welcomed the chance to rest and get some food and water inside them.

Saffron slumped to the ground, exhausted. As a twenty-three-year-old SOE trainee, she'd been marched for days and nights across the freezing, rainswept terrain of the West Highlands and thought nothing of it.

But that was a dozen years and two babies ago. I'm an old woman now!

An hour went by before Wando reappeared. He spoke to Makori, then Makori gathered his team around him.

He began with a single word: 'Kabaya.'

There was a low, gentle sound as the pseudos gasped.

'He is a very dangerous,' Makori said to Saffron. 'We served together in Abyssinia. He was a very good soldier, a sergeant like me. But when we came home, we took different paths. Kabaya chose the path of evil. He was a gangster in Nairobi, very wicked, killed many people, but no one would ever be a witness against him. Now he is leading rebels instead of criminals, but still a bad, bad man.'

He switched to Swahili as he told the pseudos what he had in mind. Wando would lead Makori and Thiga to the camp. They would infiltrate it, identify the captive, observe the layout and work out the number of rebels, then get word back when they'd worked out a plan of attack.

The pseudos nodded. One exchanged his rifle for Makori's Sterling, which was too special a weapon for the lowly Sungura to carry into a Mau Mau camp.

Saffron focused on the pseudos for a moment. She noticed that none of them asked how long Makori expected to be gone. They were used to this. They trusted their boss to get in and out alive. When the time came they would be ready.

She looked to where Makori, Thiga and Wando had been standing, but they had disappeared.

All she could do now was wait.

Makori and Thiga had taken cover behind a bush within twenty yards of the camp. There was a sentry ahead of them. Many Mau Mau treated sentry duty as a chance to relax and have a smoke. That made it easier for Makori to sneak up on them and put his knife to work. Kabaya, however, had his men well trained because this one was clearly alert and paying attention.

He would be hard to take by surprise. They would have to get in another way.

Makori put his cupped hands to his mouth, like a man imitating birdsong. Thiga nodded. He cupped his hands in the same manner and made the call of a nightjar.

The sentry stiffened and looked into the trees. The nightjar's call was the signal by which all Mau Mau made themselves known when approaching a camp.

Thiga made the call again.

The sentry made a similar call back.

Thiga stepped from behind the bush and strode towards the sentry with brash self-confidence.

'I am General Thiga,' he said. 'I am a great fighter from the Aberdares. The British ambushed my camp. Many of my men were killed, but I escaped with but a single man.' Thiga turned his head and called out, 'Sungura, show yourself!'

Makori emerged, looking sheepish, hunched and unthreatening.

Thiga turned to the sentry and said, 'Is this the camp of the mighty General Kabaya? Take me to him so we may talk together.'

The sentry frowned again. 'I cannot do that, sir. The general is conducting a trial. He cannot be disturbed.'

'Nonsense! How can a prisoner be more important than a fellow general?'

The sentry stood up tall. 'General Kabaya has captured Nguuo the Torturer. He is trying him for the killing and wounding of many of our brothers.'

'May we watch this trial?' Thiga asked.

'Yes,' the sentry said, looking downcast. 'Every other man in our company is in the jury. Only I have been denied that honour.'

'Did you displease General Kabaya?'

'I lost my boots.'

Makori looked down and saw that the sentry was barefoot.

'The general struck me twenty times with the *kiboko* and put me on sentry duty for a month.'

Thiga nodded. 'I, General Thiga, will tell you how this will go,' he said. 'You will take me and my comrade Sungura into the camp and we will observe this trial. When it is done, and justice has been meted out to the evil Nguuo, I will make myself known to General Kabaya and I will be sure to tell him that . . .' He smiled and put an arm around the sentry's shoulder. 'Forgive me, but if I am to praise you to your general I must know your name . . .'

'Kipchego,' the sentry said.

And that was the last word he uttered.

While Kipchego's attention had all been focused on Thiga, Makori had slipped behind him, unsheathed his knife and clamped one hand across the sentry's mouth while the other stabbed the knife into the small of his back.

Kipchego fell forward onto the earth and Makori fell with him. Experience had taught him that a lot could happen between the striking of a deadly blow and death itself. So it was in this case.

Muffled moans emerged from Kipchego's stifled mouth as he writhed his back and shoulders like a horse trying to buck its rider. Makori clung on as Kipchego made a last, desperate attempt to get away, digging his fingers into the earth and dragging himself forward. He managed two strong pulls that moved him half a body-length, but the strength suddenly left him. His back stilled and his limbs stopped moving.

Kipchego's head flopped forward as Makori let go his grip. He got back to his feet and helped Thiga drag Kipchego's body into the undergrowth. Then they made their way into the camp, which was laid out in classic Mau Mau style.

Around the outside were two concentric rings of foxholes the shape of shallow graves, lined with leaves. These, as Makori knew from personal experience, were surprisingly warm and cosy on a chilly night. At the back of the camp, beyond an open area that would be used to drill the troops, an open lean-to with a wooden frame and thatched roof rested against a rock outcrop. This was the general's headquarters.

The lean-to had become the judge's bench and defendant's dock. Makori saw a tall, distinguished Kikuyu in combat fatigues. He was addressing an overweight, plainly terrified white man, who was standing before him. Kungu Kabaya was the judge and prosecution in the trial of Nguuo, the hippo, alias Quentin De Lancey.

Makori could see another man, a huge, looming presence, half-hidden in the shadows behind Kabaya. He carried out a quick, rough headcount and estimated that there were twenty-five, maybe thirty more rebels sitting cross-legged in the open area in front of the lean-to, gazing with rapt attention at the proceedings. A couple of them, recognising Thiga, greeted him with the respect that his reputation deserved, but were hushed by the others around them. No one wanted to miss a single word of the trial. Thiga and Makori took their places at the back and settled down to watch the show.

Kabaya had listed at least twenty specific instances of torture and a further five counts of death. He spoke with a passionate, exaggerated tone of voice, and the outraged cries of horror and shouted abuse from the assembled Mau Mau gave the proceedings an air of pantomime. Yet this was no empty oratory. Each fresh allegation was accompanied by the name of the victim and details of the precise nature, time and place of the alleged offence.

Makori had always treated the stories of prisoner abuse with a degree of scepticism, not least because he did not want to believe that the forces he served could behave that badly. But the crimes that Kabaya was describing bore an unmistakable stamp of truth, and De Lancey knew it, too.

At first, he had reacted with furious, blustering denials and protestations of innocence, shaking his fist at Kabaya, cursing him, damning him as a liar and even turning to address the watching Mau Mau, insisting that all the allegations against him were just wicked fabrications. But as the victims and their suffering mounted up, De Lancey appeared to run out of both energy and conviction. His shoulders slumped, his head dropped and his voice was stilled.

Makori's first instinct was that De Lancey was a beaten man, who knew that his guilt was now beyond dispute, and that the only matter left to be resolved was the nature of his punishment. But as Makori watched more closely he saw something else. The grossly obese torturer was not surrendering. That was all just a front. In reality, he was planning. And while Kabaya continued with his denunciations and his audience became ever more heated, De Lancey seemed calm.

This man thinks he can escape his punishment, Makori realised. *But how?*

Kabaya's speech came to an end.

'And so,' he concluded, 'I ask the jury to find Nguuo the Torturer guilty on all counts!'

Kabaya stood facing his shouting, cheering, jeering men and waited for the hubbub to die down. He turned to De Lancey and asked, 'Do you have anything to say in your defence?'

Quentin De Lancey hauled himself to his feet. Makori knew that to white women like Saffron Courtney, who set such store by their slenderness and physical health, obesity was a moral, as well as an aesthetic affront. It suggested greed, indolence and self-indulgence. But men from poor African families, who had lived all their life in the shadow of hunger and even starvation, saw great girth as a sign of wealth and power. In their world, only the mightiest chiefs could ever hope to match De Lancey's bulk. No matter how much they hated him for what he had done, they could not help feel a degree of admiration for him.

'Yes, you filthy black baboon, I have something to say, all right.' Quentin De Lancey was holding his head high and staring at Kabaya, challenging him to be the first to look away. 'I did everything you said I did, and I'd do it again, ten times over.'

There was a gasp of astonishment from the audience. Such brazen defiance was not what they had expected, and they were uncertain how to respond. Makori's shock was as great as everyone else's. De Lancey's crimes were even worse than Saffron had suggested. How could he not be ashamed? And how dare he stand in this gathering and speak to a black man in that way? Surely that was as foolhardy as it was insulting.

Kabaya was taken aback. For once he had to search for his words before he was able to reply.

'In that case, since you have confessed your guilt, we will proceed directly to the sentencing—'

'Wait!' boomed De Lancey. 'Even the condemned man standing on the gallows is allowed to say a last few words. May I not address the people too?'

Kabaya had always been sensitive to the mood of his troops. He knew that they wanted to hear what the accused man had to say for himself. Even for men who were living outside the law, the right to speak was a matter of basic justice, which they would all want for themselves. Kabaya considered the situation and concluded that De Lancey would only condemn himself further with his outpouring of crass self-justification. He nodded and said to him, 'Speak.'

'Very well then, I shall start by asking you a question, *General –*' the rank was delivered with sneering sarcasm – 'Kabaya. Is there anything that I have done that you have not done yourself, and more often, and worse? Have you not killed? Have you not mutilated? Last night, when you captured me in my home, my wife was there also. Did you show her mercy? Did you leave her be? Or did you rape her and cut her until she died, as you and your Mau Mau friends have done to innocent white women the length and breadth of Kenya?'

'They deserved it,' Kabaya said, though there was something defensive about his tone. 'They are as responsible as their men for the subjugation of the Kikuyu and the theft of our land.'

'So you admit your guilt. That makes us equal.'

Makori saw the men around him nod in approval at the way De Lancey had caught Kabaya out. There was nothing the Kikuyu liked more than to see one man trap another with his logic, even if their own general was on the receiving end.

'Since we are now equal, let us talk as men, one to another. And let us see whether we can reach an honourable agreement that will benefit us both.'

Kabaya was intrigued. The last thing he had expected from De Lancey was the suggestion that the white man and black man were equals, or that they could work together to their mutual advantage. But he could not be seen to concede too easily.

'We can talk if you like, Nguuo. But know this . . . I still say you are guilty. I still say you will be executed for your crimes. So, go ahead. Try to persuade me, and hope that you do. For if you fail, you die.'

'I accept that challenge,' De Lancey said.

Makori whistled to himself, surprised and also a little impressed by the white man's defiance.

'I start from a simple proposition, Kabaya. You and I know what it is to hate. And what is more, we both hate the same men – upper-class bastards who think they're better than everyone else, black or white.'

'You mean the Englishmen who rule this country?' Kabaya replied.

Makori realised that De Lancey had succeeded in one thing at least. He had involved his opponent in a dialogue he had not expected to have. Suddenly he was controlling the proceedings.

But where is he going with this? Makori wondered.

For his part, Kabaya had not spotted what De Lancey was doing. He could not resist engaging in the argument.

'These men have stripped my people of their land, their rights, their freedom, their families, their homes and their lives. We have lost more than you can even imagine. How dare you compare your situation to ours?'

'I'm not comparing what we have lost,' De Lancey replied. 'I'm comparing how much we hate. And though you may not choose to believe this, there are men among this country's rulers that I have hated since you were a grubby little piccaninny, swatting away the flies from your snot-encrusted nose.'

'Why did you hate these men?'

'They're a bunch of arrogant snobs who've always looked down on me. They thought I was inferior, common, worth less than them. Oh, they were happy to let me do their dirty work. But the moment I put a foot out of place, that was it. They dropped me without a second thought.'

Kabaya shrugged, distinctly unimpressed. 'I believe that you do hate these men, Nguuo. And I hate them too – but I hate you too, as do all the Kikuyu people. You have brought us nothing but pain and misery. You have given me no reason why I should ever agree to stand alongside you. And I see every reason to kill you, slowly, before the eyes of all my men. Yes, that is what I will do . . . Gitiri!'

His baleful henchman stepped out of the shadows beside the lean-to, brandishing his panga.

'Wait! Please!' De Lancey's bold exterior began to fray. 'I can give you something you want!'

In his position at the back of the crowd, Makori gave a little shake of the head.

You showed weakness, De Lancey. Bad move.

'Yes . . .?'

Kabaya had a sly smile on his face. He was enjoying the Englishman's dread at the sight of Gitiri and the thought of what his panga might do.

De Lancey made one last attempt to regain the initiative.

'You will never win this war,' he said. 'The British government will never allow itself to be kicked out of Kenya. They could make life so much better for your people . . . But they choose to slaughter you instead. You have to find a way of ending this before they kill you all.'

'We will never surrender.'

'That's not what I'm suggesting. I'm proposing a means of forcing the governor of Kenya to sit down and negotiate peace.'

'And we will never negotiate! We will never betray the Kikuyu people!'

'Oh, for heaven's sake, man, stop striking poses and use your brain. You have a choice. Keep on the way you are, in the certain knowledge that they'll get you long before you get your freedom. Or do something so bold, so striking, so bloody shocking that it changes the whole game.'

'Changes it how?'

'By taking away your enemy's willingness to keep fighting. Listen, the whites in Kenya are as sick of this as you are. Their kids go to bed sobbing every night. Their memsahibs are half round the bend with terror. And it doesn't matter what the politicians in Westminster want. If the Kenyan whites say, "We've had enough. We want peace, right now," it's going to be impossible to keep the war going.'

'And how would I do that? You stop squealing like a fat pig and tell me that!'

De Lancey summoned a smile. 'All right, then, I'll tell you. But before I do, I need to know one thing. I know you've got these men here and at least one motor vehicle at your disposal. But can you assemble a force of a minimum forty men, preferably more, and transport them at speed to a given target, carry out an armed assault and then get them out again?'

'These are all classified matters,' Kabaya stonewalled.

'Oh, for God's sake, look around – who am I going to tell? Or is that your way of saying, "No, I haven't"?'

Kabaya bristled at the suggestion. 'The men here are not my only forces in the forest. We have trucks, not just that van. The British Army itself taught me how to plan and execute military missions.'

'Good, because I have one in mind. I know how you can strike at the heart of the white community. There's a group of people that everyone thinks are untouchable, people the whole of Kenya knows by name and reputation, even if they've never met them. If you kill these people, then all Kenya will know that no white man, woman or child is safe because you and other terrorists like you can get anyone, anywhere at any time. And when that happens, it won't matter what the British government wants. Johnny Settler and his wife will be desperate to do a deal. So . . . will you save my life?'

'Why should I? You have said much, but there have been no details, no plan of attack. So far I do not have any reason to keep you alive.'

De Lancey nodded. 'Very well then, you want my plan . . . here it is . . .'

And that was when he said the word, 'Lusima'.

From his position at the back of the onlookers, Makori could not hear every detail of what De Lancey was proposing. But he caught enough to chill his blood. Everyone in Kenya, black or white, knew three things about Bwana Courtney and his family. They were rich beyond any normal man's imagination. Their estate was like a private kingdom. And their native workers were the best-treated in the country, with no need to fight for a better life. The rest of the nation might be going up in flames, but Lusima was still a peaceful paradise.

That being the case, the deaths of Leon Courtney and his family might provoke frenzied, panicked demands for even greater savagery and oppression. As Makori had told Saffron, the British always fight back. But even they had their limits – India had proved that – and De Lancey's point that Kenya's whites were fed up with being frightened was well made. Any policeman knew how panic-stricken the settlers already were. An atrocity like the one De Lancey was proposing might just shock them into calling for an end to the civil war.

And Makori had no doubt that the attack could succeed. This was no idea De Lancey had cooked up on the spur of the moment. He'd thought of routes that would get an insurgent force to the heart of Lusima with virtually no chance of being seen. He'd considered the likely ability of the people there to defend themselves, and what would be required to overcome them.

And yet, De Lancey could not possibly have anticipated a moment like this, nor such an opportunity to put his plans into effect.

No, thought Makori, *this has just been his dream of revenge against the rich men. Yet now Kabaya will be the one to make it come true.*

Makori had given Saffron a lecture about the need to rescue De Lancey and rely on the judicial system to take its course. But even if his men achieved total surprise, the chances of a dozen attackers overpowering a force of more than twice their size were slim. And supposing they did win that fight, De Lancey could well be killed in the crossfire.

The original plan would have to be scrapped. So now what?

Makori had to make a decision upon which the fate of a family, and possibly his nation, might depend. For there was a voice in his head that said, 'Let this attack happen. Let it succeed. Let it cause chaos, bring the British to the negotiating table and take advantage of what happens next.'

But that, he quickly decided, was the voice of a fool. If Kabaya and the other men like him who were driving the rebellion ever got so much as a sniff of power, they would never let it go. They had no interest in democracy, no concern for the people. For them, this was simply the biggest robbery of their careers: the theft and plunder of an entire nation.

Makori's duty as a policeman was clear, as was his moral duty to Saffron Courtney. He had promised to keep her safe. She had shown him nothing but respect. Now he had to warn her of the threat confronting her family. If that meant abandoning De Lancey to Kabaya's mercies, so be it.

But before Makori could issue a warning that was specific enough to be useful, he had to hear what Kabaya's response would be.

The Mau Mau commander took his time, and when he spoke it was not to De Lancey, but to one of his own men, the ugly-looking brute who'd been standing beside him wielding the large and fearsome panga.

'What do you think, brother, should we do as Nguuo suggests?'

'The plan could work . . .' the brute said.

'I agree.'

De Lancey relaxed. The corners of his mouth twitched into the beginnings of a smirk. His gambit was going to pay off.

'But we must strike immediately, attack tonight,' Kabaya added.

This was better than De Lancey had dared hope.

Makori, meanwhile, was working out the quickest, safest way for he and Thiga to leave as discreetly as they'd arrived.

He didn't see the flicker of Kabaya's eyes towards Gitiri, the merest glance that carried with it all the instructions the executioner needed.

Two quick steps, a single swing of the panga's blade . . . And the first Makori knew of it was the thump as De Lancey's head hit the ground, shortly before the rest of his mountainous corpse collapsed.

But even that brutal execution was of little account to Makori. The only lives that mattered to him now were those of the Courtney family.

The moment Saffron saw Makori, Thiga and Wando emerge from the trees, she knew something was wrong.

'What happened?' she asked Makori. 'Did you find De Lancey?'

Makori nodded. 'He is dead. We must get back to the cars, fast. I will explain when we get there.'

Saffron knew better than to ask any more questions. Makori was in charge.

Makori and the pseudos were used to long, hard runs. They had been fighting in these mountain forests for the best part of two years, chasing Mau Mau gangs at pace for hours, even days at a time. Saffron was fit by normal standards. She had been born and raised at altitude, and she had trained herself into shape for the South Africa mission, but this was far more challenging than even the toughest session on her home-made assault course. The terrain was hilly, punishing to the legs and lungs on the uphill sections, but no less tricky on the downhill runs, when speeding limbs could easily trip, twist or even break on the countless holes, tree roots and patches of damp slippery leaves underfoot. After just ten minutes, she was gasping for breath, her heart was pounding fit to burst and her legs were screaming in protest.

But Saffron was never going to stop running or ask Makori to slow down. She had been trained to endure pain. She knew

that no matter how much her body might beg her to surrender, she would find reserves of strength and endurance.
Beyond that, though, her will to keep going was founded on
an intuition that Makori was afraid. But what it was that had
spooked him, Saffron did not know. And she was hurting too
much, and working so hard to overcome the pain, that she had
no mental or physical energy to waste on pointless specula-
tion. She just ran.

Wambui ran ahead of Saffron, giving her someone to follow and occasionally, when the terrain allowed, slipping back
alongside her to offer encouragement. They were halfway to
the glade where the vehicles were waiting, and the two women
were side by side when Wambui said, 'Storm coming.'

Saffron did not have the breath to answer, but she nodded.
In the momentary pause between Makori's return and the start
of the run, she had seen Wando looking up through the forest
canopy to catch a glimpse of the sky. Now she knew why.

By the time they reached the glade and Saffron was bent double with her hands on her knees, trying to catch her breath, the
first faint rumbles of distant thunder could be heard to the east,
towards the Lusima Estate.

It's going to be a wet drive home, Saffron thought, grateful that
her Land Rover had a closed, hardtop driver's cab.

She felt a pat on her back and looked round to see Makori.
Saffron managed an exhausted smile.

'Hope I didn't slow you down.'

'Not at all,' he assured her. 'You did well. But I have bad
news for you. Before De Lancey died he tried to make a bar-
gain with Kabaya, the man who captured him. He told Kabaya
how to mount a sneak attack on your father's house. Every
detail.'

'Oh God . . .' Saffron gasped.

'There is worse news. Kabaya is planning to attack tonight.'

Saffron closed her eyes, gritted her teeth and fought the
impulse to scream.

Control yourself, woman. Get a grip. You've been in tougher situations than this. Deal with the matter in hand, one step at a time.

'We have to warn them,' she said, matter-of-factly. 'Where's the nearest farm with a phone?'

'Most farmers around here cannot afford one,' Makori replied. 'To get a line connected is very expensive. But I believe old Major Brett has a phone. His memsahib made him put it in. She said it made her feel safer.'

'How far away is his place?'

'About three miles from the edge of the forest.'

'Then what are we waiting for?' Saffron said.

She dashed to her Land Rover, Wambui beside her. But as she leaned forward to put the key in the ignition she paused for an instant as a thought struck her: *Major Brett . . . where have I heard that name before?*

Kungu Kabaya commanded his Mau Mau gang with the same efficiency and competence as he had once run his King's African Rifles company. Whenever he and his men raided white farms, they did not just kill the owners. They took their weapons, their supplies of ammunition, food and fuel and any vehicles that took Kabaya's fancy. In this way he had steadily increased the quality of his four-wheeled fleet, whose flagships were three Bedford trucks, all originally army vehicles, that he had liberated from a police station, a builders' yard and a logging company.

They had each been given new paint-jobs and licence plates and were kept, along with piled barrels of diesel fuel and crates of spare parts, in a guarded encampment, covered by camouflage netting. It lay undetected by the authorities, barely four hundred yards from a road that led to Molo, and from there down into the Rift Valley, to Nakuru and on to Nairobi.

More significantly, the road skirted the northern edge of the Lusima Estate. And De Lancey, who had been given a guided tour of the property as part of his security survey, had revealed that there was a private, unmarked road that led across the estate, direct to the Courtney family home.

'A few miles past Molo, you'll see a bloody great outcrop,' he'd said. 'It's some kind of sacred place to the Maasai, apparently. You can't miss it, goes straight up like a tower, so high you often can't see the top for the clouds. Now, when you get close to that mountain, look out for a single, large boulder, standing by itself on the right-hand side of the road. That marks the Courtneys' road. Turn off there and head south. You won't see anything at first. The arrogant sods don't want the masses to know it's there. But you'll pick it up about half a mile in. From then on, keep going. It'll take you to the house. Chances are you'll go all the way and won't see a single living soul.'

Nguuo was telling the truth, thought Kabaya, when the boulder turned out to be where De Lancey had told them. *Let us hope he was right about everything else.*

The drive down from the forest had passed without incident. There had been police checks on the way. But the policemen had been Kikuyu. One reminder of their oaths was enough to ensure they let the trucks through without question.

As they drove slowly towards the lower slopes of the mountain, looking for signs of a proper, hard track, Kabaya felt a tremor of anxiety. The private road was not where De Lancey had said it would be.

Kabaya saw something ahead.

'Stop!' he commanded the driver.

He jumped down from the cab and walked across the parched earth to a depression where dust had settled. He saw a set of tyre tracks, no more than a day old. Judging by the width of the tracks and pattern of the tread, they came from a car-sized vehicle, most probably a Land Rover or jeep, since it was going across open country.

Kabaya looked at the position of the sun, which was setting to the west, and used it to judge the bearing of the tracks. They were heading south-east, towards his own destination.

He climbed up beside the driver and said, 'Follow them.'

Sure enough, the tracks led to the road. It was a matter of distance: the cunning, deceitful Courtneys had stopped it almost twice as far from the public highway as Nguuo had suggested.

Kabaya looked towards the horizon and wondered when the storm would break.

Before we get to the house, he thought. *All the better for us. In the darkness and rain, no one will see us coming.*

It was late afternoon and the light was fading fast as Makori led the three Land Rovers up the long drive from the Keringet road to the heart of the Bretts' farm.

They had no stockade around their property, which was a bungalow, surrounded by a verandah. Prettily planted flower beds and a well-manicured lawn, enclosed by a white picket fence, created the effect of an English cottage garden. Saffron knew that there would be a small settlement on the property for the farm workers, with sheds for the farm equipment. But that was hidden away somewhere, so as not to disturb the owners' view.

The drive stopped about thirty yards short of the front door. Saffron brought her vehicle to a halt and watched as Makori jumped from his open driver's seat, opened the picket fence gate and walked up the garden path towards the bungalow. Now that the engines had been switched off, she noticed the thunder was getting louder as the storm drew nearer.

Sweet Jesus, he's forgotten he's in his pseudo get-up!

Saffron knew how easy it was, when working undercover, to get one's identities confused. Makori was thinking like a policeman, seeking assistance from a member of the public with whom he was familiar. But that wasn't what the Bretts would see.

She got out of the car and started running.

The front door opened. From the corner of her eye Saffron saw a large, portly silver-haired man with an Edwardian cavalryman's moustache emerge and stand in the doorway, sheltered by the verandah. He was holding a double-barrelled shotgun. His face looked familiar, but that wasn't her priority right now.

Makori suddenly realised his mistake and stopped dead, raising a hand and calling out, 'Major Brett, I am . . .'

In a single swift, well-practised movement, Brett raised the gun to his shoulder and took aim.

Saffron threw herself full-length and hit Makori just above the knee at the moment that Brett pulled the trigger. They crashed to the ground as the lead pellets flashed just inches over their falling bodies and punched into the front of one of the police Land Rovers, smashing a headlight.

Now Saffron remembered.

'Don't shoot, Major, it's me, Saffron Courtney . . . from the Pony Club gymkhana!'

'Get up!' Brett ordered her. 'Hands in the air. Any funny business and I'll blow your bloody head off!'

Saffron did as she was told. 'Please, Major, don't be alarmed,' she said, trying to speak calmly.

Brett was an old man, living in a community that felt under constant threat. He must be terrified, jumpy, close to panic, as any of his neighbours would be if three cars filled with armed natives turned up outside their house. But Saffron needed him to relax, settle his nerves and start to think clearly. Her life and her family depended on Brett letting her use that phone.

'I promise you we are not terrorists,' she said.

Brett stepped down from the verandah, rifle still raised, and took a few paces towards her. He pointed the gun at Makori, who was lying stock-still on the ground.

'That man is a damn Mau Mau!'

'I know he looks like it, you're quite right,' Saffron said. 'But please believe me, this is Sergeant Makori of the Kenyan Police.'

'Doesn't look like any policeman I ever saw.'

'No, Major, he doesn't. He looks like a Mau Mau because he's been spying on them – in their camp – and he's got information that—'

'And what's all this about a gymkhana?'

Saffron felt her stomach tense. Brett was still as confused and anxious as ever. Then the door behind him opened a few inches, spilling a shaft of light onto the verandah, and a quavering female voice called out, 'Herbert? Herbert? What's going on out there . . .? I'm frightened!'

'Get back inside, Edwina!' Brett shouted, tilting his head towards the house. 'Back inside, this second! I've got this under control!'

No, you haven't, Saffron thought.

She raised her voice just enough that Edwina Brett could hear her, praying that she wouldn't obey her husband.

'It was 1926,' she said. 'I came second in the showjumping to Percy Toynton, who was almost twice my age. I was terribly cross and you thought it was rather poor form, me being such a poor loser.'

Brett relaxed a fraction and his gun barrel dropped a few degrees lower as he tried to make sense of what she'd just told him. Saffron judged the distance between them. It was no more than ten or twelve yards. She could probably get to him, knock him down and take the gun before he had a chance to aim and get a shot off. But it wasn't a sure thing. And she didn't want to use force against an elderly couple. No matter what the situation, that was just wrong.

She kept talking. 'That was the year my mother died. Eva Courtney, I'm sure you remember her.'

The front door to the little house opened slightly. An elderly lady emerged. She was wearing a floral housecoat and slippers, with her hair in curlers, covered by a net.

Poor thing, she was probably getting ready for an early night, Saffron thought.

Edwina Brett peered at her and said, 'Are you really the Courtney girl?'

'Yes, Mrs Brett, and I desperately need to use your telephone. My family are in terrible danger. We've got to warn them.'

Saffron was about to tell Major Brett that he had met Makori before. But he would never believe that he and the scruffy, unwashed figure before him had ever had any dealings whatever. Instead she said, 'Sergeant Makori is a King's African Rifles veteran. He's got a DCM, and bar, and Police Medal for Gallantry.'

Finally she was speaking Brett's language.

'The KAR, you say? Well, we'll soon see about that. Get up, boy, and no monkey business!'

Saffron winced inwardly at Brett's language as Makori got to his feet.

'Attention!' ordered Brett.

Makori snapped into a straight-backed, head-up pose a guardsman would have envied.

'At ease . . .'

Makori put his hands behind his back, legs apart, feet in line with his shoulders.

'So you served in the KAR, you say?'

'Yes, sir!' Makori replied. 'Second East African Brigade, then seconded to the Chindits, sir.'

'And they gave you a brace of DCMs?'

'Yes, sir.'

'Well, I'll be damned.' Brett looked at Saffron. 'And you'll vouch for him?'

'Yes, sir,' Saffron said, noting that Brett seemed to respond better if spoken to as a superior officer.

'Did I hear you say your family were in a spot of bother?'

'Yes, sir. The Mau Mau are about to attack my father's house at Lusima. We have to warn him, sir.'

'Well then, you had better come in.'

Saffron and Makori followed Brett up to the verandah and through the front door, watched by the wide-eyed Edwina, who plainly could not begin to imagine what the heiress to the Courtney fortune was doing with the ruffian making his malodorous way into her home.

'Telephone's in the hall,' Brett said, glancing back at his visitors. 'Usual drill. Dial for the operator, they'll put you through.' He turned to his wife and, knowing that she would feel better if she had something to do, said, 'Why don't you put the kettle on, old girl? Dare say our guests could use a decent cup of tea. And a couple of your delicious shortbread biscuits, what?'

Saffron dialled, as instructed. The operator answered. She gave the number of her parents' house. She heard the operator dial the number and then . . . silence.

'I am sorry, ma'am, but I cannot get through,' the operator said.

'Please try again.'

'Of course.' A few seconds later, she repeated that she could not get through. 'It is possible that the lines are down, ma'am. We have reports of storm damage across the country.'

Saffron hung up, muttered, 'Damn and blast it,' and turned to Makori.

'What did De Lancey tell Kabaya? How is he going to attack?'

'From the north. He said there was a secret, private road that leads across the estate to the main house. How far is that?'

'About twenty-two miles from the estate boundary to the house.'

'How long would it take to drive?'

'In broad daylight and dry conditions, you could do it in around forty minutes, less if you pushed it. But at night, with bad weather coming, it could take longer.'

'That will buy us more time.'

'Let's hope so,' Saffron said. 'And surely it will take time for Kabaya to summon all his troops and get them to wherever he keeps his trucks?'

'Yes, he was boasting about having more men than were visible at that meeting. They will have to come from somewhere.'

'Okay.' Saffron nodded. 'Now, was the Estate House the only place De Lancey mentioned?'

Makori shook his head. 'I'm very sorry, but he also informed Kabaya about Cresta Lodge. He said that you lived there with your husband and children.'

'Oh no! Gerhard, Zander, Kika!' Saffron exclaimed. 'For God's sake, Makori, Cresta's only three miles from the estate boundary. Kabaya could get there in no time. Why didn't you tell me sooner?'

'What good would that do? We are already doing all that is possible. And I do not believe that there is an immediate threat to your husband and children. Mister De Lancey did not seem interested in your home. It is your father he hates. He and Kabaya concentrated on your father's house. But perhaps you can call your husband now? The storm may not have reached him yet.'

'No point. We don't have a phone.' Saffron gave an angry, frustrated sigh. 'We thought it was romantic. You know, living in our own little world.'

'In that case, there is nothing more we can do. The priority must be to reach your father's house before Kabaya.'

Makori looked towards Major Brett. 'Do you have a map of the local area, sir?'

'In my study. Follow me.'

They made their way slowly into the living room, followed by Edwina, carrying a tray with four cups of tea and a plate of biscuits, through the dining room and into a study whose walls were lined with ancient, moth-eaten hunting trophies. As Edwina handed out the cups and offered sugar to go with them, Major Brett shuffled through the papers piled on his bureau.

'Found it!' Brett said triumphantly, holding up a dog-eared, heavily creased road map.

'Thank you, sir,' said Saffron.

She dashed back into the dining room and unfolded the map on the mahogany dining table, holding one end in place with her tea-cup. Makori downed his drink in one, declared, 'Ahh, very good!' and put his cup at the other end of the map.

'Where are we now?' Saffron asked.

Makori examined the map, got his bearings and pointed. 'About here.'

'Right.' Saffron swept her finger around an area of the map. 'The Lusima Estate occupies all this land. It runs in a long, thin oval, from north-west to south-east. And the road you're talking about runs from about here . . . down to the Estate House, here. The area to the south and east of the house is the Kikuyu farming country. We need to get the produce from there to market, so the only properly made-up road on the estate runs across the farming area to the house.'

'Coming in from the opposite end to the route Kabaya is taking.'

'Exactly. So we are here, to the west of Lusima, about half the way down . . . Which means that if we drive cross-country from here, we'll hit this road—'

'It looks more like a track,' Makori said, peering at the faint dotted line on the map that Saffron had pointed out.

'I know that track.' Major Brett plainly had no doubt at all now about the gravity of the situation. 'Bit bumpy, but you'll get those Land Rovers down it all right. Then you'll hit the main road through the hills to Njoro.' He traced the route with his finger. 'D'you see?'

Saffron nodded, then told Makori, 'I can guide us from Njoro to the main entrance to the estate. From there it's only about ten or twelve minutes to the house, tarmac all the way.'

There was a sudden rumble of thunder, much louder than before. Saffron glanced up at the sound.

'Lots of rain, very soon,' Makori said.

'Well, the weather will be the same for everyone.' Saffron sighed. 'It's going to be bloody tight between Kabaya and us.' She looked at the Bretts and said, 'Thank you, Major, Mrs Brett, we'll be on our way.'

Saffron and Makori ran through the house and out across the verandah towards the Land Rovers. As they went, Makori said, 'Is it true that your husband was a fighter pilot?'

'Yes – we keep a plane at the lodge.'

'Then there is nothing to worry about. When he hears Kabaya's trucks, he can just take your children and fly away. He will be as free as a bird.'

erhard had almost chased after Saffron to give her a proper hug and a kiss goodbye, and the fact that he hadn't had niggled at him all day. His wartime experiences had taught him that death could strike at any moment, and he had lost too many friends without a proper farewell. He hated the thought that such a thing might ever happen to him and Saffron. But there was little time or energy to spend for brooding with two small children in the house.

It was getting late in the day and Gerhard was thinking of that first, blessed sip of his evening drink. But Zander had other ideas.

'Please can we go up in your aeroplane today, Daddy,' he begged. 'Please, Daddy, please-please-please!'

The older they got, the more the children loved to go up in the Tri-Pacer. Zander had his sights set on becoming a pilot and was constantly pestering Gerhard to teach him how to fly. The response was always the same.

'Not until your feet touch the pedals. And maybe not even then.'

While her brother tugged at their father's sleeve with a desperation born of wild excitement at the thought that they might get the ride they craved, mixed with a terrible fear that they would be refused, Kika had gone for a more subtle approach. At the age of four, she had already begun to master the art of twisting her besotted father around her little finger. She wandered into his path as he walked across the playroom, forcing him to stand still, then looked up at him with her sweetest, most wide-eyed expression and said, 'Please, Daddy, do take us flying. I promise we'll be really good for days and days, won't we, Zander?'

Her brother took a second to catch on and then agreed with heartfelt sincerity.

'We'll be the bestest children ever!'

'Hmm . . .'

Gerhard pondered, letting the silence drag out as his children looked on with wide-eyed tension. So far as they knew, their mother was just away for the day seeing friends. Gerhard didn't want them worrying. So if he could give them something else to occupy their minds, so much the better.

'All right, then,' he conceded. 'You can come flying with me.'

Zander whooped with delight while Kika hugged Gerhard's leg.

'But it will only be a quick little hop because the sun will be setting soon. And you must give me your solemn promise to behave yourselves in the aircraft and do exactly what I say. I mean it. Flying is a serious business. So you have to do what the pilot says. Do you understand?'

'Yes, Daddy!' came the two replies.

'Right then, off we go.'

On the plateau atop Lonsonyo Mountain, in the large, thatched hut where Mama Lusima had lived and practised her healing arts, Manyoro lay on his deathbed. Naserian, his senior wife, and Benjamin were in attendance.

Manyoro's condition had been stable for the past fortnight, but suddenly, within a matter of hours it had deteriorated. He could only manage a morsel of food and a few sips of water. Even the soothing herbs that his womenfolk had gathered could no longer reduce his pain.

'Benjamin, my boy, there is no more you can do for me,' Manyoro said, and every word was an effort for him.

'But, Father . . .'

'Hush . . . let me speak . . .' Manyoro had to pause and summon up a few last dregs of energy before he could continue. 'I was wrong to say that Mbogo, my brother, should not come here. I must see him again before I die. Go to him now. Bring him to me.'

'Yes, Father.' Benjamin stood, then paused, seized by the overwhelming intuition that he would never speak to his father again. He knelt by the bed, took Manyoro's hand and said, 'Father, I . . .' He stopped short, unable to form the words that could express the storm of emotions that filled his heart.

Manyoro managed a faint, weary smile. 'I understand . . .' he said. 'You have my love, and my blessing.' He looked Benjamin in his eye, and it was as if that look swept away the years of conflict and misunderstanding and peace had been made between them, finally and forever. 'Now go.'

Benjamin stopped by the entrance for one last look at his father. The old man's eyes were closed and his mouth was hanging half-open, giving his face an even more drawn, hollow appearance.

Benjamin thought that Manyoro had died, but he noticed the barely perceptible rise and fall of his chest and the fluttering sound of his breath. He waited, then turned away and walked out of the hut.

Naserian was waiting for him in the darkness.

'I am going to fetch Mbogo.' Benjamin glanced towards Manyoro's hut and said, 'Stay with him, Mother. It will not be long now.'

The sun was setting fast. Benjamin frowned as he thought of the path that zigzagged across the precipitous rock face.

'I need a torch,' he said.

Naserian smiled. 'You have spent too long in the white men's cities, my dear. But you have the blood of Lusima the Wise in your veins. Your feet will find their own way.'

Benjamin nodded, but he went back to his hut for a thick jumper, a water-bottle and his gun, all of which would be essential if he was going to be driving by night, crossing wild country, still populated by leopards and lions.

Essential for a white man, Benjamin thought. *No Maasai would need these things. Maybe Mother was right. Maybe I should trust in who I really am.*

Naserian had been right about one thing – Benjamin didn't need a torch. As the dusk gave way to night, his eyes adjusted to the darkness and his body seemed to remember all the times he had gone up and down the mountain, from scampering as a little boy to a tall, strong, proud young man. He strode up the path as sure-footed as a mountain lion, oblivious to the drop, thinking only of what lay in store for him at the summit.

'Time to go home,' said Gerhard. 'Can you see over there . . . ?'

He banked the Tri-Pacer to make it easier for the children to see across the vast open plain towards the far horizon. Towering clouds of billowing black cumulonimbus were marching into view like the advance guard of a storm god's all-conquering army. A sudden blast of sheet lightning exploded across the sky.

The storm was still away in the distance, coming in from the east. It must have already hit the Estate House. It would be a matter of minutes before it reached Cresta Lodge.

'I want this plane on the ground and safely stowed before the first drop of rain falls on our landing strip.'

Gerhard was grateful that he had only taken the children up for a quick circuit of the area immediately around their home. He began to turn into the descent that would take them back to the landing strip, and as he did something caught his eye – a movement on the ground a couple of thousand feet down below.

He looked again. Three trucks were driving at speed, following one of the hard-beaten earth roads that cut across the Lusima game reserve. They were driving towards the storm.

Gerhard's first thought was that the truck drivers must be crazy. He looked at his compass, made a rough calculation of the direction of the wind and realised, *They're heading for the Estate House*, and, an instant later, *But those aren't Leon's trucks.*

A sudden premonition of danger struck him. For the first time in almost a decade, Gerhard felt like a combat pilot again, spotting a suspicious movement and thinking, *That's the enemy!*

For a moment he was torn. He wanted to go down and take a closer look at the trucks. But he had his children aboard and a storm was coming. They needed to be safe at home and tucked up in bed. He had lectured Saffron about keeping herself safe, for her family's sake. How could he not do the same thing?

But Gerhard's long-dormant warrior instincts were lighting up his nerve endings with danger signals. He looked at the clouds and told himself, *I'll take a look, then head for the strip as fast as I can. We can still get there ahead of the storm.*

Gerhard turned the Tri-Pacer towards the trucks and began a descent down to three hundred feet.

In the front seat of the lead truck, Kabaya saw the aircraft to his right, travelling in the opposite direction. He narrowed his eyes. It was small and single-engined, like the ones the police had taken to using.

But why is there a police plane out here?

A thought struck him: *Perhaps the mighty Bwana Courtney is so rich, he can afford his own aircraft. We must hope it does not see us.*

The hope was dashed. The plane turned and dropped into a shallow dive. The pilot had seen them. He wanted a closer look.

The Tri-Pacer dropped down towards the trucks, until it was only a few hundred feet above them. Kabaya watched it come, hating the feeling of impotence that had seized him. His men were useless to him. They could not shoot at the plane unless the trucks stopped and they all dismounted. By the time the first shot was fired, the aircraft would have flown out of range.

All he could do was hope that the pilot would be satisfied that they were delivering groceries and clean laundry to Bwana Courtney's home. But who would do that late in the evening, with a storm raging ahead?

He will not be fooled, Kabaya thought as the plane came closer. It flew for a while on a parallel course to the two trucks, practically skimming over the tall baobab trees that dotted the savanna.

Kabaya was holding his Sten gun across his lap. His fingers were itching to use it. He could see the pilot looking at him, trying to decide whether the trucks were a threat to his master, or not.

Kabaya could stand it no longer. He wound down the window, poked the barrel of the Sten into the open air, aimed at the cockpit, and emptied his magazine in a single, prolonged burst.

Kabaya was a seasoned soldier, firing at point-blank range. He wasn't going to miss.

Gerhard saw the Sten gun barrel poke out of the passenger's side window and reacted immediately. As Kabaya pulled the trigger, he threw the Tri-Pacer sideways, like a man diving for cover, banking so tightly at such low altitude that his wing tip was barely a foot or two off the earth below.

If it made contact the aircraft was as good as dead, for it would trip and fall to the ground. But Gerhard drastically altered the angle of the turn, jinking the other way and throwing one wing tip back up into the air while the other swung down towards the red-brown Kenyan earth.

But as he ducked and dived, Gerhard could not escape the Sten gun's long burst.

The Plexiglas in front of him cracked open as three rounds hit, and a line of holes was stitched across the thin aluminium skin of the fuselage.

Those bullets had entered the aircraft. But what had they hit?

As Gerhard took the Tri-Pacer up and away from the trucks, he called towards his children.

'Are you all right back there? Zander! Kika! Tell me you're okay.'

'I'm all right, Daddy,' Zander replied, but his was the only answering voice.

Gerhard was gripped by the terrible, leaden chill of fear.

'Kika! Talk to me!' he begged her. 'Are you all right?'

'I'm frightened,' the little girl's voice replied. 'I want to go home.'

Gerhard knew for sure he had stumbled upon a raiding party. If those trucks were full, there could be thirty or more Mau Mau fighters heading for the Estate House. If they could manage a surprise attack, Leon and Harriet would not stand a chance.

Gerhard tried to send a warning message over the aircraft radio, but it was a futile gesture. The storm had surely put Leon's short-wave radio out of action; if the transmitter was unscathed, the tall, spindly aerial would not have survived the pounding wind.

He glanced at the children, then looked at his fuel gauge. It was almost empty. The conclusion was inescapable: either the storm would dash the Tri-Pacer from the sky, or it would run out of gas. Meanwhile Gerhard had two tired, hungry, frightened children to consider.

He couldn't risk his babies' lives. But nor could he condemn their grandparents to certain death.

It was an impossible dilemma, but Gerhard didn't have time to come up with a reasoned solution. All he could do was follow his instincts. He took a course heading due east towards the Estate House.

He put on his cheeriest voice and told the children, 'I've changed my mind. We're going to pay Grandma and Grandpa a visit.'

He pointed his aircraft at the raging black heart of the oncoming storm.

Benjamin had seen the line of storm clouds advancing towards him as he walked down to the grasslands. By the time he reached the car their presence was manifest as a black curtain across the night sky, blotting out the stars, torn asunder from time to time by the dazzling flashes of lightning.

The deluge was almost upon him when Benjamin's headlights picked out the lines of tyre tread marks cutting across the bare earth to his left and then joining the track he was on: the route to the Estate House. He stopped the Land Rover and asked himself: *were they there when I came this way towards the mountain?*

Benjamin got out of the car, the gun in one hand, and squatted to look at the tracks. They were new, with clear, undisturbed imprints in the dust. He studied them more closely, picking out the various tread patterns and identifying individual vehicles, as he might have deduced information about passing animals from the marks of their feet, hooves or paws.

Three large trucks, he concluded. *They know where they're going, because they didn't stop or slow down when they reached the track. And if they're travelling at night, they want to arrive without warning.*

Suddenly Benjamin's journey had acquired a new urgency.

S affron and Makori's convoy was still travelling cross-country when the storm hit. In an instant, the visibility was reduced to near zero, as the charcoal clouds blocked every ray of sunlight and the relentless downpour formed an impenetrable curtain of water which no windscreen wiper could clear.

Saffron and Wambui were deafened by the hammering rain on the steel roof of the cab, but at least they were dry inside. The men in the open Land Rovers were drenched to the skin in a matter of seconds. Within a couple of minutes, Makori and Thiga were having to stop and open the doors to let out the water that had collected inside their vehicles.

In the dry they had been speeding across the rock-hard terrain at almost fifty miles per hour, heedless of the risk of a rock or animal hole that might cripple any car that hit it. Now they were crawling through the murk.

When they reached the road, matters barely improved. The rain had been falling for longer here so that they found themselves having to navigate around fallen trees and telegraph poles, ford small streams that had become raging torrents, cross bridges that were themselves under water.

Kabaya was closing on the Estate House from the north. For all that Saffron knew the storm might not have reached him yet. He was gaining ground while she was barely moving. She thought of Gerhard and the children. Despite Makori's reassurances, some primal instinct deep inside her was screaming that they were in danger. Saffron knew that if she hadn't been on patrol with Makori, there would never be a chance of rescuing her family. But still she couldn't rid herself of the feeling that bad things were going to happen, and they would be all her fault.

At last they reached a tarmac road. Though they were driving through water that was inches deep, sending up great sprays on either side, at least the carriageway beneath them was firm.

Saffron was in the lead vehicle, since she knew the way to Lusima. She pushed harder on the accelerator and changed into a higher gear. The Land Rover was constantly slipping and skidding on the treacherously slick road surface, but she maintained and even increased her speed, leaning forward over the wheel to peer through the gloom.

If she maintained this crazy pace there was a very good chance that Saffron would kill herself and Wambui. But if she arrived too late at the house, all its inhabitants and staff would certainly be dead.

She had no choice.

Gerhard had flown over Russia in worse weather than this, and done so with enemy aircraft shooting at him. As the winds tossed the Tri-Pacer across the sky like the dried pea in a tin whistle, he was confident that he would get through to the Estate House and land successfully on the sweeping lawns that surrounded the property.

But he was not alone. He had his children to consider. They were frightened out of their wits. There was crying and screams of alarm as lightning flashed around them. The wind was howling through the aircraft's rigging and blowing through the bullet-holes in the fuselage, and the plane was being hurled up and down and from one side to another.

Gerhard asked himself again and again, *Why am I flying into danger? Why didn't I just go home?*

He realised it resided in his past. He had seen with his own eyes what happened when people turned a blind eye to evil, said a prayer of thanks for not being the victims themselves and continued as though nothing was happening. Germany was guilty of that and the result had been the deaths of millions in the camps, at the battlefront and in cities reduced to burned-out rubble by Allied bombs.

If Gerhard let the trucks drive on, he might make Zander and Kika safer tonight. But the men in those trucks – or others like them – would arrive another night, knowing they could attack with impunity. The only way to keep his children secure was to confront the enemy and defeat him.

He looked at the speedometer. Gerhard had the Tri-Pacer's engine screaming into the red zone. But it only had a fraction of the power of the mighty Daimler-Benz unit that had powered Gerhard's Messerschmitt Bf 109 fighter plane. Flying into gale-force headwinds, the aircraft was barely managing seventy knots of forward progress. The trucks on the ground would be impeded by the rain and its effect on the road's surface, but the ground below was parched. The rain would be soaked up like ink into blotting paper and the trucks' heavy tyres would cut through the muddy slurry and grip on the hard ground beneath. If the drivers knew what they were doing, they could maintain a fast pace.

I'll be lucky to get five minutes' lead on them, Gerhard thought.

He had been flying by his compass and dead reckoning, relying on his familiarity with what was usually a short, uneventful hop between Cresta and the Estate House. But the sudden gusts of crosswind were making it almost impossible to maintain a steady course and visibility was near zero.

He brought the aircraft down as low as he dared above the treetops and peered into the murk. Suddenly, to his left he saw a flicker of brightness. He turned towards it and the flicker gradually took on a recognisable form: the lights of the Estate House.

Gerhard flew around the house once, to orientate himself and determine where he was going to land. Then he brought the Tri-Pacer into the wind so that the oncoming gale would act as an air-brake, to slow down the aircraft and lessen the amount of room it needed to come to a halt.

He called out, 'Hang on tight!' then came down so low over the trees that ringed the lawns that the undercarriage ripped through the upper branches. The plane hit the ground hard, bounced, skidded on the sodden grass and slewed around so violently that it was all Gerhard could do to stop it tipping over.

The children found their voices again, shrieking as the aircraft careered across the ground until brought to a halt by one of the immaculately maintained high hedges of which Leon was so proud.

Gerhard did not have time to explain anything to the children. He threw open the cabin door and leaped onto the ground. He leaned into the rear of the cabin, ignoring the soaking rain and biting wind as he unbuckled his children's seat belts and lifted them out of the aircraft so that they were standing beside him.

He got down on his haunches and shouted over the noise of the storm, 'Zander, climb on my back!'

The little boy did as he was told, clinging on with all his might as Gerhard picked up Kika and ran across the slippery lawn towards the house. Several times Gerhard nearly lost his footing, wincing with pain as Zander pulled at the hair he was holding as tightly as his pony's reins. They reached the steps that led up to the terrace.

Gerhard crossed the paving stones to the side of the house and hammered on the frame of the French windows. The moment he did it, he realised his effort was futile. No one inside could possibly hear him over the din of the wind and rain.

He crouched again, a few feet from the windows, and placed Kika on the ground. Zander scrambled from his back.

Gerhard told the children, 'Don't move. Zander, look after your sister. Hold her tight and stay where you are.'

He examined the windows, considered the damage he was about to do to the building's defences and concluded he had no alternative. He gave a hefty kick with his boot at the line where the two sets of doors met. The wood gave but the lock held. Gerhard kicked harder, again, and again. Finally, the door frames buckled inwards. He shoulder-barged his way through, then turned to his children.

'Come inside! Quick, quick! Follow me!'

They ran through the garden room and into the main hall. Gerhard heard Leon's voice coming from the dining room, followed by the sound of laughter. He and Harriet had guests.

Gerhard charged into the dining room, soaked, wild-eyed and followed by two bedraggled children. Ignoring the expressions on the servants' faces, the cries of alarm and shouts of protest, he slammed his fist down on the mahogany table.

'Listen to me!' he shouted, silencing the room. 'Leon, tell your boys to go to the gunroom and fetch every gun you've got, and every round of ammunition.'

He looked around the table at the six guests, wondering which of these middle-aged men and women in their dinner jackets and silk dresses would be up to the fight that was heading their way.

Gerhard lowered his voice. There was no need to turn alarm into panic. What he was about to say was enough.

'The Mau Mau are coming. There isn't a second to lose.'

Leon Courtney took command because it was his house and his land. He did so with the controlled urgency that came from beginning his working life as a professional soldier and serving as an officer in the First World War. He was sixty-five years old, but exuded the energy of a man twenty years his junior.

'How many of them are there?' Leon asked.

'Three trucks,' Gerhard replied. 'I couldn't tell how many men were in them. But one of them fired at me with a submachine gun.'

'So at least thirty men, possibly more than forty, all armed. How soon will they be here?'

'Depending on the surface conditions and visibility, I'd say somewhere between three to five minutes.'

'Call it three.' Leon allowed himself a few seconds' thought, then turned to Ali Mashraf, one of the two servants who had been waiting on the table. 'Ali, go to Mpishi. Tell him to assemble his staff in the kitchen, immediately.'

Leon focused on his guests. 'We're in this together, and ladies, that includes you.'

'You can count on us,' said Harriet, before any of the other wives had the chance to even hint otherwise. Her words also served to make it impossible for any of the men to back down. Dorian was the first of them to speak.

'I'm right behind you, old man. Brothers in arms, eh?'

Leon nodded at Dorian. 'Thanks, Dor,' he said quietly. 'Means a lot.' Then he turned his eyes back to the rest of his guests. 'Any who feel confident in your shooting skills are welcome to join us at the barricades. Any who don't can serve as loaders. I advise you to take off any jewellery that might attract a Mau Mau's attention, and shoes or garments that impede your ease of movement. Gentlemen, come with me.'

Leon looked at the second servant, whose name was Johnson Kiprop, and added, 'You too.'

Gerhard had kept one eye on the second hand of his watch. Leon had assessed the situation and made his first dispositions in under a minute. Harriet was already organising the ladies with a similar degree of efficiency. It was no less than he had expected, but he felt the reassurance that comes from knowing that the people managing a crisis know what they're doing.

Leon led the way to the gunroom, followed by his three guests, Kiprop and Gerhard, who was wiping the rainwater from his face and hair with a napkin he'd picked up from the table. As he walked along the hall to the stairs that led into the cellars, Gerhard considered the men who would be his comrades-in-arms tonight. Directly behind Leon came his youngest brother Dorian. He was smaller and more slightly built than Leon, and was the artist of the family, taking after their mother. His temperament was much more light-hearted than Leon's, less burdened by the responsibilities that came with being the eldest son, and he had not served in either World War. But Dorian was a Courtney nonetheless, and the way that he had reacted to Leon's announcement that the Mau Mau were heading in their direction left Gerhard in no doubt that when the time came, he would stand his ground and fight.

The other two men were somewhat younger: in their mid-forties, Gerhard guessed. He recognised their faces and knew their names, Bill Finney and Tommy Sharpe, but he had never said more than a passing word to either man. But he reassured himself with the thought that Leon Courtney did not invite men to dinner at Lusima unless he not only liked but also respected them. And that respect was not lightly won.

'Gentlemen, most of you have been to war, and you've all shot game. I don't need to tell you how to handle a gun,' Leon said, taking weapons down from the racks and handing them out to his guests. 'I suggest you fight alongside your memsahibs. Take one rifle and one shotgun per couple. The rifle will drop a man at longer range, but you can't beat a shotgun for close combat.'

As Leon dealt with the guns, Gerhard went to the cabinet where the ammunition was stored and began distributing 12-bore cartridges for the shotguns, with belts in which to place them, and three-round clips for the rifles.

'There's not as much ammo as I'd like,' Leon said. 'Put an order into Holland & Holland a couple of weeks ago, hasn't arrived yet. We'll just have to make the best of what we've got.'

'Have no fear,' Finney assured him. 'We'll make every round count.' He grinned. 'Be like Rorke's Drift all over again.'

'Good man, Bill,' Leon said. 'Listen, you and Muriel take the dining room to the left of the front door. Tommy and Jane, take the drawing room to the right. That way, any frontal assault will have to face two lines of fire. Dorian, I want you and Sophie in the garden room, covering any attack across the terrace.

'I advise you all to draw the curtains across any windows to reduce the risk of flying glass. Leave enough to shoot and see through, like the arrow-slit in a castle wall.

'Gerhard, you'll be up on the first floor. You should get a decent field of fire from the master bedroom. But keep your wits about you. There's a bathroom window to the side on the first floor. We can't have anyone getting in there.

'I will position myself in the hall, which is the easiest place from which to issue orders, and also to reinforce any room that is under particular pressure. Kiprop, you take the remaining guns and a carton of ammunition. Mpishi and his people will need them.'

'Are you sure that's wise, old boy?' Tommy Sharpe asked. 'I should have thought that the fewer black men with guns, the better.'

'I think I know my people,' Leon replied, strapping his old Webley service revolver around his waist. 'But we'll soon find out.'

Leon had reserved one other weapon for his own use – the Holland & Holland 470 Royal Nitro Express rifle that he'd been given in 1906.

'One last hunt, eh, old friend?' he murmured. 'Let's make it a good one.'

There was a sad smile on Leon's face as he picked up the final weapon in the defenders' arsenal, Eva's customised Webley, with its ivory-handled grip. Then he bucked himself up, said, 'Let's get on with it,' and led his men to the ground floor as fast as they could go.

Bill, Tommy and Dorian quickly explained Leon's plan to their wives. Gerhard found his children with Harriet. Leon joined them, loaded Eva's pistol and gave it to Harriet along with six spare rounds. She still had her evening bag in her hand. Without a thought she opened the bag, held it upside down and let its contents fall on the floor: her lipstick, compact, handkerchief and a cigarette lighter she kept in case a guest should ever need a light. Then she poured the spare ammunition into her bag.

'Right,' she said, 'I'm ready. What do you need me to do?'

'Look after the little ones,' Leon replied. 'Take them down to the wine cellar, lock the door, barricade it as best you can. I pray to God you never have to fire this gun, but if you do, I beg you, keep three rounds in reserve.' For a moment, his air of assurance wavered. 'If the Mau Mau . . .'

'It's all right, my darling. I understand,' Harriet said, resting her hand on his arm. She kissed him on the cheek. 'Go and do your duty, and I will do mine.'

Harriet addressed Zander and Kika. 'Children?'

'Yes, Grandma.'

Zander's voice was uncertain. He had heard enough to understand that the Mau Mau were coming and there was going to be a fight. He looked on his father and grandfather as his greatest heroes, so he assumed that they would win the fight. And he knew that he, as a boy, had a duty to be strong and not cry. But even so, he was very frightened.

Kika, for her part, was standing with her eyes wide and her thumb in her mouth, understanding nothing of what was happening, but feeling the tension and anxiety in the air.

'Kika?' Harriet said.

'Say, "Yes, Grandma",' Zander said, glad of the chance to seem grown up.

'Yes, Grandma,' Kika said, very softly, her lips beginning to tremble around her thumb.

'Come with me.'

The children said nothing, but turned their eyes towards Gerhard, wanting his reassurance. He crouched, embraced them both, kissed the tops of their heads and said, 'It's all right. Everything is going to be fine. Do what Grandma tells you.'

Zander and Kika nodded solemnly and followed Harriet to the cellar.

Gerhard watched them go. Then he raced upstairs, opened the curtains and looked into the night.

The storm was abating. The speed with which African weather changed was unlike the slow, gradual shifts of European weather. Within no time it would cease completely.

It took a few seconds for Gerhard's night vision to start coming back and then he saw them, away to the distance: three pairs of lights.

He ran out of the bedroom, onto the first-floor landing and shouted to the ground floor.

'I can see headlights, no more than a kilometre . . .' He corrected himself. 'Half a mile off. They're almost here!'

*

As Kiprop placed the large carton of ammunition on the kitchen table, then unhooked the five rifles he had slung around his shoulders and laid them beside the ammo, Leon looked around the room. It struck him how unfamiliar he was with it. This was Harriet's kingdom. With help from Mpishi and the house-keeper, Tabitha, she ran the household with impeccable efficiency and made it gently, but firmly clear she could manage without interference from her husband. His energies were best directed at the farms, tourist income and overseas businesses that paid the bills.

It was with the dispassionate eye of a soldier sizing up a defensive position that he considered the kitchen's layout. To his left, two dressers, laden with crockery and serving vessels flanked the door that led into the larder and storeroom, which he knew was windowless. To his right, the wood-fired range cooker occupied the centre of the room, with low wooden cupboards and shelves to either side, topped by stone work-tops. The only windows were at the end of the room, opposite the door: one above the double-sink and another in the door that led out to a small yard dividing the main house from the separate servants' quarters.

For an instant, Leon wondered whether they should abandon the house and make their stand in the servants' block, which was smaller and more defensible. But pride prevented him taking that option: *I'm damned if I'll be driven from my own home without a fight.*

But would the staff join him in that fight? They were lined up on the far side of the kitchen table: five men and three women in various states of dress and wakefulness.

'The Mau Mau are coming,' Leon told them. 'Soon they will be here and we will have to fight them. You know that if they are victorious, they will show no mercy to any black man or woman who has fought against them. I give you the choice. You may leave now. Or you can stand by me and we will battle them together. What do you say?'

Silence fell upon the room. For a moment Leon thought he might have misjudged the loyalty of his people. Perhaps, in the end, the primal, atavistic bonds of tribe and race counted for more than those of a family and a household. But Mpishi stepped forward.

The Sudanese cook had served the Courtney family for more than thirty years. His ebony skin was criss-crossed with the lines of age and the few tufts of hair on his head were all silver. He squared his shoulders, looked Leon in the eye and said, 'Courtney, Bwana, the men will stand and fight.'

'And the women, too,' Tabitha added firmly.

Leon smiled. 'Good.' He handed out the rifles to Mpishi, Ali Mashraf and the other three kitchen *totos*. 'Ladies, find the sharpest knives and largest cleavers. There will be a lot of meat to butcher. And boil big pots of oil and water. The Mau Mau have had a long drive. They will need a nice hot bath when they arrive.'

Leon heard Gerhard's voice calling from the landing. He could tell by the looks on his servants' faces that they had caught the warning message too.

'Not long now,' Leon said. 'Our enemies will surely attack the rear of the house. They will try to come in through this kitchen. But you will stop them. I know you will.'

Leon left the kitchen and made a quick tour of the other three rooms he had chosen as defensive positions. He wished all his husband-and-wife teams good luck, and gave them the same message he had been taught as a young subaltern in the King's African Rifles, almost fifty years earlier: 'Don't shoot till you see the whites of their eyes.'

Muriel Finney had never fired a gun in her life, though she had frequently loaded for her husband, who was a crack shot. They agreed to work on their usual basis, so that Bill would always have a loaded gun at his disposal. The other two women, however, were determined to do their bit on the front line.

'Try to take turns to shoot,' Leon advised them. 'That way, if one of you has to reload, the other can still keep firing.'

'I reckon I should be loading and leaving all the dirty work to Sophie,' Dorian remarked blithely, as if this were a jolly after-dinner game, rather than a matter of life and death. 'She grew up shooting duck on the Delta. Her aim is infinitely better than mine.'

Sophie smiled sweetly. 'If you want to serve me, darling, feel free.'

Leon gave a dry chuckle. 'If you two could make up your minds, I'd be much obliged. Meanwhile, let's get something across those French windows.'

There was a low wooden cabinet, about six feet long and made of heavy black wood, lined up against one wall. It was too heavy to lift, so Leon took one end and Dorian the other. They started manhandling it across the parquet floor towards the opening that Gerhard had made when he first entered.

The sound of diesel engines rumbled across the lawn, compelling the two men to redouble their efforts.

'Bloody hell, Leon, what do you keep in here? Cannonballs?' Dorian grunted, straining to get the cumbersome brute in place.

'Bits of crockery, I think,' Leon replied. One of the cabinet's doors popped open and a large china serving dish slipped out and crashed onto the floor. 'And old copies of *Punch*.'

'Splendid! If we get bored with fighting we can amuse ourselves with the cartoons.'

'No chance of that,' said Sophie. 'They're here.'

The two Courtney brothers took their places beside Sophie, kneeling behind the cabinet, looking towards the garden. While the men were moving the furniture, Sophie had opened the cartons of rifle and shotgun ammunition that had been brought up from the gunroom. She placed them within easy reach.

Three shots rang out, coming from inside the house, but above them.

'Hold your damn fire, Meerbach,' Leon muttered.

The vehicle was now visible, barely thirty yards away with its lights off. But there was no sign of any men. They were still aboard.

The truck reached the foot of the steps. The three defenders tensed, waiting for the first Mau Mau to get out and charge towards them.

But no one dismounted. The truck kept moving. As the sound of the straining engine rose still higher, Leon shouted, 'Christ! They're driving right up the bloody steps!'

He opened fire and the other two followed. At point-blank range, every round hit the truck, but it seemed as impenetrable as a great steel rhino as it climbed inexorably towards them.

As Leon, Dorian and Sophie frantically reloaded, the truck reached the top of the steps. When all four of its wheels were securely on the terrace, the driver braked.

The engine was cut and in the terrible stillness that followed, Leon said, 'Easy does it. Wait till they're out in the open, then pick your targets and—'

Without warning, the truck's headlamps were turned on. Two dazzling white beams shone into the garden room.

'I can't see!' Dorian shouted, taking his left hand off his gun and holding it up to his eye. 'I can't bloody well see!'

And that was when the Mau Mau climbed out of the truck and charged.

The trucks driving over the sodden track had left ruts that slowed Benjamin down so badly that he frequently found it easier to take to the open country. He came to a halt over a mile from the Estate House, not wanting whoever had gone ahead of him to hear his approach. When he turned off the engine, the first sound that came drifting towards him on the gentle breeze was the explosive crack of gunfire.

Benjamin was alarmed, but also uncertain. Just as a hunter could determine the breed, number and even size of animals he was tracking by the spoor they left on the ground, so a trained soldier could hear gunfire and know what kind of weapons were being fired, even roughly how many there might be. But Benjamin had not served in the war and, unlike their counterparts in

Britain, young Kenyan men were not required to do two years' National Service.

Still, he was a Maasai. He could move soundlessly, invisibly across country, particularly land he knew as well as this.

He decided to reconnoitre the area around the house and work out what was going on.

You are a doctor, Benjamin reminded himself. *First examine the patient. Make your diagnosis. Then come up with a treatment plan.*

Up in his sniper's eyrie on the first floor, Gerhard spotted the second truck making a frontal attack on the house: up the drive towards the front door. Its lights were out, so he could only detect a vague, moving mass against the pale grey colour of gravel in the moonlight that now gleamed from a cloudless sky.

When the truck was about a hundred metres away he fired a three-shot burst, aiming at the windscreen. There was little hope of putting such a large vehicle out of action with rifle rounds. But he might just hit the driver, and the firing would at least alert the other couples that the enemy were approaching.

The truck rolled on a little further, then came to a stop. Gerhard was clipping a fresh magazine into its housing when the truck's headlights were switched on, shining towards the front door and the rooms on either side. He detected shadowy flurries of movement which resolved themselves into the outlines of armed men, silhouetted against the lights. He counted fifteen of them.

The driver's door opened and a sixteenth man fell to the ground, attempted to get up and collapsed again.

'Got him!' Gerhard muttered to himself.

It was a lucky shot. But they would need all that luck and more to survive. Three sixteens made forty-eight Mau Mau, against the ten men and seven women in the house.

As the Mau Mau came closer, Gerhard saw that several of them were carrying Sten guns, giving them a huge advantage in firepower. A single Sten magazine carried thirty-two rounds.

That was more than all Leon's rifles put together. And the Sten could fire them in under five seconds.

I had better make every shot count.

From Gerhard's perch, fifteen feet off the ground, the headlights illuminated his targets perfectly. He took careful aim at the biggest, slowest-moving man in the group and fired a single shot, taking him at the top of his chest, below his right shoulder. The man dropped his gun and fell to his knees with a howl of pain that carried to Gerhard on the gentle breeze. Nature's violence had given way to a beautiful night. Now it was man's turn to wreak havoc.

Several of the Mau Mau aimed their guns up at the house and fired where they thought the shots had come from. Gerhard noticed that at least half of them fired one round, then had to retire to reload. If they only had single-shot weapons, that cancelled out some of the advantage of the Sten guns. The bullets all spattered harmlessly against the stone walls, save one which smashed the other bedroom window.

The attackers concentrated their fire on the ground floor. A couple of the Sten gunners fired long, wild bursts, smashing a lot of glass, but achieving little else. But the others were more precise. They advanced in quick sprints, threw themselves to the ground, fired quick bursts of half a dozen shots, then moved again.

They were trained soldiers. But so were the two British gentlemen beneath him and neither had fired a single round. Were they really waiting until their targets were just a couple of paces away?

And then Gerhard realised.

The lights! They can't see to take aim!

He nestled the butt of his Winchester against his shoulder, sighted, breathed out and fired at the left-hand light.

Got it!

He missed the second shot, hitting the truck's radiator, aimed again and heard the click of an empty magazine.

As another fusillade of shots crashed into the stonework and frame around his window and shattered one of the panes above his head, Gerhard spat out a couple of pithy, foul-mouthed German curses, wishing he still had a warplane and the fire-power that went with it.

The hatred of bloodshed that had possessed him since the end of the war had vanished. He was fighting to save his children's lives, his family and friends. If men had to die so they might live, so be it.

He reached for his shotgun.

One cartridge was all it took to extinguish the second light. But as darkness fell upon the scene the combat took on a new intensity. Half a dozen shots rang out from the house, finding two more targets and causing the rest to throw themselves to the ground and scrabble for cover behind the bushes and stone-work that dotted the final approach to the house.

A few more rounds fired from the windows were answered by the attackers. Gerhard still had a cartridge in his shotgun. But the moment he rose up high enough to push his gun out of the window and get a decent sighting, he was met by a volley of fire that forced him to duck back down again.

On this side of the house at least, a temporary stalemate had been reached. But it would not last for long.

Four hundred yards away, on a small hillock, topped by a copse of flame trees that gave him a view of the property, Kungu Kabaya put down the binoculars through which he had been watching the opening exchanges with a satisfied nod of the head.

'It is all proceeding as I expected,' he said.

Beside him, Wilson Gitiri said enthusiastically, 'Your plan is very fine. But can the men carry it out in time, before Bwana Courtney's farmers come running to see what is happening?'

'They won't,' Kabaya answered. 'They are too frightened. They will hide behind their bomas and wait until it is over.'

'But what if they do?'

'Then they cannot get here for at least fifteen minutes. And then it will be too late.'

'You are sure of it?'

'Of course,' Kabaya beamed. 'Look around you . . .'

Kabaya had crammed sixteen men onto each of his trucks. A dozen of the very best had been held in reserve. They were clustered by Kabaya and Gitiri.

'We will attack them, weaken them, make them fire all their ammunition. That may be enough. But let us pray that it is not. For then you and I will lead these men into that house. We will kill everyone we find. And we will bathe in white men's blood.'

Two blasts from Leon's .470 rifle knocked out the headlights of the truck attacking the garden room. But his fifty-year-old rifle was a breech-loader and there was no time to put in two fresh rounds. He took out his revolver and prepared for the Mau Mau onslaught.

A second later, the rebels charged the house like a storm wave on a cliff. A deafening crackle of gunfire smashed every pane of glass in the French windows and thudded into the cabinet.

Sophie had taken up a position at one end of the cabinet. Instead of trying to stick her head up above its surface, she darted from the side, fired off three rifle rounds, then got back under cover before anyone could respond.

Clever girl, thought Leon, deciding to do the same thing at the other end of the cabinet. He rolled out and was shocked by what he saw. One of the Mau Mau was down, but half a dozen were almost within touching distance of the wrecked French windows.

They were close enough that Leon could see the expressions on the attackers' faces. Their wide eyes and grotesquely contorted features exuded an aura of frenzied hatred unlike anything he had ever before encountered.

The intensity of their loathing hit Leon like an electric shock, sending a jolt of raw terror through his system. He gritted his teeth, shot twice, thought he saw a Mau Mau go down, then had to throw himself back behind the cabinet as a burst of Sten gun bullets chewed up the floor where he had been crouching.

Only Dorian had not fired. Leon looked around. At first he could see no sign of his brother, and then he saw him lying face down on the floor with his arms stretched out in front of him so that they were underneath the cabinet.

Leon's first thought was that his brother had been hit. But then he saw Dorian's feet move as he adjusted his position. A second later, the shotgun Dorian was carrying went off. It was followed an instant later by a sound Leon hadn't heard in almost forty years: the scream of a man who has been grievously wounded. But there was more than one voice generating this hellish cacophony.

Dorian's head and shoulders reappeared.

'Got 'em in the legs,' he grinned, reaching for two fresh cartridges.

Leon peered round the side of the cabinet. Two men were lying on the ground. One of them was clutching at a foot that was lying at a grotesque angle to the rest of his right leg, held on by a sliver of skin and flesh. The other was gazing in horror at the lone, booted foot that was standing on the floor about an arm's length from the rest of his body.

Blood was spurting from the wounds.

A third man was hopping away, supported by two of his comrades. The rest of the Mau Mau had vanished. The mutilation of their comrades seemed to have disheartened them more than their deaths would have done.

Leon watched them go. He didn't fire. He told himself it was because he had to save every round he could. But the truth was he couldn't do it. Firing on wounded men and their bearers was against the rules by which he went to war.

Sophie, however, had never been taught these rules. She saw two wounded men who needed putting out of their misery, and dispatched them with feminine ruthlessness. She had a single round left in her magazine and used it on one of the men who was helping his wounded comrade.

'No point getting the one who was hopping. He was already out of the fight,' she said.

'"And she knows because she warns him, and her instincts never fail, that the female of her species is more deadly than the male",' said Dorian, proudly. 'Dear old Kipling knew what he was talking about.'

'She'd better reload,' said Leon bluntly. 'They're coming back.'

He had heard the truck engine starting. Now it was revving and he knew what was coming next.

But there might be time . . . he thought.

He dashed out from behind the cabinet and grabbed the two Sten guns that the men killed by Sophie had been carrying. He threw one towards Dorian and kept the other for himself. A spare magazine was lying on the floor. It must have fallen from one of the men's pockets. Leon picked it up, then raced back behind the cabinet.

The truck was coming straight at them.

'Shoot at the tyres!' Leon yelled. 'It's our only hope!'

As a fourteen-year-old boy soldier, Mpishi had been among the Sudanese troops who served in General Kitchener's army. He had fought at the Battle of Omdurman where the Mahdi, lord of an Islamic empire in the heart of Africa, was defeated.

Mpishi loved to remind anyone willing to listen that this made him a comrade of none other than Winston Churchill, who had also fought at the battle. Now, he called upon this experience to rally his troops in the kitchen at Lusima.

'If there are more of them than of us, do not let fear strike your hearts,' he declared. 'At Omdurman, the evil Mahdi had five times as many men as Kitchener Sahib, and yet Kitchener defeated him. In our army, just fifty brave souls went to Paradise. But twenty thousand of the ungodly foe were sent to join Shaitan in the blazing fires of punishment. Now we will send these wicked Mau Mau to join them in hell.'

The house staff had been forced to listen to Mpishi give so many accounts of his finest hour, that they could recite it by heart. They knew he had exaggerated the scale of the Mahdi's army and its casualties. But the spirit with which the old man spoke impressed them deeply.

Mpishi confronted the approaching Mau Mau without fear. He seemed certain that the people of Lusima would prevail, and this gave courage to the assembled cooks, maids and *totos*, as the male servants were known. So when Mpishi started shouting his orders, they obeyed him with a will.

In swift succession the *totos* loaded their weapons, slung them over their shoulders and took three spare ammunition clips per man. While the women set to work preparing scalding liquids, the men went to the storeroom and took out all the large sacks of flour, millet, rice and potatoes. Two wooden serving trays were placed over the sinks, then half a dozen of the provision sacks were put over the trays and the drainers to either side. These would act like sandbags to protect the pair of *totos* Mpishi assigned to that position.

The rest of the sacks were placed in front of the kitchen table, which had been turned on its side, with the tabletop facing the door. This, Mpishi explained, would be their fortress, in the unlikely event that the Mau Mau ever got into the room. He told his men to check their weapons. Kiprop was stationed beside the door, with orders to fire at anyone who tried to get in. Ali Mashraf was given the honour of joining Mpishi behind the table.

The women went around them handing out an assortment of meat cleavers, carving knives, and other blades capable of butchering, filleting or slicing and dicing a man. Mpishi ordered the lights to be turned out, for the brighter the light inside the kitchen the harder it would be for the defenders to see out, and the easier for the attackers to see in.

Now it was a matter of waiting.

The kitchen workers heard the sounds of the fight beginning to the front and side of the house. Mpishi scanned them one by one and his heart swelled with pride at the steadfast expressions and determined eyes that looked back at him. Over the next half-minute the noise of battle elsewhere in the house rose to a deafening pitch while the kitchen remained quiet.

A single shot shattered the window above the sink, missed the two men crouching behind it and the women by the range, passed through a copper pan hanging over the cooker and embedded itself in the kitchen wall. A second later, the firing began in earnest.

The three women flung themselves to the ground as the sounds of smashing glass, gun blasts and the insect whine of flying bullets combined to ear-splitting effect. Rounds ricocheted off heavy pans and stone worktops and buried themselves in the walls or the wooden furniture. As they crawled towards the shelter of the overturned table, Mpishi was pleased to see that each woman was carrying a knife of her own. They clearly had no intention of being left out of the fight.

'I see them!' Kiprop called out.

A second later he was poking his gun through the empty space where the door window had been and firing his first three rounds. The two men by the sink also opened up and one of them gave a shout of triumph as he saw his target fall.

But they all ran out of bullets at the same time. As they fumbled with their ammunition clips and tried to reload in the dark, the Mau Mau had time to dash forward and suddenly the window above the sink was filled with the shadowy forms of three panga-wielding rebels. The two *totos* lashed out with their rifle butts, but they were being forced backwards as the Mau Mau clambered over the sacks. Mpishi and Mashraf raised their rifles to shoot, but the fighting by the window was at such close quarters that they dared not fire for fear of hitting one of their own men by mistake.

Tabitha pulled at the sleeve of the young housemaid squatting beside her.

'Come!'

She ran across to the kitchen range, followed by the girl. A large, two-handled steel pot was bubbling and steaming on top of one of the hobs. Tabitha grabbed one of the handles, then turned the pot so that the girl could take the other. They ran together across the kitchen towards the sinks.

When they were by the *totos*, Tabitha yelled, 'Get down!'

The two men were used to obeying the formidable housekeeper. They dropped like stones.

Tabitha shouted, 'Heave!'

She and the maid threw the pot upwards towards the Mau Mau.

The men on the sinks were hit by blasts of scalding hot steel and boiling water. They howled in pain and staggered backwards, tripping and falling out of the room as the *totos* helped them on their way with lusty blows of their rifle butts.

The men inside the kitchen roared with delight at Tabitha's swift thinking.

'Enough!' Mpishi roared, cutting the celebrations dead. 'Find your spare magazines. Load your weapons. They will be back and we must be ready for them.'

Leon used nearly half the ammunition in the Sten's magazine and Dorian fired even more, but they did the job. The tyres were blown. The truck stopped inches from the side of the house. The dozen or so surviving Mau Mau, who had not bothered to get in the back but were clinging onto the sides of the vehicle, jumped down and ran towards the open doors and the wooden barricade.

The ones with Stens were firing as they came, shooting from the hip, not caring what they hit but forcing Leon, Dorian and Sophie to keep their heads down.

Dorian was on the floor, hoping to repeat his trick with the shotgun, but the Mau Mau had learned fast. They were coming in from either side of the truck, avoiding his line of fire. He twisted round to the right and left but couldn't get a decent shot.

By the time Dorian extracted himself, the enemy were on them. He heard Sophie scream, turned and saw a Mau Mau coming at her.

The Kikuyu fighter was almost a foot taller than Sophie, more heavily built, and had thrown away his gun in favour of a long, sharp panga.

Dorian didn't have time to think or aim; he fired the shotgun in the direction he was looking. The 12-bore cartridge, at point-blank range, punched a hole in the centre of the Mau Mau's chest, killing him instantly and throwing his body against the wrecked door frame.

'Get out, Sophie, get out!' Dorian yelled.

Sophie looked at him for an instant, then darted for the door into the hall, keeping low as a fusillade of shots peppered the air around her. She made it to the exit, dashed into the hall and screamed, 'Help! Help! Someone . . . please!'

Dorian fired the second round in his shotgun, unable to make out any specific targets in the chaotic mêlée, hoping for the best. He wanted to reach for his Sten, which was lying on the floor at his feet, but there was no time.

Another Mau Mau was coming his way. He too had not bothered reloading his empty gun, preferring to fight with his knife. Dorian had no bayonet with which to fend him off. He grabbed his shotgun by the barrel, ignoring the scalding heat, and jabbed the gun-butt at the man's face.

The Mau Mau dodged the blow, swatted away the gun with his left hand and kept moving forward. There was a terrible grin on his face as he bore down upon Dorian, like a black panther on a frightened deer.

Dorian heard his brother shouting, 'You too, Dory! Save yourself! Go!'

He swung his gun again, hitting the Mau Mau on his upper arm but not slowing him.

Dorian had no defence left. His only hope was to flee. He turned, tried to run, but brought his foot down on the abandoned Sten gun. It skidded a few inches on the floor. Dorian lost his balance. He stumbled to his knees.

A second later an arm wrapped itself around Dorian's neck and lifted him upwards. He smelled the rank tang of the Mau Mau's sweat. He felt the arm let go of his neck then, an instant later, a hand had grabbed his hair and his head was being pulled back.

Dorian's throat was exposed. He lashed out with his arms but hit nothing but air. He stamped his feet down on the Mau Mau's boots, but that made not the slightest jot of difference.

He sensed the Mau Mau's arm bring the panga across his upper body. He sensed the cold, biting touch of honed steel against his skin. And a thought flashed across Dorian Courtney's mind.

This is what it feels like to die.

Leon emptied his Sten in two bursts, firing round the side of the cabinet without looking. It was suppressing fire, intended to force the enemy to take cover.

Leon threw the empty magazine away, slammed in the fresh one, then prepared to make a fighting retreat. He crouched down, his gun at his shoulder, ready to fire and move.

Out of the corner of his eye he saw Sophie running for the door.

Ahead of him a Mau Mau had leaped onto the top of the cabinet. Leon fired a quick burst and saw the man fall backwards.

Before another attacker could take his place, Leon was already heading in a low, crablike movement towards the door, but keeping his head and gun facing towards the oncoming enemy. He shouted at Dorian, wanting him to retreat as well.

There was no response. Leon darted his head to one side and saw his brother helpless in the grip of a Mau Mau at least a foot taller than him. The man was about to cut Dorian's throat.

Leon aimed at the Mau Mau's head.

The Sten was a notoriously crude weapon, infamous for its inaccuracy and unreliability. Leon was attempting a surgically precise shot in low visibility. He took aim as quickly as he could, then fired.

The Mau Mau's face disintegrated, like a watermelon hit by a sledgehammer. He fell backwards, letting go of Dorian's hair. The panga clattered to the floor.

Dorian picked it up and ran like hell.

Leon had barely taken two seconds to kill Dorian's attacker, but that was a lifetime in a gunfight.

He had been distracted from the danger in front of him and, as he turned towards the oncoming Mau Mau, he was hit by a sudden pulverising blow to his upper left arm.

Before the pain of the wound had hit him, Leon had registered that he had been hit, seen his arm fall away from its grip on the Sten's magazine and fired one-handed towards the enemy.

He staggered backwards for a couple of steps and then, as the screaming agony of his shattered bones and minced flesh hit him, forced himself to concentrate on the task in hand.

Somehow, anyhow, he had to get out of the garden room.

Gerhard had been crouched by the bedroom window, waiting for the sound of gunfire that would tell him that the battle at the front of the house had shifted from stalemate to action once again. Then he heard Sophie's desperate cry for help.

He did not want to desert his post. But this was not where the immediate danger lay. The threat was coming from the flanks. That was where he was needed. He slung his rifle over his shoulder, picked up the shotgun and ran for the stairs.

All the way down Gerhard could hear shooting coming from the garden room. Sophie watched him as he came down. He could see her mouth 'Thank God,' then she turned away as the door to the garden room opened again and Dorian stumbled into the hall.

Gerhard was in the hall.

Dorian shouted, 'Leon's still in there!'

Gerhard didn't stop moving. He kicked the door to the garden room open and stepped through it.

Leon was trying to fend off at least six advancing Mau Mau. Almost all of them were brandishing pangas; only one had a rifle in his hands.

Gerhard shot him first. It wasn't an immediate kill shot but it stopped the gunman in his tracks as he fell to his knees, clutching at his guts. Gerhard fired again, didn't hit anyone and took three quick strides to Leon. He grabbed Leon's Sten, fired it in a spray burst from left to right. Then he pulled Leon's good arm over his shoulder and dragged him back.

Leon's feet kept moving, helping to push them towards the door.

Gerhard fired again. But after a couple of rounds the magazine was empty.

Gerhard threw it away. His rifle was still over his shoulder. Trapped there by Leon's body.

The two of them were only three or four feet from the door. The Mau Mau were so close Gerhard could hear their breathing, smell their bodies, almost feel the blades about to cut into his flesh.

'Drop me!' Leon gasped, wincing with pain.

Gerhard kept hold of him.

He was almost at the door. It was closed.

But closed or open, it didn't matter. They were dead either way.

At the front of the house, the Mau Mau made their move. They advanced like proper soldiers: groups of one or two darting out from their cover and running to the next shelter while the others shot at the front rooms.

The ones who had gone forward first provided the fire while the others leapfrogged them to a more advanced position.

A few shots rang out from the windows on either side of the front door. But none came from upstairs. The white man who had been up there had left his post: one less danger to worry about.

Kabaya had a small, precious stock of hand grenades, captured from British soldiers. He had given three to a carefully selected trio of the frontal attackers. They were now close enough to make accurate throws.

One after another they popped up from behind their cover, threw and jumped back down again before they could be shot.

The first grenade hit the verandah that provided shelter to the front door, blowing it to smithereens. The second missed the door, hitting the wall to its right. The blast obliterated the window of the dining room where Bill Finney was stationed, parted the curtains intended to act as protective screens and studded him with a myriad needle-sharp fragments of glass and wood.

Muriel Finney screamed. She had been several feet from the blast, loading her husband's shotgun. She was thrown to the middle of the room, mortally wounded, with the gun in her hand and the window gaping open as the Mau Mau ran towards the house.

The third grenade thrower darted forward another few yards before letting go of his projectile, which flew straight and true before coming to rest about three feet from the front door.

The door was made of a single piece of mahogany, more than three inches thick. It had become harder over the years and a mere grenade was not enough to shatter it. But the hinges and lock mechanism that kept it in place were more vulnerable. The blast ripped the hinges from their mountings and shattered the lock. The door fell backwards, crashing onto the stone floor of the hall.

Tommy and Jane Sharpe were still firing from the drawing room window – one of them shooting while the other reloaded. But they could not get a bead on the flitting black figures, darting from one shadow to another in the faint grey moonlight.

The Mau Mau kept moving. They were almost at the door. And once they reached it, the house would be at their mercy.

The moment Gerhard had stepped into the garden room, Sophie Courtney had run to the kitchen and screamed, 'Come quick! Bwana Courtney is in danger!'

Mpishi reacted at once.

'Mashraf, take command here! Kiprop, come with me! And you . . .' He pointed at one of the housemaids. 'Bring hot oil!'

While the maid dunked a small saucepan into the large pot of oil boiling on the range, the two male servants followed Sophie into the hall. Dorian was standing there.

He nodded at the garden room door and said, 'In there.'

Mpishi did not hesitate. He opened the door halfway, for something was preventing him pushing it any further. Then he darted in with Kiprop behind him. He fired three shots at the Mau Mau in quick succession, not even trying to pick out individual targets.

'Cover us!' he shouted at Kiprop as he took hold of Leon, supporting him from one side while Gerhard took the other.

Kiprop emptied his magazine. The half a dozen shots fired by the two servants made the Mau Mau hesitate long enough for Mpishi and Gerhard to carry Leon out of the room.

They were in the doorway, turning into the hall, with their backs turned to the enemy, Kiprop behind them, fending off attackers with his gun.

Then a shot rang out and Leon's body jerked as if seized by some sudden spasm.

They were in the hall now. Kiprop had closed the door. Dorian had his right shoulder up against the glass-fronted cabinet, his face white with agony and strain.

The girl was standing, holding the pan filled with oil.

'Listen to me, Mary!' Mpishi ordered her. 'As soon as the door opens, throw it at them!'

A moment later, the door was pulled back. A Mau Mau warrior stood there, brandishing his panga. Mary flung the oil at his face and the man staggered backwards.

Dorian pushed the cabinet with all the strength he had left in his wiry body, so that it scraped across the floor and blocked the door.

Mpishi darted to the other side of the door and sent the grandfather clock crashing down onto the cabinet, so that it lay diagonally across the doorway.

It was only a temporary measure. The Mau Mau would soon shove their way through. But it would buy a few precious seconds.

Then Mpishi heard Gerhard calling his name. He turned around.

Leon was lying on the floor. There was a small, neat hole in the base of his back. And a pool of blood was pouring out from beneath his body and spreading in a rich crimson pool across the polished wood floor.

Once Harriet Courtney had settled the children in the wine cellar, which was tucked away at the furthest, coolest corner of the basement, she had turned out the lights. She did not want to risk the chance that one of the Mau Mau might venture downstairs and see the faintest glimmer to suggest that someone might be hiding down there.

She had hoped, though she knew she was asking too much, that the darkness might soothe two exhausted children and send them off to sleep. But there was no chance of that. They could hear the gunfire, the shouts and the screams coming from up above them. Small boys in Kenya told one another blood-curdling stories about the bestiality of the Mau Mau and now, for Zander, those stories were coming true. Kika was only in her first year at nursery school. She had no idea who the Mau Mau were or what they might do. But the sounds from upstairs were as terrifying to her as to her brother. The two of them were crying out for their mother and saying that they wanted to get out of this horrid place and asking, 'Why won't the bad men just go away?'

Harriet had no answer for them. She was as frightened as they were. But the need to look after the children and keep them quiet occupied her mind enough to keep the feeling of panic at bay.

The far end of the cellar, opposite the door, was lined from floor to ceiling with wine racks. But there was room on one of the side walls for Harriet to sit on the floor, with her back to a wall and the children to either side of her. She cuddled them close, stroked their hair and told them to be as quiet as little mice who didn't want a cat to find them.

Gradually, Zander and Kika became calmer and as they did, the sound of fighting ebbed away and a brief moment of peace descended upon the cellar.

In that moment, Harriet heard something. It was the clatter of heavy, nailed boots on a hard surface, and more than one set of footsteps. A sudden glow from beneath the wine cellar door indicated that the basement lights had been turned on. There were other people down there. And they were heading for the wine cellar.

Maina Mwangi had been given a special task by Kabaya: to lead five men around the far side of the house, where no truck had gone, and see if he could find a way in. De Lancey had told Kabaya that there were no ground floor windows on this side of the building.

'But you might be able to get in through an upstairs window. And I know Courtney has a cellar. There might be a hatch of some sort for it round there.'

Sure enough, Mwangi spotted the bathroom window and the drain that ran down from it to the ground. There was no light coming from the window, which was shut. There had been no reaction from the bathroom to their presence below it. Mwangi concluded there was no one behind the window.

But the window wasn't the only thing that had caught his eye in the moonlight. At ground level there was a long, flat piece of wood, set in a frame to which it was secured by a hefty padlock.

Mwangi had never lived or worked in a building that had a basement. Had it not been for De Lancey's suggestion, he would not have known that he was looking at a hatch. But now he looked closer and saw two sets of hinges on the side of the frame closest to the house. There was also a metal hook attached to the wood and a catch on the wall. So the wood lifted up on the hinges and was then hooked onto the wall.

But first he had to deal with the padlock.

Mwangi told one of his men to stay with him. He told the other four to climb up the drain, go into the house through the bathroom window and sweep the top floor of the house.

'If you find bwanas and memsahibs, kill them all,' he said. 'Then go down the stairs and join our comrades in the fight.'

Next Mwangi turned his attention to the basement hatch. He blew the padlock to pieces with a quick burst from his Sten, though the sound of his firing was lost in the din from the rest of the building. He lifted up the hatch, which was a single piece of solid wood and surprisingly heavy, and ordered his sidekick, who went by the name of Roosevelt, to secure it to the wall.

The hatch opened to reveal a steep brick staircase descending into the darkness. Mwangi did not like the look of that. But he could not show fear in front of a man he was leading, so he affected an air of stern determination and headed down the stairs with one hand on his gun and the other stretched out ahead of him to guide the way.

Unable to see a thing, Mwangi kept his hand brushing against the brick wall that ran beside the staircase. He hit something protruding from the wall: a light switch.

Mwangi turned on the lights. He saw an arch at the bottom of the stair, facing into the house. It opened onto a broad passage with a flagstone floor with storage bays on either side. One served as a coal bunker, a second was piled with firewood, a third was packed with old pieces of furniture and wooden tea chests.

The sight of so much material wealth – usable beds and tables, comfortable chairs, fine curtains and carpets – discarded in a chamber below the earth, infuriated Mwangi. Why should these people have so much when every man and woman he knew made do with infinitely less? And what they have they throw away.

His thirst for vengeance and bloodshed intensified further. He entered the gunroom, recognised at once what it was and was furious to discover that it was empty. At the end of the passage was another door. It was closed.

Mwangi asked himself, *If Bwana Courtney keeps so much wealth out in the open, how much more precious must be the possessions he locks away?*

He gestured to Roosevelt to follow him and marched towards the wine-cellar door.

I n Russia, Gerhard had witnessed bloodshed on the greatest scale that mankind had ever seen. He knew a fatal wound when he saw one. When he crouched beside Leon, his face was grey and bathed in sweat and breaths were coming in agonised, rasping gulps of air.

The bullet that had hit him had gone right through his torso above the waist. Gerhard didn't have to look to know that it had caused a larger, messier wound going out. The chances were that it had hit a kidney and it had certainly punched a hole through his intestines. He didn't have a hope in hell of surviving. Not here, not now.

Gerhard heard a woman's scream coming from the dining room. Before he could run to her aid the scream was cut short.

He was shouting to Kiprop and Mary the housemaid to get Bwana Courtney into the kitchen when something exploded outside the front door. Another explosion followed seconds later.

There was firing coming from the drawing room, and then the door opened and Jane Sharpe ran out, clutching a shotgun and a box of cartridges. Two shots came from inside the room and Jane stopped for a second, turned to face the way she had come and screamed, 'Tommy!'

A third explosion battered the front door, leaving it leaning inwards, barely hanging on its hinges.

Tommy Sharpe burst out of the drawing room, a rifle in one hand, a captured Sten in the other, pursued by a Mau Mau with a panga. Gerhard lifted his rifle to his shoulder and fired once, hitting the Mau Mau in the chest.

'Thanks, old man,' gasped Sharpe, as he ran past Gerhard towards his wife.

There were men battering at the door; more Mau Mau were emerging from the rooms at the front of the house.

Gerhard headed to a point where the hall was at its narrowest, a few feet in front of the kitchen, by the door to the basement. In front of him, Dorian Courtney and Tommy Sharpe were almost blocking the way. That gave him an idea.

'Dorian! Sharpe! We must form a line here, where they can only attack with two or three men at a time. Mpishi! Get something from the kitchen to shelter us. Chairs, boxes, sacks, anything!'

Two more Mau Mau appeared by the foot of the stairs. Others joined them, carrying pangas rather than guns. They looked down the tight, hemmed-in space between them and the three white men and saw what Gerhard had: anyone who went down there would be shot before they had gone a single step.

'Don't shoot,' Gerhard said to the two men beside him. 'They have more men, but we don't have many more rounds. Save them for Mau Mau with guns.'

Mpishi and a couple of the women reappeared and assembled a ramshackle pile of junk across the hall for Gerhard and the others to crouch behind. There was a pause in the assault, with neither side able to make an attacking move.

Gerhard saw one of the Mau Mau speak to another, who dashed away through the front door and into the open.

He was giving him a message, Gerhard thought, his chest heaving as he caught his breath. *My God, there are more of them out there!*

In the brief moment of stillness he heard shooting down in the basement. All Gerhard could think was, *No . . . please, God . . . not the children!*

'Be very quiet, children, and stand behind me,' Harriet whispered as she got to her feet.

She stood a foot away from the wall, with Zander clinging to one of her legs and Kika to the other. She cocked the revolver and held it out in front of her in both hands. Leon had let her fire it occasionally in the past and she knew that the recoil was too powerful for her to manage in one hand.

The footsteps were getting closer.

'I'm scared,' Kika whimpered.

'Hush . . .' whispered her brother. 'Don't let them know we're here.'

Suddenly a deafening fusillade of shots pounded their ears. The bullets passed through the flimsy door and smashed the bottles in the racks beyond.

A single kick smashed the door in. Two men entered the room, both tall, strapping Kikuyu. One of them carried the gun that had peppered the door. The other was armed with a panga.

The men saw Harriet and the children and grinned, knowing that they had stumbled upon a great prize.

Harriet was holding the gun. The men were so close she could not possibly miss. And yet she froze, unable to pull the trigger, paralysed by fear and a fundamental inability to take the life of another human being, even when her own was in danger.

Mwangi knew that this woman did not have it in her to kill. He reached forward and took the gun from her hand.

'Like candy from a baby, eh?' he said to her, speaking in English so that she would know that he was as good as her.

Roosevelt asked Mwangi a question in Gikuyu.

He replied and then told Harriet, 'He asks me if we should kill you now, or wait until our leader, General Kungu Kabaya, arrives. I told him we must wait – but you know . . .' He stroked the hot tip of the Sten gun's barrel along the underside of Harriet's chin, making her wince. 'I am not sure I will wait. I want to kill you, and them –' he nodded towards the children – 'very much.'

Just then Mwangi heard footsteps racing down the passage.

'Who is it?' he asked.

Roosevelt turned towards the open doorway. Before he could say a word, a single shoot rang out and he staggered backwards, hit the wine racks and fell dead to the floor.

Mwangi reacted in an instant. He grabbed Harriet and put a gun to her head.

Zander grabbed Kika and pulled her to the ground.

Gerhard walked into the room with his rifle to his shoulder, ready to fire.

He saw Harriet, and Mwangi behind her with his left arm around her throat and the right hand pressing a Sten gun up against her temple.

Harriet was shielding most of Mwangi's body. All Gerhard could see was his gun arm and the small sliver of his face that was not hidden behind Harriet's head.

Zander and Kika were sitting on the floor beside them.

He was about to tell the children to stay put when they saw him and dashed across to him with cries of 'Daddy!'

Gerhard noticed Mwangi's mouth widen in a grin. The barrel of his gun swung down. He was going to shoot the children.

Gerhard had a fraction of a second in which to aim and a tiny target to hit.

If he waited too long, the children would die.

If he missed, Harriet would die.

Gerhard shot. He blew the smile right off Mwangi's face.

As Zander and Kika grabbed hold of him, shrieking, and Harriet stepped aside, overwhelmed by all that had happened, Gerhard muttered something under his breath.

'What did you say?' Harriet asked.

He gave a harsh, cruel smile, an expression from another time as he said, 'It was German. I was telling him, "I shot down a hundred fighter planes, you dumb swine. Of course I was going to kill you."'

He picked up Zander and hugged him tight, while Harriet grabbed the revolver Roosevelt had taken from her and the evening bag of ammunition, hooking the trigger of the gun and the handle of the bag around her middle finger. She took Kika in her arms.

As they went upstairs to the hall, Gerhard turned and told Harriet, 'Shield her eyes.'

He held his son's head against his chest so that the little boy would not see the makeshift barrier; the men in their black dinner jackets and starched white shirts, now stained with the blood, sweat and grime of battle; the two women in their ruined evening gowns; and beyond them the line of Mau Mau, watching and waiting for the order to attack.

But Harriet saw them and gave a gasp of alarm as she followed Gerhard into the kitchen.

He looked around, searching for any kind of refuge. By the sink, Mashraf was shouting, 'Hold your fire!' to one of the *totos*, who had wasted a bullet firing at one of the Mau Mau, who were popping up at random intervals in the window or the doorway, tempting the defenders to waste ammunition. The stove was once again the site of great activity as the maids heated up any liquid they could get their hands on to fling at the enemy.

Gerhard decided that the storeroom could offer sanctuary, and let Harriet in.

He stopped and tried to warn her. But it was too late. Harriet had seen Leon lying in one corner of the room and heard him moaning in pain as Mary tried to staunch the flow of blood from his belly with nothing more than a pitcher of water and a pile of old dishcloths. Mpishi was trying to get Leon to drink some brandy to lessen the pain.

Harriet put Kika on the floor and rushed to her husband's side, while Gerhard took the children to the other side of the room.

'What's the matter with Grandpa?' Zander asked.

'He's hurt himself,' Gerhard replied.

'Did the Mau Mau do it?'

It was a bit late now to shield the children from the truth, so Gerhard said, 'Yes.'

'Were the men in the cellar Mau Mau?'

'That's right.'

'But you shot them.'

Zander held out his hand like a pistol, with two fingers for the barrel, and made shooting noises.

'That's enough,' Gerhard told him. 'You settle down here. I've got to go back outside.'

'Are you going to shoot more Mau Mau?'

'Probably – but don't think about that. You just look after Kika, and Granny Harriet will soon be back to take care of you both. All right?'

'Yes, Daddy.'

'Kika?'

The little girl's thumb was in her mouth and she couldn't talk, so she nodded.

On the way out he said to Harriet, 'I'm so sorry.' He added, 'Do you still have the gun. I'm going to need it.'

'Take it,' she said. 'I couldn't use it. And this . . .' She passed Gerhard the bag.

'Thanks.' He grabbed the spare rounds from the bag and stuffed them into a pocket. 'I'll make sure I keep three spare. One for you too, if you need it.'

Harriet gave a nod of the head, caught Mpishi's eye and said, 'You go with Bwana Meerbach. I will take care of Bwana Courtney.'

'Yes, memsahib,' Mpishi said and hurried to catch up with Gerhard.

There was a sudden firecracker burst of gunfire from the hall. A woman started screaming.

Jane Sharpe was lying across the floor, outside the kitchen door, stone dead from the bullet that had blown her brains out. Sophie Courtney was desperately trying to regather her composure. Tommy Sharpe was screaming insults up the stairs as he emptied a three-round magazine and reached for another.

Gerhard put an arm out to stop him.

'Save your bullets. You'll need every one of them.'

'The filthy Kuke savage just ran down the stairs, fired his damn gun and ran away again. And poor Janey . . . My lovely Janey . . .'

Sharpe moved towards his wife's corpse, but Gerhard blocked the way.

'There's nothing you can do for her. Go back to your position.'

'Is this what it's come to, eh?' Sharpe sneered. 'Englishmen taking orders from Krauts?'

Gerhard did not rise to the bait. He kept his voice calm and said, 'Please, for all our sakes, concentrate on the enemy.'

'He's right, old man,' Dorian said to Sharpe. 'We've got at least thirty of them to deal with.'

'Well, let's do it. Let's deal with them now!' Sharpe shouted, raising his gun towards the Mau Mau who were standing with menacing stillness ten paces away, in the broader area of the hall closer to the front door.

'No,' Gerhard insisted, knocking Sharpe's gun barrel down with his hand. 'Wait.'

'For what exactly, eh? What's the great moment we're waiting for?'

There was firing from the kitchen and the clamour of combat as Mpishi's men fought off another assault.

'Stay here,' Gerhard said. He stopped by Sophie. 'Are you all right?'

She nodded. 'Don't worry. I'll be right by Dory. And I'll make every shot count.'

Gerhard went into the kitchen. The fighting had subsided as quickly as it had begun, a wave of violence and death that had flowed in and immediately out again. There were two dead Mau Mau, and a third lying injured and helpless on the floor.

The staff had suffered casualties too. One of the *totos* was dead, as was Tabitha the housekeeper, her neck sliced open by a Mau Mau panga.

'What's the situation?' Gerhard asked Mpishi.

The old man shrugged. 'We fought them off this time. And we will fight them off next time. But we have fewer bullets now and two of my friends are dead. If they attack a third time, we will not be able to hold them.'

'How much ammunition do you have?'

'Most of my boys are down to their last clips. No one has more than two. But we will beat them. Allah, the merciful, the all-knowing, the all-powerful, will show us a way.'

'Good man,' said Gerhard, patting Mpishi on the shoulder.

He thought of the last days at Stalingrad. The food, the medicine, the guns and ammunition were all gone. Defeat was inevitable. But he had had a Messerschmitt to fly him away.

If I could get to the plane, he thought. *Maybe I could get the kids out, at least. But even if that were possible, how could I desert everyone else?*

And he remembered there was hardly any fuel left.

Mpishi had better be right. Because if Allah doesn't come to our rescue, no one else will.

He turned at the sound of Dorian calling his name. Gerhard went back into the hall.

'There's been a development,' his brother-in-law said. 'Take a look. There's more of them.'

In the storeroom, Leon opened his eyes and his bloodless face, contorted into an agonised rictus, managed the faintest hint of a smile.

'Hattie,' he whispered. 'My love . . .'

Leon struggled to say more, but no sound emerged from his mouth.

'Yes, my darling,' Harriet said softly, leaning closer to him.

Leon took three gulps of air and then gasped, 'The children . . .'

His eyes closed. Harriet could not hear him breathe. His chest did not move. When she took his wrist in her fingers, there was no pulse.

Harriet did not allow herself to compose the word for what had just happened to her husband. That would only bring her grief without limits and there was no time for that. Leon had told her his final wish and she would obey it.

She got to her feet, forced herself across the storeroom, and with a superhuman effort of will summoned a smile to her face and said, 'Hello, children, how have you two been getting on?'

Benjamin had almost completed a full circuit of the Estate House. He had spotted Gerhard's plane, buried in a hedge, and the three empty trucks. It had struck him that generals very often did not lead their men from the front, but stood behind the lines, observing what was happening and giving their orders accordingly.

If that were the case now, and Benjamin could find that leader, he might yet make a decisive contribution to the fight.

I only have one gun, he told himself, *but that is enough to kill one man.*

Then he saw the knot of men gathered by the flame tree copse. There – that was his target!

Benjamin knew every inch of the land around the Estate House. Not far away there was a spot, another rise in the land, covered only by shrubbery, which was closer to the copse than his current position, with a clearer line of sight. He ran to it now, telling himself that he would not be spotted, that any Mau Mau in the vicinity would surely be concentrating on the battle in the house.

He made it to his vantage point, crawled on his belly through the base of a large shrub, emerging just far enough out on the other side to be able to see the copse and aim his rifle. As his head emerged into the open, it suddenly struck Benjamin that the guns had fallen silent. Had he arrived too late? But then he realised something: *If the Mau Mau had won, they would be celebrating so loudly that I would hear them from a mile away. No . . . this is just a pause in the fighting. There is still time . . .*

First, though, he had to find his target.

It did not take long. The man on whose word all those around him were hanging was not the largest in the group, but he stood out to Benjamin like a professor on a ward round, surrounded by medical students. Even when some of those students were giant rugby players, the professor was always the boss.

Yes, that is him, Benjamin thought, nestling the rifle against his shoulder and looking through the sights. He thought of all the times he'd gone hunting as a guest of the Courtneys. He had found it hard enough to kill animals. But to kill another human being was immeasurably worse. It went against his principles, his training, even the Hippocratic Oath.

'First do no harm,' the oath demanded.

But Kabaya was surely the one doing that.

You're just cutting out a cancer, Benjamin told himself. He calmed his breathing, let his pulse drop as low as the adrenaline in his system would allow . . . and squeezed the trigger.

Kungu Kabaya had observed the effects of the skirmishing that had taken place in what seemed like the eternity since he had ordered the trucks to advance upon the house. Yet when he glanced at his watch, he saw that barely ten minutes had passed. In that time, the regular messages he was getting from the front lines told him his men had reduced the number of white adults from nine to five, and whittled away at the black servants, too.

More importantly, each of the attacks had obliged the house's defenders to use up ammunition. De Lancey had warned him that Mbogo had as fine an armoury as any man in Kenya. But even he was not equipped to fight a full-scale battle. In any case, Mbogo was either dying or dead. The white herd had lost their bull. Now they would be frightened cattle.

Kabaya ordered half the men standing with him by the flame tree copse to go round the back of the house and reinforce the attacks on the kitchen.

Then the man standing next to him suddenly pitched face forward onto the earth. As he lay there, screaming, Kabaya saw the hole that had been punched in the small of his back. He heard the reverberation of a rifle shot, to his left. A single gun, one shooter. Not enough to alter the course of the fight.

Unless the next shot hits me.

'Run!' shouted Kabaya. 'On me! Move, move, move!'

Benjamin swore under his breath. Another man had stepped into his line of fire at the very last second and taken the bullet intended for the leader, who was now running down the copse and onto the drive towards the house, surrounded by his men and getting further from Benjamin with every stride.

Time to find a new shooting position.

Kabaya was used to coming within a whisker of death. In the course of countless firefights, men had fallen all around him, yet he had always emerged unscathed, like a man who can walk through raging flames yet never get burned. He was not alarmed by the experience, but exhilarated.

So there was a grin on Kabaya's face as he ran along the drive to the front door. He imagined what it must be like to own a house such as this, with so much land around it. One day, men like him would have property like this. But for that day to come, the old order had to be torn down and a new one take its place.

This fight would bring Kenya one step closer to that day.

It was time to land the killer blow.

He marched through the front door and into the house that was about to be his. He would kill the white people inside, and their servants. All of them. Every man, woman and child.

To Benjamin, the logic was indisputable: if the copse had been the best spot for the Mau Mau leader to direct the battle, then it would be the best spot for him to observe it. From there he could decide where next to move. There was no point him running pell-mell into the battle by himself. He would simply die without achieving a thing. But the principle of one target, one rifle, still held good. If he could get another shot at the leader, and kill him this time, he might yet change everything.

Benjamin picked up his pace as he jogged towards the flame trees. He was a hundred yards from the hillock when he heard engines, coming towards him at full power.

He saw no lights. The engines were getting louder.

Benjamin peered in the direction of the sound and then he saw the black silhouetted outlines of two vehicles, Land Rovers by the looks of them.

Were they coming to the aid of the people in the house, or reinforcing the Mau Mau?

The Mau Mau don't drive Land Rovers!

The silhouettes stopped moving. The shadows fell silent.

'Over here!' Benjamin shouted, speaking in English.

An instant later he saw a flash, like a match being lit, and at the same time heard the blast of a gun being fired and the whining, buzzing, fluttering passage of a bullet that seemed to pass within a whisker of his skull.

Benjamin raised his hand above his head and shouted, 'Don't shoot! I'm a doctor!'

He heard a woman's voice. 'Benjamin?'

'Saffron!' Benjamin called back.

He walked towards the cars and a female figure came running towards him.

'What's happening?' Saffron asked, clutching his shoulders, her voice tight with anxiety. 'Are we too late?'

'I don't know. The Mau Mau are in the house. The shooting's stopped. But I don't know why. I almost killed their leader, but—'

'What about my family?' Saffron interrupted him.

Benjamin shrugged. He had no answer for her.

Before Saffron could say another word, the gunfire from the house suddenly started again. She had to shout to make herself heard as she told Benjamin, 'That's it! We're going in hard and fast!'

*

Gerhard had one round left in his rifle, plus Harriet's pistol and the spare bullets. He had the panga he'd taken from the dead Mau Mau, but no idea how to use it in combat. He looked at the blade tucked into his belt and reminded himself that he had been made to take fencing lessons as a boy: *think of it as a short sabre.*

Mashraf fired his last round. Kabaya gave his order and suddenly there were men running down the stairs, vaulting over the balustrade and landing in front of him. Others were leaping over the dining table and racing down the hall. One or two were carrying guns and firing as they came, so crazed by bloodlust that they did not care whether they hit their own men. The rest were waving their knives and screaming Kikuyu battle cries and curses.

'Back into the kitchen!' Gerhard shouted. As Mashraf ran by, Gerhard gave him the rifle and shouted, 'Got one round!'

He kept facing forward as his own men retreated through the door.

He crouched behind the barricade and fired the pistol four times, without pausing between shots, into the onrushing Mau Mau. They were so close that he could not miss. But only two men were stopped dead in their tracks. The pair that he wounded were so caught up in the adrenalised fury of battle that they ignored the blow and kept coming. The Mau Mau had reached the barricade and were clambering over. Gerhard shifted his gun to his left hand and pulled out his panga. He ducked under a slashing blade wielded by one of the Mau Mau, and swung his from side to side, as fast as he could, desperately trying to keep the attackers at bay as he stumbled backwards.

Suddenly a bullet cut through the left sleeve of Gerhard's jacket and he felt an impact like a sharp punch to his arm. His grip slackened on his pistol, but a hand grabbed the back of his jacket and pulled him hard.

The door of the kitchen slammed shut and he heard the key being turned.

His wounded arm was bleeding profusely, but the Webley revolver was still in his hand. He was safe. But not for long.

One glance towards the sinks told Gerhard that the men there were out of rounds too, for the Mau Mau were pouring in through the windows and the male and female servants were being forced back deeper into the room. Mashraf shot one of them dead, and that made the others hesitate as he pointed his rifle towards them, giving Mpishi and the others time to scuttle back behind the upturned table, where Mashraf joined them.

The door to the hall was shaking with the hammering of panga blades against the wood. That at least would hold for a while, but Gerhard heard a shout from the hall.

A gun started firing and he had to dive for the floor as the hot lead smashed through the lock.

He scrabbled across the floor to the storeroom door. This would be where he would make his stand. Gerhard put three more rounds in the Webley's revolving chamber, leaving three in his pocket. He prayed that he would have the courage to do what was necessary for the children when the time came.

Beside Gerhard, Dorian was telling Sophie how much he loved her, and she was replying in kind, each wanting the other to know before it was too late. Sharpe was shouting incoherent abuse at the door, daring the Mau Mau to come and get him. Across the room, Mpishi, Mashraf and two of the housemaids were lined up behind the kitchen table. There were eight Mau Mau opposite them. Three of them were wounded, but able to swing a panga.

Gerhard signalled to the staff to join him. The Mau Mau let them go. They too had run out of ammunition. Why risk their necks when their comrades were about to finish the job for them?

The sound of the Sten went on and on, getting louder and louder, taunting the surviving defenders with its incessant chatter.

The Mau Mau broke through the kitchen door.

Gerhard shot the first two who clambered through the gap in the bullet-ridden woodwork. Mashraf got a third. But then the door was smashed completely open and, though Dorian, Sophie and Sharpe hit men at point-blank range, it made no difference as one terrorist after another charged in, cheered on by their comrades already in the kitchen.

Firing the last three rounds in the Webley's chamber, Gerhard provided covering fire as the others retreated into the storeroom. Then he darted in, ducking beneath a panga blade and feeling a round fly past him into the door frame as the Mau Mau charged after him.

No sooner had the door closed and the key been turned than Mpishi, Mashraf and the two maids dashed towards it, carrying sacks of provisions which they piled behind the door. Several shots were fired through the wood, miraculously missing everyone inside. Dorian and Sharpe added to the makeshift barrier with crates of beer and then Dorian shouted, 'Grab one of the shelves! We can wedge it against the door!'

More shots and hammering smashed against the door. Gerhard could hear whoops and shouts of encouragement coming from the kitchen. They sounded like football supporters cheering on a winning team. Dorian and Sharpe grabbed one end of a freestanding shelf, filled with provisions that stood against the far wall. Mashraf and Mpishi took the other. They tilted it forward and a mass of provisions crashed to the floor. But now the shelf could be lifted and the men ran with it, still at an angle, and jammed it against the door, while the bottom rested on the floor.

Dorian's wife Sophie ran to Harriet and the children, who were clinging white-faced to their grandmother, to see how they were.

'We might as well sit on it, gentlemen,' Dorian said, placing himself on the bottom shelf. 'The weight will make it almost impossible to open the door.'

'What if they shoot us through the door?' Sharpe asked.

Dorian gave a wry smile. 'What difference would that make? If they come through the door we're goners anyway.'

Sharpe took the point. As he, Mpishi and Dorian filled up the rest of the shelf, Gerhard approached them, reloading the Webley as he went.

'Does anyone have any ammo left?'

The men shook their heads.

'I think Sophie's got one left,' Dorian said.

'I think it's best if she saves it,' Gerhard said, and Dorian nodded, knowing what he meant.

Gerhard looked at the men by the shelf and the two maids who were gathering jars, bottles and cans to use as missiles.

'You all put up a hell of a fight,' he said. 'It's been an honour to serve alongside you. But now, I've got three bullets left. I'm not wasting any of them on the Mau Mau.'

'I understand, old boy,' Dorian said. 'Go to your children . . . and God bless.'

Gerhard walked over to the children, got down on his knees and took them both in his arms.

'Are we going to die, Daddy?' Zander asked.

'Hush now, it's all right, I'm here,' Gerhard said. 'I won't let anything bad happen to you . . . Or you, sweetheart,' he added, giving Kika a kiss.

It was almost over now, Gerhard knew that. One way or another the Mau Mau would get in, even if they had to burn the house down around them to do it. A silence fell. Then there was a rattling sound, like a tin can rolling along the kitchen floor and bumping up against the kitchen door.

'Grenade!' shouted Sharpe, grabbing Dorian and pushing him to one side as he threw himself to the floor. Mpishi and Mashraf were both old soldiers; they knew the drill too. The women followed the menfolk's lead and dropped to the floor as Gerhard pushed the children down and hurled his body across them. The door and shelf exploded in a deafening hail of flying splinters that beat against the walls of the storeroom.

The two servant girls had caught the worst of the blast, but though both were badly cut, neither was severely wounded. But they, like the men, were dazed, their ears ringing, their minds scrambled.

Then a thunderous blaze of gunfire broke out. On and on it went, and all Gerhard could do was curl up in a ball around his children and hope he lived long enough to do his duty.

He had the gun in his hand. As soon as the first Mau Mau came through the door, he would kill his children first and then, if he had time, Harriet too.

The noise ended. The storeroom filled with smoke and dust. Soon the angels of death would appear through the gloom and it would be too late. Gerhard crossed himself. He thought of Saffron. He wished that they could have had just one more minute together, so that he could have put their disagreements behind them and told her how much he loved her. Then he whispered, 'Forgive me, my darling,' put his gun against Kika's head, and tightened his finger on the trigger.

The Land Rovers came tearing down the drive.

The vehicles came to a halt a few yards from the front door and everyone piled out. Saffron grabbed a Sten from Makori's stock of weapons.

'Here, take these,' he said, handing her two magazines that were taped together, slightly off-centre, open at opposite ends. 'When one runs out, just take it out, spin it and slot in the next. Means you can keep firing non-stop.'

'Never seen that before,' said Saffron. Then speaking more quietly, because she did not want to embarrass Makori in front of his own people, she said. 'This is my battle, on my land. Mind if I take it from here?'

He nodded his agreement. Saffron turned to face the pseudos and started rapping out orders.

'You, take two men and go in through the dining room, that's the window on the left. Clear it, then advance into the hall.' She pointed to another man. 'You go through the drawing room, on the right, same thing, take two men. The rest of you, come with me. You too, Benjamin. Stay tight to me and do exactly what I tell you.'

She gave Wambui her Beretta and saw her face light up as she was given the chance to fight like a man. Then she shouted, 'Let's go!'

There was no time to carry out any reconnaissance. Saffron dashed through the front door, into the hall . . . and it was empty.

There were dead Mau Mau soldiers scattered across the floor. Three or four of them were injured and still moving.

Saffron shot one and shouted, 'Kill the rest!'

There was no hesitation; her veneer of civility had been discarded. This was war and there were no rules.

As Wambui and the pseudos obeyed the order, another two Mau Mau appeared on the stairs. One of them was holding a bottle. The other was waving a gun. They thought the battle was over and won.

Saffron took one of them out. Benjamin shot the other. He had never before witnessed, still less inflicted, the destructive, blood-spattered brutality of a rifle bullet fired at point-blank range into another human being. He stopped in his tracks, sickened by what he had done.

There was not a shred of pity in Saffron's voice.

'Snap out of it! Keep moving!'

Benjamin looked at her, unable to match the callous, hardened fighter beside him with the thoughtful, elegant woman he had known all his life.

Makori appeared and shouted, 'Two whites dead! One man, one woman!'

'There's another down here,' Saffron said as she headed towards the kitchen, with Benjamin right behind her.

A woman's corpse, horribly mutilated by a myriad panga blades, lay across the opening where the kitchen door had been. Beyond her, through the door. Saffron could see a mass of Mau Mau. They were laughing and cheering, firing rifles in the air.

We're too late, she told herself.

Then she spotted the knot of men gathered round the door to the storeroom, smashing rifle butts against it and firing at the woodwork and lock. It wasn't over yet.

'There's someone in there,' she called at Makori.

He nodded, lifted the Sterling to his shoulder and walked towards the kitchen with Saffron beside him and Benjamin, Wambui and the pseudos behind them. They were outnumbered five, even six to one by the Mau Mau. But they had the advantage of surprise and plenty of ammunition.

Maybe we're going to be on time. Maybe it's going to be all right, Saffron thought.

And then silence fell on the kitchen. The men nearest the door backed away and the grenade went off.

At least four of the Mau Mau were killed by their own blast. But the rest were running for the open door and suddenly Saffron knew this was the endgame. The battle could still be lost.

She had to stop them before they could get inside the storeroom. She opened fire the way she had been taught at Arisaig, not taking careful aim, but looking at her target and letting the gun follow her eyes.

Look, burst, kill.

Look, burst, kill.

Beside her, Makori was dealing out carnage at a brutal rate. Wambui was shooting like a born marksman. Benjamin had forgotten his oath and his political principles as he took out one man after another. The pseudos were locked in combat with guns and knives.

But though the casualties kept falling, it seemed to make no difference to the men by the door. Saffron saw two faces she recognised, and realised that they belonged to Kungu Kabaya and the sidekick he had brought to the meeting with Jomo Kenyatta. Their attention was focused on killing whoever was in the storeroom.

Saffron felt a desperate hope that her father and Harriet were safe in there, mixed with a terror that all was lost. She swapped magazines, lifted her gun and fired at the two men. Gitiri went down, clutching his chest, high up by one shoulder.

That got Kabaya's attention. He saw her and shouted orders to his remaining men to turn and face the new enemy. He raised his gun towards Saffron.

She fired a lone sustained burst from her Sten gun that blew Kungu Kabaya's head to pieces.

Kabaya's men saw that their leader was dead. They started throwing down their weapons and begging for mercy. Several more of them were shot before Makori shouted, 'That's enough!'

Saffron ignored it all. She walked through the storeroom door and saw the vague outlines of people, just discernible in the dust and gloom. It occurred to her: *What if they think I'm the enemy?*

'Don't shoot!' she cried out. 'It's me – Saffron!'

And the first thing she heard was a high, piping voice calling out, 'Mummy!'

It took a second for Gerhard to realise that he wasn't dreaming. It was Saffron. She was turning to him and he saw the grim mask of the trained killer disappear as she spotted him and ran towards the corner where he was crouched by the children.

He had a gun in his hand. He looked at her and the anguish and relief in his eyes told her what she had just prevented.

They embraced, wordlessly. The two children hurtled towards her and she dropped to her knees with her arms open and embraced them both as they charged into her arms.

Gerhard pulled Saffron gently back to her feet.

'I need to show Mummy something,' he told the children.

'Are you showing her Grandpa?' Zander asked.

Saffron followed Zander's eye to the huddled body in the far side of the storeroom, then she spun round and screamed, 'Benjamin! Benjamin! Please – come here!'

Benjamin knelt beside Leon's body and felt for the non-existent pulse, but it had taken a glance to tell him that he was looking at a corpse.

Saffron broke down in tears. Her body shook with grief and between her sobs she berated herself, saying, 'I should have come sooner . . . should have gone faster . . . it was my fault.'

Gerhard took her in his arms. He stroked her head, trying to soothe her. Harriet, her cheeks wet with her own tears, said, 'Here, let me . . .'

She held Saffron and waited until she had cried herself out, then said gently, but firmly, 'Saffron, darling, look at me . . .'

Saffron raised her head from Harriet's shoulder.

'Now listen carefully,' Harriet went on, looking Saffron in the eyes. 'You have done nothing wrong. Nothing . . . You saved us. Everyone in this house owes their lives to you and the brave men who came with you. Your father is so proud of you . . . I believe he's looking down at us now and his soul is at peace because he knows that all his work, all his life, was worthwhile because it produced you. He has left you a splendid legacy and he has complete faith in you to do it justice. So don't reproach yourself. Don't worry about the things you have done. Think to the future and do what is right. That is all Leon Courtney would have asked of his daughter.'

Twenty miles away on Lonsonyo Mountain, Nascrian gasped as Manyoro opened his eyes. She leaned forward, but her husband did not see her. His vision was focused on something infinitely far away.

'I see you, Mbogo, my brother,' he whispered. 'I am on my way . . .'

Manyoro's eyes closed. His breath left his body in a long, gentle sigh. And he did not breathe again.

LUSIMA, JUNE 1964

'I'm so proud of you, darling,' Saffron said, holding Gerhard closer to her as they stood outside what had once been the front door to her family home, but was now the entrance to the Manyoro Hills Hotel.

Under Gerhard's supervision, local builders and craftsmen had converted the Courtneys' former home into the central hub of a discreet, luxurious resort. A bar, restaurant, reading room and lobby occupied the ground floor, with half a dozen bedroom suites upstairs. A swimming pool and two tennis courts had been built in the grounds, along with fifteen cabins, each of which had a bedroom, bathroom and terrace. The cabins were aligned so that they had a view of the spectacular Rift Valley landscape, but none could be seen from any of the others. Absolute privacy was guaranteed.

Gerhard had insisted that local stone, wood and thatch should be used wherever possible, and the decorative motifs in every guest room and public area reflected the traditions of the Kikuyu and Maasai people. His intention was to give the people who stayed or dined in the hotel an experience that was uniquely, unmistakably Kenyan.

'My father's spirit is looking down on this, I'm sure of it,' said Benjamin, as they entered the reception lobby that occupied the old hall and dining room. 'He is so proud of what you have created in his name.'

'Are you sure he's not off boozing with my father?' Saffron asked.

They both laughed, but their amusement was bittersweet and laced with melancholy, for passing time had dulled, but not erased, the pain of the night when the two blood-brothers had died.

A Kenyan man in an elegantly tailored grey suit, whose handsome, intelligent face was set off by gold-framed spectacles and made even more distinguished by the hint of grey in his close-cropped hair, walked up behind Saffron.

He coughed politely and said, 'Excuse me, ma'am.'

She turned and her face broke into a broad smile.

'Maku! How lovely to see you! The president's office didn't tell me you were coming.'

Maku Makori, proud possessor of a Master's degree in Public Administration from the London School of Economics, and Private Secretary to President Jomo Kenyatta, smiled back.

'I am our leader's right-hand man. Naturally, I want to make sure that all his arrangements are in order.'

'I hope you wanted to see old friends too.'

'Of course – always,' Maku said as they exchanged a social kiss. Then he held out his hand, said, 'Benjamin!' and the two men shook hands. 'So, the National Hospital decided it could spare you for a couple of days?'

'Well, I hate to leave my patients . . . but I have a good team. They will manage without me.'

'Seriously, everyone is very impressed with the work you are doing in the fight against malaria. You know we're hoping to have a new school of medicine at Nairobi University College within the next three years?'

'I'd heard, yes.'

'Well, I think you should be involved from the start, and the president agrees. We must talk about this soon.'

'That's a wonderful idea,' said Saffron. 'Our fathers would both be so proud of you, Benjamin.'

'I think they would feel the same about you, Saffron,' Maku said. He looked around and sighed. 'When I think of the last time I was here, that terrible night. This is a new world – a better world. Now, let us get down to business. I like to confirm that the arrangements for the president's visit tomorrow are in place.'

'Of course,' said Saffron. 'Now let me see ... The route that President Kenyatta's car and outriders will take through the farmlands has been checked, and the police will be posting officers at regular intervals along the roadside. You'll have to consult with them about the precise details.' She looked at Gerhard. 'Darling, have the workmen finished the presidential podium?'

'Yes, the final coat of paint went on this morning and it will be dry by tomorrow afternoon.'

'Are you quite sure?' Maku asked. 'We would not want paint stains on Mr Kenyatta's clothes.'

'Quite sure,' Gerhard assured him.

'You know the Germans,' Saffron added. 'Tremendously efficient.'

'Almost as efficient as me,' Harriet said, as she emerged from the office behind the reception desk. She handed Maku a stapled sheaf of papers. 'Here are the names and addresses of everyone attending the opening ceremony, along with the number of the seat they will occupy. A seating plan is included on the final page. I can also assure everyone that the swimming pool has been thoroughly tested by Master Alexander Courtney Meerbach, his sister Nichola and their friends. They have now produced a portable gramophone and are playing Beatles records very loudly.' Harriet peered over the top of her half-moon reading glasses. 'Don't worry, Maku. They will not be behaving like that tomorrow ... not if they want to live.'

Maku laughed. 'I would not wish to be the child who disobeyed either of you two ladies!' He looked at Saffron. 'Is everything ready for our meeting?'

'Of course,' Saffron said. 'Mr Solomons and Ms Ndiri are waiting for us in the reading room – though I admit I still think of it as my father's study.'

'Me too,' said Harriet softly.

They walked into the room, where five armchairs had been arranged in a semicircle facing the desk that had once belonged to Leon Courtney. Wangari was placing ring-binder folders on each chair. Small tables had been placed between the chairs. A uniformed waiter was standing to one side by a sideboard on which stood pots of tea and coffee, soft drinks and a large plate of freshly baked pastries.

Isidore Solomons had been seated behind the desk. He stood to greet everyone and made sure that each had whatever refreshments they required. Wangari took her seat beside Izzy's. The waiter was dismissed and the business of the day began.

'I'd like to start by thanking Wangari Ndiri for her contribution to this project,' Izzy said. 'Without her knowledge of Kenyan law and her tireless work liaising with Kenyan government departments, including the president's office, we would not be here today.'

Saffron led a round of enthusiastic applause. Benjamin beamed proudly and Wangari gave a modest smile in acknowledgement of the praise.

'You have each been given a copy of the documents that President Kenyatta will sign tomorrow, and that you, Saffron, will countersign, on behalf of the Leon Courtney Foundation. Can I confirm, Mr Makori, that the president has read the documents and he is happy with the final draft?'

'Yes, that is the case,' Maku said.

'Then I will go through the salient points, which are listed on the cover page at the front of your folders. The first is that Saffron Courtney Meerbach, being the sole inheritor of her father Leon Courtney's estate, has donated the entire Lusima Estate, save for her private home Cresta Lodge and approximately two thousand acres surrounding it, to the independent nation of Kenya, for the benefit of its people and wildlife.

'The land retained by you, Saffron, amounts to less than two per cent of the total area of Lusima. I have to say this is a truly astonishing act of philanthropy and I trust –' Izzy gave Maku a piercing stare – 'that the president will reflect that in his speech tomorrow.'

'You can be sure of that, Mr Solomons. The president is deeply moved by this act of generosity and reconciliation. It confirms the high view he has always held of Mrs Courtney Meerbach and her family.'

'That is very gracious of him,' said Izzy. 'Now, the land is being given under certain conditions. The first is that all the farmlands are to be passed on by the Kenyan government to the Kikuyu people who worked them on Mr Courtney's behalf. A further tranche of, as yet, unfarmed land is to be set aside for the use of the next generation. In this way, young Kikuyu men will be able to acquire land of their own and thereby be ready to marry and start a family, as is their custom.'

'May I say, Saffron, how deeply moved I am by this,' Wangari added. 'If other Europeans had been equally generous, we might never have had that terrible uprising and both our fathers might be alive to see this day.'

'Thank you,' Saffron said. 'I want more than anything to help make this a peaceful country, for everyone.'

Izzy continued. 'The second condition is that a game reserve is to be established on the remaining land, which occupies a little over three quarters of the total donation. This reserve, and the hotel in which we are now sitting, is to be managed for the next fifty years by the Leon Courtney Foundation.

'Thanks to the profits from the hotel and the safari holidays that will be run from it, along with the significant endowment donated by you, Saffron, the park will be staffed and maintained without making any demands on the Kenyan government's budgets.

'The third and fourth conditions relate to the Maasai people with whom Leon Courtney had such a special bond. They will be guaranteed the right, in perpetuity, to live and herd cattle across the game reserve. In addition, the landmass known as Lonsonyo Mountain, which is sacred to the local Maasai, will be designated as a protected area, over which they have complete control. They will have the right to determine who may or may not visit the mountain, and on what terms.

'Those are the essential points of the documents contained in your folders. The agreements to be signed tomorrow cover all the various legal and financial issues arising from . . .'

The rest of Izzy's sentence was drowned by a furious battering on the door to the room. It burst open to disgorge a gang of teenagers in swimming trunks and bikinis, followed by Benjamin and Wangari's sons, eight-year-old twins who were wide-eyed with excitement at being allowed to play with the big boys and girls.

'What is the meaning of this?' Gerhard asked, getting to his feet and giving the youngsters what his children cheekily called 'Dad's Luftwaffe stare', since it looked as if he was about to shoot them down.

Zander took it upon himself to be his generation's spokesman. At seventeen, he was already taller than Saffron and almost able to look his father in the eye.

'Oh, hi, Dad, hi, Mum,' he said with breezy self-confidence. 'We're all starving and we heard there were Cokes and biscuits and stuff in here, so, you know . . .' He flashed the grin that he knew could get him almost anything he wanted. 'Can we have some, please?'

Saffron watched her husband doing his best to remain fierce in the face of the son he adored. Then she cast her eyes on Kika, who, at fifteen, was already looking much too much like a budding Brigitte Bardot for her mother's comfort.

How are we ever going to keep the boys away from her? Saffron asked herself, her heart bursting with pride at her beautiful children. She thought of all she and Gerhard had gone through to get to this place, this time, and knew that it had been worth the heartache, the suffering, the bloodshed and the loss that they had endured.

Worth it all, a thousand times over.

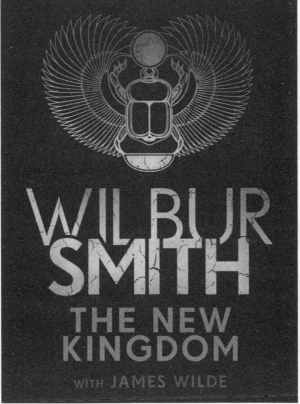

TWO HEROES. ONE UNBREAKABLE BOND.

COURTNEY'S WAR

An epic story of courage, betrayal and undying love that takes the reader to the very heart of a world at war.

Torn apart by war, Saffron Courtney and Gerhard von Meerbach are thousands of miles apart, both struggling for their lives.

Gerhard – despite his objections to the Nazi regime – is fighting for the Fatherland, hoping to one day have the opportunity to rid Germany of Hitler and his cronies. But as his unit is thrown into the hellish attrition of the Battle of Stalingrad, he knows his chances of survival are dwindling by the day.

Meanwhile Saffron – recruited by the Special Operations Executive and sent to occupied Belgium to discover how the Nazis have infiltrated SOE's network – soon finds herself being hunted by Germany's most ruthless spymaster.

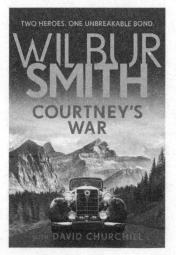

Confronted by evil beyond their worst imaginings, the lovers must each make the hardest choice of all: sacrifice themselves, or do whatever they can to survive, hoping that one day they will be reunited.

AVAILABLE NOW

BOUND BY LOVE. DRIVEN BY REVENGE.

CALL OF THE RAVEN

The son of a wealthy plantation owner and a doting mother, Mungo St John is accustomed to the wealth and luxuries his privilege has afforded him. That is until he returns from university to discover his family ruined, his inheritance stolen and his childhood sweetheart, Camilla, taken by the conniving Chester Marion. Fuelled by anger, and love, Mungo swears vengeance and devotes his life to saving Camilla – and destroying Chester.

Camilla, trapped in New Orleans, powerless to her position as a kept slave and suffering at the hands of Chester's brutish behaviour, must learn to do whatever it takes to survive.

As Mungo battles his own fate and misfortune to achieve the revenge that drives him, and regain his power in the world, he must question what it takes for a man to survive when he has nothing, and what he is willing to do in order to get what he wants.

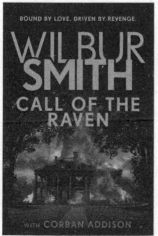

An action-packed and gripping adventure about one man's quest for revenge, the brutality of slavery in America and the imbalance between humans that can drive – or defeat – us.

AVAILABLE NOW

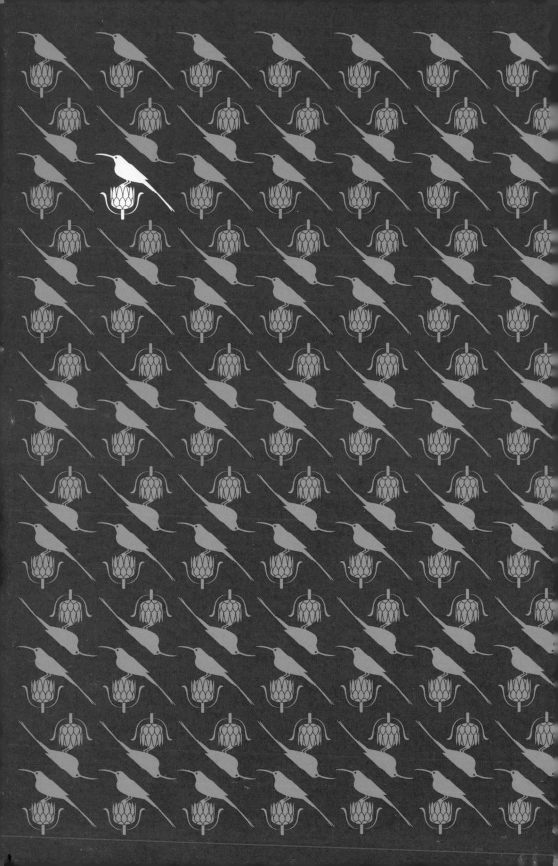